Praise for the

Hunter

Hill brings it all together for Tori in book five of this series in ways only a skilled storyteller can. Readers will no doubt appreciate the depth she brings to Hunter's story. *Hunter's Revenge* is a first-rate piece of storytelling and I guarantee Hunter fans will not be disappointed.
-*Women Using Words*

As always, Hill does a fantastic job of weaving the reader through a multi-layered path into a beautiful meadow of a perfectly told story.
-Denise J., *NetGalley*

Such a great ending to one of this genre's most beloved series.
-Patricia B., *NetGalley*

I could wax on and on about this novel, but I won't. If you've yet to read this series, crack on with it now. It is brilliant.
-Natalie T., *NetGalley*

Timber Falls

Gerri Hill is the only lesfic writer I can think of who can write absolutely any genre, and consistently produce top-quality work. Romance, mystery, paranormal...Timber Falls is no exception.
-Karen C., *NetGalley*

I would say this is a typical Hill novel but only if you understand 'typical' to mean an outstanding story, intriguing characters, beautiful settings, and unparalleled writing.
-Della B., *NetGalley*

This book may well be the best book Gerri Hill has written in years. It has everything needed to keep her readers reading into the wee hours of the morning...
-Abbott F., *NetGalley*

The Great Charade

One of the big loves I had for this book, among other things, was it is so full of rich dialogue.

-Carol C., *NetGalley*

The Great Charade really is a heartwarming, romantic holiday book that I'm really glad I was able to read this season.

-Betty H., *NetGalley*

...this was a perfect Christmas book. Not only does it nail the Christmas theme, but the premise is also engaging from the very first page... I absolutely adored this Christmas novel and it's definitely one of my favourites from Gerri Hill.

-Natalie T., *NetGalley*

Red Tide at Heron Bay

Ms. Hill has certainly done it again. I was hooked from the beginning to the end. This is a murder, mystery, romance with loveable main characters who are fully developed and has great chemistry... You can actually picture yourself in the setting watching the story unfold. This is now one of my favorite books.

-Bonnie A., *NetGalley*

This is exactly why Gerri Hill is a master in suspense and crime and romance books! Sooo good! This book was a brilliant slow burn in both ways, the romance and the crime.

-Stephanie D., *NetGalley*

Another brilliant gripping crime thriller from Gerri Hill, couldn't put it down and read in one sitting!

-Claire E., *NetGalley*

Gerri Hill writes wonderful mysteries, and this is no exception. I know I'm reading something special when I can't put a book down.

-*The Lesbian Review*

The Stars at Night

The Stars at Night is a beautiful mountain romance that will transport you to a paradise. It's a story of self-discovery, family, and rural living. This romance was a budding romance that snuck-up and on two unsuspecting women who found themselves falling in love under the stars...It's a feel-good slow-burn romance that will make your heart melt.

-Les Rêveur

Hill is such a strong writer. She's able to move the plot along through the characters' dialogue and actions like a true boss. It's a masterclass in showing, not telling. The story unfolds at a languid pace which mirrors life in a small, mountain town, and her descriptions of the environment bring the world of the book alive.

-The Lesbian Review

Gillette Park

...is a phenomenal book! I wish I could give this more than five stars. Yes, there is a paranormal element, and a love story, and conflict, and danger. And it's all worth it. Thank you, Gerri Hill, for writing a brilliant masterpiece!

-Carolyn M., *NetGalley*

This book was just what I was hoping for and wickedly entertaining... If you are a Hill fan, grab this.

-Lex Kent's Reviews

Gerri Hill has written another action-packed thriller. The writing is excellent and the characters engaging. Wow!

-Jenna F., *NetGallehy*

THE Apple DIARY

GERRI HILL

Other Bella Books by Gerri Hill

After the Summer Rain
Angel Fire
Artist's Dream
At Seventeen
Behind the Pine Curtain
Chasing a Brighter Blue
The Cottage
Coyote Sky
Dawn of Change
Devil's Rock
Gillette Park
The Great Charade
Gulf Breeze
Hell's Highway
Hunter's Revenge
Hunter's Way
In the Name of the Father
Keepers of the Cave
The Killing Room
The Locket
Love Waits
The Midnight Moon
Moonlight Avenue
The Neighbor
No Strings
One Summer Night
Paradox Valley
Partners
Pelican's Landing
The Rainbow Cedar
Red Tide at Heron Bay
The Roundabout
Sawmill Springs
The Scorpion
The Secret Pond
Sierra City
Snow Falls
The Stars at Night
Storms
The Target
Timber Falls
Weeping Walls

About the Author

Gerri Hill has over forty-three published works, including the 2021 GCLS winner for *Gillette Park*, the 2020 GCLS winner *After the Summer Rain*, the 2017 GCLS winner *Paradox Valley*, 2014 GCLS winner *The Midnight Moon*, 2011, 2012 and 2013 winners *Devil's Rock*, *Hell's Highway* and *Snow Falls*, and the 2009 GCLS winner *Partners*, the last book in the popular Hunter Series, as well as the 2013 Lambda finalist *At Seventeen*. Gerri lives in south-central Texas, only a few hours from the Gulf Coast, a place that has inspired many of her books. With her partner, Diane, they share their life with two Australian shepherds—Rylee and Mason—and a couple of furry felines. For more, visit her website at gerrihill.com.

Bella Books, Inc.
P.O. Box 10543
Tallahassee, FL 32302

Printed in the United States of America on acid-free paper.

First Edition - 2023

Editor: Medora MacDougall
Cover Designer: Kayla Mancuso

ISBN: 978-1-64247-498-5

PUBLISHER'S NOTE

THE  DIARY

GERRI HILL

2023

PART ONE: THE DIARY

CHAPTER ONE

Madilyn paused on the stairs, one hand lightly resting on the railing as she listened to her grandfather down below, the tap, tap, tap of his cane on the hardwood floor announcing his presence.

"Maddie? Where are you off to?"

She gave him a gentle smile. "I thought I'd go through Grandma Belle's things, Grandpops."

She could see the steely resolve in his dark eyes. Despite his age—eighty-nine a few months ago—and his dependence on the cane, he was still a tall, intimidating man who was as mentally sharp as he'd always been.

"Your mother will go through it all, no doubt," he said, tapping his cane for emphasis. "What she hasn't already pilfered through."

She spread her hands out. "When is she going to go through it? She already left."

Yes, she had dashed back to the city, returning to her apartment in Manhattan immediately after the burial, saying she had urgent business to attend to. Madilyn knew the urgent business was a pleasure trip to Bermuda with some new friends of hers. She'd learned that from Evan. Never mind that her own mother had just died. Never mind that her elderly father was apparently going off the deep end and planning to not only sell the estate but move to an assisted living facility, of all places. Yes, that was his plan. And her plan was to talk him out of it. Her mother, however, had assumed he really would sell, and hadn't been concerned in the least. Instead, she had sorted through Grandma Belle's jewelry, taking the most expensive pieces without asking. She wondered if her grandfather knew that.

To be fair, her grandmother had been ill for the last several years, bedridden for the last ten months. A nurse had lived here at the estate with them, tending to her until the end. And only one day after she'd died, her grandfather had surprised them all by declaring he was going to move on, saying he couldn't bear to stay there without his Belle.

He motioned up the stairs. "Whatever is up there is not worth keeping anyway. Belle moved all our things down here when she couldn't manage the stairs any longer. Years ago."

"What about in the attic? You have things in there still, don't you?"

"Mostly ancient junk. I doubt anyone has been up there in years." He waved her away. "Look through it if you want. I've already decided to have all that hauled off." He waved at the formal room where he stood. "All of this. Might as well get rid of it all."

She went down the steps a little way and leaned on the railing, looking at him. "Is there not anything you want to keep, Grandpops?"

"What for?" Then he straightened his shoulders—tapping his cane in that familiar way of his—and gave a disinterested sigh. "I won't be around much longer anyway. No sense in hanging on to stuff." He waved around him again. "No sense in hanging on to any of this. There's no one to take over when I'm gone."

"You've been saying that you won't be around much longer for the last ten years and you're still managing just fine."

"And what do you call this damn thing I have to use to walk with?"

She went down a couple more steps. "You've had that damn thing ten years too. You wouldn't be you if that cane wasn't in your hands." She tilted her head, meeting his gaze. "This is your home."

"There's nothing here for me anymore." He looked at her sharply then. "Why? What's the reason I should keep the estate? Do you want to move here when I'm gone? Take it over for me? There is no one else, Maddie. Just you."

She laughed. "I'm single. This place has eight bedrooms, not to mention several sitting areas and formal living rooms," she said, waving her hand down at him. "What in the world would I do with it all?"

His expression turned thoughtful. "Maybe you *should* take it over, Maddie. It's been in the family for generations. It does pain me to think about selling. I had hoped your mother would want to keep it, but she has no interest. She doesn't care if I get rid of it all." He scowled. "She thinks because she's got money, she's got to rub elbows with those snooty high society people in the city who don't give a damn about her. She seems like she couldn't care less about where she came from." Before she could go to him, he waved her away. "No, no. Go on up. I'm fine. Just venting."

"You don't really want to sell it, do you?"

"Like you said, it's too big for one person to rattle around in. Your mother is off in New York City and wants no part of the homeplace. She never did. And your brother? I've given up on that. Evan is…well, Evan is Evan. He's far too much like your mother. Who's going to want it, if not you? You're the only sensible one in the family."

"You know what, there's no need to rush into anything. I can stay with you for a while if you want. See how it goes."

He raised his bushy eyebrows. "What about that fella you're seeing? Your mother seems to think it's serious this time."

"Serious?" She tucked blond hair behind her ears. "He wants to marry me, yes."

He nodded. "Your mother thinks he would fit in perfectly with the family."

"Does she?" She sighed. "I don't know. I don't feel that way about him. Maybe I'm being too picky."

He smiled. "I've always liked that about you. You were smart enough not to fall for the first one that came along. Most of them see nothing but dollar signs anyway."

"Most do, yes. I don't always tell them who I am though." She smiled quickly. "Grandma Belle taught me that when I was still young."

He laughed. "Your mother never learned that lesson." Then his smile faded. "My fault. I let Belle spoil her beyond belief. We should have had more children."

Yes, spoiled was a good way to describe her mother. She had been married and divorced four times now. She and Evan had different fathers. While she was still on decent terms with hers, Evan was not.

"Now, you best go on up. Loretta will have lunch ready at noon, as always. She cycles through my favorite meals, but if you've got a hankering for something, I'll let her know. She could whip that up for you."

"I'm not particular," she said as she moved up the stairs. That was a daily occurrence whenever she visited. Breakfast, lunch, and dinner, all at regimented times. After all these years, she still wasn't used to that. She preferred to eat when she was actually hungry, not at a predetermined time.

She paused at the landing, then moved onto the wide hallway, her gaze moving to each of the closed doors. The six bedrooms up here were still furnished, yet most were not used anymore. Her mother had stayed only one night, that was the night before the burial. The first room was small and only had one window. It had been her childhood room until her mother bought the mansion, as she called it, and moved them there to Chester Heights. Now when she stayed with her grandparents, she always chose the second room. It had two large windows looking out over the once manicured grounds. Bennie had been the groundskeeper since he'd been a young man. When he grew too old and retired, they never replaced him, instead hiring a local lawn service to tend to things. They did little more than cut the grass.

She walked down the hallway to the far end of rooms. Her grandparents had slept up here for years, only moving into one of the downstairs bedrooms when Grandma Belle had grown too frail to manage the stairs any longer. She moved to their door, about to open it, when her attention was drawn to the end of the hallway and the large door in the corner. The attic.

She nearly shivered at the thought. She'd always been afraid to go up there. Probably because Evan had tormented her with ghost stories when she was young. Well, she was now twenty-seven years old. As far as she knew, despite the multitude of generations who had lived here—and died here—the place wasn't haunted. Still, she had no desire to go up there. At least not alone.

Yet before she could turn the knob on her grandparents' old room, she found herself moving slowly to the attic door, almost as if in a trance. She stood there staring at it, not quite understanding the sudden compulsion she had to go up there. It was as if a force were urging her along and she had no will to fight it.

She took a deep breath, then touched the knob, pausing only a second before turning it and pulling the door open. The stairway leading up was wide and dark. She felt along the wall for the light switch and flipped it up. A dull and dingy lightbulb swung overhead, the shadows moving lazily around her.

Something beckoned and she found herself climbing steadily up the stairs. Spiderwebs were draped from every nook and corner, and she could smell the dust as it floated about. She wondered how many years—decades—it had been since someone had been up there.

And she wondered why she was going up now.

CHAPTER TWO

Madilyn had been a young girl—six or seven—the last time she'd stepped foot in the attic. And at that, she'd only managed the stairs, running back down when she feared Evan would close the door on her. Evan was six years older than she was. They were too far apart in age to have ever played together, although they got along as well as could be expected. Still, there was always an underlying edge to their relationship. Evan never knew his father. He'd been out of the picture shortly after he was born. Her own father lasted only until she was three. He, like Evan's father, had eventually left too. And like Evan's father, he did not come around. It wasn't until she was older that she found out her grandparents had paid off Evan's father to disappear, and he had. And then they'd paid her father off as well.

Unlike Evan's father, hers hadn't completely disappeared, though. She'd been eighteen when he'd reached out to her. They didn't really have a relationship now—a phone call a few times a year—but at least she knew who he was. And where he was. He now lived in the suburbs of Chicago with his wife and two teenaged sons.

She paused to look back down the stairs, half expecting the door to swing shut. All was quiet, though, and she moved the last few steps to the top. It was darker still and she couldn't remember where the switch was. She felt along the wall, jerking her hand back as she plunged it into a mass of spiderwebs.

"Ew."

Instead of searching with her hand in the dark, she pulled her phone from her pocket, turning on the flashlight. She held her phone out, pointing it toward the wall. She found the switch and flipped it up, bathing the room in bright light. She relaxed and blew out her breath. No ghosts seemed to be lurking about. And no spiders were jumping out at her either.

There wasn't a lot up there, though. Some furniture that was covered with dustcloths that were layered in decades' worth of dust themselves. She went deeper inside, moving around a large table. There were several old dome-top trunks, the leather handles still perfectly intact. She opened one, surprised to find clothing inside. She shuffled through it, not even able to guess how many generations back they'd been worn. They seemed very old, faded, and obviously dated.

She moved to another one. This one was completely empty, and she closed the lid again. Her gaze was drawn to an old, ancient front drop desk. It wasn't covered and dust coated its surface. On impulse, she tried to open it, but it was locked. She looked around for a key, finding none. She shrugged, then went to another of the trunks. This one was filled with books. She picked one up and flipped through it, the pages yellowed and dull. She sorted through them, wondering if they were old schoolbooks. She tossed the book she'd been holding back down and was about to close the lid when, on impulse, she shoved the books to the side as if unconsciously searching for something. She saw a dark object against the side of the trunk. Her fingers curled around it.

It was an old skeleton key. She held it up to the light, then slowly turned toward the desk, an eyebrow arched. Was this the key? Yes. Of course, it was. It had to be. She slipped it into the lock, smiling as it turned and the top dropped down. Inside were tiny compartments, and she opened each drawer, wondering what treasures she would find. Instead, they were all empty. In the center was a leather strap, and she pulled it. A larger middle drawer. It, too, was empty. Disappointed, she was about to close it again when she noticed a bulge in one corner, as if the bottom of the drawer was pulling away.

She felt along the edge, excitement hitting her when she realized it was a secret compartment. She lifted the bottom, smiling when she spotted a thin book inside.

"What's this?" she murmured.

She took it out carefully, as it looked very old and fragile. The leatherbound cover was cracked and dry, held closed by a leather strap. She opened it, finding the pages filled with handwritten words. A journal? A diary? But whose? She thumbed through the pages, noting that only the first part of the book was used. The rest of the pages appeared to be blank.

She read through the first few entries—a recounting of someone's day. It was written by a woman, that much was clear. She had titled it The Apple Diary.

I walked to the orchard today. The apple blooms are mostly gone, but they were oh so beautiful while they lasted. This is my second spring to see them. I can't decide which season I like the most in the orchard. Spring is lovely with the blooms. Summer is green and lush with fruit growing. And later, when the fruit ripens and there is a crispness to the air, I enjoy that too. There is something magical about the orchard. It makes me feel less lonely somehow. I haven't decided why that is. Perhaps it's only the beauty of it that pulls me. The view of the lush valley from the trees is spectacular.

When Martha was still alive, she frowned on me doing any exploring around the estate. It wasn't proper for a Marak lady to be out on the grounds as if she were only a commoner. I fear if she'd lived and still ran the estate with her usual iron fist, I would have been stark raving mad by now. Instead, the apple orchard keeps me sane. I find myself talking to the trees as if they are old friends.

Madilyn assumed the journal would be nothing more than daily ramblings about the orchard. While not exactly exciting, she would still read it, if only to get a history lesson on the Marak family. The third entry, however, was different. Not a daily recounting, no. The author was sharing feelings.

I'm not sure why I started this journal. My life is not exciting and there is nothing much to write about. It was more of a compulsion that I couldn't seem to shake. I need someone to talk to, I suppose, other than the apple trees. James is away again. He caught the train today and is off to New York City. Business, he says. Always business. He'll be gone for several weeks this time. I get lonely when he's gone but he doesn't seem to care.

Truth is, I'm lonely whether he's here or not. We seldom talk. At least the servants are here for company, but they rarely talk to me either. Well, they do talk to me, of course, but it's not like we have friendly visits. Hattie is only a few years older than me. Four, I think. Unlike the others, she doesn't shy away from me.

Now that the weather has broken and warmer days are upon us, I shall enjoy long daily walks again to my beloved orchard and beyond. On a good, sunny day, I can walk all the way down into the valley and back before anyone worries about my absence. There is a creek at the far end of the valley, but it's too far to walk. I have a good mind to take one of the horses out to explore, but I know that would never be allowed.

James? That was Grandpop's father's name, wasn't it? So, was Isabel writing this? She would have been her great-grandmother. She died rather young she'd been told.

I met the most interesting woman today. She came up the long drive in a nice Model T Ford and blew the horn out front. Aoogha! Caused a stir with Hattie and the others, it did. I sent them back to the kitchen and went outside to greet her. She was such a striking woman. Tall. Dark hair wound up into a bun at her neck. She was sporting a black fedora. But it was her clothing that puzzled me more. She was wearing a man's trousers, right down to suspenders and a fancy ascot! My mouth must have dropped open because she laughed at me. Lorah was her name. I thought she said Laura, but she quickly corrected me, even pronounced it slowly for me. Lor-rah. How pretty. She was selling shoes and had quite a stash to choose from. I didn't need any shoes, of course, but it was nice to visit with her. I had a mind to send her on to George Class's place up the road. He and his family are renting a hundred acres way down in the back valley for farming. James takes most of what they make, but at least they have a roof over their heads in these hard times. Not a one of those kids have shoes except for the hand-me-downs they wear to Sunday church. Of course, I know they don't have the money to buy shoes from Lorah. If I see her again, I think I'll give her money. James would be angry if he knew I was buying shoes for those kids. But he doesn't need to know everything, does he?

A traveling salesman? Or saleswoman, in this case, Madilyn mused. She wondered what year this was written. There were no dates at all on the pages so far. She was about to turn to another entry when she heard a female voice call up to her.

"Miss Maddie? Are you up there still?"

She closed the book quickly and went to the edge of the stairs, seeing Loretta at the attic door down below. "Yes. I suppose lunch is ready."

"You know Mr. Albert gets very cranky if he doesn't eat by noon. Come on down, dear."

She wondered if it was Grandpops who got cranky or Loretta herself when mealtimes ran late. Loretta—in her midsixties now—had been working for the Maraks her whole life, as did her mother and grandmother before her. She imagined that the mealtimes had been set long before Loretta was in the picture.

"Be right there," she said without much enthusiasm.

She closed up the desk again, locking it with the key. She looked around the room, wondering if she should take more time to sort through things. There might be more hidden treasures like this diary she'd found. Maybe she would later. Then she debated putting the key back into the trunk. She decided not to. Instead, she slipped the key in her jeans pocket and went to the stairs, pausing to turn off the light at the top. She looked around the dark attic again, feeling none of her earlier apprehension. At the bottom, she closed the door behind her, then hurried into her room. She placed the diary beside her bed, anxious now to read more of it.

CHAPTER THREE

"Are you sure you don't want some wine, Miss Maddie?" Loretta asked.

She shook her head. "Thanks. While I enjoy a glass of wine at dinner occasionally, it doesn't sound appealing for lunch."

Grandpops took the glass from Loretta. "I do say, you are probably the only one in our family who shunned the spirits. My father was quite a drinker, although my own mother rarely touched it. A glass of fine brandy at Christmas sometimes, I do recall."

Madilyn was surprised at the mention of his mother, and she took the opportunity to ask questions. "How old were you when she died?"

"I was fourteen. After that, my father sent me off east to boarding school. I met Belle when I was sixteen. After school, I brought her back home with me and married her right here at the estate. What a crowd we had for the wedding."

Yes, she'd heard that story often. Although the way Grandma Belle told it—with much flair and detail—it was a most romantic story.

"What did she die of? Your mother, I mean."

"She was your great-grandmother. Isabel." He took a sip of wine. "We never talked about her much to you, did we?"

"No. Rarely."

"Probably because Belle never knew her, I guess. And my own father died young too. He was still in his sixties. Died right there in his study one night."

Yes. Smoking a cigar and drinking whiskey. While Grandpops never said a cross word about his father, Grandma Belle wasn't afraid to voice her opinion. "Greedy man, he was. Had more money than anyone in the Commonwealth, but still wanted more. Why, he owned most all of the land from here to Philadelphia at one time. He would foreclose on property without blinking an eye. Didn't matter to him the hardships he placed on those families." Then her grandmother would look around conspiratorially. "Don't you know people were dancing in the streets at the news of his passing."

"But what about your mother?"

His eyes turned almost wistful, and she imagined he was going back to his childhood. A smile lit his face. "She was such a sweet woman. So kind. She ran the household because my grandmother took ill. Tuberculosis. My father, like his father, was always away on business. When my grandmother died, my mother took over the running of the house and the servants. They had only been married a year at most."

"How old was she then?"

"My mother? She was probably twenty at the time. I wasn't born yet. Of course, I never knew my grandfather either. Like most of the men in the family, he died fairly young too." He picked up his wineglass and she noticed there was a slight tremor in his hand. "Such a strange thing about our family. Not only dying young—I'm the exception, thankfully—but children were hard to come by. My father was an only child and his father before him and so on. I was the only child. Belle and I so wanted a big family, but we were only blessed with your mother."

"She broke the mold, I guess, what with her having two children."

"Yes. She was also the only girl. I remember thinking the Marak name would die then with me."

"But it won't. Evan has your name."

She was surprised by the sadness in his eyes. "He has the name, yes. But I think it stops there. Evan probably will never marry, much less have children. That's most likely for the best, considering his lifestyle." He eyed her. "And you? When are you going to have some great-grandbabies for me?"

She smiled at him. "Well, I'm only twenty-seven. I have a few more years yet."

He laughed. "Yes, but I'm eighty-nine. I'm already living on borrowed time."

"What about your mother?" she prompted, bringing the conversation back to Isabel. "How did she die?"

"We don't really know. She was so pretty and died so young. I always thought you favored her." He shook his head. "She was never happy here though. She pretended, but I could see it when I got older. I'm sure my father could see it too, but he never said anything. She always had this faraway look in her eyes. So sad to see."

"She just died?"

He nodded. "During her sleep one night. She was thirty-six."

"Oh my god! That young?"

"Died right in her room."

Madilyn swallowed nervously. "What…what room was that?"

"The large second room. Where you're staying. That was always her room."

Yes, she knew that was going to be the answer, didn't she? "Where did he sleep? Your father?"

"He slept down here. In the bedroom Belle and I took over."

"I see. So, was she sick? I mean, there must have been something. Cancer?"

"No, no. There was nothing. I think she died of loneliness."

"That's so sad." Isn't that why Isabel had said she'd started writing the journal? Because she was lonely? Madilyn wondered when the diary was written. How many years before she died?

"Times were hard then. People died young," he said by way of explanation. "It was 1949 when she passed on. I don't think I was shocked by her death. She'd seemed so lifeless for so long."

"Why didn't they sleep together?" She knew the answer though, didn't she? Isabel didn't love him.

He shrugged. "I was a boy. I don't remember."

Loretta came out of the kitchen with the serving tray. Her grandfather preferred his biggest meal of the day at noon. Dinner was not much more than a light supper or snack. Today's lunch appeared to be lamb chops. Small, baby potatoes topped with gravy and a heap of green beans—with a dollop of butter on top—were crowded next to the chops. They each had a dinner roll with more butter placed next to them. Despite not being used to eating such a large meal at lunch, she thought it looked absolutely delicious.

"Thank you, Loretta."

"My pleasure, Miss Maddie. Enjoy."

She stabbed a potato with her fork, then paused before eating it. "If you sell the estate, what is Loretta going to do? She's never lived anywhere else. In fact, she was born right here in the house, wasn't she?"

"Yes, that has been weighing on me. I will, of course, make sure she's taken care of, monetarily, at least. She has a sister who lives in Cleveland. She could perhaps move in with her."

She put her fork down. "I don't think you should sell. This is your home."

"What? You think it's a rash decision?"

"Yes. You know it is. Grandma Belle died and the very next day you declare you want to sell and move away."

"Oh, Maddie. What do I want here by myself? How would I spend my time?"

"And what will you have there? Despite your name being on the building, you'll not know anyone," she said, referring to the assisted living facility the Marak Foundation had financed years ago. "Besides, you have Loretta here. You have Randy and Julia. It's not like you'd be alone."

He cut into a chop and took a bite, but his eyes were on her. "What about you? How do you spend your time?"

She, too, took a bite of the chop, savoring the taste. "You mean when I'm not representing the family at charity events?"

"That should be your mother's job. I don't know why she pushed that off on you."

"She has other interests," she said vaguely.

He nearly snorted. "I know exactly what her interests are. Unfortunately, she's not a spring chicken any longer, even if she pretends to be."

Madilyn laughed. "Yes, she did go through a run of younger men." And she had the money to buy them, she added silently.

He put his fork down suddenly and his expression turned serious. "There's something I've been meaning to talk to you about. I've been putting it off. Belle told me to tell you a year ago, at least, but…"

"What is it?"

"I've removed Margaret as executor of my estate. I've also completely removed her from the Foundation. She has no legal say as to anything regarding the Foundation."

Madilyn frowned. "I thought the way the Foundation was set up, she couldn't touch that money no matter what."

"The money is secure, yes. But I don't trust her. She doesn't have our interests at heart. When I'm gone—if she has any controlling interest at all—I fear she will dissolve the Marak Foundation and take the money and run. As you know, Belle and I started that up when my father passed." He laughed lightly. "Belle always said he was rolling over in his grave knowing we'd taken all his money and created a charitable foundation."

"If you've removed her from the Foundation, I take that to mean you want me to have complete control when you're gone?" She tried to look appropriately surprised. Her grandmother had shared that news with her last year but told her to let Grandpops tell her in his own time. It's one reason she'd taken a more active role in the Foundation of late.

"Yes. I've already done the paperwork. I simply haven't informed you or Margaret."

"I don't know that it's necessary to inform her. She already knows she can't touch that money. That's why she hasn't taken any interest in it. Same with Evan."

"Yes, I know. But I still want her to know that you'll have control over it. You're already doing the work, Maddie. Nothing is going to change."

"No. The firm you hired is doing the work. I just show up to events when I'm told."

"You can downplay it as much as you want. You have an office there and I'm told by Bob Reeves that you're there more often than not, overseeing things. Besides, he already knows of the change."

"Is that why whatever suggestions I make are never met with any pushback?"

"Probably. You've been there since college. You know how Belle and I wanted things run. I trust you to do the right thing. I don't trust your mother in the least."

She nodded. "Thank you. I have wanted to make some changes, but I was hesitant to come to you."

"Such as?"

"Offering grants for research. Health and wellness, mainly."

"I don't understand. Isn't that already being funded?"

"Yes," she agreed. "But mostly by special interest groups. I've been doing my own research on that. Take, for instance, the statin drugs for cholesterol. The majority of the research is funded by pharmaceutical companies. They make billions of dollars on the sale of statin drugs each year. But a lot of the research is skewed. If you only read the conclusions of these studies and go by that, you'd think statin drugs were the most wonderful thing ever to prevent cardiovascular disease and that the side effects were minimal. Because that's the results they pay for. But if you dig into the guts of the research—things that aren't made public—you find that, in reality, statin drugs, in most cases, do absolutely nothing in decreasing mortality due to cardiovascular disease. And the side effects are horrendous." She smiled apologetically. "Sorry. That's the latest thing I've been researching, and I've read a hundred studies on it recently so it's all still fresh in my mind. What I'm trying to say, most research is funded with the intention of getting favorable results for whoever doled out the money. If the sugar industry wants some human trials to prove that sugar is not harmful to health, they pay for studies. There has to be some neutrality involved. We can do that. We can offer grants to university labs, for instance. They won't have an agenda, and neither will we. I think that would be a good place to start. Most universities are begging for research dollars as it is."

"You've already done your homework on that, I see."

"We give to the same charities over and over. And it's the same charities that everyone else gives to. I'm not saying we stop giving to cancer research or Alzheimer's research, but we can diversify and spread it out some." She paused. "What do you think?"

"You sound passionate about it, that's for sure." He nodded. "You have my blessing, of course. I'm too old to get bogged down in the details."

"Thank you. I mentioned it to Mr. Reeves, but he didn't appear to be very enthusiastic about it."

"That's because he has things running smoothly and change will disrupt that."

"Yes. But it will give me something to do. If things continue to run smoothly, then what am I needed for?"

He picked up his wineglass. "You never did like being an heiress, did you? Your mother, on the other hand, embraced it wholeheartedly."

"I just feel like I need to *do* something, you know."

"Well, being a socialite is a full-time job according to your mother."

"You sound a little bitter. What's wrong?"

"Where is she? She barely hung around long enough to get Belle in the ground, then off she goes again. She never concerned herself with me or the estate or even Belle, for that matter. She only came around when she needed something."

"I'm sorry, Pops," she said, shortening his name as she did sometimes.

He shook his head and picked up his knife and fork once more. "I should be used to it. She was always that way. Regardless, I'm putting you in charge of the family fortune when I'm gone. The Foundation is set up to continue running as it is. The trust funds are all in order. Nothing will change there. My will is very explicit. All of the other liquid assets, the house, all the land that we still own, that will be up to you to keep or sell. I don't imagine you would want the headache of keeping up with the land and the leases that are still active."

He waved his hand. "But that is up to you. If you do end up selling, then a percentage of it would go to the Foundation and the remainder is left to you. It's all spelled out in the will. But you are in charge, Maddie. And I'll apologize now, because Margaret will not be happy that I've left you in control or that I'm leaving you the bulk of my estate. Neither she nor Evan cared one bit about me or this land. You are the only one."

To say she was floored was an understatement. The money they got from the trust funds was bordering on obscene as it was. "I don't know what to say, Pops."

He smiled at her. "You don't have to say anything, Maddie. I only hope it won't completely damage your relationship with your mother."

"You know very well we don't really have a relationship. You saw us together the last couple of days."

"Yes. You are definitely cut from a different cloth. Dare I say you remind me of my sweet mother in more than looks? Always so kind and gentle. Yet there was constantly a longing there. For you too, isn't it? It's in your eyes, Maddie, much like hers. A longing for something. I never knew what that look in her eyes meant. You have that same look sometimes."

Madilyn stared at him. "Do I?"

"Yes. A longing for something," he said again. "Longing for love, maybe?"

Was there a look in her eyes? A longing, as he suggested? She didn't know if it was truly a longing or simply an emptiness she felt sometimes. Because yes, something was missing in her life. Was it love? Perhaps. But she forced a smile, trying to lighten her own mood a little. "Are you trying to get me married off before you leave this earth?"

He pushed his plate aside and cupped his wineglass. "You're right, you know. I don't want to leave here. This is my home." He stared at her intently. "Would you consider staying here with me a bit longer, a few months perhaps?"

"Of course. Anything you want."

"You wouldn't have to rush back? What's his name again?"

"Palmer. And I can stay here as long as you need me to."

Yes, it would be nice to hang out here at the estate, she thought. It would be a good break for her to get away. She didn't want to dwell on why she thought she needed a break. Palmer would understand, surely. And if he didn't, so be it. She wasn't going to concern herself with him. Even though they'd been dating a while, she didn't consider it serious, even if he and her mother pretended that it was.

She'd met Palmer at one of the social functions she'd attended—a benefit to raise money for a children's hospital—two years ago. Palmer's family was quite wealthy, and she didn't fear his interest in her was monetary. They'd had a handful of dinner dates before he'd introduced her to his parents. She'd found his mother to be far more interesting than he was, and she'd even solicited a rather large donation to The Marak Foundation.

Yet she continued to see him, to date him. And to sleep with him. It had become—what? A pattern? Routine? Habit? She didn't love him, no. Was she even attracted to him? If she were being honest—no. He was simply safe and familiar now. He was someone to be seen out in public with and she carried on as was expected of her. While her mother rarely concerned herself with Madilyn's personal life, she'd made it known that she favored Palmer—and his parents. They would fit in nicely with the Maraks, her mother had told her on more than one occasion.

"It was a rash decision on my part, you're right about that," her grandfather said, interrupting her thoughts. "Even though Belle had been so sick this last month, and we knew the end was near, she was at least still here in the house with me. Now it's just me and Loretta. How would that look?"

She raised her eyebrows. "You're worried about outside perception? Loretta has been working for the family long before I was even born. Why would anyone assume it inappropriate that she continues to live here? And why would you care? Besides, there's Randy. Or do you plan to let him go?"

"No. Randy drives me where I need to go and takes Loretta out to do the weekly shopping. But he and his wife live in the old servants' house. That's quite different than living here in the main house."

Randy and his wife, Julia, had worked there for many years too. Julia managed the cleaning ladies who came twice a week, and she tended to the household laundry. Randy was mostly a handyman now. They were really the only full-time staff remaining besides Loretta. When she was young, the house was bustling with servants and grounds crew and most of them lived on the property. There had been five or six small houses scattered about on the immediate acres where the estate was.

"The older we got, the more Belle and I wanted to keep our life normal. All the money and land my father amassed and his father before him, what good was it doing? My father hoarded it like he was going to stuff his casket with cash on his way out."

"Is that why you didn't replace Bennie when he retired? You wanted to be normal?"

"That was part of it. We got rid of a lot of the staff, as you know. With Belle in and out of hospitals these last ten years, well, I completely lost interest in keeping up anything. She was my sole focus."

She leaned her elbows on the table and rested her chin on her hands. "I think maybe you went a bit too far with all of that. You do have a, well, I don't want to say a reputation to uphold, but there is a certain standing that you should maintain."

"What are you saying?"

"I'm saying I miss the manicured grounds and the abundance of seasonal flowers. Without all of that, it is just a huge mansion with your average run-of-the-mill landscaping. I'm saying you should hire someone again. Get it looking like it did when I was a kid. It was so beautiful then. Now? It's just a very big house. There's nothing special about it any longer."

He put his wineglass down, watching her with a thoughtful expression. "You don't really enjoy living in the city, do you?"

She shook her head. "Not really, no. It doesn't feel like home." She met his gaze. "Nothing has felt like home since I lived here as a child. When Mother moved us...well..."

He ran his finger back and forth along the tablecloth, then tapped lightly against it. "You're right. Truth is, once Belle got sick that first time, I was scared and I...I didn't really care about all of this anymore. Like I said, I lost interest. This home lost its luster for me. Belle was always on top of things, and I let her down, I guess." He rang the golden bell that was beside his place setting. Loretta instantly materialized.

"Ready for dessert, Mr. Albert?" she asked.

"No. I think I'll have another glass of wine. And bring one for Maddie, please."

Loretta glanced at her, and Madilyn nodded slightly. Her grandfather's tone had changed, and she didn't dare refuse. When Loretta left, he looked at her, his eyes again sharp and clear.

"Move in here with me. We'll get the grounds looking proper again." He held her gaze. "Run the estate for me, Maddie. We'll hire a staff again if you want. Won't you please?"

"Run it? Me?"

"Yes. Like my grandmother did. Like my mother did. Like Belle did."

"I'm hardly a matriarch, Pops. Besides, I have responsibilities with the Foundation. I—"

"Any decisions you make for the Foundation can be made from here, just like I've done these last twenty years. And as far as making an appearance at the various functions like you do, that's more of a formality than anything. Besides, we're not that far away from Philly."

Loretta came back out with another glass of wine and the bottle, which she added to his glass. She left them again and he picked his up, holding it toward her in a toast. She picked hers up as well.

"I've had many blessings in my life. My Belle being at the top of that list. You, my sweet Maddie, are the other I am most thankful for."

"Thank you," she murmured as she took a tiny sip of the wine.

Good lord, did that mean she was moving in here?

Permanently?

CHAPTER FOUR

She turned off the overhead light, leaving the room lit only by the lamp beside the bed. She looked around as if expecting to see something—someone—in one of the corners. No, she hadn't been surprised to learn that Isabel had died in this room. She didn't believe in ghosts or anything crazy like that, but there had been something guiding her into the attic that morning, she was certain of it. Guiding her to the attic and to the diary.

She placed her robe at the foot of the bed and got under the covers, still not certain what to make of the day. Had she really agreed to move here? She must have. Her grandfather had seemed positively giddy at the prospect of her living with him. So much so that he was already making plans to have one of the downstairs rooms converted into a study for her. Her own private office. And he'd even mentioned the annual Christmas ball that Belle used to host before she got sick. It had been ten years since they'd hosted one; she didn't want to disappoint him, but she had no intention of starting that up again.

Oh, she didn't want to think about it anymore. She left the lamp beside the bed on and reached for the diary that had been calling her name all day. Instead of going to where she'd left off, she flipped through it, trying to guess how many entries there were. Near the back of the book was a photograph tucked neatly between two blank pages. It was surprisingly in excellent condition, considering the age. Had it been protected in this book all these years?

She held it up to the light, her gaze moving slowly across it. What was this? Two women? It was outdoors, under a large tree. One was sitting on a chair, the other was perched on her lap, and their arms were around the other's shoulder. Madilyn frowned. The woman on the chair was wearing men's clothes—a suit jacket, a fluffy tie, and a smart-looking hat. A fedora. Her hand was touching the other's chin as she stared into her eyes. Touching her chin as if urging her closer for a kiss.

"What in the world?"

She went back to the diary, finding the passage she'd read that morning.

She was such a striking woman. Tall. Dark hair wound up into a bun at her neck. She was sporting a black fedora. But it was her clothing that puzzled me more. She was wearing a man's trousers, right down to suspenders and a fancy ascot!

"Oh, my," she whispered.

She didn't want to jump to conclusions. This was Isabel, her great-grandmother. But what in the world was this photo all about? What did it mean? She flipped it over, not surprised by what she read. *Lorah and me. Summer 1933.* She stared at the photo again. Isabel was wearing a dark dress with long sleeves and a string of pearls around her neck. Even sitting, the dress reached to the tops of her shoes. It was then that she noticed they seemed to be wearing identical shoes—lace-ups that went all the way past the ankles. They looked more like fashionable boots than shoes. A matching pair from those that Lorah sold? Her gaze went back to Lorah. Yes, she was striking, wasn't she? There was a hint of masculinity, certainly, but she was totally devoid of any manliness. She put the photo back between the pages and flipped to the front of the diary to begin reading once more.

Lorah came back today! She teased me that she wasn't here to sell me shoes this time but would love a glass of lemonade. Hattie had such a look on her face when I asked her to fetch us two glasses! Lorah was dressed as before and she looked quite handsome, I do admit! We must have talked for hours. Oh, I had such a good time, I was sad to see her go. I invited her to come 'round again sometime. I surely hope she does.

Madilyn stared against the far wall, her mind racing. *Is this what I think it is?* She flipped over to the next page, disappointed there was no mention of Lorah.

Got a post from James today. He will be home in six days, it seems. Makes no never mind, really. I'm quite used to being alone and I don't mind his absence any longer. The loneliness I felt hovered whether he was here or not. I had Hattie make up a big roast today. I think I'll take that on over to Clara, George Class's wife. Despite James saying that they were getting on fine, I know they're struggling. They've already got six children and she's pregnant again, poor thing.

It was three entries later before the mysterious Lorah was mentioned again.

Oh, what a lovely day it was. I went on a picnic! Lorah came 'round about ten. I hadn't seen her in weeks, it seemed, although she assured me it had only been three days. She had a basket of fresh fried chicken that she'd picked up at the café in town, along with fat, buttery biscuits. And a bottle of wine that her granddad made!

Yes, me! I drank some wine. It went straight to my head! It must have…I found myself holding hands with her as we sat and watched the squirrels fighting over our offered biscuits. I took her down to the valley, then we came back up to the orchard. We walked among the apple trees, then sat under the maples for our meal. What a glorious few hours it was.

I finally found out her last name—Chance. She's two years older than I am. Not married. She says she has no use for a man and will never marry. Oh, I do wish I could be independent like that. Of course, Hattie gave me a disapproving look when I returned. It was only when I caught my reflection in the hallway mirror that I realized what a sight I was! My hair was windblown and disheveled from my ride in Lorah's car. But what fun it was! I hated for our outing to come to an end.

Madilyn was smiling as she read, trying to picture the scene from way back in 1933, in a Model T Ford, no less. She closed the diary, wondering if she should be invading Isabel's privacy like she was. Had no one ever read this? Had this book been hidden in the desk all these years? For all she knew, the desk may have been moved up into the attic after Isabel's death and never looked at again.

She drew her brows together. Should she show it to her grandfather? She shook her head. No. The words written on these pages were private. She felt bad enough reading it herself. Of course, she didn't know Isabel, didn't know anything about her, really. As her grandfather had said earlier, they rarely mentioned her at all. With that, she opened the diary again.

It's been a busy few days but that's not why I haven't written. There's been nothing to say really. James came home on Tuesday. Henry drove over to the train station in Lancaster to collect him. I wish I could say I was happy he was back. But I'm not. I'm lonelier when he's here than when he's not. That both saddens me and frightens me. I still take my walk to the orchard each day. Since my picnic with Lorah, I find I miss her company. As I walked among the apple trees, bits and pieces of our conversations came back to me and I found myself smiling at something she'd said. I do miss her.

There was an ink mark at the end, like she wanted to write more but had decided against it. Maybe she was afraid to put her thoughts on paper. Afraid someone might see it? Or afraid to admit something, even to herself?

James left this morning, heading once again to New York City. While he doesn't tell me much about his business, he did say he is going into a partnership with someone to begin importing silk from Japan. Doesn't sound like a very smart idea to me. In these hard times, who is going to be buying garments made of silk? He will be away for two months, at least, he said. I shouldn't say this (shouldn't even think it), but it was a relief when Henry drove him off.

Of course, I haven't seen Lorah. She did not come 'round even once while James was here. I do miss her so. It was such a fast, easy friendship we struck up. The ladies in our circle, as James calls the few friends we have, do absolutely nothing for me. In fact, they bore me to tears. We hosted a dinner party one evening when James was here. Six couples, and Hattie had the formal dining room looking spectacular. I didn't feel like my usual engaging self. Nothing felt right about it. I was trying to have a conversation with Mrs. Straton and all I could think about was that I wished I was somewhere chatting with Lorah instead. I wonder why she invades my thoughts so.

Silk? Madilyn didn't remember ever hearing that before. Maybe the partnership never flourished. But she could almost feel Isabel's pain. And loneliness. With a sigh, she turned the page.

Lorah came by today! What a lovely surprise that was. For the last three weeks that James was here, not a sighting of her. I feared she had left the area for good. She confessed that she knew James was here and had stayed away. I missed her so. We stood out by her car and chatted away as if starving for conversation. I teased her that she would soon be in the poor house if she spent her time visiting with me when she should be selling shoes! She said the sweetest thing to me. She said spending time with me made her feel richer than selling a hundred shoes would. Oh, but I do enjoy her company so. Why is that I wonder? She makes me smile. And laugh. When I'm alone, wandering the grounds, I find myself thinking of her. I wish I could spend more time with her.

Madilyn suddenly felt very sorry for Isabel. In 1933, how old would she have been? Her grandfather said she took over running the household when she'd been twenty. He was born in 1935 so yes, Isabel would have been twenty or twenty-one in the picture, she guessed.

I haven't written all week, I know, but I've just been so blissfully happy. Lorah has come every day to see me. We took another picnic, this time Hattie making up thick roast beef sandwiches on the bread that was baked just that morning. We went to the same spot, off in the maple trees at the overlook of the valley, not far past the apple orchard. Lorah brought a nice quilt to sit on. She said her grandmother had made it for her and she always traveled with it. She said she thought this was her favorite spot with the view of the valley. Oh yes, and she brought wine again! I'm getting so daring, drinking it in the middle of the day! It was nice and sweet. I do say it relaxes me. We lay down on the blanket and watched the puffy clouds overhead. Lorah told me she grew up on a farm in Millersville but by the time she was thirteen, she knew she wanted no part of marrying a farmer. I can't see her working on a farm either. She's too lively for that. She moved to Lancaster and worked for a fine cabinetmaker for a while, she said, but she was making only pennies a day. It was her grandfather who loaned her his car and told her to get into sales. She started with selling magazine and newspaper subscriptions but found that most people wanted to barter. One time she brought back six live chickens to her family's farm! Oh, she was full of stories. Such a joy it is to be around her. I tried to give her some money when she was leaving. I know she doesn't have much, what with her not actively out selling shoes. But no, she wouldn't hear of it.

Without reading more, she flipped through the pages again, noting that the entries stopped well before the end of the book. Just blank pages followed. At the very back of the book, just past where she'd put the photograph, was a small envelope addressed to Mrs. James Marak—Isabel. It had a 2-cent stamp, and even though the postmark was faded, she could still make out the date. October 21, 1933. She opened the envelope to take out the letter which appeared to be only a single piece of stationary. Instead, she left it where it was. She would read the diary first.

She was getting sleepy, though, so she'd read more tomorrow. She carefully closed the book and placed it on the table beside the bed, then reached over and turned off the lamp. She closed her eyes with a contented sigh, her mind filled with images of her great-grandmother and a mysterious woman name Lorah.

CHAPTER FIVE

The room was cold and airy when Madilyn woke the next morning. She tossed the covers off and quickly went to close the window she'd left open the night before. The sun was rising, and she could hear birds already welcoming the new day. Instead of getting back under the covers—where it was warm—she gathered her clothes and headed to the bathroom for a shower before breakfast.

Her eyes landed on the diary, and she itched to read it, to find out what happened between Isabel and Lorah. But she could guess, couldn't she? Yes, judging by that photo, she could guess.

That thought made her nearly blush and she hurried into the bathroom, more intrigued than ever about the contents of the diary. She stripped off her sleepshirt, pausing to look at herself in the mirror. She was curvy, not rail thin. Her breasts were full, but she wasn't nearly as well-endowed as her mother. She was, however, a couple of inches taller. Her natural hair color was light brown, but she'd been coloring it blond for so long—to match her blue eyes, a gift from her father— she didn't even remember the real color any longer.

She sighed with a heavy breath. She wasn't what she would consider beautiful, but she got her share of compliments. Why, then, was she still alone? She tilted her head. She wasn't technically alone, she supposed. There was Palmer, after all. She turned away from the mirror. Being alone and not married had absolutely nothing to do with her looks. She'd made a promise to herself a long time ago that she would not settle. She longed for that euphoric, head-over-heels in love feeling for someone. Which was obviously *not* how she felt about Palmer.

She was twenty-seven. Would she eventually give up hope and accept his marriage proposal? She'd always longed for a relationship like her grandparents had. It was clearly evident to anyone who was around them that they were still madly in love, no matter how many years passed them by. They were her role models growing up, not her mother. Her mother flitted from one relationship to another—and from one marriage to another—as often as the seasons changed, it seemed.

She shook her head, in essence shaking away her thoughts as she got into the shower. She needed to make plans. If she was going to stay here through the summer, she'd need more clothes than the few she'd packed. Actually, there were very few clothes at her condo that were suitable for living out here in the countryside. Her wardrobe consisted mostly of dressy suits and fancy cocktail and dinner dresses. There were surely other things she needed as well as clothes, too. As she shampooed her hair, she wondered what that would be. She already had her laptop. She couldn't think of anything else that she *had* to have.

She stuck her face into the water, thinking how sad that was. Was there *nothing* at her home that she couldn't live without? Then again, that was probably a good thing. She prided herself on living simply, minimally. Overcompensating for her mother's extravagance, she thought wryly.

By the time she made it downstairs, her grandfather was already seated at the table. While they always ate lunch in the formal dining room, breakfast and supper were taken in the small, informal dining area at the opposite end of the kitchen. Even then, it was still on the formal side with a crisp tablecloth, sterling silver candleholders and place settings that included multiple forks and spoons. China cups set daintily on saucers, awaiting coffee, and a tiny, matching pitcher that contained the cream her grandfather used. The sugar bowl—for her—was placed near her setting.

"Good morning," she said, pausing to kiss him on the cheek before sitting opposite.

"Good morning, Maddie. Did you sleep well?"

"I did. You?"

He nodded and reached for the bell, signaling to Loretta that they were ready for their coffee. "I had one of the best night's sleep in a long while. Thank you."

She smiled at him. "So, did I really agree to stay here for an extended time?"

He laughed lightly. "We'll see how it works out. Your first order of business, call around and see about hiring a groundskeeper. I thought about it all night. You're right. I do miss the seasonal flowers. The estate used to be a showcase in its day. Not that there are visitors who come to see it, but still."

"It's not like you've let it go. The house is in excellent shape for as old as it is."

Loretta came in, a big smile on her face. "Why, Miss Maddie. Good morning." She poured coffee into her cup. "Mr. Albert tells me that you'll be staying on with him. That's such great news."

"Yes. We'll see how it goes," she said, echoing her grandfather's earlier words.

Loretta moved to fill her grandfather's cup as well, then set the carafe on the table between them. "I was dreading the thought of possibly having to leave here. This has been the only home I've ever known. Why, I can still feel the presence of my grandmother and mother here in the house. It was breaking my heart to think about leaving."

"I imagine so. The thought of him selling was breaking mine too." She glanced at her grandfather, who was smiling a bit sheepishly.

"Ring when you're ready for breakfast. I have ham this morning to go with your eggs."

"Thanks, Loretta," she said with a smile. As soon as she left, Madilyn turned to her grandfather. "You had no intention of selling, did you?" she accused playfully.

"Yes, I had an intention. Of course, I did. I just knew I couldn't go through with it. The Maraks have lived on this land for generations. Lived and died on this land. Some here in this very house. Not my great-great-grandfather, though. This house wasn't built yet when he died. He used to farm the valley. He was plowing the fields with a mule team one morning and collapsed right out there. He was only in his forties, if you can believe that."

"Heart attack?"

"Back then, I don't believe they knew for sure how anyone died. My great-grandfather took over then, and he was the one who had the real business smarts. He started buying up land all around. People thought he was a damn fool. What was he going to do with all that land?" He laughed heartily. "He, like my own father, made a fortune in real estate. Built this big, beautiful house then too. Of course, it's been remodeled and modernized so many times, I'm sure it hardly resembles the original. But the key was knowing what land to buy up, how long to hold on to it, and when it was the right time to sell. At one time, he owned all the land from Villanova to the Schuylkill River to the east and damn near down to the Delaware River to the south. Not to mention the pockets to the west that we still own today." He waved his hand. "I've told you all that before. My point is, I think they would all be very disappointed in me if I sold the family estate and the remaining land."

"Have you formally asked Mother if she is interested in taking it over or do you just assume she wouldn't?"

"Margaret? My heavens, no. Like I said, she has no interest in the place, never has. She has her own albatross to tend to, anyway—the mansion, as you're fond of calling it." He picked up his coffee cup. "Not that I consider this an albatross, mind you. But hers? She uses it a few times a year to host ballroom parties, that's about it. She spends most of her time in Manhattan, as you know."

"Yes. I'm surprised she's hung on to it this long. She mostly complains about the cost of the upkeep and keeping a staff there to run things."

"How often do you and your mother talk, Maddie?"

"Talk?" Did they talk? They spoke. They didn't actually ever *talk* about things. "Occasionally," she said, which was vague, she knew. "She'll call now and then. If there's a function she'd like to be seen at, she lets me know. We try to have dinner when she's in Philly."

"Function? For the Foundation?"

"Yes." She shrugged. "A few times a year."

"Which is about how often we saw her these last few years. That's no way to treat family."

"Our relationship is superficial only, as you know." She added more coffee to her cup. "I never quite lived up to what she wanted in a daughter. I was not tiny and petite like her. She used to make fun of me, saying I was too tall for a girl."

"You're not overly tall, Maddie."

"I know. I was tall as a kid, though. I wasn't a little princess that she could dress up and show off. I'm not the socialite she wanted for a daughter. I don't seek the limelight. Far from it. She told me once that I'd never make it in this family if I didn't learn how to play the game."

"As Belle would say, that's hogwash. There is no game, Maddie. It's business. Margaret, however, turned it into a game when she went away to college. Now here she is, nearly sixty years old and acting like she's still in a sorority."

Madilyn laughed. "She would quickly correct you, Pops. She's fifty-eight."

He picked up the bell and shook it several times. "Regardless, she doesn't have a clue as to how the real world works. That's our fault, of course. And as I said, when Belle was alive, she'd give her what she wanted most of the time. That was always a bone of contention between Belle and me."

"Was it?"

"Oh, yes. Your mother was such a beautiful young child. So easy to spoil. And with her being the only one, we had a hard time saying no to her. When she got older, it became apparent that she had no ambition or sense of responsibility. Again, our fault. Yet I couldn't seem to get Belle to take a stand with me. Margaret snapped her fingers and Belle gave in."

"Well, she has her own money. I don't suppose she comes to you for anything."

"Not so much since her last divorce. I think she came out of that one quite well. Still, after I'm gone, I'm sure you will have to deal with her in some capacity regarding the Foundation, at the very least. But you can handle her."

"I'm not so sure," she said as she refilled his coffee cup for him. "I've never had to handle her, as you say. She is the mother and I'm the daughter. There is some dynamic to that, you know."

He moved his cup and saucer closer to him. "I doubt that particular dynamic has ever come into play for you two. You lived here until you were almost ten. I wouldn't exactly say she was the one raising you. You spent more time with me and Belle than you did her. When she moved you to the mansion, there were nannies and the like, so she was still out of the picture."

"Yes, all true." Several nannies, in fact. All the while, her mother flitted off to Manhattan, coming back around to make an appearance here and there. She often wished she could have stayed here at the estate with Grandpops and Grandma Belle. Here it had at least been a little more normal. With Evan being older, he was already away at boarding school, leaving her behind. But only for a few years. She'd been shuttled off to her own boarding school in Philadelphia. She'd positively hated it. In fact, she—

Loretta came in with the serving tray, interrupting her thoughts. Just as well, she supposed. That wasn't a time in her life that she cherished, and she certainly didn't want to revisit it. The tray was laden with two plates of scrambled eggs and ham, two smaller plates with buttery toasted bread, and two small dishes that she now knew contained homemade apple and raspberry jam made by a relative of Loretta's.

"Here you go," Loretta said as she placed a plate in front of her. "I brought some more of the jam you liked so."

"Good, thank you. It was delicious."

In fact, she slathered some on her toasted bread and took a bite before even touching the ham and eggs.

"Do you need to go into the city? I'm sure you'll need some of your things," her grandfather said when Loretta left them.

"Yes. I thought I'd go tomorrow."

"Have Randy drive you."

"I can manage, Pops. I'll have some stops to make too." Namely, she should probably see Palmer while she was back.

"I'd prefer Randy take you, help you with what you need, Maddie."

She smiled at him. "Are you afraid I'll run away and not come back?"

He smiled too. "You visited us at least once a month. I doubt this will make you run." His gaze turned serious. "You're all I have left. I'm just trying to be cautious."

"You have a grandson and a daughter. I'm not all you have left." She cut into the thick slice of ham. "And I will come back. I promise."

"Evan comes around less than your mother, which is seldom as it is. Comes around when his money is running low. He took after his mother in that regard. He never stays to visit."

"I know. They didn't stick around after the burial, did they?"

"Evan has nothing but to follow in your mother's footsteps. Did you know that Margaret has been bringing him along with her to parties and introducing him to her friends?"

She nodded. "Yes. Evan told me."

He raised an eyebrow thoughtfully. "And what about you and Evan? Do you get along?"

"Well enough, I suppose. We don't really have much in common, as you know."

"In other words, you don't speak often?"

"I see him less than I see Mother and we rarely speak on the phone."

Her grandfather let out a heavy sigh. "I guess I shouldn't worry about it. It's too late to change anyone."

"You're right. You shouldn't worry about it. I do agree that their life must be very shallow—superficial—and unsatisfying. At least, it would be to me." She shrugged. "But none of my business. They seem happy. We shouldn't concern ourselves."

"Do they?"

The question hung between them, and she wondered if he expected her to answer it. She chose not to.

CHAPTER SIX

Madilyn climbed the stairs hurriedly, intending to take some time to read the diary. Instead, she found herself going toward her grandparents' old room. She paused outside the door, thinking she would just look around and see if there was anything Grandma Belle had left behind. Anything that would be a keepsake. Then she supposed she would have the room cleaned out and she would turn it into another guest room. Another room that would rarely—if at all—be used.

She pushed the door open and paused to look around before going inside. It didn't seem familiar. As he had said, Grandma Belle had moved most of their things downstairs years ago. She went over to the dresser, finding a tall jewelry box with two small, swinging doors. The jewelry box her grandmother had kept her rings and more expensive things in had been downstairs in their bedroom. A box that her mother had already been through.

She opened the doors on this one, finding several pull-out drawers—six, to be exact. She pulled out the top drawer. It contained three gold necklaces. They looked fragile and she didn't remember her grandmother ever wearing them. She closed it and moved on to the second. This one contained only a brooch. It appeared to be a flower with a jade stone in the center. She took it out and fingered it. Not a jade, no. An emerald? She ran her thumb over the stone then put the brooch back inside.

The third drawer contained rings. Eight or ten, she thought as she pushed them around, looking through them. They were all gold and seemed rather simple, some with designs carved on them, others not. If her mother had gone through this—which she doubted she had—she would have dismissed these without even picking them up. She was about to do just that when one caught her eye. She plucked it out, holding it up to get a better look at it. It appeared to be two gold bands that had been entwined, making a type of rope ring.

Without thinking, she slipped it on the ring finger of her right hand. It fit perfectly. She spun it around on her finger a few times, then was about to take it off and put it back but thought otherwise. She left the ring on her finger, pushing closed the drawer and opening the fourth one. This one contained more necklaces, although these all had pendants attached. She sorted through them, but none held her interest.

The last two drawers were empty, and she closed the jewelry box again. She absently pulled out the drawers of the dresser, surprised to find clothing in them. Garments that her grandmother hadn't wanted, apparently. She moved to the closet, but it was completely empty, as was the tall chest of drawers that was against the wall.

Instead of leaving, she went to the window and looked out, pulling aside the curtains. The ring on her finger caught her attention. There was something so familiar about it, but she was certain she'd never seen it before.

Or had she?

She hurried from the room and into her own. She closed the door behind her, then went to the bed and picked up the diary. She flipped to the middle where she'd stashed the photo last night. Her eyes widened as she pulled it out.

Lorah's right hand was in view as she touched Isabel's chin. And on her finger was…the same ring? Madilyn pulled her eyes from the photo and stared at the ring she had placed on her finger. Was it the same ring? She looked back at the photo. Isabel's left hand was in her lap, and it appeared to show a wedding ring. But her right hand was on Lorah's shoulder, and she couldn't tell if there was a ring there or not. Was this Lorah's ring? Had Lorah given it to Isabel? Or had they had matching rings?

Only one way to find out.

She took the diary to the posh chair in the corner, but before sitting down, she opened the curtains, letting in the midmorning sun. A glance down to the grounds reminded her that she promised her grandfather she'd see about hiring someone. She would speak with Randy about it. Perhaps he knew of someone locally who would be interested in working for them.

She sat down and crossed her legs, then opened the diary, going to where she'd stopped the night before.

I haven't written in a while because I haven't known what to say. Well, that's not entirely true. I've been afraid to say it. Lorah comes by every day now. I no longer worry about what Hattie and the others think or whether they'll tell James about her when he returns. There's nothing wrong with me having a friend. Besides, Lorah has completely charmed Hattie. So much so that Hattie made up a mess of gingersnap cookies for her yesterday. The problem is, Lorah has completely charmed me as well. I think about her constantly when she's not here and when she is, I just want to go off with her and sit and talk and be close to her and look into her eyes. That scares me. Because I feel things when I'm near her. I think she does too. Whatever in the world is wrong with me?

Oh, poor Isabel, she thought.

Lorah surprised me by showing up for breakfast! Hattie didn't mind in the least and whipped up a meal for the both of us. What did surprise me (and Hattie) was Lorah's suggestion that we eat outside on the porch to enjoy the sunshine. Before I knew what was happening, Hattie had the girls bring a table and two chairs out to the side porch. And what a feast it was! Fresh eggs and bacon, Dora's biscuits and jam (she is Hattie's mother), and an extra pot of coffee. It was a glorious morning and Lorah said the sweetest thing to me. She said the main reason she wanted to eat outside was because my eyes turn a deeper blue when out. Then she told me how much she enjoyed looking into them. Oh, my heart surely did flutter so in my chest. But she had to leave shortly after our meal. She said she was heading north, all the way to Morgantown. There was a new merchant there who wanted to take a look at some of her inventory. She seemed excited that he might buy some shoes from her to sell in his store. She doesn't know how long she'll be gone. Several days, to be sure. I'll miss her. But she left me with a long, tight hug that I still can't quite shake. It made me tingle all the way to my toes.

Isabel had blue eyes. Madilyn had always assumed she'd inherited her eye color from her father but perhaps it was from her great-grandmother instead. Her grandfather had said she favored Isabel. Perhaps her eyes were a mirror image of hers, not her father's.

She glanced back at the diary. The next entry was short, but meaningful.

I miss Lorah. I miss her in a way that I should miss James, but I don't. I don't give him a thought, day or night. No. My thoughts are only filled with Lorah.

She'd just turned the page when there was a knock on the door. She quickly closed the diary and placed it beside her bed again. When she opened the door, Loretta was standing there.

"Miss Maddie, I'm sorry to bother you. Your grandfather wanted me to let you know that your mother called. She's on her way up. In fact, I think she was only a few minutes away."

"Really? Isn't that odd that she'd come back so quickly? If at all."

Loretta's lips pursed. "Well, I don't pretend to understand their relationship, but your mother rarely took the time to visit, even when Miss Belle was as sick as she was." She shook her head disapprovingly. "I know this isn't news to you." She looked behind them as if making sure they were alone. "She only comes around when she wants something." Then she shook her head again. "I'm sorry. I shouldn't speak like that. It's not my place and she *is* your mother."

Madilyn touched her arm affectionately. "Loretta, you've been around the family your whole life. It's no secret how my mother is, so you're not offending me. But yes, I'll go down with you to meet her."

Halfway down the stairs, she heard her grandfather—and his cane—coming from his study. Loretta quietly disappeared and Madilyn met him at the bottom, her eyebrows raised.

"Mother is coming?"

"Yes. Apparently she has some urgent news to discuss with me."

"She was here four days ago. I'm surprised she didn't talk to you then."

"Maddie, dear, your mother's whims come and go." He leaned on his cane. "Do you want to sit in with us? This might be a good time to let her know that I've handed over the Foundation to you."

"Oh, I don't think you should tell her. She won't take it well."

The front door nearly flew open, and her mother burst inside with her usual flair. Amazing, but in four days' time, her platinum-blond hair had been changed to a glaring red color. She was wearing tight black pants, tucked into knee-high boots with at least a four-inch heel. Her blouse was a silky leopard print with a plunging neckline.

"Madilyn?"

"Hello, Mother."

"Well, I had no idea you were still here. It's just as well. I have some exciting news to share." She went to him and air-kissed both cheeks. "How are you, Father?"

"Doing really well. Especially since Maddie is going to hang around for a while and keep me company."

Her mother turned nearly accusing eyes on her. "You are? Why on earth?"

"Because he asked me to," she said easily.

Her mother waved red-tipped fingers in the air. "Whatever." She turned back to him. "Shall we talk in your study? Perhaps Loretta would be kind enough to bring us a glass of brandy." She turned to her. "Madilyn? Would you tend to that for us, please? Have Loretta bring it to the study."

"No need," her grandfather interjected. "The bar in my study is stocked. Maddie, please join us."

"Of course."

Not much had changed in his study over the years. Two large windows let in light and a credenza was between them against the wall. His desk was quite massive, and she knew that it had been his grandfather's desk to begin with. Two plush leather chairs faced the desk, and a small leather sofa was against the opposite wall. Beside that was the bar, and he moved to it, taking out three glasses.

"None for me, thanks," she said.

"You were always such a lightweight," her mother mocked. "You take after your father in that regard."

"Thank you," she said easily. She took a seat in one of the chairs and crossed her legs. She felt a bit underdressed in her casual slacks, but at least she'd had the foresight to not put on the lone pair of jeans she'd brought with her. Tight-fitting designer jeans, but still—jeans. It didn't matter, though. Her mother had told her on numerous occasions that she had no fashion sense whatsoever. And that was true, she supposed. The fact was, she simply didn't care to play the dress-up game like her mother did.

Her grandfather rolled his chair closer to the desk, then waved his hand at her mother. "Now, Margaret, what's so urgent? You were in quite a hurry to leave last week after the burial. What's going on to bring you back so quickly?"

"I have exciting news, as I said." Her mother gave a brilliant smile, then held her left hand out, flashing a huge diamond. "I'm getting married!"

His eyes widened. "Again?" he asked dryly.

"He's a wonderful man, Father. You'll love him."

"Great. When do we get to meet him?"

"Well, actually, he flew home this morning." She smiled broadly. "He's British, but he lives in Greece."

"I see."

"I'll be selling the mansion, of course. And as much as it's killing me to do it, I'll be getting rid of my Manhattan apartment too."

"Congratulations," she said. "When is the wedding?"

"We haven't decided for sure, but very soon. It will be a small, private affair only. Just a few of our closest friends. He has a villa on one of the islands. That's where we'll live. It's going to be so exciting, isn't it?"

"Sounds wonderful."

"How long have you known this chap?" her grandfather asked.

Her mother waved her hand in the air dramatically. "Oh, a while now. His wife died last year and well, you know how it is."

"How old is he?" her grandfather asked bluntly.

"He is a very young-looking seventy-nine." The smile on her face was absolutely brilliant. "And he has no children, poor thing."

Madilyn nearly rolled her eyes. How lucky could her mother get?

"I take it you don't expect us to attend the wedding," her grandfather said. "Will we even get to meet him?"

"Well, Evan will join me. Richard is going to have Evan run one of his companies there in London. Evan is nearly beside himself at the prospect."

Evan, who hasn't worked a day in his life, was going to *run* a company? Right.

"Well, you certainly seem excited by the prospect of another marriage," he said, a smile playing on his lips. "Congratulations, Margaret. This is indeed exciting news for you. And for Evan. How wonderful that he'll be given something to do."

"We are both very excited, yes. I wanted to share the news with you in person. I'm flying out in a week. Two at the most, I'd think. This was the only time I had to come out to see you. I'll let you know the details in case you want to fly out for the big event." Her mother glanced over at her. "You too, Madilyn. But I don't want either of you to feel obligated to attend. As I said, it will be a very small ceremony."

She nodded, knowing that was her mother's attempt at being polite while telling them they weren't really wanted or needed at the wedding.

"At my age, I don't think I'm up to flying across the globe any longer, Margaret. But if you're happy, I'm happy."

"Positively ecstatic, Father!"

"Good for you."

Madilyn stood. "Yes, I'm happy for you. Do you plan to stay for lunch? I'll let Loretta know."

"No, no. I can't possibly. There are a million things to do. I must get back."

"Of course." She went to her, wondering if they should hug or something. No. They weren't huggers. Besides, her mother's stiff back told her not to attempt it. Instead, she touched her arm lightly. "I guess we'll see you whenever we see you then."

"Yes, darling. I don't know when we'll be back in the States. Perhaps when we are, we could meet for dinner, and I'll introduce you to Richard."

"Of course," she said again, on cue. "Well, I have a few things to do before lunch. Good to see you, Mother. Have a safe trip."

She escaped without another word. When she closed the door, her mother was describing the villa where she would be moving off to. Madilyn wasn't really surprised by her mother's news. This would be her fifth marriage. Or was it six? And taking Evan with her? That wasn't shocking either. As far as she knew, Evan had no life of his own. It stood to reason that he would go with her. She did wonder why her mother had not hinted at this engagement when she was here for the burial. Perhaps because she hadn't known about it. Maybe Richard—the poor thing—had just now popped the question.

With a sigh, she went back through the house toward the stairs. She pushed her mother's impending marriage aside. She wanted to go back to her room.

Back to Lorah and Isabel.

CHAPTER SEVEN

We had the most wonderful day today. Lorah took us way down the valley past the peach and pear orchards and over to Brandywine Creek for our picnic. I showed her where the bridge was, and she drove us right across. Hattie put together such a wonderful basket for us and we laid the blanket under a big hemlock. We didn't see another soul while there, but I don't suppose we would have. It is still all Marak land, even though James leases out a lot of it for farming. Not on that side of the creek, though. We walked along the bank and, dare I say, we held hands as if it was the most natural thing to do. Oh, my heart simply sings when I'm around her. We stood close together under the trees and just stared into each other's eyes as birdsong serenaded us. It was all so familiar, I would swear I'd been in that very place sometime before. I hated for the day to come to an end, but it did of course. She left with a promise to come back tomorrow. I know when I sleep, I will have dreams of her. Dreams of us. Together.

"Oh, lord," Madilyn murmured. "I can't believe I'm reading this." And what bridge, she wondered. She had never heard that there was a bridge out here. The next entry, however, left her speechless.

She kissed me. I can't write about it. I'm still too shook up.

"So, it's really happening." She closed the book, again wondering if she should be reading something so personal as her great-grandmother's love affair. A love affair with another woman. The diary—journal—was hidden for a reason. To think that she might actually be the only other person to read it was quite remarkable. So remarkable, in fact, that she wanted to share it with someone else. Of course, there was no one. She certainly wouldn't show it to her grandfather.

She glanced down at her hand, the ring still on her finger. She had never worn rings before, but this one felt familiar. It truly did fit perfectly. Almost as if it had been made for her. Again, she wondered if it was Lorah's ring or if it had been Isabel's. A gift from Lorah, perhaps. She gave a contented sigh and opened the diary again.

It's early morning. The sun is not even up. But I can't sleep. What will I say to her when she comes today? Oh, but my heart hammered so. It still does at just the mere thought of the kiss. It was unlike anything I've ever felt before. Does it mean what I think it means? Can it be? Oh, I'm so scared. Yes, I am. A part of me wants to tell her not to come 'round anymore. But I don't think I could bear it. I would miss her. She's become a part of me now. My days—and nights—are filled with her. I think I would slowly die if she stopped coming to see me.

Oh, poor Isabel. Yes, she must have been frightened out of her mind to find herself attracted to another woman. A woman whose kiss made her heart hammer. Madilyn stared out into space. She was twenty-seven years old. Had her heart ever hammered in her chest from a kiss? No. She wondered what that would feel like.

But was that what had happened? Had Isabel told her to stay away? Well, obviously not right away. There was the photo. And the letter. Madilyn itched to read it. Before she could turn the page to the next entry, the alarm on her phone sounded. Time for lunch. She sighed. She wasn't hungry in the least. Not after that big breakfast Loretta had served them. She couldn't possibly keep eating like this.

With another sigh, she put the diary back beside her bed. Maybe this afternoon she would take it with her while she explored the grounds. She needed to have some plans in place for when they hired someone to replace Bennie. That was an excuse, of course. She wanted to get off by herself where she could read uninterrupted. She was dying to find out what happened between Lorah and Isabel.

CHAPTER EIGHT

Before joining her grandfather, she stopped off in the kitchen where Loretta was busy putting the finishing touches on their lunch. Baked chicken today with a lovely rice dish.

"A very small plate for me, Loretta. I'm not used to eating such big meals at lunch. In fact, I would rather you make a plate for me that I could heat up for dinner. I'll just have something very small. Maybe some of that breakfast ham in a sandwich."

Loretta looked at her disapprovingly. "But Mr. Albert—"

"He is used to eating this way. Please? After that delicious breakfast, I wouldn't do this meal justice. Just a sandwich. I'll tackle this chicken and rice for dinner. Deal?"

"Well, I don't think he will approve, but if that's what you'd like."

"Thank you. And no wine for me."

Her grandfather was already at the table, sipping on his wine. She half-expected to find her mother there as well, thinking maybe he had persuaded her to stay.

"She left?"

"Oh, yes. A million things to do," he mimicked. "She did seem very happy though."

"No doubt. A wealthy seventy-nine-year-old man with no children. How could she not be happy?"

He laughed. "Oh, your mother can find them. I keep hoping one of these days she'll marry for love and not money. Maybe this will be the one."

"Maybe so." Although she highly doubted it.

He tapped his fingers on the tablecloth. "How do you feel about it all?"

"What do you mean?"

"Well, the fact that Evan will accompany her, that he'll be a part of it."

"Do you think I'm jealous of Evan?" She shook her head. "Most of his adult life has been tagging after Mother. This is no different. Maybe he'll find some purpose to his life there. And you're right. She did seem happy. I do wonder how often we'll see either of them, though."

"The next time she sees me may very well be when you bury me next to my Belle. If she bothers to come at all."

Madilyn smiled at him. "We have a strange family."

He laughed heartily at that. "Yes, we do. I daresay we're not the first Marak to think that." He waved his hand in the air. "Now, let's talk about you. What about my idea to make a study for you down here? I want you to have your own space, but in the meantime, you could use my study if you need to."

"No, no. I thought maybe I'd turn that small first bedroom into an office for me. I noticed that there was an old dropdown desk in the attic. I could use that for the time being."

"Is there? I have no idea what's all up there." He nodded. "Of course. Do what you want. Let Randy know. He'll move the furniture for you and get it fixed up."

"Yes. I was going to speak with him later. But there's no rush for him to move things. I feel like taking some time to just relax for a few weeks. Get used to being here. Reacquaint myself with the grounds."

"That's wonderful. Yes, you should."

She nodded. "I'll also get with Mr. Reeves by the end of the month and go over some of our options on new grants. In the meantime, though, I thought I might borrow one of Randy's golf carts. The trails to the old orchard are still there, aren't they?"

"They are. Some of the trees are still producing, though they are very old. I never had any interest in keeping the orchards up. My mother used to love going out there for walks, I recall. She went daily."

"What about the orchards over by Brandywine Creek? Do we still own that land?"

"Oh, yes, of course. On both sides of the creek. But I'm sure those trees are long dead. That's part of the area that Belle wanted to set aside for wildlife. We had thought about donating it to the Commonwealth in the hopes they might construct a state park there, but we could never agree on their plans." He took a sip of his wine. "I used to swim in that area when I was a boy. We had horses back then. I'd ride down through the valley and over to the orchards and creek. Crystal clear water, it was. Don't know if it still is. Belle wasn't interested in the state turning it into a campground with people running amok, though, so we've just left it wild. I haven't been down to that area in more years than I can recall."

"Besides the land here around the estate, there is still more out there, isn't it?"

"More than we know what to do with, yes. We still lease a lot of it. I need to introduce you to Eric Bingham. He manages all of the land for me, handles the contracts on the leases and whatnot. He lives just up in Parkesburg. He swings by once a month or so and we go over it all. Formality only as he also sends me a detailed report. Everything is audited yearly anyway, but at least I still know what's going on." He sighed almost wistfully. "Oh, if I was younger, I would be more involved, I suppose. I might even be inclined to get the orchards all up and running again. But I'm past all that, Maddie." He eyed her thoughtfully. "Why? Do you think that's something you might be interested in?"

"It seems like the orchards have always been a part of our past. It's a shame they've gone to ruins."

"My mother was so passionate about them. In fact, she learned to drive just so she could venture over to the Brandywine Creek area. At least once a week, she'd take a picnic basket and go there. All by herself. But the orchard here, up against the valley—always apple— she'd walk to them once a day, every day. Even in winter. They held little interest for my father and once she was gone, he neglected them completely." He picked up his wineglass and took a sip. "My father was all about money and the orchards brought in very little compared to his other endeavors. I hate to admit it, but I wasn't much better with them. They eventually fell to ruins, as you say."

"Did…did she have any friends?"

"My mother?" His brows drew together as if recalling his childhood. "I don't believe so, no. Oh, as with all the Marak ladies, there were parties to host and of course, the Christmas ball. That was a tradition from way back. But I don't recall her having any close friends, no. To me, I always think of her as a loner. She always seemed to want to be by herself."

"Was she distant from you?"

"Oh, no. I wouldn't say that. She was very attentive and loving with me. So kind, as I said. But she was never what I would call happy. Like there was something missing. As a boy, I didn't concern myself with my parents' marriage. But as I got older, after Belle and I were married, the difference was glaring."

"They weren't in love with each other?" she asked, already knowing the answer.

"I suppose that's the real reason they slept apart. But really, it was almost as if she just drifted away from us. Every day a little bit more until one morning, she didn't wake up and she had drifted away for good."

"Sad for her," she said without thinking. "For you too," she added quickly. "You were so young."

"My father was a hard man to live with. Hard to love, I imagine. Where she was kind, he was not. Where she was soft, he was hard. Very hard. I often thought if she had lived, I would not have been sent away to boarding school, which I hated at the time. But then I wouldn't have met Belle. I can't imagine my life without her in it."

She had so many questions she wanted to ask him about Isabel, but she dared not. Surely he would be curious as to her sudden interest in his mother. Loretta came in then with their serving tray. As she'd requested, a sandwich—on toasted bread—was on her plate. It looked quite meager compared to her grandfather's full offering.

"Loretta? What is that?" he asked, pointing to her sandwich.

"I requested it," Madilyn quickly answered. "I'll save my chicken dinner for later." She smiled at Loretta. "It looks great. Thank you."

"I put a nice, thick slice of cheese on there too." She automatically topped off her grandfather's wineglass. "Ring when you're ready for dessert."

"I'm not sure I'll ever get used to eating the main meal at noon every day," she said when she picked up the sandwich that had been cut conveniently in half.

"We've always eaten at this time. Even in Belle's family, the main meal was at noontime. A sandwich such as that might be served at supper."

"Then perhaps I should skip breakfast. I might be hungry at noon then." She bit into the sandwich, noting the tangy mayo that had been added.

He laughed. "Then maybe I should tell Loretta to get back to my normal breakfasts."

"You mean ham and eggs aren't it?"

"Oatmeal and fruit most mornings. She usually only serves eggs on the weekends or when you would visit. Since you've been here, I think she's trying to impress."

"Well, that's a relief. I was afraid to decline, seeing as how much effort she's put into it." Then she smiled at him. "I actually hate oatmeal, though. A piece of toast and some of that excellent jam she has would be sufficient."

She finished her sandwich long before he'd finished his meal and she excused herself, saying she wanted to visit with Randy. Not necessarily about setting up an office for her. No, she wanted to get out onto the grounds, and she hoped he'd have a golf cart for her to use.

She hurried up the stairs, but instead of changing into her jeans, she put on the lone pair of shorts she'd brought along with her. Her wardrobe tended toward the dressy side, not casual. A lunch date at a fancy restaurant didn't lend itself to casual. Certainly not dinner dates. And when she attended functions on behalf of the Foundation, she always dressed the part. She'd at least learned that much from her mother. She hated every bit of it, however.

She didn't follow her mother's advice to "play the game." No. She didn't play her mother's game, but she was playing a game all the same. She was pretending to be someone—something—she wasn't. Oh, she was that someone in name, of course. That's as deep as it went. She would never admit this to her grandfather, but she'd often thought of running away from the Marak name and doing something shocking, like getting a real job.

That would solve nothing, she knew. The trust fund that fed her banking accounts wouldn't go away. As she got older, she realized that perhaps she could do some good things by changing how they disbursed grants at the Foundation. She'd given smaller amounts of money to under-the-radar organizations that never raised a red flag with either Bob Reeves or her grandfather. Those were the organizations that truly were appreciative of the money and the ones she wanted to focus on. Unlike the huge conglomerates that receive hundreds of millions in donations annually.

Now that she'd gotten her grandfather's permission to start up a grant program for universities, she would now have something worthwhile to keep her busy. Of course, if she stayed here—and worked from here—would her so-called relationship with Palmer dissolve on its own? Would she turn into a recluse? Only going out to functions when absolutely necessary?

Was that what had happened to Isabel? She didn't want to jump to conclusions about them, but she suspected Isabel and Lorah had fallen deeply in love. Lorah had obviously left, whether by her own accord or Isabel's request, but she'd disappeared from her life. There could be another reason, though. Maybe Lorah got sick and died. Or maybe she moved far away. Any number of things could have happened.

But in the end, according to her grandfather, Isabel had wandered the apple orchard, alone, withdrawn from the family. Until she simply wasted away and died. How very sad. She went over to her bed and picked up the diary. Maybe she should reconsider moving out here, she thought with a smile. She would hate to end up like Isabel, alone and searching. Her smile left her. Searching for what, though?

CHAPTER NINE

Randy had offered the green John Deere utility vehicle that he most often used, but she wanted the quiet of a golf cart. They had two, one of which his wife Julia used most often. The other looked brand new and seldom used, but he assured her the battery was fully charged. He also warned her not to get off the trails. With that warning, she got his number and added it to her cell phone, just in case. In case the cart died on her and in case she got lost. She'd not been to the orchard since she'd been a child, and she hardly remembered it at all. She had slipped the diary into her purse, then felt conspicuous taking a purse along with her in the first place. Instead, she'd gone down to the kitchen, finding a cloth bag that Loretta used when grocery shopping.

Beside her on the seat was an old quilt she'd found in the closet of her room. The diary and a bottle of water were inside the cloth bag. She felt rather free as she set out, leaving the estate behind her as she headed toward the orchard. Far off in the distance, she could see the beginnings of the valley. She could make out what looked like an old homestead, and she wondered if that was where George and Clara Class had lived with their children. It most likely was in shambles now, as were a lot of the other dwellings on Marak land. Isabel had written that they leased out a lot of the land for farming and her grandfather had said the same. She didn't know if the Maraks had built the houses or not. Probably. She couldn't imagine those coming here to farm would have had the money to build.

It was a warm, sunny spring day that hinted at summer. The sky was blue and cloudless. The golf cart silently traveled along the old trail, the wheels pressing down the new spring grass as she went. She recognized the orchard when she came to it—the trees all planted symmetrically in rows. Her grandfather had said these were all apples. That was all Isabel had mentioned too. She'd written that the other orchard near Brandywine Creek also produced peaches and pears.

There were a few trees in bloom still as tiny pink flowers seemed to wave at her as she got nearer, yet most of the trees were dead and leafless. When she was young, more trees had been alive than dead, the opposite of now. She remembered coming down and picking apples right off the tree. Of course, that was twenty-something years ago.

She stopped the golf cart and pulled out the diary, going back to some of the early entries. She found the one she was looking for.

We went to the same spot, off in the maple trees at the overlook of the valley, not far past the apple orchard.

She glanced around, wondering where this overlook might be. The orchard sloped slightly, then beyond it was a rise with, yes, maple trees. Her heart beat excitedly as she headed in that direction. The old trail stopped, however, and she was hesitant to go any farther in the cart. Instead, she put the diary back in the bag and swung it over her arm, then grabbed the quilt and took off on foot.

The maple trees were large and mature, yet the new leaves were just starting to pop out. She walked among them, reaching out to touch one, feeling the bark against her fingers. She stopped and dropped the quilt, knowing instinctively she was getting close. Looking around, she tried to imagine them here, hoping to find their spot. A little farther along, the rise sloped sharply downward. She stood there, her breath catching as she looked out on the expanse of the green valley far below her. The overlook. She'd found it. Surely this had to be it.

She was smiling as she held her arms out and turned in a circle. Yes. Right here. She could almost feel their presence. She took a deep breath of the clean spring air, then, without much thought, walked over to get the quilt she'd dropped. She spread it out beneath one of the trees, then sat right down, her gaze fixed on the valley below for long seconds.

She stretched her legs out finally and fished the diary out of the bag. She flipped through the pages, finding where she'd left off earlier. The kiss.

I'm not sure what to say. I'm not sure where to even start. When Lorah came by today, midmorning, she was her usual charming self. Laughing and teasing and putting me at ease. There was no mention of the kiss. In fact, Lorah acted as if she might not even have remembered it. I, on the other hand, was a basket of nerves. If she noticed, she made no mention. Hattie made us a light lunch of fried egg sandwiches on Dora's thick, homemade bread. My stomach was in such knots, I could hardly eat. Then Lorah suggested we walk to the apple orchard. She was full of stories today, making me laugh so, like only she can. By the time we climbed the rise to the overlook, we were both out of breath. Then it happened. Our eyes met and I knew right then that she had not forgotten the kiss. And I knew as she looked at me, she could tell I had not forgotten either. I don't know who moved first, me or her, but I found myself in her arms, pressed oh so close to her. Our kiss this time was so desperate, so passionate, I very nearly fainted right then and there. No, there was no mistaking what that kiss meant. I pulled away from her. Of course I did. I'm a married woman! She apologized as I knew she would. Where I got the nerve to ask her, I'll never know. But I did. Was she falling in love with me? Oh, she gave me the sweetest smile. It melted my heart right there. Issy, she said, I fell in love with you the moment I met you. Issy, she called me! I looked her in the eye and told her the truth. Yes, I was in love with her too. And then I burst into tears right there in her arms. We sat down against a tree, and she held me until I was all cried out. I still don't know why I cried so. I'm frightened by what I feel, of course. But what can we do? I'm a married woman. I have no business being out with her, not feeling the way I do. But I simply can't bear the thought of not seeing her again. James will be gone another month, at least. I'm afraid of what will happen. You hear hushed stories about people—women—like this. I've never met anyone, though. I don't even know of any, but still, you hear gossip. And now here I am, one of those women. Whatever am I going to do?

Oh, poor Isabel. Madilyn's heart broke for her, and she lay the diary in her lap, looking out over the valley as she tried to picture the two women. Yes, when she'd first seen the photo, she knew, didn't she? By the way they were looking at each other, by the way Lorah was touching Isabel, she could see that they were in love. But good lord, had they slept together? Did it go that far?

She nearly blushed at the thought. If that was the case, she had absolutely no business reading about it! Still, she picked up the diary again, unable to stifle her curiosity.

It's been three days. Lorah hasn't come by. I'm scared to death that she's left me. I haven't been able to eat, and Hattie is starting to worry. Oh, my dearest Lorah...please come back to me. I beg you. Please.

Madilyn took a deep breath, noting her hand was trembling as she turned the page.

Lorah came today. Unmindful of Hattie, I was so excited to see her, I flew into her arms, knocking her right down on the ground! We started laughing so, my stomach hurt! There was not one word spoken about my tears or the kiss. Not one. Hattie seemed excited to see Lorah too, for she cooked up such a fine meal for us. Fatty beef steak and some new potatoes and green peas that she'd sent the girls out to the garden for, along with warm buttered bread that had come fresh from the oven. She topped that off with a delicious rhubarb pie for dessert. It too was still warm and Lorah thanked Hattie so for the meal, the young woman was blushing head to toe from the compliment! Such a charmer, Lorah is. We never had a chance to be alone, other than when she was leaving. I did ask her why she'd stayed away. She said she hated that she'd made me cry. She left then, saying she had some shoes to sell. She said she would come back again tomorrow if I wanted her to. I told her yes, I did. I also told her we needed to talk. Of course, now I'm afraid of what will happen. No. Mainly I'm afraid that she'll leave me. Or worse. That she won't even come back at all. The mention of us talking sent fear into her eyes...eyes that I'm beginning to know as well as my own.

Madilyn turned the page, nearly feeling as afraid as Isabel must have been.

Lorah didn't come today. Maybe she is afraid, like me. Afraid of what will happen between us. I wish there was someone I could talk to, someone other than myself on these pages. Lorah has quickly become the best friend I never had before. Friend, yes, but so much more. The thoughts I have about her crossed the line of friendship a while ago. I think maybe there's no need to talk about it. We both know. I would dare to say Hattie may know as well.

It was the next entry that made Madilyn catch her breath.

Lorah stayed the night with me. Oh, I was a basket of nerves, to be sure. It was late afternoon when she came by. She apologized for not coming yesterday but she was all the way up in Morgantown. She wasn't going to stay, saying she had to get into town to secure a room for the night. It was Hattie who suggested to me that I invite Lorah to stay in one of the guest rooms. She said it so casually, as if it would be rude not to invite her, that the offer tumbled out without me thinking it through. Lorah had stared at me for the longest time, then finally agreed. While she took supper with me, Hattie had gone upstairs to fix up the small room next to mine. I admit I nearly jumped out of my skin at every sound I heard during the night, thinking it would be Lorah coming to me. She did not. When we met in the hallway this morning, there was such longing in her eyes I thought surely she must see the same in mine. I went to her without saying a word. She held me tightly and my heart thudded triple time in my chest. I begged her to spend the day with me. The sun is shining brightly. I offered a picnic to our spot. Yes. She could see the longing in my eyes for she drew me closer and gave me the softest, gentlest kiss. She's now gone down to help Hattie with our picnic lunch. (I'm sure Hattie will throw her out of the kitchen!) We're going to walk to the orchard. It will give us time together and I do think I'm ready to talk. Strangely, I'm no longer afraid.

Madilyn scooted back against the tree and rested there, letting her gaze travel across the valley. Yes, this was their spot. Their special place. She wasn't sure if she felt like she was invading their privacy or if she should feel privileged to be doing so. It was with anticipation that she turned the page.

Oh, I'm so madly in love! Gloriously, wonderfully, completely in love! I'm not sure if I can write it down or even put it all into words, but Lorah and I kissed and kissed and kissed some more under the maples. Then last night, when the house was quiet, I went into her room. I didn't want our first time together to be in the bed that James slept in. No. I wanted no reminder of him. What a magical night it was. I thought I would be scared (and maybe I was) but Lorah's touch felt so natural, so real, I didn't want her to stop. I have never been more thoroughly loved before. It was magical, yes, but so very sad at the same time. Sad, because I'm married to a man who never once touched me that way, who never once loved me that way. Whatever made me think that I loved James? To be fair, I didn't know any better. I thought that was all there was. I was so terribly mistaken. I now know what love feels like.

Madilyn closed the diary, her mind's eyes picturing them together, right here under these very trees…kissing. Was Lorah gay? Obviously. But was *Isabel*? She opened the book again, finding the photograph.

Only then did it occur to her to wonder who had taken it. Had Hattie taken it for them? Did people have cameras back then? She stared at the photo, trying to picture the scene. As she looked, it seemed to move, to become animated. She could see Isabel leaning closer, could see them kissing, could see Lorah's hand drawing her nearer.

"Good lord," she murmured and quickly shoved the photo back inside the diary. So, Isabel and Lorah had slept together. Wow. Just wow.

She thumbed through the diary, disappointed that there weren't very many entries remaining. Was it a short-lived affair and Isabel had quit writing after that? Or was she happily in love and could no longer be bothered to write? No longer lonely?

With a sigh, she held the diary to her chest, knowing she would be so disappointed when she reached the end of it. For that reason, she decided not to read any more today. She put the book in her bag, then sat there for several quiet moments, just staring out toward the valley.

She didn't reflect on her life often—because it was depressing. Now, sitting here, it was almost impossible not to. She didn't have a bad life and of course, she didn't want for anything. Her grandfather made sure of that. But could she honestly say she was happy? Joyous moments were few and far between. She didn't laugh often. Not true laughter. Not the kind of laughter that she could imagine Isabel and Lorah having—laughing until they cried. No. Palmer didn't make her laugh. He rarely even made her smile, other than the ones she had to force.

Maybe she should reconsider moving out here. Because it wasn't hard at all to picture herself—not Isabel—wandering through the orchards alone, day after day. Of course, she wasn't dealing with the same sense of loneliness that Isabel must have been. While she didn't have hordes of friends, she had a few who she shared dinner with. There were others, those from wealthy families that she'd met either in college or through the Foundation. And, of course, there was still Palmer.

She'd be lying though if she said any of them were *good* friends. Because of her last name, she'd learned at a very young age to be cautious of the attention of others. Evan didn't mind that women flocked to him because of the Marak name. In fact, he used it to near perfection. She, on the other hand, was always leery of men being extra attentive.

And because of that, dates were few and far between as well. She simply didn't trust anyone and that was an awful way to go through life. She sometimes wished she could be more like Evan and her mother and not give a damn if someone liked her for her and not just her name. She wasn't like them, however, and she couldn't force herself to be.

What would she do out here if she stayed? She could work from here, sure, but did she want to be that remote? And what about Palmer? What was going to be his reaction to her staying here? Granted, she wasn't *that* far from Philly. Would he expect her to make the trip back there every weekend? Did she want that? Or would he be inclined to come out here to see her? She shook her head. No. She didn't want Palmer here. The estate was almost a sanctuary for her. She didn't want Palmer to spoil that.

With a heavy sigh, she got to her feet. She'd promised her grandfather she'd stay, at least for a while. She supposed she could stay through summer and see how she felt after that. Maybe if she got the orchards replanted and looking good again, that might give her some incentive to hang around longer. She wasn't going to let Palmer's reaction determine how long she stayed. In fact, if she had any sense at all, she'd use this as an opportunity to end things with Palmer.

She went back to the golf cart and placed her bag on the seat, then took a last look around. She felt a certain peace out here. She wondered if Isabel had felt that too.

CHAPTER TEN

"Did you enjoy your outing, Miss Maddie?"

"Oh, I did. Sad to see the orchard looking so neglected."

Loretta urged her down by the small table and placed a cup of coffee in front of her. "It used to be so beautiful there. So green and lush during the summers. They were still tending to it when I was a child, but of course that was sixty years ago. When I was old enough to run down there by myself, I would sneak off in the early mornings to pick apples and bring them back to my grandmother."

"For pie?" she asked.

"Pies, yes. And jam. My grannie loved to make jam."

"You?"

"Oh, I learned how, yes. But now that there's not much left of the orchard, I only make a pie now and then. Randy will bring me apples, but there aren't that many trees still producing from what he tells me. The orchard wasn't a priority, it seems, and it fell by the wayside years and years ago."

"Was there someone who worked here named Hattie?" she asked as casually as she could.

"Hattie? Why yes!" Loretta exclaimed with a big smile. "She was my great-aunt. She lived to be ninety-one. Her mind was sharp as a tack, but her body finally just gave out, poor thing. She had arthritis something terrible."

"You knew her then?"

"Oh, yes. I'd been working here for years already when Aunt Hattie passed on. I was—oh, let me think. It was in '97 when she died. So, I would have been thirty-three, I guess. Oh, Aunt Hattie was so full of stories from back in the day."

Madilyn looked behind her, making sure her grandfather wasn't around. "She would have been here when my great-grandmother, Isabel, was running the house then. Right?"

"Yes, yes. She was here when Mr. Albert was born. Hattie lived right here in the house until she was seventy. Then she moved out to one of the small houses where her sister was living. But she still came around most days and helped with the cooking."

"Did she happen to talk much about Isabel?" She was surprised by the slight blush on Loretta's face.

"Miss Isabel died young, I'm told. Sad story to hear."

"My grandfather doesn't talk about her much. He was still a boy when she died. I'd be interested to learn more, if you know anything about her." Then she smiled. "Even if it's gossip."

Loretta tapped her chest with her open palm. "Oh, I shouldn't really tell stories, but yes, my Aunt Hattie talked freely about her. Oh, she loved Miss Isabel like a sister, she did. Hattie wasn't much older than her when Isabel came to live here."

Madilyn motioned to the chair beside her. "Why don't you pour a cup of coffee, and we'll chat."

"Well, I suppose I could take a short break. Mr. Albert said he was in the mood for a grilled cheese sandwich and some tomato soup for his supper. Won't take me long to whip that up."

"That does sound good." She smiled. "Although I'm looking forward to that chicken and rice dish you saved back for me."

Loretta filled a coffee cup and sat down beside her. "Meal planning was hard while Belle was still here. Toward the end, she wouldn't eat much more than porridge or broth. Hardly had an appetite. Reminds me of how Hattie said it was with Miss Isabel."

"Grandpops said she was only thirty-six when she died."

"Yes. Very young. To hear Hattie tell it, she wasted away because of a broken heart."

"Yet she was married," Madilyn said quietly.

Loretta looked away. "I probably shouldn't repeat the stories I was told. I mean—"

"Isabel was in love with another woman."

Loretta's eyes widened. "How did you know?" she nearly whispered.

Madilyn's plan to keep the diary a secret crumbled. Besides, she was beyond curious about it all. Even though she hadn't read all of it, she knew by the blank pages that Isabel had stopped writing.

"I found an old diary in the attic. It was hidden in a desk up there."

"It was Isabel's?"

"Yes."

Loretta nodded. "Then you know about Lorah. Oh, to hear Hattie tell it, those two were so madly in love, they couldn't hide it. Hattie says she fell a little bit in love with Lorah herself. She was such a charmer, she said." Loretta smiled. "And maybe she did fall a little. Aunt Hattie never married."

"Did her husband find out? Isabel's, I mean."

"Oh no. Hattie said they were all loyal to Isabel and Lorah and never breathed a word of their affair. Of course, there was no chance of it lasting. They—"

"What have we here?"

They both turned, finding Pops in the doorway. Loretta hopped up quickly, guiltily, but Madilyn spoke first.

"Visiting," she said easily. "I was asking her about the old orchard. She used to go there to pick apples."

"You took a trip out there today, Randy tells me. What did you think?"

"That they are in ruins." She stood, giving Loretta a smile. "Thanks for the coffee."

"Of course. Now I should get that tomato soup going."

Madilyn followed her grandfather out of the kitchen. "I think we should hire someone to tend to the orchard. Get it producing again."

"Producing?"

"I don't mean commercially, no. But I think it would fall in line with what the Marak Foundation is all about."

"How so?"

"When the fruit is ripe, we offer it free to the community. Have people come in and pick their own. Or donate the fruit to a food bank. Or to local schools."

"Where's the profit in that? Or would this be a charitable write-off?"

"Does it matter? The cost of running the orchard can't be that much. I think it would be a good thing for our brand." She smiled at him. "In case you didn't know it, the Marak name isn't spoken of fondly by the locals."

"Of course, I know that. It's always been that way. Jealousy. And back in the day, most of the locals worked for the Maraks in some capacity. My father, for instance, leased out land all over for tenant farming. He provided a house and—"

"And they did the work, yet he kept most of the profits."

"What makes you think that?"

"Grandma Belle told me that years ago."

He tapped his cane several times on the hardwood floor, then smiled. "She was right. My father was ruthless. He didn't care what anyone thought of him. He always said he was in the business of making money, not friends."

She raised her eyebrows. "So? The orchard?"

He nodded. "Yes, fine. If that's something you'd like to do, then I think it's a good idea. You may want to take a look at the land over by Brandywine Creek too. Most fertile over there if I remember. It was more diverse, though. Peach and pear, as well as apple."

"Thank you, Pops. Maybe I'll get Randy to drive me over there sometime." She glanced at her watch. "I think I'll go to my room and get cleaned up before dinner." She leaned over to kiss his cheek. "See you later."

CHAPTER ELEVEN

Madilyn had hoped to catch up with Loretta again after dinner, wanting to finish their interrupted conversation, but instead, she joined her grandfather in the study as she'd been doing lately. He had taken the liberty of speaking with Randy about hiring someone for the grounds. Randy knew of three locals who might be interested. Pops wanted her to call them and set up interviews for next week. She'd also put a call in to Palmer to let him know she would be in the city tomorrow. She only got voicemail, so she left a quick message asking if he wanted to have lunch. She wasn't looking forward to that. She could already imagine his reaction to the news that she'd be living out here for the summer. But, she reminded herself, that could be a good thing.

By the time she'd finished with that, she stopped off at the kitchen, but Loretta had retired to her quarters already, so she headed up the stairs. It was far too early for bed, but she was so anxious to read that she changed clothes and brushed her teeth, then crawled under the covers, leaving on only the lamp beside the bed. She took a deep breath before opening the diary.

It's been two weeks since I wrote last. Lorah has been here every day and every night. I'm beside myself with happiness. Hattie must surely know about our affair. I'm sure it's written all over our faces. If not that, she must know I've not slept in my own bed at all during that time. Even so, she's not said one word to me about it. In fact, she goes out of her way to include Lorah in everything, as if she's a part of the family. Lorah, in turn, treats Hattie like a friend, not like the servant she is. She left today, though. She said she would indeed be in the poor house if she did not sell some shoes! She has not had to pay for boarding or meals so I'm sure that has helped her out. I do miss her already. My day feels empty when she's not here. However did I stand it before Lorah came into my life?

Madilyn turned the page slowly, knowing there were only a handful of entries left for her to read.

A card came from James today. I could see the smile in Hattie's eyes when she handed it to me. As expected, he was announcing his return. He apologized for staying away longer than the expected two months, saying it would be another six weeks before he returned. My heart seemed to swell in my chest. Six more weeks with Lorah. I handed it to her to read. She looked so relieved, but she said nothing. She simply looked into my eyes like she does, and I'm filled so with love at what I see there. I suppose we should talk. Talk about us, that is. She had an appointment in town this afternoon to show some shoes to Mr. Greenburg at the mercantile store. Maybe we will talk when she gets home. Yes, home. For the first time since I moved here, it finally feels like home to me. I so dread James's return. I have a huge ache in my chest just thinking about it. Therefore, I won't think about it. Maybe we won't talk after all. We have six more weeks now.

Madilyn could almost feel the relief in Isabel's words. Relief that her husband wasn't coming home.

I love Lorah. I love her like I could never love James. She loves me too. Yes, we talked. But what was there to say? I'm a married woman. I'm having an affair and cheating on my husband. Cheating on him with another woman. A woman I love with all my heart. As I told Lorah last night as we lay in bed together, we have six more weeks. Let's not ruin that by worrying about James coming back. Oh, but I could see the pain in her eyes. She loves me so.

"Oh, Isabel," she murmured quietly. And poor Lorah. How she must have felt. It was almost with trepidation that she turned the page.

I think Hattie may be dreading James's return too. She, like me, knows that Lorah will leave when he returns. Hattie seems to be extra attentive to us. Today, for instance, she made us a picnic basket and nearly shoved us out the door. It was a pleasant day for being the end of July. Not so hot that we couldn't sit under our trees and enjoy the view of the valley. Lorah said something, though, that broke my heart. We were walking among the apple trees, and she said she so hated it that she wouldn't be around when they ripened. I completely broke down and started sobbing. We fell to the ground there, under the young apples, and she kissed my tears away. She then said we would do an outing to Brandywine Creek tomorrow. She thought the peaches or maybe the pears there would be ripe enough. We're going to pick some and ask Hattie to bake a pie for us. That made me cry more and I didn't stop until Lorah made love to me right there under the apple trees.

Madilyn didn't need to read the rest of the diary to know what had happened. James returned and Lorah was forced to leave. Was that the end of their affair? Had Isabel considered divorce? Or was divorce deemed taboo at that time? She turned the page, knowing the only way to find out was if Isabel wanted to tell her.

There was another card from James today. By the look in Hattie's eyes, I knew without reading it that he was returning soon. Four days. I can't believe it's been six weeks already. Henry is to meet him at the train station on Friday. Four days. Four days until my world ends.

Madilyn turned the page slowly, fearing what would happen.

It was the best and the worst day. It was our last picnic. We didn't take it under the maples though, like we usually do. We drove out to Brandywine Creek again. The orchards were full of men working as the peaches need picking. We drove just south of the orchard and went to the bridge and on across the creek, far away from them, and put down Lorah's blanket in the thick grass. I had no appetite but forced down some of the chicken that Hattie had packed for us. There was also wine and Lorah poured us each a glass. Instead of talking about tomorrow, which will be our last day together, we reminisced about the summer. It had flown by so fast, it seems, but what a wonderful summer it was. As we talked, we both cried, yet there was nothing we could do about it. James is coming back whether we want him to or not. We didn't do justice to Hattie's picnic basket. Instead of staying there, Lorah said she wanted to be home with me. So back we went. We spent the entire afternoon in her room, loving and crying. We slept fitfully during the night, waking to love again often. I'm exhausted as it is. She is still asleep. Dawn is approaching, the morning of our last day. I'm going back to bed. I want to be with her.

Madilyn flipped the page over. There was only one other entry.

Lorah has been gone five days. I can't stop crying. James thinks I'm sick and maybe I am. Heartsick. Hattie has tried to comfort me but that only seems to make it worse because Hattie knows exactly why I'm crying. Lorah begged me to go with her. I just didn't have the courage to say yes to her. She seemed to understand. She slipped off the ring she always wore and put it on my finger. A reminder, she said. As if I need one. She will forever be in my heart as it is. She left then and now she is gone from my life forever. How will I live without her? My heart is shattered, and I fear it will never mend. I simply want to die.

Madilyn wiped at the tears that had formed in her eyes. She could feel Isabel's pain. How in love they must have been. She had no frame of reference for that. Maybe her grandparents. Even then, she couldn't imagine anyone being more in love than Isabel and Lorah must have been.

She took out the photo and stared at it, surprised that there was no mention in the diary of it. Who had taken the photo? Had it been Hattie like she suspected? She put the photo back and took out the envelope. It was yellow and faded and the paper felt fragile as she removed the single piece of stationery. The handwriting was elegant and beautiful.

My Dearest Issy. I know James has left again. It would be so easy for me to come by to see you. I've had to fight with myself to stay away, in fact. But I can't go through the breakup again. I don't think my heart could survive it. You already know how much I love you. I will go to my grave with you still in my heart. You and only you.

Do you remember on one of our picnics I told you that I was certain we had met before, had loved before? In another lifetime, Issy. I'm certain of it. That's how I know that we will meet again and love again. Just like now. I know that in my heart. And I can't wait for that time. I hope you believe that too. Please believe that, Issy.

I am getting off the road. I am going back to the farm. Back home. I will plant an apple tree or two while there, I think. Something to connect me to you. Then I may go back to Lancaster to find work, or I may stay there with my new apple trees. If you ever need me for anything, you can send a note to my family's farm in Millersville. They will know how to get in touch with me if I'm not there.

Please know that I think of you each day and I go to bed with a heavy heart each night. I promise, my love for you will never die. Not in this lifetime... and not in the next. Or even the next, Issy.
Yours forever. Lorah.

Madilyn's tears ran down her cheeks as she folded the letter carefully and put it back in the envelope. How could it be that she felt like she knew these two women intimately, like they were friends of hers? The diary wasn't long by any means, but it was filled with such love—and pain—that she could literally feel it herself. She didn't understand it, really, but she could certainly feel it.

She wiped at the tears on her face, then leaned back against the pillows, absently twisting the ring—Lorah's ring. The diary had ended, but she so wanted to know more. She hoped that Loretta would be able to shed some light on Isabel's later years. This was in 1933. Her grandfather was born two years later. How long had Isabel continued to share a room with James? How long and painful were those years until she died? And what about Lorah? What happened to her? Had she never come around again? Oh, she had so many questions and she feared she would not get answers to them.

She was jarred out of her thoughts by the ringing of her phone. It was Palmer. She let it go to voicemail, not wanting to disturb the quiet mood she was in.

Instead, she closed her eyes, picturing the two women as they walked among the apple trees. They were holding hands and smiling at each other—she could see that vividly in her mind. Yes, like seeing two friends on a sunny summer's day.

Oh, how she missed them already.

Again, the soft ding of her phone—letting her know Palmer had left her a message—interrupted her thoughts. With a sigh, she reached for it.

"Madilyn, it's me. Sorry I missed your call earlier. Can't wait to see you. However, can we do dinner instead of lunch? I already have a lunch date with a client. I'll make reservations at Clines. I know you love their prime rib. See you tomorrow, love."

She nearly groaned. Apparently her plan for a quick day trip would turn into an overnight affair. That thought did elicit a groan. *He's going to want to stay the night*, she thought with dismay.

She put the phone down and stared at the ceiling, but her thoughts quickly returned to Lorah and Isabel, easily pushing Palmer from her mind.

CHAPTER TWELVE

When Madilyn got to the restaurant, Palmer was nowhere in sight. She took a seat in the lobby, ignoring the comings and goings of other patrons by feigning interest in the paintings that adorned the walls. Clines was Palmer's favorite restaurant, and they came here frequently. She often got the prime rib or the steak and lobster. Tonight, she wasn't sure she was in the mood for either of those. She wanted something different.

She took a deep breath, wishing she was already back at the estate. She was certainly ready to go. Her car was packed with the few clothes she'd decided to take with her and some toiletries. As she'd gone through her wardrobe, she saw how terribly lacking it was for casual wear. Even shoes. There was nothing suitable for traipsing around the orchard. She'd immediately gotten online and gone shopping. Hopefully her new clothes would arrive at the estate within a few days.

"Madilyn?"

She glanced up, seeing Palmer coming her way. She stood, forcing a smile to her face. She leaned closer to meet him as he placed a light kiss on her cheek.

"You look as lovely as ever," he said as he took her hand. "I've missed you."

"Thank you. But it's only been what? A little over a week?"

"Ten days."

They were led to a table in one of the enclaves where it was dark and quiet. Two candles were burning and as always, she was impressed by the romantic setting here. Shame it never resonated with her. Wine was being poured into glasses and she arched an eyebrow at him.

"I ordered ahead. Prime rib for you and I requested the roasted duck with that orange and ginger glaze that I like."

She nodded and smiled at the waiter who bowed slightly. "For your appetizer, we have mushrooms stuffed with Pecorino Romano, garlic and topped with crispy breadcrumbs."

"Thank you," she automatically.

When he left them, Palmer leaned closer. "It's so good to see you, Madilyn. We hardly spoke while you were gone. Did you miss me at all?"

Her thoughts suddenly became jumbled as she stared at him. He was a handsome man, five years older than she was. He was pleasant enough, she supposed. He was from a prominent family and had already made partner at one of the most prestigious law firms in Philadelphia. Although even he admitted he wasn't certain that was because of him or his father. As his eyebrows raised, she finally found her voice.

"Of course, I missed you." *Was that a lie?* Yes. Yes, it was. And on the heels of that, why did she feel the need to lie?

"I never expected you to stay away this long."

"I know. And about that." She folded her hands together on the table. "My grandfather has asked me to stay with him for a few months. Through the summer, at least."

He leaned back, obviously shocked. "Are you serious? Whatever for?"

"His wife of sixty-seven years just died and he's suddenly alone in a very big house." She picked up her wineglass and took a tiny sip. "He was distraught enough that he'd considered selling and moving."

"Distraught? Hadn't she been sick for years? It's not like it was a shock she died."

"I've been away ten days. I guess I'd forgotten how blunt you are about some things." She slid the wineglass away from her. "Yes, she'd been ill. That didn't make her death any easier for him."

"And he wants you to stay with him? Through the summer? What? Four or five months?"

"We haven't set a date, Palmer. We're going to see how it goes."

He picked up his wineglass for the first time. "Why on earth, Madilyn? There's nothing to do there. You'll be so isolated."

"We're forty minutes from Lancaster and not much more than an hour's drive to Philly. I wouldn't call that isolated."

"But what are you going to *do* there?"

"I still have responsibilities for the Foundation. That won't change. And I want to get the old apple orchard going again. That's going to be my main focus, actually."

At that, he seemed at a loss for words. "An apple orchard?"

She smiled and nodded. "Yes. Apparently back in the day they had quite a large orchard near the creek there. And a smaller one up by the estate. That's the one I'm most interested in."

"Well, that's certainly a surprise. I would have never guessed you'd be interested, as you say, in an apple orchard." He gave her a fake smile. "That sounds so very exciting. How often will you come back here? Once a week? Or do you expect me to come there to see you?"

She returned his fake smile. "I don't expect you to come to the estate, no. As you said, there's nothing to do there."

He slid his wineglass to the side and folded his hands in front of him. "What's going on, Madilyn?"

"Why do you assume something's going on?"

"Because this isn't like you at all. You don't ever do things on the spur of the moment."

"No, I don't. But this is something I want to do for my grandfather."

"And you'll come here, what? On the weekends?"

"I don't know, Palmer. We'll see how it goes."

He stared at her quietly for a bit, then his gaze landed on her right hand. "You have a new ring? I rarely see you with jewelry."

She automatically touched the ring, then covered her hand, hiding the ring from his gaze. "It was my grandmother's ring. Or perhaps my great-grandmother's," she clarified. "I wanted a keepsake."

"I see."

The remainder of their dinner passed in almost frosty silence, and she was surprised at how taken aback he seemed to be at her proposed absence. They both declined coffee and dessert, and he led her almost abruptly back to the lobby.

"Should I plan on finding a date for the wedding then?"

She frowned. "What wedding?"

"Jason Redmond. You met him and his fiancée at one of my parents' dinner parties. Their wedding is coming up next month, remember? We've already discussed this. They're renting the ballroom at the Ritz-Carlton in Center City. Most of the guests will be staying at the hotel. I've already reserved a suite for us."

"I had forgotten. A few weeks? It depends if I've hired someone by then, I guess."

"Hired someone?"

"For the orchard."

"Ah, yes. The very important apple orchard," he said sarcastically.

"Okay, Palmer. I think I've had enough for one night. Yes, why don't you find a date for the wedding. I think that would be easier for both of us." She paused before leaving. "Thank you for dinner. It was an absolutely lovely evening," she said, her sarcasm matching his.

He followed her outside. "So what are we doing here, Madilyn? Are you breaking up with me or something?"

She turned to meet his gaze. Yes. Tell him yes. "I don't know, Palmer. Right now, all I know is that I'm going to be with my grandfather for the next several months. After that, we'll see where we are."

"We'll see where we are? Does that mean you expect me to wait around for the next four or five months so you can 'see where *you* are'?" he finished with emphasis.

"I expect no such thing. Do as you wish," she said curtly.

His expression hardened. "Fine. Give me a call if you want to get together."

He left her standing there alone on the sidewalk as he hurried away from her. She blew out her breath. What just happened?

I think we broke up.

Is that what she wanted? While, no, she wasn't in love with Palmer, he was at least someone she was accustomed to. Someone she was comfortable with. She knew he had no underlying agenda when it came to her or her name. That made her frown sharply. Or did he? Why were they even still dating in the first place? There was little passion between them and when it came down to it, did they even like each other all that much?

Why were they still dating? She knew what her answer would be. Safe and familiar. But what about him? What was his reason? He was a successful, handsome, wealthy man. Why would he settle for what they had? She blew out her breath. Maybe for the same reason she had settled.

So, had they ended things with a spat in front of Clines? She decided she didn't really care.

She headed toward her car, surprised at the relief she felt. Surprised by the smile on her face. Instead of going back to her condo, she headed west, away from the city.

Back to Lorah and Isabel…and back to the apple orchard.

PART TWO: THE ORCHARD

CHAPTER THIRTEEN

Madilyn paused, seeing her grandfather standing on the large expanse of the back porch watching as the new lawn crew was unloading flats of colorful flowers. He seemed pleased with the progress that had been made in the last few weeks and she was glad hiring a crew had been her first priority.

The apple orchard was her second. She had such an undeniable urge to get it looking presentable again—to get it looking like it was when Isabel and Lorah had walked there. Nearly every afternoon she took the golf cart down there herself—or walked the lane—trying to picture how it had once been. Most of the trees now were long dead, only a hardy few hanging on.

She'd learned from Loretta that back when Isabel had been alive, she'd forbidden the workers from harvesting the apples there, sending them on to the orchards at Brandywine Creek instead. In their place, she'd allowed in the families who were leasing and farming the Marak land nearest the estate to come in and pick their fill. Her grandfather didn't recall that happening, though. He only remembered his father ignoring the orchards because they weren't as profitable as his import businesses, and he had no time for them.

She had visited with Loretta a bit more about Isabel and Lorah, but Loretta didn't know much other than what she'd already learned from the diary. As far as Loretta knew, James never learned of the affair. After her grandfather had been born, Isabel made it clear that she would not share a room—or a bed—with James. James then made it clear that if she wouldn't perform her wifely duties, he would find someone who would.

"He never brought them around, though," Loretta had told her. "Hattie said he rarely came home at all, staying in the city instead, which suited Miss Isabel just fine." Loretta's expression changed. "Oh, Hattie loved her like family. Hattie's heart broke as she watched Isabel fade away from them. She said it was like Miss Isabel willed herself to die."

Yes, Madilyn imagined that's how it had been. Even having a child to love and care for couldn't mend her broken heart. And while she now knew of Isabel's fate, she did wonder what had happened to Lorah. Had she died young too? She supposed, if she did some searching, she could find out. She knew her last name—Chance. Knew she'd been from Millersville, then Lancaster.

A part of her didn't want to know, though. It was such a sad, tragic love story as it was. She would rather think of Lorah as she'd been in the photo—a bit dashing in the suit and tie…and a bit rakish with the fedora shadowing her eyes. Thinking of the photo made her smile. Like Isabel, and perhaps Hattie too, she seemed to have a little bit of a crush on Lorah, all from a photo. That thought nearly made her stumble. A crush? On a woman? With a shake of her head, she walked on, going around to the large shed where Randy was interviewing the men who had applied for the orchardist job.

He had told her they'd likely get more applications if she didn't insist they live on the property. She, on the other hand, wanted this to be someone's sole focus, not just a job they came to and left. Besides, there were five or six vacant houses on the Marak property going to waste. After touring them, though, she realized that most of them needed major work done to get them livable again. Truthfully, most of them needed to be torn down. The old George Class place down at the far end of the valley was falling apart at the seams and looked as if it would collapse any day now.

She'd picked out the nicest house—at the upper edge of the valley—which needed both a kitchen and bathroom upgrade and was in desperate need of painting, both inside and out. Really, though, it was the only house that was even suitable for a remodel. Randy had hired someone for that chore, despite his pleas that he could do it himself. She'd convinced him to supervise instead. And it wasn't that she didn't think he could do it—he was the handyman, after all—she simply wanted it done quickly. After the remodeling, she would get Julia to send the cleaning ladies over to get it ready for new appliances and furniture.

There were four trucks parked at the shed. She wasn't quite sure why it was referred to as a shed. It seemed much too large for that, and it functioned more as an elaborate garage. There was a nice room inside with a bathroom attached. Randy had added a coffeemaker and a small fridge to the room, calling it his office. He'd also added a small TV, and she wondered if this was where he came if he needed to escape from his wife.

Two men and a woman were standing in front of one of the trucks, talking. She knew there were four appointments scheduled, but she did wonder who the woman was. Perhaps one of them had brought his wife along. Then she mentally shook her head. No. This young woman, with her boyish haircut and faded jeans, wasn't a wife to these middle-aged men. She watched her as she spoke, her hands moving animatedly, a smile on her face. The woman turned then, as if feeling her watching. Dark eyes matched her dark hair and Madilyn's breath caught. She had such a strong sense that she'd met her somewhere before, she very nearly went over to her now. The woman smiled at her, and Madilyn returned it. She shook herself, then made herself move. She opened the side door to the office and went inside, finding Randy speaking with, yes, another middle-aged man. He was short and stout, his voice rather loud as he listed off his attributes.

"And I can grow some fine peaches and pears too. That's most of my experience, but I've dabbled in apples before. Ran a fifty-acre apple orchard back about ten years ago. Quality fruit."

She walked up to them, holding her hand out. "I'm Madilyn Marak."

"How do you do, ma'am. I'm Jimmy Fisher."

"Pleased to meet you," she said with a smile. "Where are you from, Mr. Fisher?"

"Over near Smithville."

"And you'd be willing to relocate here?"

"Well, as I was telling Mr. Shaffer here, my wife and I are currently renting a house there. I've got four months left on that lease. But it's not that far of a drive to come out. It only took me about forty minutes to get here."

She nodded and smiled at Randy. "Please continue. I want to look over the résumés."

She let their voices fade to the background as she picked up the papers. She barely glanced at Jimmy Fisher's. He wasn't the one. She didn't care how good his résumé was. Two of the others had similar experience to Mr. Fisher. The other, Dylan Hayes, had the least amount of experience. In fact, he listed nothing other than tending to his family's apple trees. She frowned, seeing no other jobs mentioned. She tossed it aside, focusing on the other two.

"What do you think?"

She looked up at Randy, not realizing that Mr. Fisher had left them. "Are these the only four we received?"

"Afraid so. Like I said, requiring them to live on the property is going to limit your choices. But we only really advertised in this area. We could do a state-wide search."

"No, no. Let's go ahead and speak with these first." She picked up Dylan Hayes's very brief résumé. "This one shouldn't take long. No experience at all."

"Yeah. I almost didn't even bother with an interview, but I called anyway." He went to the door. "Dylan Hayes? Come on in."

Madilyn's eyes widened when the woman walked inside. She supposed surprise showed on her face because the woman—Dylan Hayes—gave a laugh.

"Yeah, I know. My name always throws people. It's a family thing." She came closer, holding a hand out first to Randy, then to her. Her grip was firm, her gaze direct. Again, Madilyn would swear she knew her from somewhere. "I took a drive through your orchard on my way in. I hope you don't mind. I saw the apple trees from that side road and thought I'd take a look. You've got some old gnarly trees in there and I was shocked that some were still producing. That's crazy. Looks like they hadn't been pruned in decades. Apple trees start declining at thirty, and by fifty years, they're pretty much spent, if people even keep them around that long. Although my uncle swears that two on his farm are ninety years old and they still have fruit. Anyway, if they produce fruit for up to fifty years, it's an exceptional tree. Judging by some of those in your orchard, they're getting on to be a hundred years old themselves. If I were you, I'd graft some of those and get some new trees started from them."

"Well, you seem knowledgeable," Madilyn said. She held up the résumé. "Not much here, though."

"No. I've not ever worked at a big orchard. Truth is, I never had much desire for farm life. Spent a lot of time on my uncle's farm when I was growing up, though. I went to college, got a job thinking I'd never live on a farm." She gave an easy laugh. "Life throws you curve balls sometimes, doesn't it?"

She didn't elaborate and Madilyn was too polite to ask.

"What size is your uncle's orchard? We're looking to not only get the one here going—it's rather small and only three acres—but there is another area along Brandywine Creek that is over a hundred acres. It's fallen into neglect and needs a complete redo. I haven't decided if we will attempt to revive the full one hundred acres or not. We'll probably start small and see how it goes."

"My uncle's farm is sixty acres, but only about ten of that is orchard. Peach, pear, and apple. He farmed the rest at one time or another."

"If you got this job, what size of a crew would you need to manage an orchard this size?" Madilyn asked.

"Well, removing the old trees and getting new ones in the ground is labor-intensive but you can hire out for that. Managing the orchard itself…" The woman scratched the back of her neck thoughtfully. "I can manage the three acres by myself with no problem. But you start talking a hundred acres? That will host a hell of a lot of trees. At my uncle's farm, I do all the pruning myself. And the harvesting. And that about kills me," she said with a quick laugh. "Three acres would be a piece of cake. A big orchard, though? A hundred acres? You're going to need ten or twelve guys, easy. That's just to maintain it. You'd have to hire seasonal workers come harvest time. And from what I understand about some of the larger farms, they're all fighting for the same seasonal workers. So, there's that. Of course, new trees, you're looking at four, five, six years before the production really kicks in."

"And what about living here on the property?"

"Well, to be honest, that's the main reason I applied for the job." Again, an easy smile. "I'm soon to be homeless."

"I see." Madilyn raised an eyebrow, waiting.

"My uncle, well, we're going to have to sell the farm. It's about to kill him, but he's—" She shrugged. "Anyway, yeah, we're going to put it up for sale. Soon. Like any day now."

"And the farm is where?"

"It's over near Millersville."

"I take it you're more interested in a place to stay rather than a job then?" Randy asked, his tone a bit dismissive. "Since you're about to be homeless and all."

Dylan Hayes laughed quickly. "Is that how it sounded? No. But it would certainly be convenient, that's for sure."

Madilyn could tell by Randy's expression that he was already rejecting her. And why not? She had no experience to speak of.

"Well, thank you, Ms. Hayes. We have four applicants, and we'll certainly keep you in mind," he said.

She expected disappointment on Dylan Hayes's face, but the woman only smiled and shook their hands again. "Thanks for seeing me. I know I don't have a lot of experience. At least, not on paper. But I've been tending to my uncle's orchard for the last six years. I'm twenty-nine, in case you were wondering. And I know a thing or two about apples." Then she laughed and Madilyn couldn't help but return the smile. "Well, more than just a thing or *two*," she clarified and even Randy laughed at that.

It was then, when Dylan Hayes met her gaze head-on, that Madilyn was absolutely certain she'd met the woman somewhere before.

When she left, Randy turned to her. "Likeable woman, but not what we're looking for. I think she'd be in over her head." He picked up the other two résumés. "Do you have a preference on who is next?"

Madilyn shook her head. "No. Doesn't matter." For one thing, she knew nothing about orchards or fruit trees and wouldn't know who would be best suited to hire. She would most likely leave that up to Randy.

While she sat in on the other two interviews—and contributed with a few questions—she found her mind wandering to the woman. She seemed to have a constant smile on her face despite her assertion that she would be homeless soon. She wondered why they had to sell her uncle's farm. She also wondered what had prompted her to apply for a job she was obviously not qualified for. Desperation, perhaps? Yet her demeanor had not seemed desperate at all. No, she seemed to be one of those perpetually happy people. Madilyn had felt drawn to her, which was strange. She was never one to warm up to people easily. Quite the opposite.

She pushed Dylan Hayes out of her mind and forced her attention to Mr. Dennis, the last of the interviews. He wasn't much different than the other two. In fact, all three men's résumés were almost identical, with all of them having plenty of experience. She stood and shook his hand.

"Thank you. We'll be in touch."

"Yes, ma'am, thank you." His handshake with Randy was much firmer. "Like I said, I can get started right away."

After he left, she and Randy went out into the sunshine, and she took a deep breath as she glanced into the blue sky overhead.

"What do you think?" he asked.

She gave him a brief smile. "I think maybe I was overzealous. I had no idea the labor needed to maintain a large orchard. Perhaps we should wait and see how this turns out before attempting to revitalize the Brandywine Creek area."

"Yes. I think that's one reason why your grandfather—and his father before him—got away from the orchards. Profit margin is slim if things don't fall right."

"I know. But in this case, I'm not really interested in a profit margin. Now, about them," she said, referring to the guys they'd interviewed. "They were all pretty much alike. None stood out above the others. Who did you like most?"

"Well, Todd Dennis here can get started right away. And he has no problem moving out here."

She nodded. Mr. Dennis and his wife were living with her parents over in Wakefield. He seemed to be in a hurry to move away from them. "Yes. But let's think on it overnight. Now, what about the remodeling? Did you get the appliances ordered?"

"Sure did. They'll be finished with the bathroom by Friday, they think. Another week before the kitchen will be ready. As far as the outside goes, they're stripping that tomorrow and will get on to painting that in the next few days. They found some wood on a couple of the eaves that needed replacing. Nothing more than that."

"Good. Thank you, Randy. It seems like it's coming along then. I want to focus on the orchard here first. We'll hold off on Brandywine Creek." She turned to leave, then stopped. "How long has it been since people have lived in the houses? They really should be destroyed rather than attempting to revitalize them."

"Oh, it's been a while. Most of those were already vacant when I started working here. As leases ran out, and your grandparents got older, they just didn't want to mess with the upkeep on the houses is what I was told. They stopped leasing out the farmland closest to the estate years and years ago. The last one to be lived in is the one we're fixing up."

"The estate here sits on what? Five hundred acres?"

"More than that. I'd say seven or eight hundred here surrounding the house. Maybe even close to a thousand. That includes all of the valley and miles along Brandywine Creek too."

"Wonder why he didn't have the old houses torn down then?"

"Truth be told, Mr. Albert seemed to have lost interest in the land. Like when Bennie retired. He didn't care what the grounds looked like anymore."

"Yes, I know. He lost interest in a lot of things when Grandma Belle got sick. That's something I'd like to do, Randy. Let's see about hiring someone to tear down those old houses and get it cleaned up. Okay?"

He nodded. "Sure thing." He looked away for a moment, then back to her. "It's not my place to say this, but I'm awfully glad you're here, Maddie. I had been afraid your mother was going to swoop in and—" He stopped, and a slight blush lit his face. "I'm sorry. I didn't mean that like it sounded."

She laughed. "Afraid she'd swoop in for the kill?"

He relaxed. "I never got on well with your mother. She doesn't care two cents about this place. Never did."

"And that hasn't changed, I'm afraid." She touched his arm as she moved past him. "Thank you, Randy. I'll see you later."

"You want to discuss who we'll hire in the morning then?"

"I suppose," she said without much eagerness as she turned away from him.

Truth was, none of the men excited her in the least, which was disappointing considering her enthusiasm for getting the orchard going again. In fact, of the four interviews, the only one who seemed truly passionate about the job was Dylan Hayes. Todd Dennis seemed more eager to move away from his in-laws than anything else.

The excitement she'd started the day with faded now at the prospect of hiring one of these men. She paused to look skyward. Why was she so eager to get the orchard going again? Was she only doing it for Lorah and Isabel? Did she feel some sense of responsibility now that she'd read the diary? With a sigh, she continued back toward the house. The fact was, she missed Lorah and Isabel. It was almost like two friends had left her without saying goodbye. Which was crazy, of course. The diary wasn't that lengthy, and she'd only had a very brief glimpse into their lives.

Almost as brief as their love affair had been.

CHAPTER FOURTEEN

Dylan held the spoon out to him, but he shook his head. She then shook hers as well. "Kathleen said you didn't eat again today, Uncle Frank. You need something in you." She scooped up another spoonful of the soup.

He looked away from her. "The doc said when my appetite goes, well…"

"You act like you're going to die tomorrow."

"I think I might," he said, his voice rough and gravelly from the cancer.

She put the bowl down. "Don't give up on me. You're all I have left."

He patted her hand affectionately. "Have I told you lately what a good niece you are?"

"Not today, no."

"You gave up your life to come take care of me. And what do I leave you? A bunch of medical bills and an old farm that's not worth much at all."

"Uncle Frank, I didn't give up my life. I've loved living here on the farm with you." She took a deep breath, wondering if she should even tell him. "Actually, I applied for a job today."

"Is that where you went off to?"

"Yeah. The Maraks. It's out east of Cochranville."

"The *Maraks*?"

"I've never heard of them before. Have you?"

"Who hasn't? Probably the richest family in the Commonwealth. But I don't know anything about them personally. They own a lot of land, that's all I know. What kind of job do they have?"

She grinned. "Running an apple orchard."

His laugh turned into a cough. "Girl, what the hell do you know about that?"

She laughed too. "Not much, that's for sure. But our trees out here all look good. I've been babying them for the last six years. And as a bonus, Madilyn Marak is really cute."

He leaned back against the pillows and closed his eyes. "Did I ever tell you the story about how our orchard started?"

He'd told her plenty of stories over the years but never one about the orchard. She scooted her chair closer to the bed. "No. Tell me."

"It was already established when I came along. My Aunt Lorah planted the first two in the spring of 1934. Those two old ones up here by the barn—told you they were ninety years old. She would have been your great-aunt. She was fun and I loved her. She was feisty, though. Never married." At this, he opened his eyes. "Much like you."

"You think I'm feisty?"

"She never took a husband either."

She smiled. "Maybe she was gay like me."

He scoffed. "There weren't no gay people back then."

She laughed loudly. "Sure there were. They just weren't out in the open." She waved her hand. "Go on. Tell me the story."

"She used to sell shoes."

"Shoes?"

"Yes. Like a traveling salesman. Didn't want no part of the farming life. Then one day, they said she showed back up right out of the blue and never left again. She planted those two apple trees. Fussed over them good, she did. They say she would sit there between the two and talk to them for hours on end." He wiggled his hairless eyebrow and smiled. "She was an odd bird, Aunt Lorah. She wore men's clothes and worked out in the fields with them. She was already middle-aged when I came along, but she was still working. And boy, those apple trees could sure turn out some fruit. Had more apples than we knew what to do with, just from those two trees."

"Did she plant the other trees too?"

"She helped with them, yes, but she didn't seem to favor the new trees. Even when I was a boy, I remember her going to sit up against the trunks of those two old ones. You'd see her talking up a storm. Musta been talking to God or something—she never said. Anyway, the new trees did good, but they weren't nothing special. Not like those two old mother trees."

"Is that why you started grafting them?"

"Yep. But my father used to say that we weren't talking to them enough, like Lorah used to do."

"When did she die?"

"Oh, she had a good, long life. Eighty-something. Shame she didn't hang on, though. You would have loved her. She died just a few days after you were born."

"Really?"

"Yep. She went with us all to the hospital to take a look at you. She picked you up and held you for the longest time, she did. Wasn't but a couple of days later, she died in her sleep." He had a smile on his face. "Aunt Lorah was always a little odd, sure, but I used to tag after her when I was a boy. She was so full of stories." His smile faded. "Always felt sorry for her, though. She seemed so lonely. Like I said, never took a husband. Don't think she had any friends, either. She very seldom left the farm."

"I don't think I've ever seen a picture of her," Dylan said as she picked up the soup bowl again.

"No. She and your mother didn't really get along." He chuckled. "Your mother was so prim and proper. Lorah, with her men's clothing, never quite fit in." He held his hand up when she offered him the spoon again. "No, Dylan. That soup won't help anything."

She put the bowl down once more. "My mother never really knew what to do with me. I never really fit in either."

He patted her hand. "Your mother loved you. Don't think she didn't."

"I know she did. I just wasn't the daughter she wanted. And now…"

"And now they're all gone and it's just us." He met her gaze. "And I'll be leaving you very soon too."

She squared her shoulders. "I hate when you talk like that, Uncle Frank."

"Can't run from it, girl." He tapped his chest. "I can feel it. Won't be long now, thank god. But don't you fret. I'm ready. I'm tired of fighting it. So tired."

She stood up and stared out the window as darkness settled around the old farmhouse. No, it wouldn't be long. It was nearly six months ago that his lung cancer had advanced to stage 4. At the doctor's visit last month, he'd told her he was surprised Uncle Frank was still hanging on. And at the visit last week, he'd pulled her aside. "Make sure all his affairs are in order."

And they were. She'd moved here to stay with him six years ago when he'd first been diagnosed. She and Uncle Frank were the only two left. Well, there were a few distant relatives of Aunt Linda who lived in Minnesota, but none that Uncle Frank had kept in touch with. No, it was just them. Soon to be just her.

"You'll be okay, Dylan."

She turned around slowly. "Will I?"

"Sell the farm and go back to Philly. Pick up where you left off."

"I think it's been too many years for that. Besides, after living out here, I can't imagine going back to work in a big office building again." She shoved her hands into her jeans pockets. "Maybe this job will pan out."

"Where will you live?"

"They provide housing out there. That's the main reason I applied." She shrugged. "Can't see me getting the job, though. Like you said, what the hell do I know about managing an apple orchard."

His eyes closed. "Maybe you got some of Aunt Lorah's charm with the apple trees. Maybe you just need to talk to them." He fell silent and she touched his arm. His eyes fluttered open for a moment, then closed again. "I love you, Dylan."

She nodded and pulled the covers up higher around him. "I love you too." She squeezed his arm again, then picked up the soup bowl. "I'll check on you before bed."

She watched him a bit longer, wondering if tonight would be the night. She shook her head as she closed the door. She'd been having that same morbid thought for the last week. Yes, she had. And one of these times, it would be true.

She had a sinking feeling that it would be very soon. All the signs were there. The doctor had told her he would refuse to eat. His appetite hadn't been much for the last couple of months, and he'd lost even more weight. Yet this week, he hadn't eaten at all that she recalled. She'd watched for the signs that the doctor had told her to be on the lookout for. Shallow breathing, clammy yet cool skin. His constant need for sleep. The increased need for pain meds.

Maybe she would sit with him tonight. She didn't want him to die alone.

CHAPTER FIFTEEN

Dylan put two ice cubes in the tumbler, then added the bourbon whiskey to it. Knob Creek Single Barrel. She'd never even heard of it before she'd moved in here with Uncle Frank, and she never thought she'd like whiskey straight up. He'd had a bottle and they'd shared a toast on her first night. As the months and then years ticked by, she noticed that Uncle Frank drank less and less, and she was drinking more. She'd stopped that nearly daily habit, only enjoying a nightcap on occasion now.

She took her drink out to the porch. It was cool enough for her to slip on a sweatshirt. The moon was already up—two days from full—and as its light bathed the two old apple trees, her gaze was drawn to them. She went down the steps and made her way over. Yes, these trees were old and gnarly, much like the ones at the Marak place. They had no business still being alive, much less producing fruit. It was unheard of that a tree this old was still bearing. Nonetheless, they had bloomed like always and she imagined in the fall, they'd have fruit on them again. Like always.

She sat down on the ground and leaned against one of the trees, surprised at the calmness she felt. Her life was going to be turned upside down very soon, yet she felt at peace. She wished she could keep the farm—it had become home—but she'd have to sell it to pay for the medical bills that had piled up. Besides, what would she do with it? The small orchard barely turned a profit and that was only because she did all the picking of the fruit instead of hiring a crew. And the rest of the land? Uncle Frank hadn't been able to farm it in the last four years. It was just getting weedy and overgrown.

She glanced at the house. It was old and wasn't in the best shape either. Whoever bought the farm would have a lot of work cut out for them. That alone told her she probably wouldn't get the price she wanted for it.

She took a sip of the whiskey and sighed. What in the world was she going to do? Maybe Uncle Frank was right. Maybe she should go back to Philly and get a job. She nearly rolled her eyes. Six years removed from the workforce. Technology changes fast. She probably wouldn't even be qualified for entry level PC support, much less falling back into a networking job. Anyway, she'd lost touch with her contacts and old coworkers. She wouldn't know where to start.

Didn't matter. After living out here this long, she knew going back to the city and working in a damn cubicle wasn't for her and it never had been. No, she'd find something. If she could sell the farm for a fair price, then she'd have enough left over for her to get by on. Then it wouldn't be imperative that she find a high-paying job. She didn't need any place fancy to live. Besides, Tanner had already offered his place if she needed somewhere to bunk for a while.

She smiled as she thought of Tanner Wilson. He was her best friend. She'd met him that first week. He worked at the farm and ranch store here in Millersville and he'd proven to be a wealth of information when it came to fruit trees. She'd shared steaks at his place, and he'd been over here to the farm on countless occasions. The old rusty smoker out back that Uncle Frank said hadn't been used in decades had been cleaned and transformed. Tanner had come over many an early morning to put on a rack of ribs or a pork roast that he'd smoke first, then slow cook for hours. And they'd sit around drinking a few beers and talk football and apples while the delectable smell of the smoker wafted about. Yeah, good times.

She leaned her head back against the bark of the tree and looked into the sky, the stars obscured somewhat by the bright moon. Yes, she would miss the farm. She'd been born in Lancaster, but her parents had moved to Philly when she was three. She'd grown up in the city, yet she had fond memories of the farm as they would visit at least once a month. Uncle Frank and Aunt Linda didn't have children, and they'd spoiled her like their own whenever she stayed with them, often spending several weeks each summer out here.

She'd been nineteen when tragedy struck their family, yet she remained in the city. And she'd been twenty-three—just getting good and settled in her job—when Uncle Frank got his diagnosis. Six years ago, she'd been pulled back to the farm, and it was now home. But Uncle Frank would be leaving her soon and then what would she have?

She took another sip of the whiskey and closed her eyes. It would all work out. She didn't know how she knew that, but she did. Maybe that's why she felt at peace. She sat there against that old apple tree, the breeze blowing about. Yes, it would work out. Maybe that cute woman at the Maraks—Madilyn—would hire her. Maybe.

As she listened, she thought she heard someone—a woman—whispering to her. She glanced around her, but the words kept coming. She squeezed her eyes closed, trying to make them out, but they were just mumbled sounds in the night. Then the breeze blew them away entirely and all was quiet again. She opened her eyes, looking up into the opposite apple tree, its branches bathed by moonlight. Her breath caught as she was certain she saw a shadowed face among the leaves, watching her. She wasn't afraid, although a part of her questioned if she wasn't losing her damn mind. She stared at the face—or what she thought was a face—crazily wondering if that was who had been talking to her. Before that thought could settle, the face disappeared into nothingness, making her doubt that it had been there at all.

For some reason, an image of Madilyn Marak popped into her head. An involuntary smile lit her face. She was cute. Blond hair, blue eyes. There was something about her that was so familiar, though. They'd never met, obviously, yet…there was something.

She nodded. Maybe she was having a premonition or something. Maybe she *would* get the job.

CHAPTER SIXTEEN

Madilyn joined her grandfather in his study for a brandy after dinner, something she'd been doing nightly. Instead of sitting behind his desk, he eased down onto the leather sofa, and she did as well.

"I say, they've got the grounds looking so nice again, Maddie. Don't you think?"

"Yes. I think they actually squeezed more flowers into the beds than Bennie used to."

"I'm glad you talked me into it." He took a sip of his drink. "Now, what about you? You had interviews today for the orchardist?"

She nodded. "Four. I believe Randy wants to hire the last one we talked to. Todd Dennis."

"That's not who you want?"

"Not really, no." She gave him a quick smile. "There were three men and one woman who applied. All three men were pretty much identical in their experience, and ages, for that matter."

"And the woman?"

"A young woman. A couple of years older than me. Limited experience. Very limited. She ran a small orchard on her uncle's farm. A farm they are apparently having to sell for some reason."

"I take it by your tone that you liked her better than the men."

She laughed lightly. "Do I have a tone?"

He smiled but said nothing.

She took a deep breath. "Yes, you're right. I liked her much better. She seemed very friendly, pleasant. She might possibly be someone I could become friends with. The men—"

"Friends? Maddie, the Maraks do not make friends with the hired help."

She reached over and patted his shoulder. "I warned you. I'm not a matriarch. I don't fit that aristocratic prototype that you seem to think the Maraks should still be molded in. Besides, if I'm going to live here, it would be nice to have a friend."

He eyed her thoughtfully. "You don't mention friends very often. If at all. Are there none?"

"A few. It's the same reason there haven't been a lot of men in my life. Most have ulterior motives."

"Yes. That does follow us, doesn't it? I think that was one reason my mother was so lonely out here. The main social event was the Christmas ball and most of the guests were business acquaintances of my father. A few of the well-to-do locals would be invited too. That's how it remained even when Belle ran things."

"Grandma Belle didn't have friends either," she stated.

"No. Truth was—and is—the Maraks were never looked upon fondly by the locals even though we donated money to most of the churches and schools in the area."

"We were always out of touch," she added. "Literally. The estate is massive and sits in the middle of hundreds of acres of land. The entrance is blocked by a huge fence and a locked gate. It's not like people could come visit if they wanted."

He nodded. "My father put the first gate up not a week after my mother died. He'd threatened to do it for years, but she wouldn't hear of it for that very reason—someone may want to come visit." He laughed. "Of course, no one ever did."

Had Isabel been hoping that Lorah might come back to her? Was that why she didn't want a gate? Even though Lorah's letter to her stated that she wouldn't come around, had Isabel held on to hope? At least for a while?

"Why don't you hire this woman if that's who you like?"

She took a sip of her brandy. "She doesn't have much experience. Randy thinks she would be in over her head."

"So what? It's not like you need the orchard to turn a profit or anything. You want to donate the fruit anyway."

"True. I hadn't thought of it that way." She leaned back, picturing Dylan Hayes. "You wouldn't have a problem if I hired someone like that? Without experience?"

"Maddie, this is your project. Do with it what you like."

"I don't think Randy will approve. He—"

"Randy's last name is not Marak and therefore, he is not running things. You are."

She nodded. "Thank you, Pops. I think I do want to hire her." Yes, she did. She felt like she was *supposed* to hire her. She'd been thinking of her all day.

"May I ask though, about your sudden interest in the orchard?" He waved his hand. "I know what you said and all, but what's the real reason?"

She raised an eyebrow. "You think I have an underlying motive?"

"Not at all. You're not conniving like that. But there's something, isn't it?"

How did she explain her compulsion to replant the orchard without mentioning the diary?

"You've talked about how your mother liked to walk to the orchard every day, how much she enjoyed it there," she said carefully. "Loretta mentioned too that her aunt—Hattie—was working here when Isabel was alive."

"Oh, yes. Of course, I remember Hattie. She cried so when my mother died."

Madilyn nodded. "Hattie told Loretta how much the orchard meant to Isabel. You don't mention her much. It's almost like she's been forgotten. I thought it would be nice to get the orchard going again in her memory." That much was true, at least.

"Really?"

"Yes. I know very little about her, but I feel an affinity for her—a kinship. Maybe because I'm staying in her room, but I feel I know her. I think what you said was true. She was lonely out here."

"And you? You're lonely too?"

She nodded slowly. "Yes."

"I take it you are already regretting your decision to move out here with me?"

"Oh, no. I didn't mean it like that, Pops. It has nothing to do with being here. Even living in Philly, I felt lonely. And I don't mean to imply that I had *no* friends. There were lunch and dinner dates. There were parties." She paused. "And there is Palmer."

"Yes, the man in your life. You never said, how did he take the news of you moving?"

"He wasn't too thrilled," she said honestly. She waved her hand dismissively. "That doesn't matter. His reaction to this has no bearing on my decision. But what I'm saying is that I wasn't starved for company. It was just…different."

He nodded. "I sometimes think the Marak name was both blessed and cursed. Like I said before, children were hard to come by. Going back to the beginning, our family tree is rather short with very few branches. No children, no friends. My father had business associates and acquaintances only. He most assuredly had no friends. Enemies, yes, but not friends. As I said, he was ruthless. And me? The Marak reputation was already set in stone when I came of age. Even though Belle and I changed direction when we created the Foundation, it was too late for an image reset. By that time, we didn't really care about all that anyway. We lived our lives here, just the two of us. We had the annual Christmas ball and functions out for the Foundation. That was enough of a social life for us."

"Did my mother ever enjoy living here at the estate?"

"No. All she cared about was being the center of attention and surrounding herself with adoring friends. Unlike you, she wasn't concerned whether they wanted to be around her because of her name or not. That didn't matter in the least to her and she was quite good at buying friends. So no, she hated being isolated out here. In fact, she loathed it, she told me once."

"Why did she live here then after her early divorces?"

"Sad to say, but I forced her. We were concerned for Evan, then for you. Belle didn't buck me on that. At first, anyway. She eventually gave in to her. That's when Margaret bought the mansion. It wasn't so far away that we couldn't check on you and it was still close enough to the city for her to be satisfied." He waved his hand. "She wasn't satisfied, though. Nannies and servants to run things while she flitted off to her parties—it's amazing you turned out as wonderful as you did. I wish I could say the same about Evan."

"Thank you."

She found herself absently twisting the ring on her finger and his gaze was drawn to it. "New ring? I didn't think you wore jewelry."

"Actually, I found this in Grandma Belle's jewelry box upstairs."

"Really? I don't recall her ever wearing that one."

"No?" she asked innocently. She held her hand out, eyeing the ring. "There were several up there. This one caught my eye and it fit. I hope you don't mind."

"Oh, not at all, Maddie. Belle would love that you're wearing it."

"Good." She stood. "I think I'll head upstairs." She moved closer and bent to kiss his cheek. "Goodnight, Pops. I'll see you in the morning."

She made her way carefully up the stairs, lit only by two lamps along the wall. The stairs were shadowy, and she remembered being afraid to go up alone when she'd been young. Evan teasing her of ghosts hadn't helped matters.

She went into her room, going to the bed to turn on the lamp rather than the overhead light. She reached out for it, then stopped. She turned around, her gaze darting into the shadows of the dark room. The curtains were still spread open, letting in bright moonlight.

"Isabel?" she whispered, the word floating in the air around her.

She shook her head quickly, feeling foolish. She turned the lamp on, but nothing seemed out of place. Nevertheless, she couldn't shake the feeling that she wasn't alone. She certainly wasn't frightened, though. Instead, she opened the drawer where she'd hidden the diary. She took it out carefully and opened it, finding the picture of Lorah and Isabel. She held it under the light of the lamp, a smile forming on her face as she imagined Lorah pulling Isabel closer for a kiss.

CHAPTER SEVENTEEN

Dylan stood in the doorway, watching as they prepared to take her uncle. He had been in and out of consciousness all day yesterday. The nurse—Kathleen—had stayed with her, sitting beside him, tending more to her than she had to him. Kathleen seemed to sense his pain as she'd placed morphine drops in his mouth on several occasions.

She had feared he would die during the night while she was there alone. She'd sat with him again, like she'd done the night before. Kathleen had come earlier than normal that morning, thankfully.

They'd watched as his condition worsened, and she'd felt helpless, especially when he had been gasping for air. She panicked then, but before she could call 911, Kathleen had stopped her with a firm hand on her arm.

"There's nothing anyone can do, Dylan. It's his time. Let him go in peace."

The words hung in the air, and she had nodded. She had paced beside his bed, his breathing so shallow then, several times she'd thought he'd taken his last breath. Then suddenly he had. Kathleen had hovered over him, her stethoscope held to his chest.

Now as she watched, she blinked back the tears that were threatening again. She turned away as they lifted him from the bed to the gurney. She walked numbly out of the back of the house, taking deep breaths of air.

It was over. Just like that. He was gone.

And she was all alone.

She moved farther away from the house, her gaze on the two old apple trees and she went toward them. She'd been prepared. Sure, she had. They'd been talking about this day for the past several months. Nearly daily for the last few weeks. Yet the quick finality of it all surprised her.

"Ms. Chance?"

She turned, seeing the funeral home director himself at the door. She retraced her steps. "It's Hayes. Dylan Hayes."

"Oh. I'm sorry. I keep thinking you're his daughter."

"Niece."

"That's right. Of course. I know he made all the arrangements months ago but are you sure there's to be no service? Something small with a few friends or family?"

"No. He didn't want anything. He just wanted to be buried next to Aunt Linda. Besides, there's no family left."

He nodded. "Of course. We'll take him now. Again, I'm very sorry for your loss."

"Thank you, Mr. Banton."

He paused. "Do you wish to be there at the cemetery?"

She remembered her uncle's words just last week. "Have Banton plop me in the ground beside Linda without ceremony, Dylan. I don't need or want a bunch of hoopla."

She nodded. "Yes. I'd like to be there."

"Of course. I'll call you tomorrow and we'll set up a day and time. Perhaps Friday morning?"

She nodded and he left her then. She made her way back to the apple trees, reaching out to touch the bark with her hand as if for comfort. She wondered what would happen to these two old trees when she sold the farm. They were in desperate need of pruning, but they were too tall for her to manage. They'd been left to their own accord for years now. They probably hadn't been pruned since Lorah died. She would guess they were over forty feet tall now. She hated to think of them being cut down, but that's surely what would happen.

She heard doors slamming and she turned, seeing the funeral home's car pull away. Kathleen had left too, a good half hour ago. A deep breath and a long sigh—she was truly all alone. She pulled her phone out of her pocket. She needed to call Tanner. He would want to know. In fact, she thought he'd join her at the cemetery. He and Uncle

Frank had gotten along well. Before she could call him, though, her phone rang.

"Hello, Dylan here."

"Yes. Hi. It's Madilyn Marak. We met the other day, about the orchardist job."

She raised her eyebrows. "Orchardist? Is that what it's called?" She was surprised by the laugh she got.

"Yes. Or so I'm told. I'd like to offer you the job, Ms. Hayes."

"Wow. *Really?*" She shook her head. "I mean, wow, that's great." She paused. "Did the other guys turn you down?"

Another quiet laugh. "No. And I'll be the first to tell you that Randy—Mr. Shaffer—thinks I'm crazy to hire you."

"But? I mean, I like crazy."

"I think you would be best for this job, not them. Are you still interested?"

She walked back to the apple trees and stood between them. "Yes. I'm very interested."

"Great. When can we get started?"

"Well, there's a little complication. My uncle...he died this morning."

"Oh, I'm so sorry."

There was silence for a moment, and she looked up into the sky. "It was expected. He had cancer."

"I see. I'm sorry," she said again. "If you need some time, I understand. The house where you'll be staying is being remodeled and it won't be ready until the end of next week, at the earliest."

"Yeah, if I could have a little while, that would be great. We'll probably bury him on Friday so maybe I could come out next week and go over the particulars. We could talk more then."

"Of course. Whatever you need. Why don't you call me on Monday, and we'll go from there. I should have a better idea of the remodeling timeline then too."

"Thank you, Ms. Marak. I'm frankly shocked that you called, but it couldn't have come at a better time."

"Please, call me Madilyn. I take it this is why you said you would be homeless soon?"

"It is. I've got to sell the farm."

"I see. Well, again, I'm very sorry. We'll talk on Monday."

Dylan pocketed her phone, having forgotten about Tanner. She couldn't believe it. They hired her. They actually hired her.

Were they crazy?

CHAPTER EIGHTEEN

Madilyn walked off the porch, wearing one of the new pullover sweaters she'd ordered. It was a cool evening, not cold, and the sweater was perfect. All the clothes she'd purchased online had already trickled in and she'd had fun wearing them. There hadn't been much at her condo that was suitable for wear here. She'd sorted through her suits and dresses, not bothering to bring even one with her. Unfortunately, casual clothes—jeans and such—she owned little of. A couple of pairs of dressy jeans, that was it. So, she'd ordered—and was wearing—her very first pair of Levi's jeans. Other things had been delivered too, things she thought she would need for the summer. Besides several pairs of jeans, she had gotten some boots for outside walking, some casual shorts for summer, and a handful of comfortable T-shirts, things she'd owned none of. Her mother would be positively appalled.

She let her mind wander to Dylan Hayes. Had she made a mistake by hiring her? Randy certainly thought so. The truth was, now, after speaking to her, she felt sorry for her and was glad she'd gone with her intuition, despite Randy's protests. There was something about the woman that drew her. She'd only met her the one time and talked to her on the phone just the once—hard to form a concrete opinion on someone—yet she got the impression that Dylan was one of those inordinately happy and positive people. People she'd heard existed but none that she'd ever met. She apparently lived with her uncle, who had died, and she was about to be homeless. Yet her words, her tone, did not reflect the desperation she must be feeling. She wondered at the circumstances that were making her sell her uncle's farm instead of keeping it.

The ringing of her phone startled her, and she pulled it from her pocket, sighing as Palmer's name stared back at her. She almost sent it to voicemail, something she'd done yesterday when he called. She looked skyward for a moment before answering.

"Hello, Palmer."

"Madilyn. I was beginning to think you were avoiding me."

Should she lie? She walked farther away from the house. Yes, that would be the polite thing to do. "No, of course not. I've been busy."

"Oh, yes. Your apple orchard."

She blew out her breath. "Did you call for a reason?"

"Do I need a reason?" He paused for only a beat. "I miss you."

She moved farther away from the house, her gaze drawn to the moon as it hovered over the trees. Was it full tonight? Not quite. "Palmer, nothing has changed. I'll still be here through the summer."

"Can't we compromise on this, Madilyn?"

"Compromise?"

"Yes. Why can't you come here on weekends so we can get together?"

"Get together? Have dinner? What?"

"Yes, dinner." Then he gave a quiet laugh. "You could plan to stay at my place."

Ah. Dinner and sex. She shook her head. "I can't promise anything. I have a new orchardist starting next week. I'll be heavily involved in that project. Frankly, I don't know what all it will entail."

"Surely you'd be able to get away on a Saturday."

Able to and wanting to were two completely different things, she mused. "I'll have to see how it goes."

His sigh was loud in her ear. "Have you at least given any thought to the wedding?"

She rolled her eyes. The wedding again? "No."

"I've got a nice suite reserved. Room service. Breakfast in bed," he said in a seductive voice.

"Palmer, I can't commit to anything now. I'm sorry. Like I said at the restaurant, perhaps you should find another date if you need to."

"You were serious?"

"Yes, I was."

He paused a long moment. "I thought we were moving in a different direction, Madilyn. I'm ready to seriously talk about marriage and you seem like you want to slow things down. Is that how it is?"

Did she? Did she want to drag it out, just in case? She frowned. *Just in case what?* "Look, do what you need to do. I'll be here for several months. When I get back, we can see how things are going. But right now, you are not my primary focus, Palmer. My grandfather is."

"Yeah, your grandfather and some stupid orchard." He laughed then, but it wasn't a laugh she recognized. "You know, I ran into Brandon Raush the other day."

Of all the things she expected him to say, that was not it. She hadn't thought of Brandon Raush in years. "Really?"

"Yeah. He called you the Ice Queen."

"Ice Queen?"

"He said you were rather frosty in bed."

"How would he know?" she shot back quickly. "But it is so mature of the two of you to discuss me like that. Goodbye, Palmer."

She ended the call rather rudely, she knew, but she simply didn't care. The Ice Queen? That thought caused another roll of her eyes. Is that what they thought of her? She folded her arms around herself, wondering at the validity of the name. She could count on one hand the number of men she'd slept with, and she wouldn't need all five fingers. Brandon Raush wasn't one of them, however. She'd found him to be completely dull and uninteresting. She'd had the same feelings about Palmer at one time, hadn't she?

It was true. She tended to be rather guarded when it came to dating, and she certainly didn't sleep with her dates often. Yet she knew—or hoped—that she would throw caution to the wind should she meet someone who completely swept her off her feet. That hadn't happened, of course, so she really didn't care that men she'd once dated called her an ice queen.

She really didn't care if Palmer thought that about her either. And when her phone rang again, she promptly sent it to voicemail. No, she didn't care what Palmer thought. God, he actually had the audacity to mention marriage. Was he completely clueless?

CHAPTER NINETEEN

She and her uncle had cleaned out most of the "junk," as he'd called it, months ago. They'd even had a yard sale one weekend last summer. The house itself only had the bare necessities now. It wouldn't take long for her to pack up her things considering she hadn't brought much with her to begin with.

She looked around the kitchen, her gaze going to the coffeepot, the toaster, the microwave. She supposed she would need those things when she moved into her new place. Dishes, pots, and pans, too.

She went down the hallway to her uncle's room. She'd already stripped the bed. She'd donated all the furniture in the house to a local charity in Lancaster and they would be over Monday morning to collect it. The hospital bed that they'd had set up in the living room had been removed too. Hospice had come and picked it up Thursday afternoon. And she had called Francis Stumer of Stumer Realty to let him know it was time to list the farm. Her uncle had had everything arranged. All she had to do was put it in motion.

His farming equipment had been sold two years ago. She would take some of the tools and other odds and ends with her from the shed. The rest would be left for the new owners to do with as they may. His truck had been sold too. In fact, they'd sold his truck and her car at the same time, trading them both last year on a brand-new truck for her.

She stared at his empty room for a long moment, amazed at how quickly life comes…and then goes. She was prepared for her loss, and she thought she'd handled it well. Still, it was a little disconcerting to face the fact that she was truly all alone now. There was Tanner and a handful of friends she'd made here. No one else.

Before depression and loneliness could settle—and that impending sense of feeling sorry for herself—she let out a deep breath and turned from the room. She went through the quiet house and out the kitchen door. It was a cloudy day and storms were expected for the weekend. Nonetheless, Tanner was coming over tomorrow—Sunday—and they planned a last meal on the old smoker. Judging by the rain forecast, she imagined they would end up cooking steaks on the grill instead. It was on the porch, under cover. The smoker was out in the weather.

She glanced toward it now. It was too big and cumbersome to move. That was something else she'd miss. She blew out another deep breath and went toward the shed. Now was as good a time as any to sort through the tools and decide what she would take with her and what she would leave.

She opened the double doors on the shed to let more light in. When she'd been a kid, it still had an earthen floor. Uncle Frank had added the crude concrete floor not more than ten years ago. It was still a cluttered mess to be sure, but the tools she used most often were kept on the small workbench nearer the front, mainly the tools she used for pruning the trees each year. The hand pruners, the loppers, and the pruning saw.

She had gone by the hardware store yesterday and picked up two large, canvas tool bags. She'd done nothing more than toss them into the shed yesterday evening. She opened them now and started putting in items she thought she might need—assorted screwdrivers, open-ended wrenches, pliers, the socket set, the cordless drill and driver, and the bits to go with it.

There were so many tools, collected over the years by not only her uncle but his father and probably his grandfather as well. She didn't remember Grandpa Dave really. Only from pictures. She had fond memories of her grandmother, though. Another life cut short.

She walked around the shed, eyeing all the stuff there. In the back was a closet. The junk closet, Uncle Frank had called it. She opened the door, the rusty hinges squeaking. There were shelves on one side, surprisingly filled with Christmas decorations and wads of tangled lights. Old, dusty, and ancient from the looks of it. There were two brooms leaning against the back wall, the straw rubbed down to a near nub. Metal buckets were stacked upside down and there were six or eight metal T-posts that she thought would have come in handy had she known they were in there.

She was about to close it up again when she spotted a box on the floor, under the bottom shelf. It was an old cardboard box with a lid, the writing on the sides long faded away. Out of curiosity, she bent down and slid it out, taking it into the shed where the light was better. Dirt had settled on top of it, and she wiped it off before removing the lid. A felt fedora was on top and she took it out. The felt nearly disintegrated under her touch. She set it aside and pulled out a wooden box. It appeared to have been hand carved, the wood smooth. She ran her fingers across the top, feeling the indentation of two letters in the center—LC. The box had been sanded down and was smooth, yes, but the wood was in its natural state, not stained.

With a shrug, she opened it. The first thing she saw was a yellowed envelope addressed to Miss Lorah Chance. She held it up to the light, the postal stamp nearly faded. June 26, 1934.

"Wow," she whispered.

She opened the envelope, cringing as the corner tore a little. She carefully took out the lone piece of paper.

My Dearest Lorah. I never knew a heart could hurt as much as mine does. The pain just will not go away. My days are spent walking the path we took to the orchard. I'm sure the apple trees are sick of me by now. All I do is walk among them and talk to you. I swear I can still hear your voice as it whispers to me. Hattie worries, I know. I'm not eating much, not sleeping. She knows why my heart aches. I think she misses you nearly as much as I do.

I don't wear my wedding band any longer. James hasn't seemed to notice. I do wear the ring you gave me. Always. Not that I needed anything to remind me of you, but I'm so glad to have it as it was once yours.

I won't write to you again, my love. I wanted you to know how I was getting on is all. I hope you are well. Have you settled on the farm? Did you ever plant those apple trees for me?

I should stop now. My tears are falling as I write this. I miss you so much, Lorah. My life is completely empty without you. I live solely through my memories of last summer, the best months of my life. The best time of my life.

I love you, my dearest. Every beat of my heart is a longing for you. Forever yours, Issy.

"Oh my god. What the hell *is* this?" Well, obviously it was a love letter. From a woman.

She looked back in the box, seeing a faded newspaper clipping. This, too, was yellow with age. She carefully took it out. July 14, 1949. It appeared to be an obituary. Mrs. James Marak.

She looked up and frowned. Marak? She picked up the letter again, rereading it. *James hasn't seemed to notice.* She read through the obituary quickly, picking out words here and there—age thirty-six, one child—as she looked for a name. There. Isabel.

"Issy." She laughed. "Well, I'll be damned. So Aunt Lorah *was* gay."

But Marak? Was it the *same* Marak? Surely it was. Did Lorah have an affair with Isabel Marak? A sexual affair? She stared out at nothing. Did her Aunt Lorah have a lesbian affair with her new employer's relative? She wondered who Isabel was in relation to Madilyn. Could be an aunt like Lorah was to her or even a cousin or something.

She looked back in the box. The only other thing in there was an old leather pouch with a drawstring. She took it out and opened it up, pouring out the contents into her hand. She smiled and nodded. Apple seeds. Were they from the two old mother trees? Perhaps. She nodded again. Most likely, yes.

She put the seeds back in the pouch, then placed it inside the box again. The letter and the obituary went in next, and she closed the lid. She eyed the cardboard box for a moment but knew she wouldn't leave this treasure behind. She took the wooden box and the old fedora out with her. How had it ended up in the junk closet? She paused. Had someone shoved the box in there after Lorah had died? Or had Lorah herself put the box there, forgotten for all time? She supposed she would never know the answer to that because there certainly wasn't anyone left to ask.

She stopped up short at that thought. No, there wasn't anyone. It was with little ceremony that Uncle Frank had been buried yesterday. Tanner had stood beside her as they'd lowered the casket into the ground next to Aunt Linda. She then took Tanner over to her parents' graves. She had been nineteen when she and Uncle Frank had buried them all. She didn't stop by often enough, she knew.

She was halfway to the house when it hit her. She turned slowly, her gaze going to the two old, gnarly apple trees. What had the letter said? "Did you ever plant those apple trees for me?"

Is that why Lorah had planted them? For this woman named Issy? Is that why she sat there, day after day? Is that who she'd been talking to?

She nodded slowly. She had no way of knowing for sure, but the romantic side of her wanted to think that very thing. She paused and shook her head. Romantic? When was the last time she'd felt romantic about something?

CHAPTER TWENTY

"Frank was a good man." Tanner tapped his beer bottle with hers. "Damn shame his life ended like this."

"He was ready. I think when the doctor told him the end was near, he was relieved."

"And you're okay?"

She nodded. "Got no other choice. And he made it easy. Everything was already taken care of."

"I hate that you've got to sell the farm, Dylan."

"I know. But it's the only asset and there are medical bills to pay. Besides, what the hell would I do with this farm? It's already seen its better days."

"And this all goes?"

"Yeah. You want any of it?"

Tanner shook his head as he plopped down on the couch. "My place is crowded enough."

The forecasted rain had hit with a vengeance. So much so that they'd not only canceled the ribs on the smoker but the steaks too. Instead, she'd whipped up one of Uncle Frank's famous casseroles—ground beef, pasta, a bag of frozen mixed veggies, and marinara from a jar. She had doubled the cheese that he normally put on it.

"Well, after I meet with Madilyn tomorrow, I'll find out if I'm going to need anything or not. But yeah, getting rid of it all."

"Can't believe someone hired you to start up an orchard," he said with a laugh. "Are they crazy?"

She laughed too. "Yeah, that was my first thought. But you know, it sounds like I'll get to hire some guys to help me out if we get the large orchard going. You could always come work with me."

"Apples?"

"Yeah. A hundred acres or more eventually."

He laughed harder. "Good lord, who in their right mind hired you to manage a hundred acres?"

"Exactly! That's why I need you."

He shook his head. "Sorry, my friend, but I'm not quitting my job." Then he laughed. "A hundred-acre orchard? You'll be fired within the year."

She laughed with him although she'd thought that very thing. "We're just going to start with three acres. I'll worm my way into their good graces by the time we aim for the hundred. They'll never know I'm a fraud."

"Three acres? That's it? You can hardly call that an orchard. Won't make any profit with those few trees."

"I don't think making a profit is what she's after. Besides, I think the orchard would just be chump change. I doubt the Maraks are worried about income from that."

"Holy shit! The *Maraks*? That's who hired you?"

"Yeah. Who are they? My uncle said they were filthy rich."

"Back a hundred years ago or more, they owned most of the land between here and Philly and down to the Delaware. I don't know if that's where they made their fortune, though. Kinda standoffish from what I hear. Keep to themselves. Always have."

She took his empty beer bottle and went to the fridge for a cold one. "I didn't get that impression from her. She seemed nice enough."

"So who hired you?"

"Madilyn Marak. Young. About my age." She twisted off the cap before handing him the bottle. "Blond hair, blue eyes." She grinned. "Cute. Really cute."

He shook his head. "Never heard of her. Maybe a granddaughter or something. The old man's name is Albert, that's about all I know other than they're rich as hell." He laughed. "And she's way out of your league."

"Yeah. That's too bad." She let out a heavy sigh. "Maybe this job is too big for me, huh?"

"No, you can do it. Three little acres, you can do that in your sleep. But getting a big ass hundred-acre orchard up and running?" He shook his head. "That's a whole different ballgame, Dylan."

"Yeah, that's what I'm afraid of." She sat down beside him. "Where's Jenna?"

"Why? It's not like we're together every night."

"Right. Every night other than when you come over here."

"Yeah." He met her gaze. "You think I should ask her?"

"To marry you? I told you that last year already. You keep dragging it out, you're going to lose her. Hell, Tanner, you're older than I am. Get on with it already."

"What if she says no?"

She laughed. "She's not going to say no. She's as crazy about you as you are her."

"Yeah, I am pretty crazy about her. I've been seriously thinking about asking her. I mean really serious."

She nudged his arm. "Just do it."

"You think you and I can still hang out?"

"I would hope so. But judging by the security out at the Marak place—electric gate that needs a special code to get in—it'll be me coming to see you."

"So where are you going to be living?"

She shrugged. "I haven't seen the place. They're having it remodeled. There's a lot of wide-open land out there. Pretty. Pockets of woodland, then fields and meadows, then more woodland. There is a big-ass mansion there that looks to be in the middle of hundreds of acres. Man, it was quiet out there. I'm going to love that."

"What are you going to do there by yourself?"

"I'm going there to work. I'm not worried about my entertainment." She got up to check the casserole. "Besides, you're already predicting I'm going to get fired within a year."

"They're not going to fire you. You're too likable." He followed her into the kitchen. "We need to have a date night."

"You and me?"

"Yeah. Like every Wednesday or something. We can meet in Quarryville. Grab dinner or go to a bar."

"Yeah." She pulled the casserole from the oven. "Let me get settled and see what my routine is going to be. And if I'm bored out of my mind there, then Jenna will just have to share you."

He bumped her shoulder. "You need to find your own girlfriend."

"Yeah, I do. Because I sure as hell ain't getting any younger."

"What about Crystal? You still avoiding her?"

She took out two plates and handed him one. "She's not my type. We had three, four dates, and it was just…meh." She scooped out a portion of the casserole onto his plate. "So, yes, I'm avoiding her."

CHAPTER TWENTY-ONE

Since Madilyn had conducted the interviews for the orchardist job and hired Dylan Hayes, she'd done a lot more research on the operations of an apple orchard. Something that she should have done much earlier in the process, to be sure. If she had, there was no way she would have hired a woman with such little experience. In fact, Randy had suggested she call Dylan and tell her that they'd changed their mind.

And really, if she hadn't spoken to her, if she didn't know that her uncle had just died, know that Dylan was going to be homeless, she might very well do that. But not now. It was too late for that. So, she would do as she'd originally planned. Get the orchard going here—Isabel's orchard—and then reevaluate at Brandywine Creek. Because in truth, she had only been concerned with the orchard here at the estate. It was her grandfather who had suggested she invest in Brandywine Creek as well, which she had learned was not *the* Brandywine Creek. It was the West Fork of Brandywine. But that could wait. Her focus was going to be Isabel's orchard first. And she had no idea how much fruit three acres would produce but hopefully enough to serve her purpose—allow the locals to come in and pick the apples at will and maybe eventually change the impression the locals had of the Marak family.

Dylan Hayes was on her way now. Randy had called, saying that Dylan had buzzed in from the locked gate. She supposed she would need to give her the code so she could come and go without relying on someone being around to remote open the gate for her. She should have given it to her on Monday when they spoke on the phone.

She headed out toward the shed, wearing a pair of her new jeans and the boots she'd purchased. She saw a truck coming up the long drive and she assumed it was Dylan. She hadn't paid much attention to the vehicles that were there during the interviews. She shielded her eyes from the sun as the truck got closer—maroon in color, she noted.

Randy's utility vehicle was parked out front, and she supposed he was waiting for Dylan. He had a list, he said. Things that he thought needed to be done to get a good start. She could already tell that he had inserted himself in the role of supervisor. She hadn't yet told him that *she* would take on that job, even though she knew little to nothing about orchards. As her grandfather had reminded her, this was her project, not Randy's.

She stood beside the John Deere, waiting for Dylan to park. She wondered if she should purchase a utility vehicle like this for Dylan as well. It would be much quicker to get to the orchard using the trail rather than taking the road around.

"Good morning, Ms. Marak," Dylan greeted cheerfully. "Beautiful today, isn't it?"

She nodded automatically, realizing that she hadn't given the day much thought. She looked around then, noting the blue skies and bright sunshine. She matched Dylan's smile. "Yes, it is. And please call me Madilyn." She pointed to the John Deere. "Would you like one of these?"

Dylan raised both eyebrows. "Excuse me?"

"To get to the orchard."

"Oh. Well, I thought I'd be using my truck. The road—"

"There is a trail to the orchard and valley from up here. Easier to get to than taking the road around."

"Okay." Then a smile. "In that case, sure, I'd love one."

Madilyn nodded. "I'll have Randy get one for you then. This is his." She motioned to the door of the shed. "Come inside. We'll go over the particulars, as you called it."

Randy was pouring himself a cup of coffee when they entered. Madilyn knew he still wasn't convinced that Dylan could do this job—neither was she, for that matter—but his greeting to her seemed genuine.

"Good morning, Ms. Hayes. Coffee?"

"Good morning, Mr. Shaffer, but please call me Dylan. And no, I've had my fill of coffee. Two cups and I'm done for the day."

He nodded. "And call me Randy." He motioned to the small table. "Please, sit. I have a list of things I want to go over."

"Okay. Sure."

"Maddie? You want a cup?"

"No, thank you."

She sat down opposite Dylan Hayes and Randy took the end chair. He sat and placed his list in front of him. She glanced at Dylan, noting that she appeared to be a little nervous as her hands were folded together and tapping lightly on the table. Randy cleared his throat, appearing very businesslike this morning. Madilyn assumed he had little to keep him busy all day and he was embracing this new project.

"I think the first order of business is to remove all the old trees from the existing orchard. You, as well as the other applicants, all mentioned hiring out for that. Now—"

"Well, if I could interrupt here," Dylan said with an apologetic smile. "When I took a look at the orchard that day, you still had some that looked healthy and were still producing."

"Some, yes. But even those are old and nearing end of life. Like you said yourself, it's rare for them to still have fruit. I think we should raze all the trees and start completely over."

"I see."

Clearly, Dylan Hayes didn't agree with that suggestion. "What would be your proposal?" Madilyn asked her.

Dylan looked at her, a smile on her face now. "Well, there are a couple of reasons to keep the old gals that are still producing. One, they seem to be a superior tree to most and I'd like to try my hand at grafting. Granted, I've never done it before, but I heard plenty of stories from my uncle on how they grafted off those two old mother trees at the farm." Dylan looked over at Randy now. "Plus, we're going to need some pollinators for the new trees. Might as well be these old ones, provided they live another three or four years." Then she smiled broadly. "And third, I make a mean apple cobbler. I'd sure hate to have to wait three or four years before I had one."

Madilyn knew without a doubt that her assumption of Dylan Hayes was on target. She was a happy and positive person and she found herself gravitating to her. "I agree."

Randy shot her a look. "You do?" He then turned again to Dylan. "But what happens when those trees do die off?"

"We can replace them then. There's nothing wrong with having several age differences in a small orchard like this. Now your big orchards? Sure. They keep everything nice and neat and orderly. They also remove the trees once their production starts to slow. They would never allow something like those old ugly trees to hang around." She shook her head. "No, they remove the trees and put new ones in and cycle through the orchard like that. Keeps the production up."

"Isn't that what we want?" he asked, the question directed at her, not Dylan.

Madilyn shook her head. "I'm sorry to disappoint you, Randy, but this orchard is almost entirely nostalgic. I'm not concerned about production. Now, if we venture over to Brandywine Creek eventually, that would be different."

"So you basically just want trees then?" he asked.

"I want a functioning orchard. Once the fruit comes in, I want to open it up to the local communities to pick for free." She smiled at him. "Unheard of in this family, I know." She quickly turned to Dylan. "I'm sorry." Then she motioned to Randy's list. "What else?"

Randy sighed and glanced at the papers in front of him. "Well, I mainly wanted to go over the removal of trees and the planting of new ones. I've called around and I found some places where we can buy young trees. We can—"

"Actually, I've got a buddy who works at the farm and ranch store there in Millersville. He always gives me a discount on the cost. He can—"

"A discount?" Randy shook his head. "This is the Maraks we're talking about. I think we should pay top dollar and get the best trees. We don't want discounted varieties. There'll be no shortcuts, Ms. Hayes."

Madilyn was shocked by Randy's tone and words. What in the world was going on with him?

"Of course. Sorry." Dylan smiled good-naturedly. "I'm used to working on a very tight budget. Not sure I'll know how to act without one."

"I assume you'll want me to handle all of the purchasing, not Dylan?" Randy asked her.

That was something else she hadn't considered. But she shook her head. "No. I think Dylan should handle all of that."

Randy's eyes widened. "But—"

"We can discuss that later," she interrupted. "In fact, I'd like to go out to the orchard now. Show Dylan around and inspect the trees."

Randy nodded. "Okay, sure." He stood. "I can run her out there. I'll—"

"Actually, Randy, if we can use your utility vehicle out there, I'll take her myself." She smiled. "And I'd like a word with you, please."

Dylan looked between the two of them, then stood too. "Okay, so I'll…" She pointed to the door. "I'll wait outside."

Madilyn nodded, then motioned for Randy to sit again. When he did she leaned closer. "What is going on?"

"What do you mean?"

She only arched an eyebrow, saying nothing.

He looked away from her. "Well, Mr. Albert told me to make sure things went smoothly. He was concerned this woman—who has little experience—might try to take advantage of you."

"Is that right?"

Randy nodded. "He was afraid you might…well, give her free rein. I mean, we don't know this woman at all, Maddie. And you're already telling her she's going to be in charge of purchasing?"

"While I appreciate your—and my grandfather's—concerns, I'm not a naïve young woman with no business sense. And I'm not one to trust easily. When I said she would be in charge of purchasing, I didn't mean we'd give her a blank check to do with as she wanted. But I also don't want her to feel like she's got to look over her shoulder all the time."

She stood up and rested her hands on the back of the chair. "This little orchard is a pet project of mine, Randy. So, I'd like to be the one to see it through. I'd like to have it done my way and I plan to be involved in it." She stood up straighter. "Now, I do have a project for you, though. I spoke with my grandfather last night. He's in agreement that the old houses should be removed. I'd like you to take care of that. Okay?"

"Of course. I've already called around and got some bids. I'll get the ball rolling on that."

"Good. And I'd also like you to purchase another of those John Deere vehicles for Dylan to use. If you would like to keep the new one for yourself and give her this one, that's fine with me."

"Oh, this one is not even a year old. I'll keep it. I've got it fixed up the way I want it." He got up too. "I didn't mean to upset you, Maddie. I was just doing what Mr. Albert said."

"I know. And I'll speak with him today. He's being overprotective, that's all." She went toward the door. "Want to give us a quick tutorial on driving that thing?"

"Sure, but there's nothing to it."

CHAPTER TWENTY-TWO

Dylan leaned against her truck, wondering what kind of conversation was going on inside. She also wondered if she'd made a mistake by taking this job. Of course, it wasn't like she had a lot of options. None, actually. She'd already had an offer on the farm. It was well below what she wanted but at least there was interest. Mr. Stumer said he'd had several calls about it and planned to show it to another interested buyer in a couple of days. He'd also hinted that maybe she needed to come down on her asking price a little. Maybe so but certainly not the first week it had been on the market. She'd let it ride for a few months, at least. She had already let the hospital know that she would be paying off her uncle's bill in full as soon as it sold. They weren't hounding her, so she had time.

When she heard the door open, she turned toward it. Madilyn came out first and gave her a reassuring smile. Dylan returned it, not sure why she thought it was reassuring. Maybe because she wasn't getting fired on her first day. When their eyes met, though, she had that same nagging feeling that she'd met Madilyn Marak somewhere before. Of course, she knew that was impossible. They *so* did not run in the same circles. Yet there was something familiar about her—thick, blond hair parted slightly off center, reaching a few inches above her shoulders, blue eyes. But no, she was certain they'd never met. She would have remembered meeting someone this attractive.

"Randy is going to let us take this," Madilyn said, pointing to the Gator. "Why don't you drive? Get familiar with it before you get your own."

Dylan looked over at Randy for confirmation. She'd gotten the feeling that he either didn't like her or didn't trust her. Or both.

"It's pretty straightforward," Randy said. "Or have you driven one before?"

She nodded. "I have. My buddy has one. An old one, though. Not fancy like this with the roof and doors and all."

Randy motioned to it. "It's all yours then. Maddie's got my number in case something happens."

"Thanks."

She opened the door and got inside, waiting until Madilyn was seated before starting it up. The gearshift was between the two seats, and she moved it from N to R, pausing to release the brake first. It nearly purred as she backed up before flipping it to F and pulling away.

"Nice," she murmured. She glanced over to the woman sitting next to her. A woman with brand-new boots and jeans that hadn't yet been broken in. "Where to?"

"Go around the back of the shed." She motioned. "There's a trail. It's rather overgrown now, but I would assume with you driving this way, you'll get it knocked down again. I've only taken the golf cart out there a few times."

She nodded but made no other comment. She found the trail as it curled between two large maple trees, the leaves still young and vibrant green. She drove at a slow pace even though the trail seemed to be relatively smooth and bump free. They moved through clumps of trees, then out into the open again. To her right, she caught a glimpse of lush green, and she slowed even more.

"Wow," she murmured without thinking. "That's beautiful."

"The valley? Yes."

Before too long, the old orchard came into view and Madilyn was right, it was much quicker taking the trail rather than the road. Their path seemed to dive right into the heart of the orchard then it disappeared into nothingness, as if there'd been no trail at all. She finally stopped.

"I guess we're here."

"Yes."

They eyed each other for a long moment before either of them moved. Dylan finally opened the door.

"Okay. Let's take a look around."

* * *

Madilyn watched as Dylan went to one of the trees that was sporting leaves. She reached up, bending a limb down to inspect it. She was wearing jeans that looked old, soft, comfortable. Unlike her own which were still a bit stiff. Dylan had a smile on her face, and she motioned her over.

"Come look."

Madilyn moved to stand beside her, looking at the tip of the limb. "What am I seeing?"

"A tiny baby apple. Not much fruit has set on this tree, though."

Dylan moved on down the row, past the four obviously dead trees to the next live one. There appeared to be a cluster of live trees here. She counted six that had leafed out. Beyond them, there were mostly all dead trees until you got closer to the edge where the maple trees shielded them from the north. There was another cluster growing, and she couldn't help but wonder if those were the ones Isabel visited the most...on her way to their old picnic spot under the maple.

"More fruit here," Dylan said. "Easier pollination when you've got several trees all blooming together. Even though three acres isn't huge to us, to a bee it is. Why travel way over there," she said, pointing to another live tree about four rows over, "when you can stay right here and hit all of these?"

"What is your plan?"

"Do I have a plan?" That was followed by a big grin. "Teasing. Of course I have a plan. I'll get some of that pink tape to use as flags. I'll walk the entire orchard and mark the ones that I want to keep. This group here, probably. If there are any live ones on the perimeter, I'll keep those too. Even if they don't produce fruit, the blooms will attract bees and help with cross-pollination for our new young trees."

Dylan walked on and Madilyn followed. When Dylan stopped, she was no longer looking at the orchard. Her gaze was on the valley. Madilyn followed suit, her eyes lingering on the green lushness spread out before them. It was becoming a familiar sight yet one that still made her catch her breath. It was—

"God, that's gorgeous." Dylan turned a circle. "If this orchard wasn't here, this would make a wonderful place for a house. What a view to have."

"Yes. I'm glad you like it because it'll be your view."

Dylan faced her. "What do you mean?"

"Your house. It's at the edge of the valley." She pointed up ahead. "It's past the woods here. There's no trail, though. Only the road. I'm sure you'll make your own trail."

Another smile. "Is there a porch to sit on with this view?"

Madilyn shook her head. "The porch is in the front. Opposite the view. There is a small sitting area in the back, but it's not covered, I'm afraid."

"Oh. Well, that's okay."

They came to the edge of the orchard and Madilyn's gaze went to Isabel and Lorah's spot beneath the maples. Dylan walked in that direction, passing by the tree that Madilyn had sat against to read the diary. Instead, she moved to the edge where it sloped downward to the valley. Again, she had a look a bewilderment on her face.

"You like it?" she asked quietly, surprised to find herself holding her breath as she waited for the answer.

"I love it," Dylan answered without turning around.

Dylan stared out a few more seconds, then moved back. Amazingly, she pointed to the exact spot under the maple. "I can see myself packing a lunch every day and sitting right there to enjoy it."

Madilyn smiled and nodded, thinking that Isabel and Lorah would be pleased that someone else was enjoying their picnic spot.

"So, back to my plan," Dylan said, moving again toward the orchard. "Once everything is marked, I'll have to hire someone—a crew—to come in and remove the old trees."

"What will they do with them?"

"Oh, they'll sell the wood. But yeah, they'll clean everything up. They'll have one of those trucks with a mulcher for the smaller limbs. They'll dump that mulch out here so we can use it around the new trees. Now you'll need to decide how much you want to spend. We can leave the stumps and plant around them, or we can get them to grind the stumps down."

"Which do you recommend?"

"Well, if money isn't a factor, I'd get them to grind them down. Get them gone and out of the way."

"Then let's do that."

Dylan ran a hand through her short hair a couple of times. "Are you going to be my supervisor or is Randy?"

"Do you need a supervisor?"

"Well, you know, to run things by. Costs and all." Dylan shoved her hands in the pockets of her jeans. "I got the impression that Randy didn't like me."

Madilyn started walking back toward the orchard and Dylan fell into step beside her. The coolness of morning was fading, and it was quite warm now. So much so that she wished she'd worn shorts.

"It's nothing personal with Randy. He wanted to hire one of the men who applied." She smiled apologetically at her. "Actually, he wanted to hire *any* of the three besides you."

"He doesn't think a woman can do the job?"

"I think it was the experience factor."

"That's understandable. Then why me?"

Madilyn shrugged. "I wanted to hire you. This project—as I had to explain to Randy earlier—is *my* project. I didn't anticipate Randy being involved at all. My grandfather is being overly protective and asked Randy to handle things."

"I see."

"No, you don't. It's *my* project," she said again. "I think I have made that clear to Randy now, and later today I will make it clear to my grandfather that I don't need babysitting."

"If you don't mind me asking, why did you want to hire me? I didn't talk to all three of those guys, but I talked to two of them. They had way more experience than me."

"Intuition, perhaps, but I didn't get a good feeling about them. I wanted someone who I could work closely with."

Dylan laughed lightly. "So, I made a good impression on you, huh?"

She returned her smile. "You did." Then she asked the question that had been bothering her. "Why do you have to sell your uncle's farm?"

"Oh. Yeah." She gave a quick shrug. "Medical bills. Lots of them. He'd been sick for the last six years. The last year, well, the last five or six months really, the bills kinda piled up especially after his lengthy hospital stay. The farm is the only asset. The hospital is being very cooperative though. It's just, the farmhouse is very old, and the land, well, he couldn't really farm it for the last several years. The only thing still functioning out there was the orchard." Dylan smiled. "You know, *my* orchard."

"Will you miss it?"

"Yes. Especially the two old mother trees. While they do still produce some fruit, they are ugly as hell," she said with a laugh. "And it's not like they're hidden somewhere in the back. No, they're right out near the house. I guess whoever buys the place will cut them down."

Madilyn looked at the trees around them. "I'm glad you aren't suggesting we eliminate all these trees. And my reason is totally sentimental. It has nothing to do with cross-pollination."

"Is this where you grew up?"

"My younger years, yes." She didn't elaborate. "I have a condo in Philly. My grandmother died recently and—" And what? "I've agreed to stay with my grandfather, at least through summer."

"Oh. So, when you move, I'll be on my own? Or will Randy then oversee things with the orchard?"

"I haven't thought that far ahead." That certainly was the truth. She hadn't given the end of her stay much thought. She paused at the green vehicle. "Now, what do you need? Tools? Materials?"

"I have some tools. Those that I use at the farm. That'll get me started. Once we get the trees out of here and order the new ones, then I'll need stuff. Is there a tractor out here with a small backhoe or something?"

Madilyn stared at her. "I don't think so. Backhoe?" *What was a backhoe?*

"For digging holes to plant the new trees. Can't dig them by hand." She laughed. "Well, I guess I could, but it would take me until Christmas to finish. Or we could hire a crew to plant, but I'd rather do it myself. I'm a bit of a control freak."

Madilyn found herself smiling back at her. "Okay. Well, let's buy a tractor then."

"That would be really great if you could. Just a small one, nothing big. We had to sell the one at the farm. I didn't know I would miss it so much. It was just your basic tractor with a front-end loader which is great to haul stuff, like mulch and fertilizer and stuff. And a backhoe would—"

Madilyn held up her hand. "You don't have to convince me. Tell me what you want, and I'll have Randy buy it." Then she shook her head. "Better yet, I'll set up an account for you with a card. You can use that to buy whatever you need."

Dylan raised her eyebrows. "Like carte blanche?"

"Like you let me know what you need before you buy it. How's that?"

Dylan opened the passenger door for her, smiling broadly. "I think I'm going to *love* this job."

When she got behind the wheel and started it up, Madilyn motioned between the trees. "If we can find the road, I'll show you the house we're remodeling for you."

"Okay, sure."

"And it just occurred to me, we have not discussed salary."

"I wasn't really too concerned about it because just the fact that you're giving me a place to live is worth it."

"Well, I've researched salaries for orchardists and there is quite a range. I've settled on a midpoint. I hope it will be satisfactory for you. It's not a huge salary, but like you said, housing is provided. How does sixty thousand a year sound?"

Dylan actually stopped the vehicle and turned to her. "Sixty?"

"I know it's not a lot and if you think you deserve more, we can—"

"Madilyn, it's only three acres." Dylan shook her head but there was a smile on her face. "Look, that's way too generous an offer. I'd feel like I was stealing from you."

"You think it's too much? Really?"

"Yeah, it's too much. You obviously didn't run it by Randy and your grandfather. I'm sure they would balk. It's just three acres."

Madilyn smiled at her. "Now see, this is why I hired you. I had a feeling you'd be honest and trustworthy." She motioned for her to drive on, still smiling. "But the salary stays as is."

CHAPTER TWENTY-THREE

Dylan still couldn't wrap her head around the fact that Madilyn was going to pay her sixty thousand to manage the measly three acres. And give her a place to live. That was just crazy. She pushed that away as she made her way through the orchard to the narrow road that would, if she stayed on it, hook back up with the main driveway. It was the road she'd taken that first day when she'd come for the interview. Instead, though, they turned to the right, following what was once a road but now seemed long neglected. The weeds and grass that had grown over it had been smashed down recently. Probably by the construction workers doing the remodeling, she guessed.

"Has the house been vacant for a while?" she asked Madilyn.

"Yes. There are several houses on the property that have been vacant for years. Most are beyond repair. This was the nicest of the bunch. Actually, I'm having the others torn down and moved."

Like on most of the property, there were pockets of trees and cleared land. The road emerged from a stand of oaks into a clearing, and she spotted the house. A small, wood-framed structure with an obvious fresh coat of paint. The walls were beige in color with a darker brown trim. It looked nice. There were five or six large trees surrounding the house, two pines and two big hemlocks and a couple of red maples.

"I hope you'll like it. It's nothing fancy, but we did remodel the kitchen and bathroom and there will be all new appliances installed once it's finished."

"I'm sure it'll be fine."

There were two trucks parked out front and she pulled the Gator next to them. Buckets of paint and paraphernalia were on a drop cloth on the small front porch.

"They're still painting the inside," Madilyn explained. "They'll be finished by Thursday, at the latest."

Dylan let Madilyn go in first and the smell of fresh paint was nearly overwhelming. There was a ladder in the living room, and they skirted around it. A nice long bar separated the room from the kitchen.

"There was a wall here," Madilyn said, pointing to the bar. "The kitchen was so small and closed in, I had them take it out and put the breakfast bar in instead."

"I like it."

Madilyn raised her eyebrows questioningly. "Do you cook?"

"I do. But I had to fight my uncle for kitchen duty. He loved to cook too. Of course, not so much the last year."

"I'm sorry."

Dylan shook her head. "No, no. It was a long battle he fought, but at the end, he was more than ready for it to be over with."

"Do you have other family in the area?"

"Actually, no. He was the last."

She knew that Madilyn was about to utter "I'm sorry" again, but they were interrupted by a man carrying a roller brush. His face was smeared with white paint.

"Oh, Miss Madilyn, I didn't hear you drive up."

"Hello, Brad. This is Dylan Hayes. She'll be living here. I wanted to show her around."

He held a paint-stained hand out to her, and Dylan laughed but shook her head. "Nice to meet you," she said instead of shaking his hand.

He laughed too. "My wife often wonders if I get more on me than the walls." He motioned behind him. "We're in the bedroom, but you can take a look at the bathroom. That's done. Turned out real nice."

"Thanks, Brad," Madilyn said, letting him pass by them and outside before moving down the hallway.

The bathroom did indeed look nice. "New fixtures?"

"Yes. They gutted the whole thing. New shower, everything." She opened a small closet. "For towels and such."

Dylan nodded. "Is there a place for a washer and dryer?"

"Yes. There's a small utility room off the kitchen." Madilyn gave a quick smile. "And I do mean small."

"I guess I should measure it then. The washer and dryer at the farm are both old and big and clunky. I might have to get new ones."

"No, no. Randy ordered new appliances. Come take a look at it. As soon as they're through painting, I'll have Julia give it a thorough cleaning and then Randy will get the appliances installed." Madilyn opened the double doors against the far wall of the kitchen. "Like I said, small."

Above where the washer and dryer would sit were two cabinets. She reached around Madilyn to open one, revealing two shelves inside. She nodded.

"Perfect."

"I'm glad you like it. I didn't order furniture yet because I didn't know what you'd want to bring with you."

"Yeah, actually, all the furniture was my uncle's. When I moved in with him, I didn't bring any of my own. It's been donated to charity, but I haven't had them pick it up yet because I didn't know if I'd have to bring stuff with me."

"Then let's get everything new unless you have some sentimental attachment to some. That's fine too."

"Well, truth is, most of that furniture is old and has seen better days. But all of this," she said, waving at the room, "plus new furniture is probably costing a fortune as it is."

Madilyn touched her arm briefly and smiled. "We'll get new furniture."

"Okay, then." Dylan shrugged. Hell, what did she know about it? This little remodeling job was probably a drop in a bucket for the Maraks. "Can I take a look out back?"

"Of course." Madilyn pointed to a door at the end of the kitchen. "There."

The back door opened onto a small concrete slab. At first glance, Dylan calculated it to be maybe eight-by-eight. Nothing huge but big enough to fit a small table and a chair. Maybe she'd get resourceful and lay some bricks down or something to enlarge it. Make it big enough for a grill, at least. The view was spectacular. She could imagine sitting out here and having her morning coffee. She could hear birds singing in the trees, and she made a mental note to bring her uncle's old bird feeder along with her.

"Do you think deer come out into the valley?"

Madilyn walked up beside her, following her gaze. "I don't know, really."

"I hope so." She turned to her. "This is great, Madilyn. Thank you. I feel like I hit the jackpot with this job. I was…well, when I knew the end was near, I was feeling a little sorry for myself, not knowing where I'd live or if I could even get a job." Madilyn turned to look at her and Dylan met her gaze. "A couple of nights before he died, I went and sat out against one of the old apple trees and I had such a sense of peace settle over me—a feeling that things would all work out. I knew I had no business getting this job, but I think I was holding onto hope that maybe I would."

"When we advertised for the job, I had no idea who I wanted to hire or what my expectation would be. When we interviewed the four of you, I knew who I *didn't* want to hire." Madilyn looked back toward the valley. "I told my grandfather I wanted to hire you despite your lack of experience. For one thing, we're about the same age—I'm twenty-seven—and being isolated out here like we are, it would be nice to have a friend." Madilyn turned back to her. "My grandfather informed me that the Maraks do not make friends with the hired help."

Dylan nodded. "Ah. I see."

Madilyn smiled at her. "I told him I did not follow that rule."

"Good." Dylan matched her smile. "And to be honest here, I have no idea who you are or who or what the Maraks do."

Madilyn laughed. "And you have no idea how refreshing that is."

CHAPTER TWENTY-FOUR

"I in no way thought you needed a babysitter."

Madilyn looked at her grandfather skeptically. "Really? Randy just took that upon himself?"

Her grandfather finally smiled. "Okay. I may have told him to oversee—"

"I can handle this," she interrupted. "You're trusting me with the Foundation, yet you're concerned about the orchard? That hardly compares."

"You're right, of course." He waved his hand in the air. "I apologize. I'll speak with Randy in the morning."

"No need. I think I've already conveyed my feelings to him." She pushed her plate aside. "You mentioned the other day about setting up an account for the orchard and whatever expenses we'll have for it."

"Yes. It's already done. I've got the account information on my desk. Mr. Holdren took care of that for me," he said, referring to his accountant.

"Good." She smiled. "Because I need to buy a tractor. With a backhoe."

He nodded, apparently not surprised by her request. "Yes, I knew you would need some equipment. Back when I was a boy and the orchards were working—especially the one over at Brandywine Creek—the crews had several tractors, if I recall. Get what you need, Maddie."

"Thank you."

"Does this woman know what she's doing? I suppose she was the one who mentioned the tractor."

"Yes. She seems quite versed in it all. I'm pleased. I like her."

"Good. Then I won't worry over it. Like you said, you can handle it. I'm sorry I overstepped my boundary."

Madilyn laughed. "Well, it is *your* land and *your* money. I wouldn't call it a boundary, exactly."

"Maddie, I've been on this earth for eighty-nine years. When you get to be this old, you feel lucky just to wake up in the morning. Everything that I own, you own. Honestly, I'm glad you've taken an interest in the orchard." He picked up his wineglass. "Maybe that will keep you around longer."

"Still afraid I'll run away?"

"I don't know. You seem to be settling in. I've noticed the new clothes, of course."

She nodded. "That's been fun." She folded her hands together. "Truth is, I feel like a different person out here. I'm certainly more relaxed. And I like Dylan. She will probably be sick of me and think I'm underfoot."

"Oh? You don't trust her to manage things?"

"Yes, I do trust her. But I want to be out there too and involved in the daily activities."

"Like...*work?*"

She laughed at the look on his face. "Yes, like work. I'm looking forward to it. And who knows? I may learn to drive a tractor."

CHAPTER TWENTY-FIVE

"Where would you like it, ma'am?" he asked, referring to the sofa they'd brought in.

Dylan turned to Madilyn. "What do you think? I'm not exactly a decorator."

Madilyn walked over, pointing to the open space near the bar. "Here." Then she turned to her. "I assume you'll want your TV against the wall."

"I didn't even think about a TV." She smiled. "You got me one?"

Madilyn smiled too. "I did."

"Thanks." She moved out of the way, letting the guys place the sofa down. "How did you get this here so fast?"

Madilyn shrugged. "As my grandfather likes to say, our last name is both a blessing and a curse. In this case, a blessing."

"Well, I do sincerely thank you. I've been staying at Tanner's the last few nights. They've already taken all the furniture out of my uncle's house."

"Tanner? Is he your boyfriend?"

Dylan laughed. *Boyfriend?* She hadn't been asked about a boyfriend in probably fifteen years. "I don't have boyfriends. No, Tanner is that buddy I was telling you about. He works at the farm and ranch store over in Millersville."

"Oh yes. The one who'll give you a good price on new trees."

"Yeah." She tilted her head. "What about you? You have a boyfriend?"

Madilyn shifted uncomfortably. "Sort of. Maybe."

"Sort of?"

Madilyn sighed. "Palmer. I keep trying to break up with him. He—as well as my mother—thinks we'll get married someday."

"Yikes." Then she arched an eyebrow. "Is that why you're out here with your grandfather? Hiding from this Palmer guy?"

Madilyn laughed. "Not the sole reason, no, but it did factor into it." Madilyn took her arm and pulled her aside as the guys brought in a nice leather recliner. "Put it over there." She pointed.

As soon as they placed it down, Dylan sat in it. "Oh yeah. Super nice." She grinned at Madilyn. "You're like the best boss ever."

Madilyn laughed. "Glad you like it." She motioned to the door. "Maybe we should get out of the way."

Two men came in carrying a bulky headboard. "Want to show us where you want the bed?"

"Oh, sure." Dylan went into the bedroom, pointing against the far wall. "Headboard there. And the dresser against this wall here."

They nodded and she stepped aside, then went out to the porch where Madilyn was waiting. They were still in the way, though, so they went around to the back. Dylan was surprised to find two chairs and a table on the small patio.

"You put down bricks," Madilyn said, pointing to the concrete squares she'd added. "It looks nice."

"Needed a place to put a gas grill. And when did you sneak those out?" she asked, referring to the chairs and table.

Madilyn pulled out a chair and sat down. "I had Randy pick them up in Lancaster. He takes Loretta once a week for shopping."

Dylan sat down too. "Loretta?"

"She's my grandfather's cook. She's worked here her whole life, as did her mother and grandmother before her."

"Wow. So this place has been around a while, huh?"

"Yes. It was my great-great-grandfather who built the estate. There are servants' quarters in the house—that's where Loretta lives now—but there were also two other houses nearby where servants lived. One got torn down and the other is where Randy and his wife live." Madilyn held her hand up. "I actually hate the word 'servant,' but that's the word my grandfather still uses and it's kinda stuck."

She thought back to the obituary and wondered if Isabel Marak ever lived out here. She was about to ask but then kept quiet. Did she really want to get into a discussion about her Aunt Lorah's lesbian affair? Instead, she kept her gaze on the valley. "Am I ever going to get to meet him?"

"My grandfather? Yes, of course. I was trying to let you get settled first. He can be rather abrupt sometimes. Even at his age—he's eighty-nine—he's still a bit intimidating to some."

"And you recently lost your grandmother?"

"Yes. Like your uncle, she had been ill for some time, so her passing wasn't a shock. My grandfather still took it hard, which is why I'm here." She smiled. "Well, one of the reasons."

"Oh, yes. Palmer," she teased. "Your future husband."

Madilyn actually groaned. "Palmer is an attorney from a very wealthy family, and he bores me to tears." Then she smiled. "He probably thinks the same about me."

"Then why does he want to marry you?"

Madilyn stared at her for a moment. "Because of my name."

"Oh. So it's not love and romance related then."

"Not in the least, no."

"Like an arranged marriage?"

Madilyn laughed. "No. Not quite that obvious. My mother knows his parents. I'm sure they've discussed it. My mother has mentioned several times how wonderful it would be if Palmer and I wed. And I would venture to say that his parents have said the same to him."

"And have you and Palmer discussed it?"

"Not exactly. He's offhandedly mentioned it a couple of times. I mostly ignore him."

"I don't guess I understand. If you don't like the guy, tell him to hit the road."

"We had dinner a few weeks ago. I thought we had ended things." She sighed. "But he called." She held her hand up. "I don't want to talk about Palmer. I don't even want to think about him." She smiled. "Let's talk about apple trees."

CHAPTER TWENTY-SIX

Madilyn crept along the trail in the golf cart, noting how well-worn it looked already. For the third day in a row, the sound of chainsaws filled the air. But there was something different today. She wondered if they had started grinding down the stumps. Dylan had thought they might.

She spotted her green Gator parked near the maple trees, out of the way of the orchard. She noticed that the doors had been taken off, something Dylan had told her she wanted to do. She pulled up beside it, but Dylan was nowhere in sight.

She looked out among the remaining trees, spotting her walking between them. She had such a sense of déjà vu while watching her, she put a hand on the cart to steady herself. Dylan turned and came back down another row. She guessed that Dylan was counting trees. When Dylan saw her, she motioned for her to come out. Madilyn gave a quick smile, then went to meet her. She was surprised at how quickly they had become comfortable with each other.

"I still can't believe how many trees they crammed onto three acres," Dylan said. "Eighty trees per acre is about standard, unless you're planting dwarf species. There were over four hundred trees total. Of that, I marked twenty-five to save."

"That's a lot of trees to take down."

"Yeah, but this is all that's left." She pointed to where she'd been walking. "They'll get these knocked down by this afternoon. Gonna take a few more days to get all the stumps done, though."

"It looks different already."

"It's coming along. And I've ordered the new trees. They'll start delivering them next week. I staggered the deliveries." She broke off a dead limb from one of the live trees. "I didn't want to be overwhelmed with them all at once. It'll take a while to get everything planted as it is."

"What about the tractor?"

"Oh, Madilyn, that's going to be great," she said with a smile. "It's going to be like Christmas when I get that thing. I hope by Friday. He said he'll call me."

"And they'll deliver that too?"

"Yep." Dylan wiggled her eyebrows. "Why? You want to learn to drive it?"

Madilyn smiled too. "Can I?"

"You're the boss. You can even help me plant trees if you want." She paused. "I mean, unless you don't want to get that dirty. Because—"

"I'm looking forward to getting dirty. It'll certainly be something different." They walked back toward the vehicles. "Did you get your kitchen set up?"

Dylan shook her head. "Not really. Enough to cook dinner last night, that's about it. I'll need to go to a grocery store too. I didn't bring much with me."

"And how did it sleep?"

"Really good, thanks. Quiet. Extremely quiet."

"Compared to the farm?"

"Yeah. We were right off one of the main roads heading into Millersville and then Lancaster. Traffic noise is something you get used to. Until it's gone," she said with a laugh. "I was sitting out on the little back porch last night and I didn't hear a single vehicle, not even way off in the distance."

"The estate here is several hundred acres. Close to eight, I believe Randy said. We're in the middle of it so there are no nearby roads. Not public roads, anyway."

"This other area you were telling me about, Brandy-something or other?"

Madilyn smiled at her. "Brandywine Creek. Well, actually the West Fork of Brandywine."

"Yeah, that's it. How far is it from here?"

"Actually, I don't know. I've never been there," she confessed. "Why?"

Dylan pointed at the orchard. "Well, not much we can do until these crews are out of here. I thought maybe we could take a drive over there, look around, explore."

"I suppose we could, but you know I think we're going to wait before we attempt any improvements on the orchard there."

"I know. I just thought..." She shrugged, not finishing her sentence.

Madilyn stared at her. Drive to the creek? Explore? That would definitely be something different for her. So, she nodded. "Yes. Let's go. We'll get directions from Randy. I don't believe it's far. Down on the other side of the valley, I think."

That warranted a smile. "Great. We can take my truck. I'll meet you at the shed."

Madilyn nodded again, watching as Dylan hopped into the Gator and sped away. She was heading into the woods, and she assumed Dylan had found a shortcut to her house instead of taking the road around. She stared after her for a while, aware that she was still sporting a smile. She took a deep, pleasing breath, then got into the golf cart, going back toward the shed.

CHAPTER TWENTY-SEVEN

"Is your truck new?"

"About a year." She glanced over at her passenger. Madilyn was wearing shorts today with a navy cotton shirt. As usual, both looked brand-new. And as usual, she tried not to stare at her legs.

"Did you recently get a new wardrobe?"

Madilyn seemed surprised by her question. "Is it obvious?"

"Well, I didn't know if it was new or if you don't keep things long enough to look old." She plucked at her own shirt—a faded green T-shirt advertising the Millersville Farm and Ranch store. "I think Tanner gave me this shirt six years ago when I first moved here."

Madilyn seemed to relax then. "No, it's all new. Nothing in my wardrobe was suitable for life out here." She smiled at her. "And I mean nothing. So I ordered some things. I realize now that I'll need much more."

"Well, if you want to actually shop in person, there's a great place over across the river, by Clarke Lake. They're like an outfitter. They rent kayaks and paddleboards. But they have a lot of outdoor clothing and pretty cool stuff." Then she laughed lightly. "Big name brand outdoor clothing is usually way out of my price range, but I've bought a few things there."

Madilyn frowned. "Truthfully, I'm not that familiar with things out here. Is this the Susquehanna River?"

"Yeah. It's where Clarke Lake is. It's like a mile wide there. Very pretty." She paused, wondering if she was out of line by offering. "If you want to go sometime, I wouldn't mind taking you. Like I said, we're kinda at a standstill for probably a week."

Dylan slowed when she came to a side road to the right. She'd noticed it before, but it was obviously not well used, and she assumed it went nowhere in particular. When giving her directions to Brandywine Creek, Randy had assured her this was the old road that skirted the valley. He said they would find numerous sideroads where old homesteads used to be, occupied by those who had leased land from the Maraks back in the day.

"Really? You would take me shopping? You don't seem the type."

Dylan laughed. "No, I hate shopping as a rule. But this place is really unique, right on the river. Kinda like you're shopping outdoors."

Madilyn studied her for a long moment, then nodded. "Okay. I accept."

"Great. We can go tomorrow if you like."

"Thank you. Yes, tomorrow is good."

The little-used road was bumpy, and Dylan slowed her pace. "Is there any public access to Brandywine?"

"No. From what my grandfather told me, when they harvested the fruit, this was the road they used. We own the land on both sides of the creek, but I have no idea how to access the other side. The old orchard is on this side."

The valley was to their right, and it was vast. As Randy had said, there were crude roads here and there, some leading to long-ago farmland and others to old homesteads. She slowed when she saw what appeared to be a stone fireplace still standing.

"Want to explore?"

Madilyn raised her eyebrows. "What do you mean?"

She pointed out the passenger's window. "There. Looks like the remnants of an old house or something."

Madilyn nodded almost eagerly. "Yes. Please."

She could make out a road, but the grass and weeds had nearly reclaimed it. A few trees grew behind the fireplace, but that was all. Their front door must have opened out right onto the valley. She could imagine the crops growing right up to the house itself.

She stopped and got out, walking over to where she assumed the house had been. Madilyn came up beside her, and Dylan glanced at her.

"There's nothing left."

"When my grandfather stopped leasing the land here by the estate, I think they had some of the older houses torn down. Not all, obviously, as you're in one of them. The others, well, I have Randy on that project. Get them removed and cleaned up."

She walked closer to the fireplace, seeing fallen stones around the ground. "This one must have been really old. Look at these stones. Like they were hauled up from the river or something."

"Maybe so." Madilyn reached out to touch the fireplace, running a hand over the smooth stone. "So much history here. I wish there was a better accounting of it all." She glanced over at her. "My grandfather...well, he changed directions on the family businesses. My great-grandfather had owned two companies, but when he died, my grandfather sold them and started the Marak Foundation. He also stopped leasing the land here around the valley for farming." She motioned to where the house used to stand. "The valley is back to its natural state now and the houses fell to ruins, much like the orchard did."

"To be honest, I love the valley like this. Natural. But I'm sure a lot of people would think it's just wasted land."

"I'm sure the wildlife loves it. Actually, that was the wish of my grandmother. They wanted to donate the land around the creek to the state, hoping to make it into a park."

"What happened?"

Madilyn smiled. "My grandmother didn't want a big campground here with 'people running amok' as my grandfather told me."

"Well, let's go take a look then." As she walked back to the truck, she looked again at the old fireplace. "You think your grandfather would mind if I confiscated some of these stones?"

"Of course not. He probably doesn't even know this is here anymore."

"These would make a nice base for a firepit." She drove back to the main road and continued on. "And I could put a spit or something on it too."

"For cooking?"

"Yeah. Well, mostly just to have a campfire and sit around. But yeah, cooking too. Nothing better than a steak cooked over a wood fire."

"I'll have to take your word for it."

"At my uncle's place, he had this old smoker that was about to fall apart. His grandfather built it way back when. They had a firepit next to it. They would keep a fire going, then take the coals out to feed the smoker. Back then, they used it for smoking sausage and other meats that they were curing. When I was a kid, my uncle didn't use the smoker much, if at all, but he would often cook steaks over the firepit."

"I envy you that. And I don't just mean the steaks but having those kinds of memories. My family is very small, and when I came around, there was no one left but my grandparents. We lived here at the estate until I was ten, but there are no memories like you have. Loretta tended to the meals then like she does now. Everything was always proper and formal and,"—she paused—"with little levity." Madilyn gave an embarrassed smile. "That just now occurred to me, I think."

"The lack of levity?"

"Yes."

"Are you an only child?"

"I have an older brother. We're not close. We have different fathers." A quick laugh. "That's not the reason we're not close. Evan models his behavior after our mother."

"So you're not close to your mother then?"

"No. I was raised by nannies, went to boarding school, then college. She didn't have much of a presence in my life."

"No joyous childhood memories?"

"None whatsoever. My early years living here at the estate were a little more normal because I was always very close to my grandparents. Even then, everything was regimented. Still is. My grandfather hasn't deviated from that either." Madilyn held her hand up before she could ask any more questions. "What about your family?"

Dylan shrugged. "Got none. Uncle Frank was the last."

"What happened? Your parents?"

She glanced at her quickly, then back to the old road she was following. "There was a bad car accident. I was nineteen. My mom and dad, my grandmother, and my Aunt Linda—Uncle Frank's wife—were all killed. That was a tough time, but we carried on. I stayed in Philly but came out to the farm most weekends to see him. Then when he got diagnosed—and we knew that his time was short—I moved out here with him. Six years ago."

"So you really have no one?"

"Just me." She swallowed down the lump in her throat. Even though she knew it to be true, of course, saying it out loud made it hit home a little harder.

"Why don't you date?"

Dylan glanced at her, surprised at the question. "I never said I didn't date."

"You said you didn't have a boyfriend."

"Right. I don't date guys. You never asked if I had a girlfriend, though."

"Oh." Madilyn's eyes widened. "*Oh*," she said more slowly.

Dylan laughed. "Now don't tell me I've shocked you. I haven't been mistaken for a straight woman since, well, since I was probably a teenager."

"I see." A pause. "And do you?"

"Do I what?"

"Have a girlfriend."

Dylan shook her head. "No. Crystal was the last one I dated and she…well, there wasn't any kind of a spark there for me. I knew it wasn't going to go anywhere so I'm kinda avoiding her."

"Oh. I guess there was a spark for her then?" She held her hand up. "I'm sorry. I'm being nosy."

"Don't have any gay friends?"

"No."

"I hope it's not a problem. I promise I'll try really hard not to flirt with you." Yeah, flirting with her boss was probably not a good idea. It would help if she wasn't so cute.

"So Crystal? A spark?"

Dylan shook her head. "I don't know. I think maybe she just *wanted* there to be one. She still calls, wants to go out." She shrugged. "Wants me to give it another try."

"I'm familiar with people not taking a hint," Madilyn said with a smile. "Palmer doesn't call that often, thankfully. I only answer every third one or so."

Dylan slowed when she saw the telltale sign of a creek—trees lining the shore. But where was the orchard?

"Did they have the old fruit trees removed?"

"I'm not sure. I wouldn't think so."

She stopped. "Don't see any skeletal trees. Or live ones."

"Did we miss a turn? Or take a wrong road?"

Dylan pointed up ahead. "That's the creek." She drove on a little closer. "Let's take a look."

The crude road was swallowed up by the valley before they got to the creek, so she made her own road, driving right up to the trees.

"Nice creek. Bigger than I expected."

"I'm not really sure what I expected," Madilyn admitted. "My grandfather said he used to ride his horse here and swim."

Dylan got out and Madilyn did the same. They walked through the tall valley grass to where the trees became thicker along the creek bank.

"This would be an awesome spot during the heat of summer," she said absently. "Perfect place for a picnic."

Madilyn stared at her, a smile forming. "I wouldn't picture you as the picnic type."

"No? I like being outside. Maybe it was those few years I was stuck in a cubicle in a high-rise office building, but I'd just as soon be outside as in."

She walked along the creek, heading upstream. She stopped suddenly, seeing motion on the other side. Without thinking, she wrapped her fingers around Madilyn's arm to stop her movement. "Deer," she whispered. "Three of them."

"Where?"

She moved ever so slowly behind Madilyn, then raised her arm into her line of sight. "They're behind that small bush. Looks like a mother and her two fawns." She felt Madilyn tense.

"I see them." Her voice was tinged with excitement. Then Madilyn turned to look at her. "Would you believe me if I said this was a first?"

"A deer? Or a fawn?"

"Both. They're beautiful."

She stood still as the doe's tail flickered, then she moved off, her two fawns hurrying after her. "I imagine since there's no farming out in this area and no people around, then the wildlife is plentiful. Who knows what we'll see?" She walked on. "It's kinda early, though. I didn't think they started giving birth until later in the month. Although those two were very young still."

"Did you have deer at your uncle's farm?"

"We'd see them around, but other than the orchard, there weren't any clumps of trees on the property. There are pockets of woods along the river—the Conestoga—which is pretty close, but all around our farm is just other farms."

"Will you be able to sell it?"

"Sure. The question is whether I'll get the price that I want. The house isn't in great shape to begin with, and, like I said, since the land hasn't been farmed for several years now, it's going to need some work. I may have to take less than I want." She shrugged. "I'll give it a couple of months. If no takers, then I'll drop the price." She smiled. "Why? Are the Maraks interested in adding to their farmland?"

Madilyn shook her head. "No. I think my grandfather is out of the farming business. He does still lease land, but he has someone who manages that for him. I believe most of the acreage is to the east of the estate."

Dylan stopped again. "Look way over there. I think there's our orchard." It was still some distance away, but she could make out the stick figures of long-dead trees. "Guess we missed the road."

"Wow. There's nothing left of it. It looks far worse than the other one."

"Come on. Let's see if we can find the right road."

CHAPTER TWENTY-EIGHT

"You were gone most of the day."

Madilyn nodded. "Yes. We went over to the creek. Took us a while to find the old orchard. The roads out there are almost completely grown over."

He handed her a glass of brandy, then sat down on the sofa. "What was it like?"

"The orchard? Nothing but dead trees. The valley grasses had grown over it too. As Dylan warned, it'll take a major undertaking to get it going again." She took a sip of the brandy. "I'm not sure that's something I'd want to do anyway. I think Grandma Belle's idea of leaving it for the wildlife was a good one." She smiled. "I saw deer. A mother and two babies. They were on the other side of the creek, but we were still pretty close."

"We used to hunt down there when I was a boy. It wasn't something I was ever fond of, though. Once Belle and I married, she wouldn't hear of it," he said with a chuckle. "That was my excuse then."

"Where did you used to swim? Was it near the orchard?"

He nodded. "There were a couple of spots I would go. The old road there forked into two and they each went around the orchard. I would take the upper road to the creek. There was a nice swimming hole there. Now that's not where my mother used to go. I think I told you, once a week she'd drive out there with a picnic lunch. All by herself, usually, but she did take me a time or two. Showed me where she would picnic. Lovely spot across the bridge. I took Belle there too, but I don't recall that we ever had a picnic. When I was a boy, though, I would swim near the bridge too."

She thought back to Isabel's diary. Wasn't there an entry where she said Lorah had driven them across a bridge?

"That was a nice spot," he continued. "I put a rope swing up in one of those big hemlocks one year."

She frowned. "What bridge, Pops? I don't remember you ever mentioning that before."

"Oh, I'm sure that old thing is long gone. My grandfather had it built well downstream of the orchard. He used it to get to the other side instead of having to drive all the way around and come in from the north." He took a sip of his brandy. "I don't think he got to use it much. He died shortly after that. My father would use it some. There wasn't really anything for him to check on over there. He never leased any of that land out, but I do recall him venturing down there some. Maybe it was his escape."

"His escape? You mean from here? Or from you and Isabel?"

He smiled at her. "Probably, yes. As I told you, he and my mother didn't have an ideal marriage, although I don't recall there ever being any fighting between them. They simply didn't communicate with each other." He waved his hand. "He was gone a lot anyway. But yes, he did escape across the creek now and then. Not sure what he did there."

"Well, I'll have to explore that area and see if the old bridge is still there." She thought for sure that Dylan would be happy to explore with her.

"And how is this woman working out?"

"Dylan?" She smiled. "I like her. In fact, she's taking me shopping tomorrow."

"Shopping? Whatever for?"

"For some more suitable clothes for working an orchard." She held her hand up. "And yes, I do plan to work. Get my hands dirty. Plant some trees." She laughed at the look on his face. "What? Unheard of?"

"I'll say. What has gotten into you?"

She laughed again. "Maybe I was switched as a baby. I may not actually be a Marak."

He laughed too. "Except for the fact that you have an uncanny resemblance to my sweet mother."

"So you say." She got up and placed her empty glass on the bar. "I was thinking when Dylan comes around tomorrow for our shopping trip, you might want to meet her."

"Meet her? To get my approval?"

Madilyn smiled at him. "No. Just to meet her. Say hello."

"You've been spending a lot of time with her."

"Yes. Like I said, I like her. We're becoming friends. It's nice to have someone to talk to. Another woman my age," she explained.

He made a face. "She's a commoner."

She laughed loudly at that. "You mean as opposed to royalty like the Maraks?" She leaned against his desk, watching him. "She's had a bit of tragedy in her life. Her parents were killed in a car accident and now her uncle has just died. She has no remaining family. While I can't totally relate to having no family, besides you, there are only three others. My relationship with Mother and Evan is totally superficial and my father is but an occasional voice on the phone."

"I thought you got on well enough with him."

"I do. But it's different. He has a family, kids. We talk a couple of times a year, maybe, but we only scratch the surface of each other's lives." She pushed off the desk. "So? Do you want to meet her?"

"Well, if you think I should."

She went to him and bent down to kiss his cheek. "Actually, it's more that I want her to meet you. When I talk about you, I'd at least like for her to have some semblance of who you are."

"Do you talk about me?"

"Of course." She smiled at him. "Goodnight, Pops."

"Goodnight, sweet Maddie. See you at breakfast."

She closed the door to his study and made her way through the house and up the stairs. She was looking forward to the shopping excursion tomorrow. Looking forward to getting off the estate and seeing an area she'd not been to before. Other than the drive back and forth between here and Philly, she wasn't familiar in the least with the state that she called home. But really, the truth was, she was looking forward to spending time with Dylan—a gay woman who was going to try not to flirt with her. She smiled at that thought, then sobered. Did she mind that Dylan was gay? Would she mind if she flirted with her?

She went into her room and closed the door, moving across the floor to turn on the lamp. She opened the curtains on one of the windows, glancing out into the night sky. Had Isabel been curious about Lorah like that? She had called Lorah interesting and charming well before their relationship changed. Had Lorah flirted with her? She smiled. Yes, most likely so.

Unconsciously—or perhaps consciously—her gaze was drawn in the direction of the orchard. She was glad that Dylan hadn't wanted to remove all the trees. She couldn't help but wonder if those trees that were still alive were the ones that Isabel had wandered between, reliving precious moments with Lorah, perhaps even talking to her as if their affair hadn't ended.

That thought made her feel sad and she stared out into the darkness for a few seconds longer, picturing the lonely young woman walking through her beloved orchard all alone, trying to nurse her broken heart.

With a sigh, she pulled the curtains closed, chasing Isabel from her mind. She turned her thoughts again to Dylan, the woman she'd hired to tend to Isabel's orchard. What a joy she was to be around. There was no underlying agenda, no pretense. No fawning over her because of her last name. Dylan treated her like…well, like an ordinary person. How often had that happened in her lifetime?

They had walked along the bank of the creek for a bit, but she never got a sense that that was where Isabel and Lorah had walked. Based on what her grandfather had said, they weren't far enough upstream to his swimming hole by the orchard nor far enough downstream where the old bridge would have been. She would get Dylan to take her there again. She wanted to explore both there at the orchard and also to see if she could find the bridge. If it was even still standing.

She paused as she pulled the covers back on the bed, wondering at this new, budding friendship she and Dylan had started. It was a little strange, she knew. For one thing, she didn't make new friends. She was too guarded. And of the handful she would call friends, they were ones who traveled in her social circle, some she'd known since before college. They were ones she saw out at parties and functions or when one of them threw an elaborate dinner party.

Dylan was the complete opposite of those people. They all portrayed forced happiness. Dylan's was genuine, despite her circumstances. Dylan was also gay.

Madilyn stared across the room for a moment, then got into bed. Had she been surprised by Dylan's declaration? Even though it wasn't something she had considered—or concerned herself with—she wouldn't say she was surprised.

What surprised her more was the fact that she could talk freely to her and that they had become friends so quickly.

"I like her," she murmured in the darkness.

Yes. She liked being around her. Near her. Dylan made her smile, made her laugh. The smile on her face faltered a bit as she thought back to Isabel's diary. Isn't that how she described things with Lorah? That Lorah made her happy. Lorah made her laugh.

She shook her head quickly and closed her eyes. No. That wasn't what was happening to her. She barely had any attraction to men. Why on earth would she have any for a woman?

CHAPTER TWENTY-NINE

Dylan had gotten a text from Madilyn, instructing her to go up to the house. The big house. She also said that they would take her car.

"Wonder what she drives."

Hopefully it was something fancy and fast. But no. She didn't picture Madilyn in a sports car. In fact, she thought she'd drive something a little more conservative than flashy. She also didn't think Madilyn was one to flaunt her wealth. She didn't anticipate there being a Ferrari or a Bentley. Maybe a Mercedes.

She drove around the shed, seeing Randy's Gator already parked out front. She went past, following the small lane that she knew would take her to the house. She felt a bit nervous, wondering if Madilyn would take her inside to meet her grandfather. She glanced down at her bare legs. Maybe she should have worn something other than shorts. But she shook her head. No. She was what she was. No sense trying to put on airs.

She slowed as the mammoth house—mansion—came into view. Good lord, but it was huge. Painted a pristine white, it was quite formidable. Colorful flowers were painstakingly planted along the edges and among the shrubs. The lawn was cut to perfection. A neat, white picket fence surrounded the lawn and she pulled to a stop next to a gray SUV. She smiled with a bit of relief at seeing the vehicle. Not a Ferrari or Bentley, no. Not even a Mercedes. A nice, smart BMW. She glanced at the back, seeing it was an X5. She had no idea what that was, but, yes, it fit Madilyn.

She went through the gate, watching it swing shut behind her. She hesitated only a moment before going up the wide stairway to the front porch. Before she could knock—for she saw no doorbell—the door opened. An older woman stood there, her hair more gray than brown and cut in a short, no-nonsense style. She had a friendly smile on her face.

"You must be Ms. Hayes. Come in, please. Miss Maddie ran upstairs to her room. She'll be right down."

"Good morning. Please, call me Dylan."

The woman nodded. "I'm Loretta. I tend to Mr. Albert's needs. And now Maddie's too while she's here."

Dylan nodded and moved past her into an enormous room. A large, curving staircase wound against the far-left wall, and she followed its length, her gaze landing on Madilyn as she stood at the top. *God, she's cute.* Their eyes held for a second, and she smiled, matching Madilyn's.

"Good morning."

Dylan nodded. "Morning."

Madilyn came down the stairs, gliding almost gracefully along the steps. "Good. You wore shorts too." Then she winked. "Nice legs. Nice tan."

Dylan felt a blush light her face. Was she flirting with her? "I…I usually work in shorts."

"Really?"

"Well, out at the farm I did."

Madilyn nodded. "You met Loretta, I see. Come meet my grandfather." She looked at Loretta. "Is he in his study?"

"Yes. Shall I bring coffee?"

Madilyn looked at her with raised eyebrows. Dylan shook her head. "No, thanks. I've got a mug outside for the drive."

"None for me either. Thanks, Loretta." Madilyn motioned with her head. "This way."

Dylan again had a case of nerves. She looked around them. "Big-ass house," she murmured.

Madilyn laughed lightly beside her. "Yes. And most of it does not get used at all. I was known to get lost in it when I was a kid."

They went into another large room. It looked much like the other with fancy couches and antique furniture. Several large paintings adorned the walls in this one. Madilyn went to the far end where a set of double doors were. She knocked once, then opened one.

"Grandpops?"

"Yes, come in, Maddie."

Dylan pushed her nervousness down and followed Madilyn inside. Her grandfather was sitting behind a massive desk. He had a head full of thick, bushy gray hair with equally bushy eyebrows that were revealed when he removed black-framed glasses. She was surprised to find a laptop opened in front of him. Instead of allowing Madilyn to introduce her, she stepped forward and held her hand out.

"I'm Dylan Hayes, Mr. Marak. Pleased to meet you finally."

His eyes were dark and alert, and he stared her down for a second before taking her hand in a firm shake. "Albert Marak, Ms. Hayes. Nice to meet you."

She gave him a smile. "Please call me Dylan."

"Dylan is taking me shopping today," Madilyn supplied. She turned to her. "I forgot the name of the place."

"It's over near Clarke Lake. It's like a giant L.L.Bean store. It's called Old River Outfitters."

"On the Susquehanna River?" he asked.

"Yes, sir."

He nodded. "The Maraks used to own a lot of that land along the river south of there. Peach Bottom it was called. Owned the land all the way to the Maryland border." He waved his hand. "That was sold when I was a boy." He pushed his chair back and got to his feet, then reached for a cane that was leaning against the desk. "Maddie tells me you're all moved into the house she had fixed up. Does it suit you?"

"Oh, yes, sir. And you can't beat the view I've got of the valley."

"Perhaps Maddie will give me a tour soon. I haven't been out to the old orchard in years."

"Not much to it now. Hopefully in a week or two, I'll start getting the new trees in."

"Maddie tells me she plans to assist."

Dylan laughed. "Yes, she tells me the same thing."

Madilyn smiled too. "And I will." She motioned to the door. "Ready?"

"Sure." She nodded at Mr. Marak. "I hope to see you again."

He gave a brisk nod. "You be careful driving. Take care of my granddaughter."

"Yes, sir. Of course."

Madilyn closed the door behind them, and Dylan let out a relieved breath. "So that went okay, right?"

Madilyn laughed quietly. "Yes. Were you afraid he would throw you out or something?"

"He wasn't really intimidating until he stood up. He's eighty-nine. Does he know how to use the laptop?"

"Oh, yes. He gets a daily report from Mr. Reeves. He's the manager of the Marak Foundation. And he also gets a report detailing all the land that is still leased out. Someone else manages that for him, but he likes to be involved. That's one aspect of the family business that I'm not familiar with."

"What? The leases?"

"Yes. I have no idea how much land or where it all is. I've been involved with the Foundation since college so that's more my niche." Madilyn opened the front door. "I'm actually looking forward to shopping, something I normally hate to do."

"Your shopping is done in fancy boutiques?"

"If I need a fancy, elegant dress for something—usually a function for the Foundation—I have it made and designed for me. Of which I now have a closet full. Other clothes, yes, one of the boutiques in Center City or more often, I order online."

They paused beside Madilyn's car. "You want me to drive?"

Madilyn nodded. "If you don't mind."

"Sure." She hurried around to the passenger's side and opened the door for her. "Hop in."

She grabbed her coffee from her Gator, then went around to the driver's side and slid onto the cool, black leather seats. "Sweet," she murmured as her gaze traveled the length of the dash. "New?"

"Yes."

Dylan pushed the start button which was down on the console by the gear shift. The car purred to life, and she smiled. "You may have to show me how everything works. There's a lot more stuff in here than my truck."

"I don't know what even half of it does."

Dylan backed up, then pulled away from the house. "It looks like an SUV, but it kinda drives like a sports car." Then she laughed. "Well, like I imagine a sports car would drive." She turned to Madilyn. "After you texted me, I was trying to guess what kind of car you drove."

"And this wasn't it?"

"I was hoping it was a bright red Ferrari or something."

Madilyn laughed. "That is so not me."

"I know. I settled on something a little more conservative. A sedan. Mercedes. Not an SUV."

"That would have been my previous car. I liked it. I'm not sure what prompted me to change and get this one."

"It's nice. Comfortable."

Madilyn leaned back against her seat. "You think I'm a snob, don't you?"

Dylan looked over at her. "No, not at all. Why? Is that the impression you have of yourself?"

"No, not really. I try hard to be…well, normal." Then she smiled. "Which I realize is impossible in my position. It took me a long time to come to terms with that."

"You can't help who your family is."

"No. Tell me about you. You said you had no one else after your uncle died. Only child?"

"Oh. Yeah. My mother had some complications when I was born. Nothing she liked to talk about, but they couldn't get the bleeding stopped. Did an emergency hysterectomy right then. So, one and done. They got me."

"And your name? You said it was a family thing."

"Yeah. It came from my grandmother—my mom's mother. She was the youngest of five sisters and the only one who got married. Anyway, their last name was Dylan. And their father—my great-grandfather— was an only child too, so the Dylan name died with him. I think my mother felt obligated to name me that, whether I was a boy or not."

"That's kinda sweet."

She laughed. "I'm just thankful the last name wasn't Googanhoff or something like that."

Madilyn laughed too. "Surely you would have been spared that. Were you close with them?"

"My parents? Yes. Very. I was born out here, in Lancaster, but they moved to Philly when I was young. Three. But they were real tight with Uncle Frank and Aunt Linda—Frank was my mother's brother. We came out to the farm at least once a month for a weekend stay. And I spent summers out here too. Until high school and other interests came along, that is. Uncle Frank and Aunt Linda didn't have any kids, so I was it. After the car accident, Uncle Frank and I got really close. I was out here on weekends a couple of times a month."

"And you've been living here six years, you said?"

"Yes. At first, it was more emotional support than anything. He could still get around fine and could still tend to the farm. It's really been the last two or three years that he had to give that up. The last year, well, it was bad. He had two stays in the hospital where we thought that was it, then he'd bounce back." She shrugged. "I had him around longer than we thought."

She stared ahead, surprised by the sudden sense of loss that hit her. She blinked back tears, stunned by them. She'd been doing so well. A soft hand on her arm nearly made her choke up.

"I'm sorry, Dylan."

She nodded but didn't look at her, embarrassed by her tears. "I did most of my grieving before he died. It sneaks up on me sometimes."

Their conversation shifted to less personal things and Madilyn seemed to enjoy the drive through the farmland. Instead of going north to hit the highway, she went west and meandered through the countryside as they made their way to the other side of Millersville and on up to the bridge outside of Columbia that would cross the river.

"If you're interested, we can have lunch here later," she offered, thinking of the old greasy spoon diner that Tanner had introduced her to. "There's a place on this side of the river with a nice view."

"Sure. Sounds good."

Dylan smiled at that, guessing that Madilyn had never set foot in a place like that before. She was quiet as they crossed the bridge, noting that Madilyn was staring out her window, apparently enjoying the scenery.

Before long they were following the river downstream and Madilyn turned, looking at it through Dylan's window now.

"The river is huge." She scooted closer. "There are islands. Are those houses on them?"

"I guess. I don't know if they're like weekend homes or summer homes, maybe."

"Not much privacy, though."

"No. I think during the heart of summer, this lake is full of boats. Not like having a big-ass house in the middle of a zillion acres," she teased.

"I know. It's always a little culture shock when I visit. Now that I'm living out there, it's culture shock to go back to Philly. My grandparents rarely left the estate."

"Where is your grandmother buried?"

"Oh, there's a family plot on the property. It goes back several generations. I think the first was my grandfather's great-great-grandfather. Like your family, ours is rather small too. My immediate family is all that is left—my mother, my brother and me. Well, besides my grandfather."

"No cousins? Aunts or uncles?" *Any of them named Isabel?* she thought to herself.

"No. My grandfather was the only child. My mother too. Evan is six years older than me, and I don't see him getting married, much less having children."

Dylan slowed as she came to the road that would take them to the river's edge and the shop she was looking for. "What about you? I know there's Palmer hanging in the wings, but what about children?"

Madilyn shook her head. "No. I've never wanted children." Then she smiled. "I've just not told my grandfather that."

"Why not? Children, I mean."

"This isn't an easy family to be born into. Not if you want to have a normal life. You never know what people's intentions are, what their motives are. You never know who you can trust."

Dylan turned into the parking lot of the Old River Outfitters. She found a space away from other cars and stopped. "So, the old saying is true? Money can't buy happiness, can't buy love?"

"Exactly. It's very true. For me, anyway. I would guess that my mother and Evan have no such feelings. But what about you? You ever want kids?"

"No. For one, I'm way too much of a tomboy to ever consider getting pregnant and actually giving birth." She shuddered. "Yikes. But really, I've never been around kids enough to actually want one."

"That's true for me too."

They got out and headed toward the entrance. "You're really not close to your mother and brother?"

"Not at all, no." Then Madilyn held up her hand. "Enough of that. Show me around. Let's buy some clothes."

CHAPTER THIRTY

Madilyn couldn't remember the last time she had so thoroughly enjoyed an outing. It was probably the first time in her life that she would have called a shopping trip fun. Dylan had made it so. She'd been so patient with her as she'd sorted through clothes, not knowing what to buy. Dylan had finally made suggestions and ended up picking out most of the things she'd bought. Mostly all casual summer clothes. At first, she'd refused to try on what looked like men's cargo shorts. Dylan had then pointed to the shorts she was wearing.

"Oh. Well, they look very nice on you. But—"

"They're comfortable. They're practical." Dylan had grinned at her. "And I don't have to carry a damn purse because everything I need fits in a pocket."

Madilyn had laughed. "Do you even own a purse?"

"No. Never."

So, she'd tried them on and yes, they were very comfortable. She bought three—two khaki and one denim. All told, she bought six pairs of shorts, two more pairs of jeans, numerous T-shirts and loose-fitting blouses, and two pairs of shoes. Oh, and sports socks. They were both laden with bags when they left. But instead of heading back, after they'd stashed the bags in her car, Dylan had taken her down to the river where the kayak launch was. There was a trail going upstream and down, and they'd taken a leisurely walk in both directions, watching as kayakers paddled about.

Then they'd had lunch at what appeared—at least on the outside—to be a rather rundown establishment. Not a place she would have ever dreamed of stopping at herself. But an outdoor patio, right on the river, had been inviting. They sat out in the sunshine, now on the opposite side of the river from where they'd walked earlier. She'd taken Dylan's advice and ordered a burger and fries, and it was the *best* burger and fries she'd ever had.

She made her way down the stairs now, a smile still on her face. The best, yes, because she couldn't recall the last time—if ever—she'd eaten at such a casual, informal place as that. Their lunch had been served in plastic wicker baskets with paper napkins and plastic forks. Again, she'd followed Dylan's cue and ignored the fork, using her fingers to eat the fries. Now she was still pleasantly full and had already told Loretta not to fuss over dinner.

She knocked lightly on her grandfather's study, opening it when he beckoned. He was in his chair, but it was turned away from the desk, spun around so that he could see outside. The groundskeepers were mowing around the trees in the back.

"I asked them to plant some roses," he said as he turned around. "Belle loved roses. Bennie used to have a whole garden of them. Do you remember?"

"Yes. What happened to them?"

He sighed. "Like most things, they were neglected after Bennie left." He studied her. "You're looking relaxed. Did you enjoy your day?"

"Very much so. I had a great time. And Dylan got a call while we were out. The tractor is being delivered Friday morning." She laughed. "I've never seen a grown woman so excited before. Over a tractor."

He nodded. "You like this woman?"

"Oh, yes. And despite your declaration, we have become friends. She's so easy to talk to." She sat down opposite his desk. "She has no clue as to the Marak name and she doesn't care. It makes no difference to her. In fact, she bought my lunch today. Her treat, she said. I can't remember the last time someone bought me lunch, other than Palmer."

"I was wondering if you'd stopped somewhere to eat."

"It was a little dive of a place on the river. A nearly dilapidated building." She laughed. "You would have thought it scandalous."

His face showed as much. "She's a commoner. It stands to reason she would frequent places like that."

"I like her, Pops. And now that I've gotten to know her, I don't think she would be offended by you calling her a commoner." The smile left her face. "I am, however. So let's stop with that, okay?"

He waved her request away. "It is what it is, Maddie. You are a Marak, she is not."

She didn't bother arguing with him. His view of the Marak name was ingrained in him. Brought on by his father, though. Certainly not Isabel. Judging from the words in her diary, Isabel thought no such thing about the Marak name. She would like to think that she held the same views as her great-grandmother.

She stood. "I'm going to take a quick run out to the orchard. See the progress they made today. Would you like to come along?"

"I don't think so. I'll wait until the new trees are in, as your Dylan suggested."

"Very well. I'll see you at dinner."

CHAPTER THIRTY-ONE

Dylan scooted her chair away from the small table, enough to stretch her legs out. She'd added a splash of the Knob Creek whiskey to her glass, pausing to shake the ice cubes around before taking a sip. Clouds had rolled in earlier, obscuring the stars. With the clouds had come wind and she'd donned a sweatshirt before going outside. She still wasn't used to the quiet. At the farm, there were always trucks on the road, their hum fading to the background as she didn't even notice them anymore. Funny how the absence of sound seemed louder to her ears.

But there were other things too. An owl was calling from way down in the valley. Maybe as far as Brandywine, she thought. From her view here, the valley seemed to go on forever, yet she now knew that the line of trees just on the horizon was the edge of the creek. An answering call—whether from a mate or a rival—came from behind her. It was much louder, and she assumed the owl was in the pocket of trees not far from the house.

Yet, still, it was quiet. Lonesome. She took another sip, then leaned her head back, staring up into the dark, starless sky. Was she lonely? Yeah, a little. She was still adjusting to not being at the farm, not having her uncle around to talk to. The day had been fun, though. And when was the last time she called a shopping trip fun?

She smiled now, picturing the excitement on Madilyn's face as she tried on—and bought—new clothes. The smile turned into a laugh when she remembered the look on her face when their lunch was delivered to the table. But Madilyn had been a good sport and had practically devoured the burger.

No, she didn't guess she was really all that lonely. She and Madilyn had become friends, as strange as that seemed. They had been together for hours today and there'd not been any awkward silences or uncomfortable lulls in the conversation. They were just two people getting to know each other—new friends. It would help if she wasn't so damn cute. Because she really liked her. She was easy to talk to, easy to be with. And Madilyn had told her she had nice legs. She smiled but shook her head. No, no, no. Madilyn was straight. She was also her boss. She needed to stop flirting with her. She smiled again. But it *was* fun.

She took a deep breath and her sigh this time was content. Maybe she'd get Madilyn to help her haul some stone up from that old fireplace tomorrow. Tanner was coming on Saturday to help her build the fire ring or at least get started on it. She looked at a spot not far from the little sitting area. Yes. It would go good right there. Then maybe one night next week she would cook a couple of steaks over the fire. She wondered if Madilyn would like that.

CHAPTER THIRTY-TWO

"Good lord, these are heavier than they look."

Dylan nodded as Madilyn placed the stone she'd been carrying on the back of the truck. "Yeah. Maybe I should downsize it a bit." She wiped at the sweat that had beaded up on her forehead. "Or maybe I should ditch the idea altogether."

"Oh, no, you don't. I think you promised me a steak. I intend to hold you to it."

"Okay. Then we need about fifteen more of these. That'll get us started."

Madilyn groaned as she went back to the falling-down fireplace. Dylan watched her go, her eyes following the sway of hips covered by jeans today, not shorts. One of the new pairs, she guessed. They hugged in all the right places too.

"Are you coming or are you going to make me do all the work?"

Dylan looked up, nearly blushing to have been caught staring. Instead, she smiled and went over to her. "I thought I was supervising."

"Oh? Is that what you call it?" At that, Dylan did blush, and Madilyn laughed. "And she blushes. How cute."

Dylan gave an awkward smile. "I'm sorry. I was—"

"I know what you were doing." Madilyn gave her a rather flirty grin. "I'm flattered. Now come on. We've got stone to move."

She pushed away her embarrassment, mentally chastising herself as they carried stone from the fireplace to her truck. Madilyn seemed genuinely interested and asked tons of questions about how she planned to build the firepit. Dylan explained it the best she could, considering she'd never built one before.

"So mortar? Like what they use on a brick home, for instance."

Dylan nodded. "Kinda, yeah. I watched a couple of videos on it. It looked easy enough." She paused. "Why? You want to help?"

"Yes." Madilyn leaned against the truck to rest. "You have no idea how freeing the last three weeks have been. Definitely out of my comfort zone but in a good way. My life has always been so regimented and structured. Safe."

"Dull?" she guessed.

"Exactly."

"Well, this doesn't really rank very high on the entertainment scale. At least, probably not to most."

"It's something different. Especially for me. I've been a relatively indoor person for so long, I feel like I'm being transformed by being outside like this." Madilyn held her arms out. "Sun on my skin doing something other than lounging by the pool at the condo." She smiled at her. "Thank you for including me in your project."

"Sure. I enjoy your company. I'll probably start on it this weekend, but I doubt I'll get it finished. And next week, I'll be busy with the new trees. The first group gets delivered on Monday. Fifty trees."

"You're going to put in three hundred?"

"I think that's enough. They had way more than that crammed in there." She paused. "Unless you want me to do more. I mean, you are the boss."

Madilyn waved that away. "I have no clue. That's why I hired you."

They went back to get more stone. "Yeah. Me with no experience. What were you thinking?"

"I was thinking that I liked you."

Dylan met her gaze and nodded. "I'll try not to let you down."

Madilyn stared at her for a long moment before speaking. "You won't let me down. Now, what about the materials you need for the stones? When will you get that?"

"Oh, Tanner is going to bring it out tomorrow." She picked up a large one. "I hope that's okay. He wanted to see where I'm living, and I thought I'd get him to give me some pointers on building this thing. Tanner is one of those guys who knows a little bit about everything. Might even get him to help me get started."

"I see. Sure, that's fine."

Dylan was surprised at the disappointment she saw on Madilyn's face. "You'll love him. He's a nice guy."

Madilyn raised her eyebrows. "You want me to meet him?"

Dylan smiled. "Well, yeah. Unless you don't want to help build it. I thought—"

"Oh, yes, I do," Madilyn said quickly. "I didn't know if you wanted me…I mean, I thought maybe—"

"No, no. I want you to come. We're going to throw some chicken on the grill. Nothing fancy."

"That sounds like fun."

Dylan smiled at her. "Just taking a guess here, but you've never done a cookout before, have you?"

"I have not. And when did you get a grill, anyway?"

"I bought one in Lancaster and brought it out with me when I moved my things. I only put it together this week."

"And what have you cooked on it?"

"Pork chops."

Madilyn smiled. "Pork chops, huh."

Dylan nudged her arm. "You've never had pork chops before, have you?"

"Not that I recall. Loretta usually prepares lamb chops. I'll expect a dinner invite sometime so I can try them."

Dylan was smiling as they went back to her truck. Yeah, this was nice. She'd made a new friend and apparently someone to have dinner with. No. She wasn't lonely.

CHAPTER THIRTY-THREE

Madilyn was admittedly nervous. She maneuvered the golf cart along the trail that Dylan had made to her house, bypassing the old road from the other side of the orchard. Her grandfather had seemed quite surprised that not only had she been invited to join Dylan and her friends for a cookout, but that she was actually going.

"And who is this friend that is coming? Do we really want her inviting strangers out here to the estate?"

"Tanner is her best friend. He's the one we're buying the new trees from. And I believe his girlfriend is coming with him."

"Oh, Maddie. Really? You're going to be socializing with—"

"Don't say it," she had warned him.

And he hadn't. The disapproving look on his face said it for him, however. *Commoners*. She shook her head, wishing he didn't still view anyone other than a Marak as a commoner. But at eighty-nine, he was so set in his ways, she had no hope of changing him.

She stopped the golf cart when she came to Isabel's maple trees. It was late afternoon, and the sun was making its way over the valley, the green lushness of it tempered somewhat by the bright light. She turned to look back at the orchard. It had been completely transformed. All of the dead trees were removed and only a few clusters of the remaining live ones were scattered about.

Dylan's new yellow tractor—much smaller than what she had planned to buy, but Dylan had said she didn't need a massive one—was parked near the road on the far side. It had been delivered yesterday morning as scheduled and Dylan had been practically giddy with excitement. And now Madilyn knew what a backhoe looked like. Dylan had gotten a quick tutorial and had even dug two holes for the new trees. After watching that, she understood why Dylan had wanted the backhoe. It had only taken a couple of minutes for each hole.

She was actually pretty excited herself about the planting, which would start on Monday. Dylan had told her to wear old jeans—of which she had none—because she would get plenty dirty. She had then added, "Unless you don't want to help. I mean, I'm the one getting paid for this." She had assured Dylan that, yes, she did want to help. It was something that six weeks ago she would not even have fathomed doing.

Reading Isabel's diary had changed all that. It made her realize that being a Marak could have very different connotations than what she was used to. She had assumed that her great-grandmother would have been much like her own grandmother and probably the same as the other Marak women who came before her. But she'd gotten a sense that Isabel was nothing like that. Reading how she'd wanted to buy shoes for the George Class family told her that. Well, just the fact that she'd befriended Lorah in the first place—a commoner. She rolled her eyes at that thought and finally continued on to Dylan's house.

Reading the diary had changed her. Prior to coming here, she'd been simply going through the motions of living. She had a certain image to uphold—something that had been ingrained in her since birth—and there was no deviating from that, no matter how badly she wanted to. It was why she was still technically dating Palmer. Were they still dating? Her lone variance had been the monthly trips out here to visit her grandparents. Even then, it was still structured. Get up at a certain time to make sure you didn't miss breakfast. Lunch and dinner were always at the same time each day. Brandy in the study afterward. Even bedtimes were regimented.

She had a sense of freedom today, though, didn't she? She didn't have any rules to follow. She realized she was smiling as she made her way along the path, coming out of a cluster of trees to see Dylan's house up ahead. Her smile faltered though as she spotted the black truck parked next to Dylan's. The nervousness she'd started out with crept back and she had a near death grip on the steering wheel. What if Dylan's friends didn't like her? What if she didn't know how to socialize with them?

Just as quickly, that nervousness faded as she saw Dylan come from around the back of her house. She could see the smile on Dylan's face as she waved at her, causing one to form on hers as well. She stopped next to the trucks and Dylan came over to meet her.

"Hey, I was just about to call you. Thought maybe you'd decided not to come."

"No. I wasn't certain what time you wanted me over. I—"

"You could have come anytime." Dylan motioned her out. "Come on. Meet my friends. They're out back. Tanner is designing my firepit and trying to talk me into covering the little patio." She grinned at her. "I did remind him that I didn't actually *own* the house."

"If you want a cover, I can—"

"No, no. If I want a cover, I can pay for it myself."

"Dylan, I—"

"Nope. Come on."

She was whisked around the house, finding a man squatting on the ground, making marks in the dirt with a stick. A dark-haired woman was sitting in one of the chairs watching him.

"You guys, meet my boss. Madilyn Marak. Madilyn, this is Tanner and Jenna."

The man stood up and he gave her a friendly smile, the tops of his eyebrows brushing his reddish-blond hair. "Nice to meet you, Madilyn."

"Thanks. Pleasure to meet you as well." She turned to the woman. "And you, Jenna."

"Yes, thanks. Dylan has told us a lot about you."

Madilyn glanced over at Dylan who appeared to be trying to temper a blush. "Not, you know, a *lot*." Both Tanner and Jenna laughed.

"I think you impressed her by helping move all these stones," Tanner supplied. "Can I get you a beer?"

Again, she glanced at Dylan. A *beer*? She was certain she'd never had a beer before. Dylan answered for her, though.

"Yeah. Bring me one too, would you?"

Madilyn finally found her voice. "Yes, please."

Dylan came closer and nudged her arm playfully. "You've never drunk a beer before, have you?"

Madilyn matched Dylan's smile with one of her own. "I have not. I'm beginning to think I've been terribly sheltered."

Tanner came back with four bottles, handing one to each of them. Madilyn followed suit as they all clanked bottles together in what she assumed was a ritual. She took a small swallow of the beer, not sure what she was expecting. It had a bitter taste yet seemed light and crisp at the same time. Dylan gave her a wink and motioned her over.

"Let me show you what we're going to do here."

"Maybe you should let me tell her," Tanner suggested. "You're going to put three layers of these stones. And you don't have nearly enough. I think it should be this big." He pointed to the circle he'd made in the dirt, which seemed quite large to her.

"Yeah, so we're going to have to get some more stone," Dylan added.

"I won't mind," she said easily.

"Okay, then I was telling Dylan about this cooking spit that will fit across it. It has different attachments. You can even do a rotisserie. And it's got a rack for steaks." He walked around to the back side of the circle. "I suggested she put the spit toward the back here. That way you can regulate the temperature better." He tapped the toe of his boot against the line. "You can also have your campfire up front there and only move enough coals to the back to slow cook your meat, if you want. Or build the fire right under it for a sear."

"But the spit is not permanent, right?" Dylan asked.

"No. The ones I've seen get stabbed into the ground on both sides of the pit. You can move it around. Pain in the ass, though. They're anchored down about a good foot or more, I'd guess."

Before Madilyn knew what was happening, she was handed a pair of gloves—the same ones she'd used the other day—and she and Jenna were lugging the stones over to the pit from the back of Dylan's truck.

"How did we get this job?" Jenna asked after their third trip.

"I'm not sure. I don't think my arms have recovered from the first time." She leaned against the truck as they rested. "How long have you known Dylan?"

Jenna's smile was quick. "Since I met Tanner. A little over three years. At first, I was jealous of their relationship. I even thought that maybe they were dating."

Madilyn laughed but said nothing.

"Dylan is just the nicest, though. She and Tanner are very close, and I like to give them time together."

"Did you know her uncle?"

"Uncle Frank? Yes. Such tragedy that family has had. Poor Dylan is all alone now. Tanner was afraid she'd pack up and head back to Philly after Frank died. We were as excited as she was when she got this job."

"Was she excited?"

Jenna smiled. "Excited and shocked, to hear Tanner tell it. But you won't be sorry you hired her. She's very dependable. Trustworthy."

"Yes. I've found that out already."

"Yo, girls! We need some stone," Tanner called from around back.

Jenna looked at her and rolled her eyes. "Again, how did we get this job?"

They not only had to haul the stones, but they had to hold each one in place as Tanner and Dylan lathered mortar around them. By the time they'd finished, her hands were a mess and she sat down on the ground beside the half-finished firepit, peeling off the mortar that stuck to them. Dylan sat down beside her, then reached over and rubbed at a spot on her cheek.

"You've got it everywhere."

Madilyn sat still, barely breathing as Dylan gently wiped across her skin. Their eyes met and Dylan smiled. Madilyn matched it.

"I had fun," she said honestly.

Dylan nodded. "Good. I hoped you would."

Madilyn nodded too, then watched as Dylan's fingers moved to her hand, rubbing against the ring she wore.

"I like this. It's unusual."

She said nothing as she stared at Dylan's finger that was touching Isabel's ring. Or should she call it Lorah's ring? She felt a chill run across her body as Dylan's fingers touched her skin.

"I sometimes think I've met you before." Dylan's words were quiet, nearly whispered. "Isn't that strange?"

Madilyn shook her head. "Not strange. I've thought that too."

"Maybe that's why we became friends so easily."

"Maybe so."

Their eyes held for a long moment, then a slow smile formed on Dylan's face. "Do you want me to take your picture?"

Madilyn raised her eyebrows questioningly. "Why?"

"Because you have mortar spots on both cheeks, and you look absolutely adorable."

"Adorable, huh?"

Dylan was still smiling. "And I'm not flirting with you."

"No?"

"No. It can't be considered flirting if it's the truth. Right?"

She returned Dylan's smile. "Okay. I need proof that I worked today anyway." She pulled her phone out of her pocket, but it rang before she could hand it over to Dylan. She groaned, then showed Dylan the phone.

Dylan's smile disappeared. "Ah. Palmer. I forgot about him."

"I did too." Madilyn silenced the ringing, sending it to voicemail. "I didn't return his call from yesterday, so this is his follow-up."

"I bet he'd be shocked to see you out here."

"To say the least." She handed her phone to Dylan. "A picture. A reminder of what a fun day it was."

"Was it?"

"The best."

She sat still, not knowing whether she should smile or not. The grin on Dylan's face caused her to match it, however. It always did. A quick snap, then Dylan handed the phone back to her.

"Are you as dirty as I am?" Jenna asked as she scooted a chair closer.

"I am. In fact, Dylan was just documenting the occasion with a picture."

Tanner came over then, nudging Dylan's boot with his own. "You going to be able to finish this?"

"I think so. I'll get Maddie here to help me. I've promised her a steak as soon as it's built."

The shortening of her name wasn't lost on her. No one called her Maddie except her grandparents and therefore Loretta and Randy. To everyone else in her life, she was Madilyn. She decided she didn't mind in the least that Dylan had used her informal name. In fact, she loved it.

She accepted another beer and she and Jenna sat in the two outdoor chairs while Dylan and Tanner got the chicken on the grill. Chicken that had been marinating since last night, Dylan had informed them. She assumed that was a good thing.

Then Tanner—in the half-finished firepit—had started a fire. As the sun set over the valley, they sat out, watching it pass behind the trees. Dylan had brought two chairs out from the kitchen, and they'd all sat around the fire, watching as the sun disappeared beyond the valley. Disappeared down behind Brandywine Creek, she assumed. She made a mental note to ask Randy to pick up two more chairs to match Dylan's outdoor set.

She looked around then, seeing the others still staring out over the valley. Jenna and Tanner were sitting side by side, holding hands. Dylan sat across the fire from her, and she had such a contented look on her face, Madilyn wondered if her own mirrored that. As if sensing her watching, Dylan turned, and their gazes collided. Matching smiles formed and it wasn't lost on her how comfortable she felt around Dylan.

"I brought wine," Jenna said, interrupting the silence—and their stare.

"Great! Then let's eat."

Madilyn took one last look to the west, the sunset colors fading quickly. What an absolutely wonderful day it had been. She took a deep breath, smiling to herself as she joined the others inside.

CHAPTER THIRTY-FOUR

Dylan leaned back in the chair and rubbed her full belly. "That was so good."

Tanner nudged her legs out of the way as he scooted his chair next to hers. "That barbeque sauce must have been my recipe."

"Why do you think everything I make is yours?"

"Because it is."

She smiled at him. "Yeah, you're right."

He leaned closer. "What's going on with you and Maddie?"

"Absolutely nothing."

"Oh, come on. You're flirting with her. She's flirting with you. You're—"

"I am not flirting." Then she smiled. "Okay, well I maybe am. Because I'm kinda attracted to her."

"Marak and all, I would have guessed she was straight."

"Yeah, well, there's that to contend with," she said dryly. "And some guy named Palmer."

"Looks like you've got your work cut out for you."

"Oh, there's nothing to work on. We're friends. And like you said, she's straight."

Maddie and Jenna were inside doing the dishes. Maddie was the one who had volunteered for the job, not Jenna, and she had waved her and Tanner outside.

"But you like her?"

"I do. A lot. We just clicked. I like spending time with her. Why can't I find someone like her who is actually gay? I have the worst luck."

"Oh, well. There are worse things. She's really cute."

"Told you she was. Now what about you? Did you ask Jenna to marry you?"

He kicked her leg. "Not so loud. I haven't decided yet."

"You have decided. You're just too scared to pull the trigger."

"Okay, yeah. That's the truth. I am scared."

The back door opened, and Jenna was the first out. "What are you two whispering about?"

"Nothing," they said in unison.

Jenna bent down and kissed Tanner's cheek. "Gorgeous night, isn't it?"

"Sure is," Dylan agreed. She elbowed Tanner. "Why don't you get the fire going again?" She looked behind her, seeing Maddie joining them. She motioned to the chair beside her. "Come sit."

Maddie gave her a smile as she sat down. "I love it out here."

"Yeah. It's nice. I need a couple more chairs, I guess. The ones from the kitchen are brand new and shouldn't be out here."

"I'll have Randy get two for you. I don't know why I didn't ask him to get four to begin with."

"Because you thought it would just be me and you here," she teased.

Maddie leaned closer to her, her voice quiet. "I like your friends."

"Good. I'm glad."

Tanner got the fire going again and the four of them sat there quietly, watching the moon as it hovered low in the sky. She looked over at Tanner and Jenna who were sitting close, their hands clasped. She was surprised by the jealousy she felt. Well, jealousy was a bit strong. Envy, maybe. She turned her head, finding Maddie's gaze on her, not the fire.

The sweet, gentle look in Maddie's eyes made her heart skip in her chest.

CHAPTER THIRTY-FIVE

Madilyn stood on the porch, watching as Dylan drove away in the Gator. After Tanner and Jenna had left, Dylan insisted on driving her back. While she protested that she could make it perfectly fine in the golf cart—it did have lights, after all—she was still thankful that she didn't have to make the trek alone in the dark. Knowing her, she would have most likely gotten lost.

"I know you probably have better things to do on a Sunday, but if you want, I thought we could go back down to the valley and get some more stones. Then maybe go back to the creek and explore around there."

Madilyn had readily accepted the offer. For one, she would love to try to find the old bridge. Of course, it would also give her time with Dylan—time she suddenly seemed to crave. Even though the taillights of the Gator faded away, her smile did not. What a fabulous day—and evening—it had been and now she had something to look forward to tomorrow.

Before going inside, she pulled her phone out. The picture that Dylan had taken was absolutely ghastly. Her hair was disheveled and wind-blown, and her cheeks were smeared with gray mortar. It amazed her that Dylan had said she looked adorable. Despite that, though, the smile on her face and the brightness of her eyes were indicative of the fun she'd had. She smiled back at herself. She'd spent the afternoon and part of the evening with Dylan—a woman she'd known barely a month—and two complete strangers. Yet she'd had more fun than she could recall having in years.

Just as she clicked out of the photo, her phone rang, startling her. Palmer again. She had half a mind to ignore it but answered anyway.

"Hello, Palmer," she said rather curtly.

"Madilyn? I called you earlier. I called yesterday. I haven't heard back from you."

Was his tone accusing or was she imagining that? She leaned against one of the massive pillars, resisting the urge to sigh loudly. "I've been busy."

"That's it? You've been busy? Too busy to return my call?"

Should she lie? No. "Actually, I didn't want to return your call." There was a long pause before he replied.

"Whatever for?"

This time she did sigh. "I didn't want to talk to you." Another pause.

"So you're still mad at me?"

Mad? Was she mad? She thought back to their last conversation and nodded. Oh, yeah. She was the Ice Queen. She'd hung up on him. She'd actually forgotten. "Should I be?"

"What is wrong with you, Madilyn? Are you having some sort of a crisis?"

"A crisis?"

"Like a hormonal crisis."

"Hormonal?" She shook her head. "No, I'm not. I have other things on my mind, Palmer. That's all. I thought I'd already explained that to you."

The pause this time seemed to be exaggerated and she tilted her head, wondering if he expected her to elaborate. She didn't.

"Madilyn, you know I love you."

She closed her eyes for a moment. "You don't love me, Palmer," she said, her voice quiet. "Just like I don't love you."

"What are you saying?"

She blew out her breath. "I'm saying that we have no chemistry between us. We have no business dating. There's no possible future. That's what I'm saying."

"You can't mean that, Madilyn. The last two years, I thought we were heading toward marriage. We've talked about it. We—"

"*You've* talked about it," she corrected. "I have no intention of marrying you, Palmer. I won't be in a loveless marriage."

"Then maybe you should think of it as a business arrangement. It would benefit both of us, I think."

"I see you've been listening to your parents and my mother. I don't happen to hold their views on a merger. Besides, my mother is off to Europe soon, if she's not there already. She has apparently convinced some billionaire to marry her. I doubt she's given you and me much thought lately."

"You're kidding. Margaret had dinner with my parents just a few weeks ago. They've not mentioned that to me."

"Because it's none of your business," she said bluntly.

"My, but you've changed, Madilyn. It's like I don't even know you anymore."

She rolled her eyes. "Don't be so dramatic, Palmer. And don't act like this is a shock to you. The last time we had dinner, I thought we had—well, I thought you knew. At the very least, our last phone conversation should have given you a clue."

"So you're serious? You want to end things? Over the phone, you want to end things?"

"Yes, I do."

"Madilyn, let's meet somewhere. Let's discuss it. We can—"

"We've been discussing it, Palmer. I'm not attracted to you. I don't love you. I don't want to date you. That's not going to change so there's nothing further to discuss."

"Wow. Hit me where it hurts."

She laughed. "Good lord, Palmer. Don't act like you're emotionally invested. Let's stop pretending. We've just been going through the motions. Surely, you're as tired of it as I am."

"Okay, so what? Are you saying you need some space, some time?"

She glanced up into the dark sky with a shake of her head. God, how hard was it to break up with someone? "Okay, let's say that. Yes. Space and time. Indefinitely. That means don't call me anymore. Goodbye, Palmer."

"Wait! You can't—"

"Yes. I can."

She pocketed her phone, but instead of going inside, she took the porch around to the back. She found her grandfather's chair and sat down with a weary sigh. The soft glow of the garden lights illuminated the flowers, and she could see moths flying about. Was what he said true? Had she changed?

She didn't think so. Her feelings for Palmer—or lack of—were the same as before she'd left. What had changed was her assertion. She should have made it clear to him on their last dinner back in Philly. Or on their last phone call, which had also ended in anger. In her mind, she had made it clear, yet verbally, probably not. Because Palmer was safe and familiar, she reminded herself. Yet, after this phone call, surely, he knew they had no future. As she'd said, she was tired of pretending that they did.

It should have felt more freeing, though, shouldn't it? She wouldn't have to concern herself with Palmer any longer. She wouldn't feel obligated to make a trip to Philly to see him. She wouldn't have to dodge his phone calls. But at some point, she'd have to leave the estate and go back to Philly to resume her life. Then what? If there was no Palmer, then what? Would she try to meet someone else? Would she go to parties more frequently in the hopes of meeting someone? Or would she toil away at the Foundation on the pretense that it was urgent she be there? Because it would be a pretense. The Foundation ran like a well-oiled machine. Mr. Reeves and his team handled the contributions, and the investment firm handled the money. She would have little to do there other than shifting funds to smaller charities—like she'd been doing—or reviewing grant requests.

Her mother was off to Greece with some man none of them had met and Evan apparently was going to tag along. Her grandfather was eighty-nine years old and wouldn't be around forever. Now she'd ditched Palmer, the only other person in her life.

She leaned her head back, surprised by a feeling of lonesomeness. Is this how Dylan felt after her uncle had died? No. She had a best friend in Tanner. She knew people. She was normal. She didn't have to worry about whether someone liked her for *her* or for her name. But still, she must have felt this way at some point.

She got up suddenly and went to the railing. She pulled her phone out, calling before she could reconsider.

"Hey. What's up?"

Madilyn chewed her lower lip. "Are you lonely?" There was only a slight pause before she answered.

"Not right this moment, no." She could hear the smile in Dylan's voice. Then she asked, "Are you?"

Madilyn smiled at the question. "Not right this moment. No."

"But you are sometimes?" Dylan asked in a gentle tone.

Madilyn let out a breath. "My mother—who I don't really even have a relationship with—is moving to Greece. My brother is moving too." She paused. "And I just broke up with Palmer."

"You did? Good for you."

Madilyn laughed lightly. "Good for me?"

"Well, you didn't love the guy. Why waste your time going out with him?"

"You're right."

"So, all of that had you feeling lonely?"

"Yes." She moved along the porch slowly. "I don't have a lot of friends. Well, there are some." She shook her head. "No. I'm lying. There are…people I know. People I go out with sometimes—lunch, dinner. Acquaintances more than friends."

"You and I are friends. Aren't we?"

She gripped the phone tighter and nodded. "Yes. Yes, we are."

"Good."

"I'm sorry I called. I—"

"Don't be sorry. I don't mind."

"What were you doing, anyway?"

She heard Dylan yawn before she answered, "Getting ready for bed. I'm beat."

"Yes. Me too. It was such a fun day, Dylan. Thank you so much for including me."

"Yeah. Your first cookout. But you know, a real cookout means you eat outside too. Maybe when I cook you a steak over the firepit, we'll eat at the little table."

"I'd like that."

"Great. Okay. And we're still on for tomorrow, right?"

"Right. I'm looking forward to it."

"I'll pick you up in the morning. About ten?"

"I'll be ready."

"Okay. Goodnight, Maddie."

She smiled at Dylan's use of her nickname. "Goodnight, Dylan."

This time when she pocketed her phone, there was no sense of loneliness. Because she wasn't completely alone. Dylan was in her life. A woman who made her smile, made her feel good about herself. A friend. The smile was still on her face when she went inside. She headed up the stairs, then paused when she heard her grandfather's cane as he walked.

"Maddie? Is that you?"

"Yes. Are you heading to bed?" She peered over the railing, seeing him down below in the muted light.

"In a bit. Did you enjoy your outing?"

"I did. It was fun. Her friends were very nice. And I helped build a firepit."

"You did *what?*"

"I'll tell you about it over breakfast. Goodnight, Pops."

CHAPTER THIRTY-SIX

Dylan rushed over as Maddie struggled with the large stone. She put her hands under it just before it fell.

"Thanks. I think I overestimated my strength or else I'm still sore from yesterday."

Dylan walked backward to her truck as they carried it, laughing when Madilyn stepped on her foot, nearly causing her to stumble. They put the stone on the tailgate, both blowing out their breaths with relief.

"Oh, yeah. I forgot you and Jenna did most of the heavy lifting yesterday." She counted how many they had. "We need four more."

Madilyn patted her shoulder. "Great. I'll get one of them. You get the other three."

It was a warm, sunny day and they both wore shorts. Maddie was wearing a baggy T-shirt and looked about as comfortable as Dylan had ever seen her. When she'd picked her up that morning, they'd chatted on the drive over, but there was no mention of last night's phone call. Madilyn's eyes were bright and alive, much like they'd been yesterday.

"What do you normally do on Sundays?" she asked as they made their way back over to the old fireplace.

"Nothing, really. I have a little work I do for the Foundation. Busy work, nothing more."

"You keep mentioning the Foundation. What is that?"

"The Marak Foundation. My grandparents established it shortly after his father died. It's a charitable foundation. We offer grants, donations, things like that. I'm trying to establish a new program, offering grants for university research. That's mainly what I've been working on."

"That sounds like a worthwhile endeavor."

Madilyn smiled at her. "As opposed to?"

Dylan laughed. "Well, since I don't know anything about your family, I didn't know what the normal processes were."

This time Madilyn laughed. "Meaning do we just flit around and spend money like crazy?" Her smile faded a little. "My mother does, yes. And Evan too. They have no interest in the Foundation. Their income comes from trust funds. As does mine. They can't touch the Foundation's money, so they don't concern themselves with it."

"That's all so over my head."

"It's all I've ever known."

She stood beside the fireplace, eyeing which stone she was going to pick up. "Was dating easy or hard?"

"What do you mean?"

"Rich girl at school. You could have any guy you wanted, right? So? Easy or hard?"

"Very hard. You never knew who you could trust, who was being sincere. I never knew what their true intentions were. That applied to friends too. Thus, why there were so few of them."

Madilyn leaned against the portion of the fireplace that was still standing. "There was an incident in college once. I was considered aloof. Untouchable." She smiled. "The Ice Queen. There was this party. Everyone was drinking but me. Drinking a lot. After a few hours, I wanted to leave, but I'd ridden there with a couple of friends. To this day, I'm not really sure what happened. Two guys came on to me. They were totally drunk. They—" Madilyn swallowed. "They got me into a room."

"Oh my god."

"I was terrified. But they were drunk, and I wasn't. I hit one of them with a lamp and managed to call 911. Campus police got there within minutes. I was totally embarrassed."

"Why embarrassed? Christ, they were assaulting you."

"Yes. But everyone said I'd overreacted. I know I didn't, but that seed was planted. I didn't press charges. I didn't need to. My grandfather's money was enough to get them kicked out of school." A quick laugh. "I never had a single date after that."

Dylan knew Madilyn was trying to make light of it, but she could tell she was still affected by it. Instead of picking up the stone, she went to Madilyn and pulled her into an embrace. There was only a slight hesitation before Madilyn relaxed against her. She squeezed her tight, then released her quickly, hoping she hadn't encroached into her personal space too much. Madilyn had a slight blush on her face.

"What was that for?"

Dylan shrugged, trying not to feel embarrassed. "You looked like you could use a hug."

Madilyn met her gaze. "Yes. And it was a very good one." Then she smiled. "I don't ever get hugs."

"No? What about from Palmer?"

"Palmer is not a hugger. I don't suppose I am either. My family is not what you would call affectionate."

"That's too bad. My family were huggers. So much so that my mother often embarrassed me in public."

"You still miss them, I suppose."

"Yeah. It's been ten years, but I miss having them, yes."

"You were nineteen, you said? Practically still a kid."

She nodded. "Yeah, I guess I was. I became an adult real quick, that's for sure." She bent down and picked up a stone. "You haven't mentioned your father."

Madilyn picked up a stone too. "They divorced when I was young. We keep in touch some. We talk a few times a year." She walked beside her as they made their way back to the truck. "He's remarried and has a family now. He's in the Chicago area."

They put their stones on the truck with the others, then she jogged back to the pile, picking up another one. Madilyn had hopped up on the tailgate and was sitting, swinging her legs back and forth.

"One more," she teased, and Dylan nodded.

"Does this mean you're not going to help me unload them?"

"Oh, I'm sure I will. The sooner it's done, the sooner I'll get the promised steak."

A mere ten minutes later they were back in the truck, bouncing down the old road toward the creek. She took the same one as last time, but Madilyn motioned to their left and she slowed.

"There. That's the upper road. It circles around the orchard."

Dylan stopped the truck, eyeing the alleged road. "Are you sure? It looks less used than this one."

"My grandfather said the upper road goes above the old orchard and to the creek. That was the one he took when he rode his horse here."

Dylan nodded but looked at the road skeptically. The valley had all but reclaimed it. "You want to try it?"

"Actually, no. I'd rather try to find a road that goes downstream. My grandfather says there was an old bridge across the creek." She glanced at her, then smiled. "I also read about it in a diary I found. My great-grandmother's. It was from 1933."

"Really? That's kinda neat. You think the bridge is still there?"

"He doubted, but I'd still like to look. There may be something left of it."

Dylan continued down the same road they'd taken the last time. It was easy to follow as the grass was still smashed down. She kept an eye out, hoping to spot an old road, but there was none. She came to the place where they'd stopped the last time.

"What do you think? You want to just drive along the creek?"

"Do you think it's safe? I mean, all we can see is grass."

"I think it'll be okay. I'll go slow."

And she did, driving at a near crawl between the edge of the valley and the trees that lined the creek bank. Madilyn had her eyes fixed on the creek and there was a contented smile on her face. That, in turn, caused her own smile to form.

CHAPTER THIRTY-SEVEN

Madilyn found herself holding onto the grab handle above the door as Dylan drove them along the creek. She was looking for the ruins of a bridge, but she didn't really know *what* she was looking for. Some wooden beams that were still standing, perhaps? Or maybe even part of the flooring? Or maybe there was nothing at all. Maybe some long-ago flood had wiped it out and carried it downstream. There might be no evidence whatsoever that a bridge ever existed.

With those thoughts bouncing around in her mind, she was absolutely shocked to see…yes, a bridge! She reached out and grabbed Dylan's arm.

"There!"

Dylan stopped, her gaze following where she pointed. "I'll be damned. It's still standing."

Madilyn was already opening her door, but Dylan stopped her. "Let me take a look. Maybe we can drive down to it. I mean, obviously someone used to drive here."

Madilyn nodded and closed her door again. "Okay. Good." Then she grinned. "I'm so excited. I didn't think it would still be here."

She stayed in the truck but leaned forward to watch Dylan's progress. She has nice legs, she thought absently. And that wasn't the first time she'd thought that. Then she blinked several times, wondering why "nice legs" had popped into her mind. Dylan walked back and forth where she would presumably drive, then moved closer to the creek bank and the bridge.

Madilyn took the time to look around her. They seemed to be surrounded by green—not only the thick grass of the valley but the trees lining the creek were all leafed out in vibrant colors. She imagined in the fall this would be a pretty spot when the leaves changed.

She saw Dylan coming back and she had a smile on her face. She gave her a quick thumbs-up motion with her hand. Madilyn smiled too, taking that to mean they could drive right down to the creek and the bridge. She felt her anticipation grow. Is this where Lorah had taken Isabel for their picnic? She'd reread the diary entry just that morning.

We had the most wonderful day today. Lorah took us way down the valley past the peach and pear orchards and over to Brandywine Creek for our picnic. I showed her where the bridge was, and she drove us right across. Hattie put together such a wonderful basket for us and we laid the blanket under a big hemlock.

Yes, that was the entry where they'd walked along the creek and held hands.

We walked along the bank of the creek and, dare I say, we held hands as if it was the most natural thing to do. Oh, my heart simply sings when I'm around her.

Dylan got back in the truck, still smiling. "You can tell there used to be a road there. There's still a bunch of rocks and gravel. We can park right there by the bridge."

Even so, she found herself holding her breath as Dylan headed straight toward the creek and bridge. She stopped several feet from the water and Madilyn couldn't contain her excitement as she got out of the truck. She didn't know if she was more excited about the bridge or the prospect of finding their picnic spot under a hemlock.

"I can't believe the condition of this. It doesn't look rotted at all," Dylan said as she stood near the wooden planks that still stretched across the creek.

The bridge itself was nothing more than a flat surface to cross over the water. The sides were only about a foot tall with a large beam on each side. Dylan was touching one now, running her hand across the smooth surface.

Madilyn touched the opposite beam. "You think we can walk across it?"

"Yeah. Carefully." Dylan took a step onto the planks and stomped on it. "Damn. Seems solid still. When was this built?"

"Probably in the '20s, I guess."

"Wow. A hundred years old."

They walked across tentatively, both holding their arms out as if balancing on a cross beam. The middle section seemed a little wobblier than the end and she stopped, but Dylan kept going. She figured even if it broke and she fell into the creek, it wasn't really that deep. No worries, as it turned out. Dylan had a grin on her face when she reached the other side, and she quickly joined her.

She turned in a circle as she looked around. "Amazing. I can't believe we found it."

"So what's all on this side?"

"Nothing. Just land. Well, as far as I know." She looked up into the tall trees. "Show me a hemlock." Then she smiled. "A big one."

"A big one, huh?" She looked up too, her head moving from one side to the other. "There are a couple down there along the bank. Got a nice one there," Dylan said, pointing upstream.

Madilyn walked away from the bridge, trying to imagine where Lorah and Isabel had picnicked. The hemlock Dylan pointed out was indeed huge. The underbrush had grown up around the trunk of the giant tree. She walked around it, thinking she could almost feel Isabel's and Lorah's presence. Or perhaps that was just wishful thinking. She had romanticized the diary so much that she was probably only imagining things.

"Pick a spot for our picnic."

Madilyn turned to look at Dylan, that word causing her heart to beat just a little too fast. "Picnic?" she asked quietly.

"Yeah. Nothing fancy, but since you're helping me with the stone, I thought I should at least feed you lunch." Dylan winked at her. "Peasant fare. Plain old turkey sandwiches. With cheese."

Madilyn reached her hand out and squeezed Dylan's arm. "That was kind of you. Thanks."

Dylan nodded. "Nothing fancy, like I said."

"Do you think I need fancy?"

Dylan looked at her, her gaze thoughtful, then shook her head. "No. I don't think you do." She turned around. "We could eat on the bridge. Or we could mash down some of this grass along the bank."

She took a deep breath, savoring the freshness of the air as she listened to the gentle gurgling of the creek. "I think the bridge is a wonderful spot."

"Great. Let me go get the stuff."

She watched for a minute as Dylan hurried back across the bridge, then turned to look into the forest. Amazing how the valley just stopped at the creek. She supposed all of the valley had been farmed at one time or another. Over here? Apparently not. It looked undisturbed with towering trees and thick brush. She was so thankful that her grandparents hadn't given this land to the state. She imagined it wouldn't have remained wild like it was now.

Dylan came back carrying a blanket under one arm and holding a soft-sided cooler with the other. "Just to be safe, let's get closer to the edge than the middle."

She spread the blanket out over the planks, then bent down and untied her boots and kicked them off. Madilyn watched her, then quickly did the same.

"Now, it's not much," Dylan warned again as she opened the cooler. "Spur of the moment so I didn't have a lot of choices."

"It doesn't matter."

Dylan took out two sandwiches wrapped in a plastic wrap. "I didn't know if you liked mustard or not, so I just brought the bottle." She held it up. "But I put mayo on."

She took the offered sandwich and also took the mustard. "I like both."

"And I brought some pickles." Dylan placed the jar between them. "Oh. Wait. I forgot the chips."

She put her boots back on but didn't bother lacing them before hurrying to the truck. She came back with a canvas bag. From it she pulled out a wad of paper napkins and an already opened bag of Doritos.

"Sorry. It was all I had."

Madilyn laughed. "Will you stop! It's nice."

She took two water bottles from the cooler and handed her one. "Wine would have made it better." Dylan shrugged. "I like a cheap, sweet wine. Which I know is so wrong and a big faux pas. You probably know exactly what wines would go with what meals, right?"

"You would be wrong. I'm not much of a drinker. My grandfather has wine for lunch every day. And after dinner, we go into his study for brandy. He pours me not much more than a swallow, though I will admit, it has grown on me." She opened the sandwich and squirted on some mustard. "I liked what Jenna brought."

"Yeah. She knows what I like. And you know, I'm not talking about super syrupy sweet or anything like that. Just not so damn dry." She took a bite of her sandwich. "When I moved in with Uncle Frank, he had this bottle of whiskey. I had never had whiskey in anything other than a cocktail before. But he put a couple of ice cubes in a tumbler and splashed this whiskey in and we had a toast on my very first night there. I like to drink beer, especially when me and Tanner get together. And sometimes I'll have a glass of that sweet wine. But at night? I'll have that same whiskey nightcap. I guess it'll always make me think of Uncle Frank."

Madilyn bit into her own sandwich, nodding. "I envy you that. I never had that closeness with anyone. My grandparents were nurturing, but I was ten when my mother moved us away from here. I was raised by nannies, mostly." She waved her hand. "I told you that already. Boarding school, college. I don't recall ever really *living* with my mother. There was a household staff, and she had an apartment in Manhattan and rarely made an appearance at the house."

"That's sad."

Madilyn shrugged. "I didn't know any better, I guess. Once I could drive, I spent more time here with my grandparents. And the last few years, with my grandmother being sick, I tried to spend as much time as possible with them. Despite everything that goes along with the Marak name, things felt a little more normal here." Then she laughed. "That's relative, I suppose. I told you before, I try to be normal only I'm not sure what that means anymore."

"True. Normal means something different to everyone, I guess. I think instead of trying to be normal, you should just be yourself."

"That goes along with it too. I'm not sure who I am. What I am. I mean, I broke up with Palmer, the only man I've ever dated for any length of time. The person I was with him is who I thought I should be. Who I tried to be."

"Why?"

Madilyn met her gaze. "I don't know," she said honestly. "I want to say because that was what was expected of me. But I've never fit into the mold that my mother did. She assumed I would follow in her footsteps. On the occasions that she tried to shape me, I wasn't receptive to it."

"Maybe because you resented her."

"I...I disliked her. And I knew I didn't want to be like her. She's very flamboyant. She's not apologetic at all about her wealth. In fact, the opposite. So, I didn't want to be like her, I didn't want to dress like her, I didn't want the extravagance of it all."

"But?"

"But I found myself going to fancy dinners and parties and dressing the part. And I had functions to attend on behalf of the Foundation and of course, that meant being dressed to the nines."

"Thus, you needed a shopping trip for normal clothes?"

She laughed. "Yes." She plucked at the baggy T-shirt she wore. "I'd guess no one would recognize me in this. Maybe that's what I mean when I say I don't know who I am. I feel so comfortable and free out here with you. Like this huge weight has been lifted and I didn't even know it was there."

"Like you can let your hair down and be your true self?"

"I guess. Like I don't have to pretend." She met her gaze again. "With you, I don't have to pretend to be somebody—something— that I'm not. That is so refreshing, Dylan. You have no preconceived notions of who I am or what I am. I can just be *me*."

Dylan smiled sweetly at her. "Glad you hired me, huh?"

She smiled too. "Very glad I hired you." Without thinking, she touched Dylan's arm, giving it a gentle squeeze. "I didn't realize how badly I needed a friend."

Dylan nodded, then leaned back on her elbows. "Tell me about last night."

"What do you mean?"

"The phone call."

She swallowed. She'd been wondering if—when—Dylan would bring that up. "I was assessing my life, I guess, and I was feeling, well, lonely. I had just ended things with Palmer, and I had a bit of a panic. I thought maybe that might have been how you felt after your uncle died."

Dylan nodded. "If I dwell on the fact that I have no one, then yeah, it's a little scary. I left good friends behind when I moved out here. We kept in touch at first. I'd go back to Philly every weekend for the first couple months. Then every other weekend. That dwindled to every other month. I was still trying to hang on to that life, I think. I eventually realized that my life was out here now, not in Philly."

"Do you still talk to your friends?"

"Sure. A quick phone call here and there. But I've changed since living out here. Priorities are different. I'm older. Being a caretaker for someone makes you appreciate things more, I think. You certainly don't take anything for granted."

"So you've grown apart from your friends?"

"I guess that's a good way of putting it. Erica was my closest friend. We met as freshmen in college. She even came out here to the funeral when my parents died. I probably talk to her the most. She's married now and has a kid. But even then, I can tell that we've drifted. Her husband and kid are her main focus now and I sometimes feel like I'm intruding on that. What we had in common during college is long gone." Dylan reached over and took a couple of chips from the bag. "Life goes on, though, and you meet new people along the way." She smiled. "Like you."

Madilyn nodded. "Yes. I've never made friends easily, for obvious reasons, but I never once felt any awkwardness with you. I don't know if that has more to do with you or me."

"Maybe being away from your real life has left you more open."

"Perhaps."

Dylan lay back on the blanket and stretched out along the bridge, folding her arms behind her head. "So, Palmer is really out of the picture?"

"I would hope so. While he is a nice enough man, I don't think I was ever really attracted to him." She shook her head. "No. I don't *think* that. I *know* that. I wasn't attracted to him, yet I let it drag on for two years." She leaned back too. "What scares me is that had I not come out here, if I'd stayed in Philly and continued my life as it was, I might have ended up marrying him."

"I don't think so. Regardless of the circumstances, I think you, like everyone, wants to find that true love."

She thought of Isabel then. James obviously wasn't her true love, but she married him anyway. When her true love did come around— another woman—she didn't have the courage to leave James. Of course, it was 1933. No, she wouldn't have expected Isabel to leave. She rolled her head to the side, finding Dylan watching her. She let their eyes lock, hold, and she was struck by such a sense of wholeness— completeness—that her breath caught.

"What about you?" she asked quietly. "What about your true love?"

Dylan gave a quiet sigh and turned her gaze to the sky. "I don't know. When I was younger, I was never really looking for true love." She smiled. "Just dating and having fun. Nothing serious."

"But?"

"But I'll be thirty before the year is out and time kinda got away from me."

"Meaning maybe you *should* have been looking?"

"Is true love something you search for, or does it just happen?"

Madilyn leaned back fully, mimicking Dylan's position. Was that true? Did it just happen? Maybe in a romance novel, but was it true in real life? Well, it was certainly true enough for Isabel and Lorah. She turned her head, finding Dylan watching her expectantly.

"Yes. I think it just happens."

Dylan gave her a soft smile. "Yes. I think so too. Like one of those out-of-the-blue chance meetings with someone."

Madilyn nodded. "Yes."

They lay there on the bridge, saying no more. The contentment she felt then was almost foreign to her. She was completely relaxed and at ease. She turned to look at Dylan. The other woman had her eyes closed and there was a hint of a smile on her lips. She allowed her gaze to linger, noting the smooth skin, the strong jawline, the disheveled hair that rested on her forehead. She had to resist the urge to brush it away. That thought surprised her, but she kept her hands still while allowing her eyes to continue to stare.

"Are you ready to leave?"

Madilyn pulled her gaze away, looking into the trees along the creek. "It's nice here. Beautiful, in fact."

"Yes. Beautiful."

She turned her head again. Dylan's eyes were no longer closed. They were watching her. She had an odd sensation travel through her body, making her heart flutter. She wondered if this was what Isabel had felt when she had looked into Lorah's eyes. That thought made her sit up with a jolt.

What?

Dylan sat up too. "You okay?"

Good lord, where had that thought come from? She swallowed nervously, refusing to look at Dylan. No, she didn't look at her. She needed to put some space between them and *quit* looking at her.

"I think...yes, maybe we should go."

CHAPTER THIRTY-EIGHT

Dylan hopped off the tractor, pausing to watch Madilyn, on her knees, scooping mulch around the tree with her hands. Madilyn's face was relaxed, her lips formed in a smile, but Dylan could tell she was concentrating mightily on her task. As she stared, she was aware of the smile on her own face, aware of the contented feeling she had.

She admitted that she had more than a little crush on Madilyn Marak. She nearly groaned as that thought sunk in. She hadn't had a crush on a straight girl since high school, but man, did she have one now.

"Why am I doing all the work?"

She shook herself out of her stupor. "I was supervising."

"Uh-huh."

"I was." She grinned. "And you were doing everything exactly right."

Madilyn got to her feet, brushing off the knees of her jeans with her gloved hands. "This is harder than it looks."

"We've got four trees in the ground already."

Madilyn laughed. "And two hundred and ninety-six to go!"

"Yeah. Sounds daunting when you think of it that way." She went over to the new hole she'd dug. "Are you changing your mind about helping?"

"Of course not. I'm enjoying the heck out of it."

Anytime she had to replace trees at the farm, she bought bare-rooted trees that were usually two years old. This time, though, since money wasn't an issue, she'd opted for three-year-old trees that were in five-gallon planters. A little harder to maneuver and plant, but they would bear fruit sooner.

As before, Madilyn held the bottom of the planter while she carefully lifted the tree out. Bags of peatmoss and compost had been delivered with the trees and she had used the front-end loader of the tractor—the bucket—to bring the bags over. She backfilled the hole with the topsoil she'd dug out, then Madilyn started adding the peatmoss and then the compost.

"I'm going to dig three or four holes at once, so you don't have to do all of this by yourself."

Madilyn glanced at her. "I don't mind."

"You'll be exhausted by noon."

Madilyn laughed. "Try ten."

Four holes later, she shut the tractor down and climbed off, pausing to stretch out her back. The day had started out sunny, but clouds were building now. Before joining Madilyn, she pulled her phone out, checking the weather forecast. Only a slight chance of showers in the afternoon but tomorrow looked to be a rainy day. She glanced over to where they'd unloaded the new trees. Fifty of them. If they got twenty-five or thirty in the ground today, it would be good progress. She supposed if thunderstorms were expected, she could simply tie the new trees together so they didn't get toppled.

"What's wrong? You're frowning."

She pointed to the clouds in the west. "I was checking the forecast, in case there was rain coming."

"And is there?"

"Tomorrow."

"Will the trees be okay?"

Dylan nodded. "Yeah. I'll keep an eye on things. These in the ground should be fine. In fact, they're all nice and straight. I don't believe we'll even need to stake them."

They worked diligently, getting a good routine down. By the time they'd had ten more planted, they were working seamlessly together. However, at eleven thirty, Madilyn plopped down on the ground and pulled her gloves off.

"I need a break."

"A break? Reached your limit?"

"I have. Between stone hauling and this, my arms feel like overcooked spaghetti."

Dylan sat down beside her. "I guess we could break for lunch now."

"Right. What are you going to feed me?"

She did a quick mental inventory of her fridge. "Well, Tanner brought me some sausage links that he'd picked up in Lancaster. I could grill some of that and we could make sandwiches."

Madilyn tilted her head, one eyebrow arched.

"Pickles, onions. Lots of mustard," she continued.

Madilyn smiled at her and nodded. "I accept."

Driving the Gator on the trail she'd made took only a few minutes to reach her house. Once inside, she motioned to the bathroom.

"Go clean up. I'll get started."

She used the sink in the kitchen to wash her hands, then pulled the sausage from the fridge. He had brought three links for her. She took one out and put it on a plate. Then she took out the pickles and half an onion that was left from a previous meal.

"Need help?"

"Sure. You can slice the onion and a couple of pickles." She pointed to a drawer beside the stove. "Knives are in there. Cutting board is back there."

She went outside to start the grill, eyeing the little table. She supposed they could eat outside. The sun was drifting in and out behind clouds and it was still pleasant. When she went back inside, Madilyn was fishing a pickle from the jar. There was already a pile of onions on the cutting board. She was surprised that Madilyn was as proficient as she was.

"I don't suppose you have any chance to cook here with your grandfather."

"No. None. Actually, I would be hard-pressed to put a meal on the table. But I used to love to sit in the kitchen and watch them—the cooks."

"When you were young?"

"Yes. There were two ladies dedicated to preparing the meals. When I think about it now, they would prepare the meals for me, as if I was a princess for them to serve. Evan was away at boarding school and my mother rarely made an appearance." She put the knife down. "They would make some elaborate meal, but since my mother wasn't there, they'd serve me in the back kitchen, and I'd eat with them." A quick smile that didn't reach her eyes. "My mother would never have approved of that."

"What was the alternative? Have you eat alone in a big, fancy dining room?"

"Yes. With me properly dressed, of course."

She went closer to her. "You did a fine job with the onion."

A genuine smile this time. "I used to love to watch cooking shows too."

She reached around her to get down two plates from the cabinet. "You had a lonely childhood." It was a statement, not a question.

"Yes. Very."

"What about school?"

Madilyn shook her head. "I had a private educator until I went to boarding school."

"Like homeschooled?"

"Yes, I suppose like that."

"Wow. So, no interaction with kids your own age?"

"Rarely. Boarding school wasn't quite the shock I thought it would be, though. Many of those kids were coming from similar situations." She shrugged. "I didn't know any better. That was just the way my life was."

She motioned with her head. "Come on out. I'll put the sausage on."

Madilyn sat in one of the chairs and brushed the hair away from her face as a gust of wind blew it. The knees of her jeans were dirt-stained as was her T-shirt. Dylan thought she looked absolutely beautiful. She shook that thought away. A crush on a straight woman. Her boss. Good lord, what was wrong with her? She put the sausage on the grill, then, because she couldn't help herself, her gaze slid back to Madilyn, whose own gaze was still fixed on the valley.

"This really is a nice view. It's so peaceful."

Dylan nodded. "It is. I feel comfortable here."

Madilyn turned her head slightly. "I think I'm jealous."

She pulled out the other chair. "Why is that?"

"Because I don't feel comfortable at the estate." Madilyn shook her head quickly. "That's not what I meant. I grew up there until I was ten. I've known Loretta my whole life. Randy has been there for years. It's not that I'm *uncomfortable*. It's just…it's my grandfather's house. I have a room. Loretta does the cooking. Julia the cleaning. The laundry. There's no…freedom. Maybe that's the word I'm looking for."

"Meaning you have no say in anything?"

Madilyn turned to look at her and she was surprised by the look of sadness in her blue eyes.

"Maybe that's why I've enjoyed my time with you so much. You don't tell me what we're going to do. You ask if I want to."

Dylan bumped Madilyn's foot with her own playfully. "I haven't forgotten you're the boss." She stood up to turn the sausage. "I take it you don't have a whole lot of control over your life."

"I guess some of that is self-inflicted. I feel boxed in—trapped—by the Marak name." Madilyn stood too, coming over to watch as she flipped the link over. "I don't mean to sound like I have no free will. I do."

"I think you feel pressure because your mother and your brother aren't concerned with the family business and you're all that's left so you have no choice."

"Yes! Exactly! When my grandfather is gone, the responsibility will fall to me whether I want it to or not. He didn't give me a choice."

"Okay, so say some dashing rich guy came in and swept you off your feet. He wants to move you to his private island in the Caribbean. You're madly in love with him and running the Foundation is not high on your list any longer. Then what? Do you go with him, or do you honor your family commitment?"

Madilyn laughed. "Can't I do both?"

"Can you?"

"Of course. At this point, the Foundation runs itself and my grandfather has hired good people. And he's a firm believer in very thorough audits so there's no worry that someone is making improper investments or anything. Our presence in it is more for show than functional at this point. I mean, there are decisions to be made, but that doesn't mean you have to physically be there."

"Maybe that's what your issue is. It's for show only. You know you're not *really* needed there."

Madilyn brushed the hair away from her face only to have it blow back. "You're very insightful, aren't you?"

Dylan reached out to tame the hair herself this time, unable to resist. It was an intimate gesture, one she had no business making. "Everyone needs to have a purpose in life. I was a caretaker. Now I'm not. Now I'm trying to get this once beautiful orchard going again. Because, right now, that's your purpose too."

Madilyn held her gaze, nodding slowly. "Yes, it is. I have this almost compelling need to get it looking like it used to. For sentimental reasons or nostalgia, as I told Randy, but yes, it's my *purpose*. You're right, I needed to do something and working at the Foundation was the logical choice. The only choice, really. Until I came out here and learned about Isabel's orchard, I was a little empty inside. Being able to work out here, to be a part of this, has changed my whole outlook, I think."

Dylan turned the fire down to low and moved the sausage away from the flame. *Isabel?* Finally, a mention of the mysterious Isabel Marak—Issy. Should she tell Madilyn about the letter? No. What would she say? *I think my great-aunt Lorah had a lesbian affair with your Isabel.* Of course, she couldn't blurt that out. "Who was Isabel?" she asked instead.

A slow smile formed on Madilyn's face. "She was my great-grandmother. She died young—at thirty-six—and my grandfather rarely spoke of her. But I found her diary, like I told you. It was hidden in an old desk up in the attic. She wrote it in 1933 and—" There was a pause. "Well, she mentioned the apple orchard frequently. And fondly. It was her place of solace, I think." Madilyn looked at her. "The diary wasn't lengthy, but there was enough there to know that she wasn't happily married."

No, she guessed not. Not if she had an affair with Lorah. Again, she pushed the thought of telling her to the back of her mind.

"Well, only a three-acre orchard, I don't guess it was that profitable."

"I don't know. Loretta said that Isabel wouldn't allow them to pick it commercially. Instead, she let those leasing Marak land come in and pick what they wanted. Loretta learned this from her aunt, although my grandfather was only a boy then and doesn't remember." Madilyn sighed. "I'm not sure what my grandfather *really* thinks of this endeavor of mine. Part of me thinks he's only humoring me, hoping to keep me around longer."

Dylan pulled the sausage off the grill and plated it, then motioned for Madilyn to follow her into the house.

"Have you thought about what you're going to do after the orchard is planted?" She pulled out a knife to slice the sausage. "Grab the bread, would you?"

Madilyn did and placed two slices on each plate. "How much mustard?"

"I like a lot."

Madilyn squirted all four slices with mustard, then leaned against the counter beside her, and Dylan heard her sigh. "I'm not sure what I'm going to do," she said, answering her earlier question. "The thought of going back to Philly and my condo is not very appealing. Depressing, in fact."

"You've lived there a while, though, right?"

"Yes. I bought the condo four years ago." Another sigh. "It's just a place to stay. It doesn't feel like home."

She scooted the plates closer and put sliced sausage on the bread. "So stay here."

"Here?" Madilyn topped each sandwich with pickles and onions. "Yes, my grandfather would love that. But will I turn into a lonely old woman like Isabel?"

Dylan looked at her. "Was she lonely?"

"Yes. Very. Especially after—" Madilyn stopped and shook her head.

"After what?"

"I don't know anything about Isabel, yet I feel so connected to her. In tune with her. Isn't that crazy?"

"Everything you know about her is from the diary?"

"Pretty much. My grandfather was only fourteen years old when she died. And like I said, he seldom spoke about her. Since I found the diary, I've asked him more questions about her and he's elaborated some, but I honestly don't think he remembers all that much about her."

She cut each sandwich in half, then slid a plate over to Madilyn. She should probably tell her about the box she'd found. And the letter. But would that tarnish Isabel's image in Maddie's mind? Would it spoil her impression of her?

"This is really good."

They were still standing at the counter, eating. She eyed the table and heard Maddie laugh quietly.

"You're trying so hard to be proper, aren't you?"

Dylan laughed too. "Well, yeah, sitting at the table would be the civilized thing to do." She motioned with her head. "Let's go back outside to eat."

The clouds were thicker now, but the sun still peeked out occasionally. She hoped they could get most of the trees in the ground this afternoon. "Tell me about the diary."

Madilyn nearly jerked her head up, her eyes a little wide. "It's… well, it's a recounting of that summer in 1933. Nothing too exciting."

Dylan was amazed by the slight blush on Maddie's face. That blush told her everything. Madilyn already knew about Isabel's affair with Lorah. What had the letter said? *I live through my memories of last summer* or something like that. The letter was written in 1934.

"So, it was just about the orchard and stuff?"

"Yes."

Dylan nodded. "Maybe I should read it then. I might learn something about apples."

Maddie had a slight look of panic on her face, then she smiled. "I thought you already knew a thing or two."

CHAPTER THIRTY-NINE

Madilyn stood at her window, looking out at the rain that had been falling all morning. Cursing it, really. The rain meant she wouldn't get to see Dylan today. She felt restless. Caged in. With a sigh, she pulled the blinds closed, blocking out the rain. She tried not to mind. As Dylan had said, a nice soaking rain would be great for the new trees, and it would save them having to water each one.

That had not been something she'd thought about, and she was thankful to learn that there were already water lines there. Dylan had pointed them out to her as they'd scrambled to get the last of the trees in before dark. She'd been exhausted and sore—pleasantly so. She'd missed dinner, but Loretta had saved a plate for her. She'd heated it in the microwave and ate at the small kitchen table instead of in either of the dining rooms.

Her grandfather had voiced his displeasure later when she'd ventured into his study.

"Marak women do not *work*, Maddie. For the life of me, I can't understand why you're putting yourself through all this."

Sad to say, but she thought that James Marak was probably the last one to actually work at anything. By the time her grandfather returned home and married Belle, the family fortune was already pouring in.

He'd done little more than manage his father's companies before selling them for quite the profit, to hear Grandma Belle tell it.

He had scoffed at her declaration that she enjoyed the physical work. It was true, though. It was nice to sit back and take a look at the trees they'd managed to get in the ground—thirty-two of them—and know that she'd had a part in it. A big part, really. She'd been thoroughly spent by the time they'd finished, but she would admit the day had been fun.

Dylan made it fun. They'd chatted like old friends, not new ones. And they'd teased and made the day playful. Teased and flirted, she had to admit. And what in the world was she doing flirting with a gay woman?

At four, while she rested against the trunk of one of the maples, Dylan dashed off to her house, coming back with two cold beers for them. They'd sat quietly, looking out over the valley as they enjoyed the break. Even to her untrained eye, she could sense the impending rain. And while Dylan said they needed the rain, she secretly hoped it would miss them.

Because of this. Because of being stuck inside. God, what did she do at her condo all the time? If she was at her condo, she was usually on her laptop. More often than not, she was at the Foundation, desperately looking for something to do, something to keep her busy, something to make her feel like she was needed. In reality, she knew she wasn't, but she continued to pretend that she was.

Here? The orchard? Yes, it was her project, her baby. She was in charge. In control. She smiled. Well, she was supervisor in name only. Dylan was in charge. And that was okay because Dylan never once made her feel like she wasn't needed. Quite the opposite.

She opened the blinds once more, then went to the plush chair and sat down, her gaze still drawn to the window. She liked Dylan. She liked her a lot. Dylan was good for her. She treated her like an equal. Not like her boss. Not like she was a Marak. She smiled at that thought. She didn't treat her like a Marak because Dylan had no clue as to who the Maraks were. No, Dylan treated her as a friend. And there weren't many of those, she knew. *Oh, let's don't pretend*, she told herself. There were none. People she knew in passing, people she went to dinner parties with. Not real friends.

Dylan was a friend. Yes. But sometimes, Dylan felt like more than a friend. It was that *more* that troubled her. More *what*? Sometimes the look in Dylan's eyes told her yes, there was more. Was Dylan attracted to her? For that matter, was *she* attracted to Dylan?

She thought back to their picnic the other day, the way she felt when she looked into her eyes. No, that wasn't a feeling she'd ever had with a friend. And this flirting they were doing. What did that mean?

Her phone rang and she got up, going over to the bedside table to get it. She smiled at the name displayed, as if thinking about her had conjured her up.

"Hey," she answered.

"Hey yourself." A slight pause, then, "I'm bored," Dylan said.

Madilyn smiled. "Me too."

"What are you doing?"

"Sitting in my room, watching it rain."

"I keep telling myself the rain is good. But I'm ready for it to stop."

She sat down again, aware of the smile still on her face. "When are they bringing more trees?"

"Tomorrow. Why? Are you anxious to get to planting again?"

"I was so sore this morning," she said with a laugh. She stretched her left arm out to the side. "Still am. I'm not sure how much help I would have been today anyway."

"Yeah, I guess we needed a break."

"I don't know about you, but I know I did." She had another call and she glanced at the screen. "Oh, crap. *Why?*"

"Huh?"

"I've got another call. Palmer."

"Oh. Okay. Well, I guess I'll see you tomorrow then."

"No! Wait. I sent it to voicemail. I don't want to talk to him." She leaned her head back with a sigh. "What do you say to someone who you've broken up with and they don't believe you?"

Dylan laughed. "I don't have a lot of experience in that. None with guys, as you know."

"And what about this woman? Crystal?"

"Yeah, well, she called maybe three or four times after I told her. I took the first two calls. After that, no."

"And she stopped?"

"So far. I mean, she's not like a stalker or anything. We got along fine. There just wasn't that, you know, that spark, and I didn't want her to think that there was."

"Yes. A spark. I wonder what that feels like," she said almost wistfully. Isabel and Lorah definitely had a spark. Was that the *more* she was afraid of with Dylan? She rolled her head toward the window, looking out at the rain. "I missed you today." The words were out before she could stop them, and she mentally shook her head.

"Oh, yeah?"

"Yes." Then she forced a laugh. "You're my only friend."

"Is that it? I thought maybe you missed my lunches."

She smiled. "I do."

There was just a slight pause before Dylan spoke. "I missed you too, Maddie."

"Did you?"

"Yes. If it's nice tomorrow, maybe we can have another picnic. At the overlook there. I love that spot."

She gripped the phone tighter. Isabel's and Lorah's spot. Dylan wanted to have a picnic. Should she panic? Should she decline? "That sounds nice. How about I ask Loretta to put something together for us?"

"So you really *didn't* miss my lunches then."

She laughed, letting go of the tension she felt. "Yes, I did. But you're busy with trees. And I know she wouldn't mind doing that for us."

"Okay. Because you know, I'm limited to sandwiches."

"When am I going to get a steak?"

"When you help me finish the firepit."

She sighed. "Damn this rain."

"How about we get started on the trees early in the morning? Early. Like at daybreak. Then we can knock off early and try to get another layer of stone up. We just need two more."

"Yes. I'm game," she said eagerly.

"Great. And I mean early, Maddie. Like beat the sun."

She nodded. "I'll be there." She made a mental note to set an alarm. "Don't you be late!"

"Okay. It's a plan. I guess I should let you go."

"Thanks for calling, Dylan. I…I missed talking to you today. I look forward to tomorrow."

"Yeah. Me too, Maddie."

She put the phone in her lap, ignoring the quiet ding she heard alerting her to Palmer's message. She was feeling a blissful peace right then and she didn't want to chase that away by listening to Palmer. Because yes, she was looking forward to tomorrow, and yes, she did miss Dylan today.

She closed her eyes, wondering at the changes she felt. Wondering at the contentment that Dylan brought to her. Wondering if she should be afraid of it.

Or simply embrace it.

CHAPTER FORTY

The smile came to her face automatically when she spotted Madilyn's golf cart parked at the edge of the orchard. She had indeed beat the sun there. She pulled to a stop beside her, seeing a matching smile on Maddie's face.

"You're late," Maddie chastised her.

"I can't believe you beat me." She tossed a banana over to her. "Breakfast."

"Thanks." Maddie pointed at the Gator. "How did you keep it dry yesterday?"

"Oh, I threw a tarp over it, but yeah, I was wishing I hadn't taken the doors off. It's cold this morning." She assumed Maddie was cold too as she had on a sweatshirt. They sat in their respective vehicles across from each other, peeling bananas.

"Loretta questioned my sanity at going out this early, but she did send me off with a picnic basket."

"Great. And if this is all we have for breakfast, I'm sure we'll want to eat early."

Before long, she had the tractor fired up and they began the chore of planting trees. Like yesterday, she dug four or five holes at once, then they both got the trees in the ground. While she dug the next set of holes, Madilyn finished off the set with peat moss and compost. She had to admit that Maddie was doing most of the physical labor, yet she'd not complained even once.

At nine thirty, when they had only two trees remaining, she heard a truck approaching. A truck with a trailer—more apple trees being delivered. She was surprised to find Tanner driving, though.

"Yo, Dylan," he called with a wave.

"Hey," she greeted him when he got out. "I thought this type of work was beneath you."

"Yeah, it is, but I missed you." He turned to Madilyn. "Hey, Maddie. Can't believe she's making you work like this."

Madilyn came over to them. "Hi, Tanner. And I volunteered. Crazy, I know."

"Admit it. You're having fun," Dylan said.

Madilyn smiled at her. "I'm having fun, yes." She turned to Tanner, motioning to the orchard. "What do you think?"

"I think you two have been busy. It's looking good."

"That rain set us back," Dylan said. "Wasted day." She glanced at the trailer where two guys were starting to unload the trees. "That looks like way more than fifty."

"Yeah. Got another place to deliver to. And don't rush getting these in the ground. My next order got delayed. Probably be out here late next week at the earliest, but don't hold your breath."

"That's fine. It'll give us a chance to work on the firepit."

"How's it coming?"

"Haven't done anything since you were here. But Maddie has been wanting a steak, so…"

"I'd offer to help over the weekend, but Jenna's family is having a big birthday party for her grandmother. She'd kill me if I didn't go."

Dylan clapped his shoulder. "Did you ask her yet?"

Tanner glanced quickly at Maddie, then back at her. "No. I chickened out."

"Ask her what?" Maddie asked.

"To marry him," Dylan supplied. "He's dragging his feet. He said he was going to do it."

"If you love her and you want to be with her, then you should ask her," Maddie said reasonably.

"What if she says no?"

"What if she does?"

"It would break my heart, I think."

Maddie nodded. "The chance you take." Then she patted his arm. "But I don't think she'll say no."

"She's crazy about you," Dylan added. "You know that."

"Yeah, well you're not the one asking. It's scary as hell. I mean, do I go to a fancy restaurant, wine and candles? She'll know something is up if I do that."

Madilyn shook her head. "I obviously don't know Jenna well, but I don't think that's what she would want. Someplace quiet, just the two of you. A walk outside somewhere. Tell her how much you love her. Tell her you want to spend your life with her."

"Then drop down on a knee and ask her," Dylan finished.

"That might work," he said. "Because if she starts freaking out or something, I can just skip the dropping to the knee part and continue our walk. She'll never know I was going to ask her."

She and Maddie both laughed. "Okay, Tanner. Sounds like a plan," she said. "Let us know how it turns out."

CHAPTER FORTY-ONE

By eleven, she was starving. She was also sitting on the tractor, trying to dig a hole. Dylan was standing off to the side—and safely away from the backhoe—giving her instructions. She lowered the bucket slowly, as Dylan had told her, and dropped the teeth into the ground. Dylan gave her a thumbs-up, and she let out the breath she had been nervously holding.

"Okay, doing great," Dylan called. "Now scoop it out."

Dylan had gotten so good at it that she was able to dig deep holes with only three quick digs. She peered over the tractor, noting that she'd barely broken the surface with her first dig. She glanced over at Dylan, who gave her a reassuring smile. She tried again. After five scoops, she finally had it deep enough.

"This will take us all day," she yelled over the rumbling of the diesel engine.

"No, it won't. Three more."

The second one also took five scoops, but she was able to get the other two after only four tries. Dylan motioned for her to kill the engine.

"That's harder than it looks," she said when she hopped down.

"It just takes practice."

"I guess you want to plant those four, huh."

Dylan shook her head. "No. I'm starving."

"Oh, thank god. Me too."

They put their dirty gloves on the back of Dylan's Gator, then used water from the jug to wash up a little. She grabbed the picnic basket Loretta had put together for her and Dylan took the blanket.

"I'm glad you remembered a blanket," Dylan said as she spread it out under the maple tree.

"Yes. I put it out last night so I wouldn't forget."

She set the basket on one corner, then kicked her boots off before sitting down with a relaxed sigh. "I'm so tired."

"Yeah. And we get to haul stone this afternoon," Dylan reminded her.

"I think that will be easier than what we've been doing." Then she nudged Dylan's foot with her own. "Because I'm hoping you'll have some beer."

"For someone who had never had beer before, you seem to enjoy it."

"Oh, I do." She opened up the picnic basket, curious as to what Loretta had packed for them. There were two containers and she pulled them both out. There was also a sleeve of crackers. One of the containers held a variety of cheeses. The other, meats. There were also two bottles of water. A meager lunch, she mused. Not the thick roast beef sandwiches that Hattie had fixed for Isabel and Lorah.

Dylan had already snatched a piece of cheese. "You look disappointed."

"Do I? I didn't really know what to expect."

"This is great. We've got some chicken here. And this looks like ham. And turkey." Dylan opened the crackers and piled one high with a piece of meat and another slice of cheese, then added another cracker to the top.

Her hunger pushed her disappointment aside and she mimicked Dylan, making a cracker sandwich. They ate silently at first—and rather quickly, a testament to how hungry they were. After four mini-cracker sandwiches, she finally relaxed. Dylan was staring at the valley, a smile on her face. Even though she'd thought before how attractive Dylan was, sometimes it shocked her how much she enjoyed looking at her.

Dylan turned then, capturing her eyes. Again, that fluttery feeling hit her, and she sucked in a shaky breath.

"I love this view here," Dylan said quietly. "It's similar to mine, yet different somehow."

Madilyn swallowed down her nervousness before speaking. "I think this has more of a pronounced drop-off into the valley. More like an overlook."

"Yeah. An overlook."

Dylan lay back on the blanket like she'd done the other day at the bridge, folding her hands under her head. "Do you ever feel like when you do something, see something, that it's like, you've been there before?"

"Like déjà vu?"

"I guess. Sitting here, looking out at the valley, I could swear I've done this before." She turned her head toward her. "Of course, I know I haven't."

Like when they'd met, Madilyn thought. The feeling of familiarity was so strong, she was certain they must have run into each other at some point before. She knew they hadn't. Maybe that's why this friendship was so easy with Dylan. But was there something else? The elusive *more*? Was the only reason she was out here planting trees because she wanted to get the orchard going as soon as possible? Was that it? Or was it the fact that she craved Dylan's company? That she wanted to be around her. Wanted to be close like this?

She pulled her gaze from Dylan, wondering what was happening to her. Was she taking Isabel's diary to heart? She mentally shook her head. No. Of course not. She wasn't Isabel. But there was *something* here, wasn't it? Yes, there was, but she dared not put a name to it. What in the world was she thinking?

Dylan sat up then and took another cracker, topping it with meat and cheese. "These are pretty good. This is like real meat."

She smiled at that. "Real?"

"Yeah. Meaning not deli meat." Dylan surprised her by patting her thigh affectionately. "Better eat up. Got those four holes to fill."

"Then we'll stop for the day?"

"Yeah. Then we'll go play with stone."

Madilyn could feel the skin of her thigh burning where Dylan had so casually touched her. Whatever was wrong with her?

CHAPTER FORTY-TWO

Dylan watched as Madilyn seemed engrossed in her task—stirring the mortar. She was sitting on the ground, cross-legged. Her blond hair was hanging across her face, obscuring one side, and there was a smile on her face. After planting over fifty trees now, that task had surely lost some of its luster for her, but she still seemed genuinely interested in the firepit. Or maybe it was the future steak she was interested in. As she stared, Maddie brushed the hair away, only to have it fall down again. She had such an overwhelming urge to reach out and tame the hair herself that she had to forcibly stop herself.

"You're staring."

Yes, she was. "Just, you know, making sure you're doing it correctly."

Maddie turned her head slowly, meeting her gaze. One of her eyebrows disappeared into the hair that covered that eye. God, was that a sexy look or what? Then she shook herself, pulling her gaze away. A stupid crush. For god's sake, she had a stupid crush on her.

"And?"

"And you were doing it perfectly," she managed as she moved to the other side of the firepit. She chanced another glance at Madilyn who was still smiling.

"Planting trees has become work. I mean, I still enjoy it, but yeah, it's work." Maddie motioned to the still unfinished firepit. "This is fun."

"Glad you think so." She selected a stone and took it over to where Maddie was. "Ready for me?"

"I am."

Madilyn had a thick layer of mortar down and she placed the stone on top of it, shifting it a little to get it straight. Maddie quickly added mortar to the sides and into the space that was left between it and the previous stone. They repeated this process with six more stones before she called a halt to their task.

"Let's let these set. Beer break."

"You won't get an argument from me."

Dylan went into the house to get two beers. Maddie stayed where she was, still sitting on the ground. When she came back out, instead of taking a chair, she plopped down beside her.

"Another six or so should finish it out."

Maddie took a swallow of beer and sighed contentedly. "For not ever having beer before, I really do like the taste." She laughed lightly. "Maybe it's good I never tried this in college."

"I only really started drinking it after hanging out with Tanner." She smiled too. "And now you."

"I'm a bad influence?"

Dylan leaned closer to her. "How do you get so dirty?" She couldn't resist rubbing the spot of mortar on Maddie's cheek.

"And you," Maddie said quietly as she too reached out to wipe away dirt from her cheek.

She found herself holding her breath as Maddie touched her. She held her breath and she held Maddie's eyes. She saw Maddie swallow as her hand fell away and she swore her eyes turned a deeper shade of blue.

"I've...I've kinda enjoyed getting dirty," Maddie said. "It's not something I've ever done before. Even as a young child, I don't ever remember playing outside, getting dirty. Truth is, I don't really remember playing at all." She brought her knees up and rested her arms on them. "A child in a grown-up world. Maybe that's why I've always been so serious about things."

"You think you come across that way? Serious?"

"Yes." Then a quick smile. "In the past. Not recently. Not with you."

"I imagine it's exhausting trying to maintain this perfect persona all the time."

"It is, yes. That's one reason I enjoy being with you so much."

"What about with Palmer? Were you still trying to maintain an image with him?"

"I didn't really like the person I was when I was around Palmer. Yes, there was an image to portray. Although, at the time, I didn't realize that it was a false presentation of who I was. It's only since my grandmother died that I feel like I've changed. Of course, that also coincides with moving out here, finding my great-grandmother's diary, meeting you."

"What was it about the diary that allowed you to change?"

Maddie nodded. "Yes. I like that word. *Allowed* me to change. Gave me permission to change." She put the beer bottle down and stretched her legs out. "Isabel was terribly unhappy, although she didn't *know* she was unhappy. Not at first. She was stuck in a loveless marriage, she didn't have any friends, and she had no identity." She turned to look at her. "That was going to be my fate. If I'd married Palmer, it would have been a loveless marriage. I have no close friends and my identity is my last name. I was becoming Isabel."

"How do you know she was unhappy and didn't know it?"

Maddie held her gaze. "Because she fell in love with someone. A short-lived affair that shaped the rest of her life. And it was a very short life at that."

"So the diary is about this love affair?"

Maddie nodded. "It started out about the orchard." She laughed quietly. "When I read the first few entries, I thought there was no way I'd read the whole thing. What did I care about apples? But it quickly became more than that."

Dylan reached out and took Maddie's hand, tugging playfully on her index finger. Madilyn already knew of the affair. It was time to tell her about the letter. "Did they call her Issy?"

Madilyn's gaze was full of wonder as her eyes locked on hers. She was surprised to find their fingers entwining.

"How did you know?" Maddie breathed.

"You found a diary. I found something too."

Maddie frowned. "What do you mean?"

"It's the weirdest thing. I was going to ask you weeks ago, but I thought maybe it would be inappropriate to suggest what I think happened."

"Dylan? What are you talking about?"

"Well, I found this box. When I was cleaning out the old shed. It belonged to my great-aunt. She was my mother's and Uncle Frank's aunt. Anyway, I've never even seen a picture of her, and they didn't talk about her at all. In fact, I'd forgotten she even existed. But a few days before he died, Uncle Frank told me the story of how Aunt Lorah planted those two apple trees. She—"

"Oh my god." Maddie squeezed her hand almost painfully tight. "*Lorah?*"

Dylan held her gaze. "Isabel fell in love with Lorah."

Madilyn's mouth opened in disbelief, and a whispered word came out. "Yes."

"There was a letter she wrote to Lorah, and she signed it Issy," she continued.

Tears filled Maddie's eyes and she slowly nodded. "I have a letter that Lorah wrote Isabel."

Dylan smiled. "This is kind of a weird coincidence, isn't it?"

Madilyn's eyes closed. "Her last name was Chance."

"Yes. That's my middle name. My mother and Uncle Frank were the only two left in that family. Lorah was their aunt. Uncle Frank had no kids, so my mother named me Dylan for her mother's family and Chance for her father's family."

The eyes opened again. "Lorah was your great-aunt."

"Yes."

A smile. "I can't believe this." Maddie sat up straighter, finally dropping her hand. "When I found the diary, I was almost embarrassed to read it. I felt like I was intruding on her privacy. *Their* privacy. But it was so fascinating, I couldn't stop. After I read it, there were so many questions I had and there was no way to get answers. I knew of Isabel's fate but not Lorah's."

"Do you want to read the letter?"

"Can I please?"

"Of course. Come on inside. I'll show you the box."

She stood, then held her hand out to help Maddie up. Yes, what a strange coincidence it was. It was almost surreal. She could tell by the look in Maddie's eyes that she thought the same.

She went into the bedroom, motioning for Madilyn to sit on the bed. She opened up the closet and took the box from underneath the old felt hat.

"Oh my god! Is that her fedora?"

Dylan took the hat out too. "This was with the box. I have no idea if it was hers or not, but I couldn't bear to leave it behind."

Madilyn's hand was shaking as she reached out to take the hat. Again, that look of wonder in her eyes. "Yes. It's Lorah's fedora. Isabel spoke of it in the diary." Maddie met her gaze. "I have a photo of the two of them. She's wearing it."

"You're kidding? I'd love to see it."

Maddie nodded and handed the hat back to her. She went and sat down beside her. Her hands ran across the smooth wood surface of the box. "There's not much in it. A letter and Isabel's obituary. And a leather pouch with seeds."

"Seeds?"

"Apple seeds. I'm guessing from those two old mother trees of hers." She paused. "After I read the letter, well, there was no way I could get rid of this. I know very little about Lorah, just what my uncle told me. I certainly had no idea who Isabel was." She handed the box over to Maddie, who also ran her hands over its surface.

"Lorah used to work for a cabinetmaker in Lancaster," Maddie said quietly. "I'm certain she made this box herself."

Dylan watched as she opened it. Maddie took out the envelope first and gently removed the letter from inside it. Dylan found herself leaning closer, reading it again as Maddie did.

My Dearest Lorah. I never knew a heart could hurt as much as mine does. The pain just will not go away. My days are spent walking the path we took to the orchard. I'm sure the apple trees are sick of me by now. All I do is walk among them and talk to you. I swear I can still hear your voice as it whispers to me. Hattie worries, I know. I'm not eating much, not sleeping. She knows why my heart aches. I think she misses you nearly as much as I do.

I don't wear my wedding band any longer. James hasn't seemed to notice. I do wear the ring you gave me. Always. Not that I needed anything to remind me of you, but I'm so glad to have it as it was once yours. I won't write to you again, my love. I wanted you to know how I was getting on is all. I hope you are well. Have you settled on the farm? Did you ever plant those apple trees for me?

I should stop now. My tears are falling as I write this. I miss you so much, Lorah. My life is completely empty without you. I live solely through my memories of last summer, the best months of my life. The best time of my life.

I love you, my dearest. Every beat of my heart is a longing for you. Forever yours, Issy.

She heard the quiet tears that Maddie wasn't trying to hide. She hesitated, wondering if Maddie needed some comfort, wondering if she was overstepping. She put her arm around Madilyn and pulled her closer. She wasn't prepared, though, when Maddie turned her head and buried her face against her neck. Her heart lodged in her throat, and she only barely resisted taking Maddie fully into her arms.

"My heart just breaks for them."

Dylan closed her eyes as Maddie's breath tickled her skin. "You've read the diary. I guess you have a better understanding of their affair."

"I'm sorry." Madilyn pulled away and wiped her cheeks. "Yes, I do. They became like friends to me." She folded the letter up carefully and placed it back in the envelope, then took out the obituary. She read it quickly, then nodded. "Yes, this is exactly what I meant when I said Isabel had no identity. Mrs. James Marak died. Not Isabel."

"I think that's how it always was back then."

"They were so in love."

"Yes, it sounds like it."

Maddie looked at her and smiled. "I really can't believe this." She slowly shook her head. "Lorah. You're Lorah's great-niece."

Dylan smiled too. "What do you know about her?"

"Lorah? I don't know much, really. She was a traveling salesperson who showed up in a Model T Ford."

"Shoes."

Madilyn nodded. "Yes. Shoes. She sold shoes."

Dylan nodded too. "My uncle told me that. Said she showed up one day back at the farm and never left again."

Madilyn took her hand and squeezed it hard. "*Your* farm? That was *Lorah's* farm?"

"The family farm, yes."

Madilyn leaned her head back and looked at the ceiling, then lay down on the bed completely. "What are the chances of this happening?" She turned her head slowly. "I can't believe this," she said again.

Dylan had to agree. "I don't know anything about her other than what my uncle told me that one time. He said she planted those two old apple trees in 1934. He called her an odd bird. Said she wore men's clothing. Said she would sit under those trees and talk, like she was having a conversation with someone."

This caused more tears to form in Maddie's eyes. "Yes. She was having a conversation with Isabel. Just like Isabel talked to the apple trees here. But she was really talking to Lorah, not the trees."

"Is this the real reason for the orchard?"

Maddie rolled her head to the side again, looking at her. "Yes. Because of the diary. Oh, Dylan, you've got to read it. You'll fall in love with them just like I did. And it'll break your heart." She sat up. "When did Lorah die?"

"My uncle said just a few days after I was born. She was eighty-something, he said."

Madilyn reached into the box again and took out the leather pouch. She opened it up and poured out a few seeds into her hand. "You know we're going to have to plant these, don't you?"

Dylan smiled. "I guess so."

Madilyn looked at her, holding her gaze, as if trying to make sense of it all. "This is so crazy, isn't it? I had so many questions after I read the diary, yet there was no one to ask. Then it turns out that Hattie was Loretta's great-aunt. She—"

"Who was Hattie? Her name is in this letter."

"Hattie was a servant at the time. She did the cooking. She was only a few years older than Isabel and Lorah, I think. Anyway, Loretta remembered stories that Hattie used to tell, and she shared some with me, but I still never knew of Lorah's fate. I wondered if she had died young like Isabel had."

"No. But she lived a terribly lonely life, I imagine. Uncle Frank said she rarely left the farm."

"That is sad. According to the diary, Lorah was a fun and outgoing person. Amazing how a broken heart can kill someone's spirit like that."

"Is that what happened to Isabel?"

"Yes. My grandfather said she just drifted away. Died in her sleep one night."

Dylan nodded. "I would like to read the diary if you think that it would be okay. It would be nice to learn something about Lorah."

"Yes. The photo of them is in there too." Madilyn seemed to study her. "Maybe that's why I thought I'd met you somewhere before. I think you favor Lorah." Maddie reached out and touched her jaw, running a finger slowly along her skin. "Yes."

Dylan felt her heart spring to life, and she nearly shivered from the soft touch. Then Maddie's hand fell away. Her hand fell away, but Maddie's blue eyes still held hers tightly.

"I...I like you a lot, Dylan. I'm a little afraid by it." A quick smile. "More than a little, actually."

Dylan was aware of the intimacy of their positions—on her bed. She was having a hard time believing what she'd just heard. She was the one with the crush. She was the one, not Maddie. Right? However, the look in Maddie's eyes said something completely different. And that look terrified her.

She stood up and moved away from the bed, away from Madilyn. "It's been a long day. Maybe…maybe we should—"

Madilyn stood up too. "Right. We should call it a day." She paused. "I'm sorry."

Dylan wasn't sure what she was apologizing for. "Maddie, I like you a lot too."

Madilyn nodded quickly, then took a step away from her. "I should go."

Dylan stood rooted to the floor, watching as Madilyn fled from the room. She shook her head slowly.

What in the hell just happened?

CHAPTER FORTY-THREE

Madilyn lay in bed, the covers pulled almost to her chin. She was still wide awake even though she'd been in bed for over an hour. She turned her head, looking out the window that she'd opened earlier. Her mind was a jumbled mess, and she couldn't seem to focus on anything. She hadn't been able to even think about her and Dylan's conversation. She was afraid of what it meant. Besides, she had yet to wrap her head around the fact that Dylan and Lorah were related.

Hard to believe, but was it really? As she'd told Dylan, there'd been such familiarity from the very beginning. But was that all?

She closed her eyes, trying to chase away the thoughts that had been teasing her—trying to push them away like she'd been for the last hour. She wasn't a toucher. She never had been. She wasn't a toucher, wasn't a hugger. Then why did she find herself touching Dylan? Touching her without even thinking about it. And holding hands with her. *God.*

Then her eyes widened, and she leaned up on an elbow. She looked around the room, half expecting to see Isabel there watching her.

"I'm losing my mind," she murmured out loud.

She reached out to turn on the lamp. The diary was there beside the bed, and she picked it up, flipping through it until she found the photo. She scooted up higher against the pillows, holding the picture to the light. Her eyes were on Lorah. Yes, she could see a resemblance. She slid her gaze to Isabel, only it wasn't Isabel she was seeing. No. She saw herself there, sitting on Dylan's lap, staring into her eyes. It was Dylan's fingers touching her chin, drawing her close for a kiss. It felt so real, she could feel her thundering heartbeat, could feel Dylan's lips on hers. It was so real, she felt the sensation of the kiss all the way down to her toes.

She closed her eyes and took a deep breath, finally letting in the words that she'd been fighting off all evening. Words she knew to be true.

I'm attracted to her.

Yes. Crazy as it seemed, she was attracted to Dylan physically. Sexually. Was this how Isabel had felt? Married to a man she didn't love, not knowing that she was unhappy. Not knowing, that is, until Lorah walked into her life. Was she traveling the same path that Isabel had? Was that possible?

She looked at the photo again. It was Lorah and Isabel. Not her and Dylan. She wasn't Isabel. Dylan wasn't Lorah. It was ridiculous to even think that.

She turned the lamp off once more, but her eyes were still wide open, staring into the darkness. She'd been dating a man she didn't love for two years. A man who wanted to marry her. Unlike Isabel, she knew she wasn't happy. She also knew that Palmer didn't love her either. Yet she continued on. If her grandmother hadn't died, if she hadn't agreed to stay out here, would she have simply carried on, dating Palmer and pretending? If she hadn't read the diary, would she think that was all there was?

Sadly, she thought that yes, she would have stayed the course. For a while. But surely, she wouldn't have married him.

Right?

Right. Because she wanted to be in love. Like Isabel and Lorah, she wanted to be in love like that.

Yes. She wanted to be madly, crazily in love.

CHAPTER FORTY-FOUR

Dylan wasn't really surprised to find no sign of Madilyn at the orchard. It was still early, not yet eight o'clock, but she thought that maybe Maddie needed some time to herself. Or was she being presumptuous? Had she read her wrong? Had she misunderstood her words?

No. She didn't think so. But what the hell did they do now? Should they talk about it? She got out of the Gator and headed over to the tractor. Talk? She shook her head. No, that wasn't her strong suit. Especially about something like this. Christ, Maddie was *straight*.

She shook her head again. No, no, no. She wasn't going to go there. She was smart enough to not even *think* about getting involved with a straight woman. She climbed up on the tractor and nodded. Right. So maybe they should talk. Clear the air. She started it up. Yeah. They should probably talk and clear the air. They could blame it on just being in the moment…or whatever.

She was on her fifth hole when she saw the white golf cart coming along the trail. The nervousness that she felt at the sight tempered when she saw that Maddie wasn't alone. Her grandfather was with her. She moved the tractor back away from the new holes and shut off the engine.

Instead of stopping where she normally parked, Madilyn drove the golf cart right up to the new trees. Dylan hopped off the tractor, going to meet them.

"Good morning," she greeted. "Out for a tour?"

"Maddie thought I needed to see the progress." He nodded. "I haven't been out here in years, but it looks very different with all the old trees gone."

She followed his gaze. "Yes, we only kept a few of the hardier ones. For cross-pollination purposes."

"And to make a cobbler, Maddie tells me."

Dylan smiled and turned her gaze to Madilyn. The smile on Maddie's face belied the tension that Dylan could see in her eyes.

"It was my Aunt Linda's recipe," she offered.

"I hope you'll share with me if you make it," Maddie said, finally speaking. "I was going to show my grandfather what we've done so far, and he was curious about your house. You wouldn't mind if I took him by there?"

"Of course not. Go on inside. Show him around." She pointed to the five holes. "I've got trees to plant."

"I'll be out later to help."

"Okay. Great."

She watched them leave, hoping that this tension between them wasn't going to stick. And hoping that she'd made up her bed properly and put her breakfast dishes up.

* * *

"Not that I know much about the infancy of an orchard, but it looks very professional." He glanced at her. "At least the trees all appear to be in straight lines."

Madilyn laughed. "Yes. Everything's been measured and spaced evenly. And I even dug some holes yesterday."

"With the tractor?"

"Yes. But I have yet to actually drive it."

He shook his head slowly. "A Marak woman doing manual labor. Let's hope word doesn't get out. People would think we've lost our fortune."

"I don't look at it as labor. It's been fun. Certainly, something different."

She hadn't been sure that she would be brave enough to face Dylan today. At least not alone. So, she'd lingered after breakfast, finally talking her grandfather into a quick tour of the orchard. Dylan, though, appeared perfectly normal and her usual charming self. Although she did notice that she was hesitant to meet her eyes. Or maybe it was her who was hesitant. In her mind's eye, she kept seeing them in the photo, kept seeing them kissing.

What in the world was she going to say to her? Should she apologize? And if she did, what would she be apologizing for? Maybe they could just pretend that nothing out of the ordinary had happened and go on like they'd been.

"I forgot to tell you, Maddie, but Eric Bingham is coming by tomorrow. I'd like you to meet him."

"He's the one who manages the leases?"

"Yes. I think I told you that he comes by periodically. Not that I don't trust him—like everything else, I believe in audits—but we can't just blindly let someone run our business for us."

"Why haven't you sold that land? I don't think it's something that you've ever been interested in, has it?"

"Yes, it's been on my mind to get rid of the last of it. Belle and I sold more than half the acreage years ago, but I haven't bothered with it since. Probably because Bingham does the work and it's not been a chore for me. But you're right. I never took an interest in it. That was my father's doing. My grandfather bought up all this land for pennies, then it just sat. He started leasing it for farming, but it was my father who turned it into a business."

She drove through the last group of trees before Dylan's house came into view. "How many acres are here around the estate? You don't plan to sell any of this, do you?"

"No, no. This is Marak land. It's close to a thousand acres here at the estate and the valley and all. Then on the other side of the creek, another five hundred, I believe."

"That's the land that you were going to donate for a park?"

"Yes."

She stopped next to Dylan's truck. "We were out at the creek the other day and we found the old bridge. It's in pretty good shape still. Not that I would chance driving across it, but we did walk to the other side."

"Really? It was still there?"

"Yes. I was surprised when we found it."

"I imagine that's all grown up over there now."

"Yes. Thick woods and brush on that side of the creek. Huge trees. Very beautiful."

He eyed her thoughtfully. "You've taken an interest in the land out here, haven't you?"

She smiled and nodded. "I have. All these years, whenever I visited you, I never left the house. I never took the time to explore around and learn to appreciate it. There are so many different little parts to it. The woodlands, the valley, the creek. And the orchard." She got out, then went around to his side to help him. "Come on. I'll show you what I've been working on."

He stopped at the bottom step of the porch and tapped his cane several times on the wood. "It doesn't even look like the same old house. Of course, it's been years since I've been out this way. I like the new paint colors."

"The outside structure was in surprisingly good shape. Randy said they found a few areas along the eaves that needed replacing. Now the inside, it was awful." She opened the door and went inside. As usual, it was neat and tidy. "There was a wall there, and the kitchen was so small you could barely turn around in it. So, we took the wall out and put in the bar to open it up."

He nodded. "Can't say I remember what it used to look like."

She pointed down a hallway. "The bedroom and bath are back there. They gutted the bathroom and completely redid it. It looks nice." Then she went into the kitchen. "Come out here. I'll show you the firepit."

She went out to the little back patio, noting how inviting it was. How familiar it was to her now. "Dylan added the bricks here to enlarge the sitting area and to house her grill." She moved one of the chairs out of the way. "And this is the firepit. Not quite finished, but close."

He leaned on his cane as he surveyed it. "You helped build this?"

"I did. We found the stones at the site of an old homestead down in the valley. There was nothing left except a fireplace and a lot of it had fallen. Dylan and I hauled the stones up from there."

He nodded. "Yes, I think I know the place. About halfway down?"

"Yes."

"That was where Douglas Linen farmed when I was a boy. He had a son about my age."

"Were you friends?"

He looked at her for a moment, then shook his head. "No. It wouldn't have been proper. They were nothing more than sharecroppers."

"Did you have any friends, Pops? When you were growing up?"

"I had a horse. And a dog."

His eyes had a faraway look in them, and she thought he might elaborate, but he didn't. Instead, he moved slowly around the firepit, using his cane to tap on the stones. "This looks real nice." He motioned to the ash left inside. "Already had a fire in it?"

"Yes. We had one when Dylan's friends were here. She's going to get some kind of a spit so that she can cook over it. She's promised me a steak."

He turned to look at her. "You seem quite taken with this woman."

She nodded easily. "We've become friends, Pops. Good friends, actually. And you know why? Because she doesn't know—or care—anything about the Marak name. She likes me for me, not my name. And because she doesn't know anything about the Maraks, I don't have to pretend to be someone I'm not."

"What does that mean? Pretend."

"I don't make a very good heiress and I'm not a matriarch. When I'm out in public representing the Foundation, those are two things I must pretend that I am." She waved her hand. "Even when I'm not representing the family, I *still* have to play the part." She spread her arms wide. "Out here, that never comes into play. I'm just me—Maddie. Not Madilyn Marak."

He tapped his cane a few times, then nodded. "Your mother always put expectations on you. I did too, I suppose. Taking for granted that you would follow in everyone's footsteps—the Marak women."

"But not your mother," she said quietly. "Not Isabel."

He looked off, his gaze traveling across the sun-splashed valley. "No. My mother was never happy being a Marak. In fact, she most likely loathed the elaborate dinner parties she had to host and the Christmas ball." He brought his gaze back to her. "She wanted me to make friends with him. Henry was his name. The boy."

"Then why didn't you?"

"My father wouldn't hear of it. The Maraks don't make friends with people like that." He took a deep breath. "You're right. My mother ignored most of the expectations—the rules—placed on Marak women. She was more at home in the orchard, on her daily walks. She was *alive* out there. Back at the house, no. She was but a shell. Always such sadness in her eyes." He tapped his cane again. "I certainly don't want to see you like that, Maddie. Because I've noticed a change in you. Of course, I have. Your eyes are bright. Happy."

"Yes. Having a purpose—something to do—makes all the difference."

"The orchard?"

"Yes. And getting to help build it—do the work—is rewarding. Thank you for allowing me that."

He looked at her thoughtfully. "Allowed? Is that how you see it?"

"It was a bit of a whim on my part."

"No. Not a whim, I don't think. You seem too passionate about it to only be a whim. And you're enjoying it, as you say. I see that." He tapped the ground a few times with his cane. "You better take me on home so you can get back to work."

"Thank you." She moved closer to him, leaning in to kiss his cheek. "I love you, Pops."

His eyes misted over. "I love you, too, sweet Maddie."

As they stared at each other, she wondered if that was the first time they'd said those words to one another. How sad, if so.

CHAPTER FORTY-FIVE

Dylan was on her knees, piling mulch around the base of the latest tree she'd planted when Maddie came out to join her. She sat back on her heels, and Madilyn stood there, her arms folded almost protectively around her. Neither spoke and Dylan wondered if she should be the one to break the silence. However, it was Maddie who did.

"We should talk. We should probably talk."

"There's not much to say, Maddie." She swallowed nervously. "I'm gay and you're not. So…nothing to talk about."

Madilyn unfolded her arms, but she continued to stare at her. She saw her take a deep breath, saw her lower her gaze. Then a smile formed. A tiny one, but a smile, nonetheless.

"My grandfather was impressed with the firepit. Or maybe impressed that I helped build it."

Ah. So, Maddie didn't *really* want to talk. Okay. That suited her fine.

"Good. Glad he wasn't upset that we confiscated those stones."

"Not at all."

"Good," she said again. Then she pointed to the tractor. "You want to dig some holes?"

Their eyes met and she saw that Madilyn was still hesitating. She got up off her knees and brushed her hands off on her jeans.

"Do you want to talk?" she asked quietly.

"No. I mean, yes. But no."

Dylan smiled. "I completely understand."

"Do you?" Maddie turned her back to her for a second, then turned back around quickly. "I'm attracted to you, Dylan. There. I said it out loud. I'm attracted to you." She paused. "And you're attracted to me."

She stood still, letting the words sink in. She finally nodded. "Yes. I am."

Madilyn held her gaze, her words quiet. "And you're gay and I'm not."

"Yes."

Maddie stared at her, and she could see the uncertainty in her eyes, imagined she saw terror there. She wanted to go closer. She wanted to hug her and tell her that there was nothing to be frightened of. Instead, she moved away from her, putting space between them.

"We're friends, Maddie. That's all." She went over to the tractor. "Now, I need to get to work before my boss yells at me. Do you want to stay and help? Or…"

She saw Maddie visibly swallow, saw the indecision in her eyes. Then Maddie gave a slow nod.

"I want to stay."

CHAPTER FORTY-SIX

To say the afternoon was strained was an understatement. There was very little conversation and when there was, it was trivial. She missed their normal talk and banter. She missed the comfort she typically felt when around Dylan. It was her fault. She couldn't stop thinking about the damn kiss. The *imaginary* kiss, she reminded herself. An imaginary kiss that made her heart spring to life, made her pulse race, and caused her stomach to flip over. An imaginary kiss did all that. What would a real one do to her?

Had Isabel felt that too? Had she been this frightened? Yes. She'd said so in the diary. Her feelings for Lorah had frightened her. She'd said—

"Not that I'm complaining—since you are cheap labor—but you're kinda lagging behind."

Madilyn looked up, only then realizing that she'd stopped in her task of adding mulch and was three trees behind Dylan.

"Sorry."

"Well, you are the boss. I guess you can go at your own pace."

Madilyn tried to match Dylan's smile. She did. Only it wouldn't come. Instead, words tumbled out, words that she couldn't take back.

"I think about kissing you. Or rather you kissing me."

Dylan stared at her. "I see."

They were both on their knees, both dirty. And this was so not the time or place to have this discussion. But—

"I don't know what's happening."

Dylan tilted her head. "Don't you?"

Madilyn looked skyward for a moment, then back at Dylan. "Yes. Yes, I do."

"Okay."

Madilyn's eyes widened. "Okay? That's it? That's all you have to say?"

Dylan smiled. "I think about kissing you too." She pointed to the tree. "Now hurry up. I'm going to dig some more holes."

Madilyn watched as she went to the tractor and climbed up on it with ease. The diesel engine rumbled to life and soon Dylan was doing just that—digging holes. And there she sat, staring at her as she worked.

I'm attracted to her. I'm attracted to a woman, she thought. *And I'm thinking about kissing her, for god's sake.*

And she thinks about kissing me too.

Oh, Maddie, what are you going to do? she asked herself. Just what in the world are you going to do?

CHAPTER FORTY-SEVEN

Dinner had been a tedious affair and she struggled to keep the conversation going. If her grandfather thought anything was off, he didn't mention it. He, too, seemed quiet. He reminded her that Eric Bingham was coming tomorrow. He also said that he had decided to go ahead and terminate the leases and would put the land up for sale. She had no feelings on it one way or the other. She had too many other things on her mind to care about the leases.

She and Dylan had pretty much called a truce on the kissing talk. She wasn't sure if that was a good thing or not. Because it was there. Every time their eyes met, it was there. Dylan went to great lengths to keep some normalcy between them, and after a while, she finally pushed all that "I'm attracted to you" stuff out of her mind.

When Dylan had called a halt to the work for the day, she'd dashed off to her house for a couple of beers. They'd sat under the maples by the overlook, enjoying the drink. Dylan told her about the orchard at the farm and how she managed it. And she told her about the two old mother trees, as she called them. Lorah's trees. No, she supposed they were Issy's trees, since Lorah had planted them for her.

Dylan had asked her if she'd be interested in seeing them and, of course, she readily agreed. Besides wanting to take a look at the old trees, she was beyond curious about the farm and where Lorah had spent her solitary life without Isabel. Curious, too, about where Dylan had spent the last six years.

So, they would go on Friday morning. They'd also go into Lancaster for some shopping and Dylan had offered to take her to lunch. "Someplace fancier than last time." To which she'd replied, "I don't need fancy."

All normal things, yes. Dylan needed to restock her pantry and fridge and she said she wanted to get some steaks. She'd promised to cook one for her over the grill if the spit she'd ordered didn't come in by Saturday. So yes, normal things.

Which would all be great and fine if she didn't constantly think about kissing her.

CHAPTER FORTY-EIGHT

Dylan wasn't sure how she felt about going back to the farm. Would it look unkept? Probably. The grass would need cutting, for sure. She supposed she should get with Stumer Realty and see about hiring someone to do that for her. Francis Stumer hadn't called her in a few weeks. She hoped that wasn't a sign that no one was interested in buying it.

"Are you looking forward to seeing the farm again?"

She turned to Madilyn. "I was just thinking about that. All the little things there that aren't getting done. Keeping the grass mowed, for one. But looking forward to it? I don't know. I had never intended to stay there once my uncle was gone. At first, I thought I'd go back to Philly. Resume my life there." She shook her head. "As the years went by, that became less appealing. And I know I call it a farm, but it's really not anymore. The only thing left is my orchard."

"What did he grow?"

"The last few years, mostly corn. When I was a kid, I remember he had soybeans on probably half of the land, and he grew potatoes for a number of years too. I think during the years when he was young, they grew wheat and tobacco, too."

"I guess if you don't sell it, you'll have to see about harvesting the fruit there."

"I'm hoping that'll be a selling point. Not that our ten-acre orchard produced a huge profit, but that would be something for a buyer to consider." She smiled. "That and dropping the price. If it doesn't sell by the end of summer, then I'll lower the price and hope someone buys."

"When did you normally harvest?"

"September. That's all I did. Every day, all day. Pick apples." She pointed to their left. "This is the Myers' farm. Joey Myers was my uncle's best friend. He was killed two years ago when his tractor ran over him."

"How did that happen?"

She slowed when she approached their property. "Tragic accident, really. He was getting off of it and his sleeve caught the gearshift. Uncle Frank took that hard. He'd known Joey since they were boys." She turned onto their long driveway. "This is it."

On both sides of the driveway were the weedy, grassy fields of her uncle's once pristine farmland. "There are thirty acres here in front. Then the house. Behind the house are thirty more acres. That's where the orchard is."

The old farmhouse came into view, and it looked even more shabby than she remembered. Maybe she should take Mr. Stumer's advice and lower the price already. She glanced at Madilyn, wondering what she thought of the place. She could tell by the look on her face that she wasn't seeing the raggedy house and overgrown grass around it. No, she had a look of curiosity, and she was most likely picturing Lorah out here in years past.

She drove around to the back and parked. "Come on. I'll show you the trees."

She didn't plan to take her into the house. She didn't see the point. The furniture had all been removed and it was bare. And after seeing the mansion that Madilyn lived in, she'd be embarrassed to show her the farmhouse.

"Oh, here's that old smoker I was telling you about. Tanner got it fixed up enough to use."

"You didn't want to bring it with you?"

"Well, I kinda did, but Tanner thinks it'll fall apart if we try to move it. Besides, it's ugly as hell."

"It has character. Who built it?"

"My grandfather, I guess." She walked on, pointing up ahead. "The two old mother trees." Then she frowned. Something was wrong. "Oh no."

"What is it?"

"The trees." She hurried over, a frown on her face. "I can't believe it."

"What's wrong?"

She reached up and pulled a limb down. "They're dying. The leaves are shriveling." She was struck by such a sense of loss that she went to the tree and wrapped her arms around the trunk. "I can't believe it's dying."

Maddie went to the other tree and pulled a branch down like she had. "This one too. What do you think happened?"

"I guess it was just time. Old age."

She sat down on the ground and leaned against the trunk like she used to do. She wasn't really surprised to see Maddie do the same on the other tree. They sat there, looking at each other.

"You're going to think I'm crazy, but I feel such a sense of peace being here," Maddie said quietly.

"Not strange. I feel it too. I used to come and sit out here. Like this. A couple of nights before my uncle died, I came out here. I knew the time was near and I knew my life would change, but I sat here and, yeah, a sense of peace settled over me." She thought back to that night. "You're going to think *I'm* crazy, but that night, the wind was blowing, and I swore I heard a woman's voice, talking to me. I couldn't make out the words though. Then the moon came out and I thought I saw a face in the branches." She pointed up to the tree where Maddie sat. "Up there."

"Lorah?"

"I don't know. Maybe that's why the trees are dying. Maybe they were lonely. Nobody was here anymore."

"Oh, Dylan, that breaks my heart."

She wasn't really surprised to see Maddie's eyes turn misty with tears as she stared at her.

"I love that about you."

Maddie raised her eyebrows. "What?"

"Your sentimental side. How you imagined Lorah and Isabel were, how the trees that they loved have become more than just trees." She smiled. "And that you think it's possible that I may have heard and seen Lorah that night."

Maddie nodded. "Yes. I'm staying in Isabel's room. The room she lived in. The room she died in. I've thought on several occasions that she was in the room with me." Then she smiled. "And thought maybe I was losing my mind."

Dylan smiled too. "No, don't think that. Some things we can't explain."

No. There were things they couldn't explain. Like why would Maddie hire her, someone with no experience? What even made her apply for the job in the first place? Maddie found a diary, she found a box. Was all of that just a coincidence? Fate?

"Dylan?"

"Hmm?"

"Do you think—" But she didn't finish her question. She shook her head. "Nothing."

Dylan frowned. "Do I think what?"

Maddie shook her head again, then smiled. "Nothing. Show me your orchard. Show me what ours is going to look like in a few years."

Dylan stood and offered her hand to Maddie. Their eyes met, then Maddie took her hand. Dylan pulled her up and they stood there between the two old—and now dying—trees. Maddie didn't let go of her hand and Dylan could swear she could feel the energy between them. Maddie, who had confessed she'd thought about kissing her. Maddie, who hadn't yet released her hand.

"I think you're more afraid than I am."

Dylan didn't have to ask what she meant by that. She simply nodded. "I knew I was gay in high school. I never had any doubt. You—"

"I don't have a label to put on this. I don't need one. I'm attracted to you." She shrugged. "And I'm not blind. I've seen the way you look at me sometimes. What does all of that mean?"

She finally let go of Maddie's hand and took a step away, only to back into the trunk of Lorah's tree. "There's...there's Palmer. There's—"

"There's no one, Dylan." She smiled then. A sweet smile. "I'm glad we're having this conversation and not hiding from it."

"Oh, yeah, me too," she said dryly.

Maddie laughed, easing some of the tension. "How about you show me your orchard?"

Dylan let out a nervous breath and nodded. "Yeah. Okay. The orchard. Come on."

CHAPTER FORTY-NINE

Madilyn was surprised by her bravery and thankful that they'd been able to talk. Sort of. Dylan had had a look of pure terror on her face. She wasn't quite sure what that meant. Was Dylan afraid to start something—physical, emotional—for fear she might lose her job if it ended up being a mistake? For that matter, what about her? Could she truly contemplate having a physical, sexual relationship with Dylan? Just the thought brought a blush to her face.

Dylan unlatched a gate and pushed it open. "Here we are. My labor of love."

"Wow. It is much bigger than ours at home."

"Ten acres, so yeah, more than triple the size."

"And you managed all of this yourself?"

"I did. Like I said, it about killed me. But there are different varieties, so they don't all ripen at once, thankfully."

"Are you doing that for ours?"

"Because it's so small, I only used two varieties." Dylan walked in among the trees, and she followed. "Some of these are different ages too. I replaced about fifty trees, oh, four years ago, I think it was. Those are on the back side." She reached up to pull a limb down, then showed it to her. "Baby apples."

"These baby apples look much bigger than the ones at home."

"Yes. This is an early variety. There are four acres with these. They'll ripen in August. Once I get done with these, then the others start ripening. I'm out here dawn to dusk in September picking apples."

"What if you don't sell the farm?"

Dylan looked at her and smiled. "Well, then I hope my boss will let me take some time off to work here." The smile faded. "Truthfully, I'm not looking forward to that. Maybe I'm getting older, but just the thought of having to be out here working like that is overwhelming."

"Why don't you hire someone to pick them?"

"Can't afford it. And it's not big enough for the seasonal workers to bother with anyway. They wouldn't make enough money here. They stick with the huge, commercial orchards."

"I could pay for—"

"No, Maddie. It is what it is. If September comes around and I've not sold the farm, then I'll deal with it then. We still have all summer." Dylan wiggled her eyebrows. "Maybe I could talk a friend into helping me."

"You think you can sweet talk me into that, do you?"

As their eyes held, she saw a change in Dylan's. It was enough for her breath to get caught in her throat, enough for her heartbeats to nearly choke her.

"Maddie…"

She couldn't tell if that whispered word was a plea or a warning. She didn't really care which at this point. Any rational thoughts she may have had vanished as her gaze dropped to Dylan's mouth. The only thoughts in her mind were those of kissing Dylan—certainly not rational, no.

She was surprised that she was the one who moved first, not Dylan. She reached for her, her eyes never once leaving Dylan's dark ones. Their kiss was nearly desperate, hard. Not soft. Not tentative. She found herself pressed fully against Dylan's body and she moaned at the contact. Her mouth opened to Dylan, and she was certain she had never been more thoroughly kissed before. She was also certain she'd never been this aroused from only a kiss. She became lightheaded and her knees felt weak, causing her to cling to Dylan tighter as they kissed.

The ringing of her phone interrupted them, and Dylan pulled away first, her eyes nearly wild as she stared at her.

"I'm so sorry."

Madilyn held on to Dylan's arm to steady herself. "You took my breath away," she said unevenly. "Don't be sorry."

She pulled her phone from her pocket and frowned. It was Loretta. She never called her. She looked at Dylan. "Loretta," she explained before answering. "Hello."

"Oh, Miss Maddie. You need to come quick. Mr. Albert has collapsed."

Her heart jumped into her throat. "What? Collapsed?"

"Randy is here. I've already called for an ambulance." Her voice cracked. "I don't know if he's okay or not. Randy—"

"I'm on my way." She squeezed Dylan's arm. "She said my grandfather has collapsed. Ambulance is on the way."

"We won't beat it there, Maddie. They'll take him to Lancaster. Let's find out what hospital. We can meet them there."

Dylan was already leading her back to her truck and Maddie simply followed along, Loretta's call chasing the sweet memories of their kisses from her mind. She couldn't think straight. Part of her wanted to race back to the estate, but Dylan was right. They would never beat an ambulance there.

Before she knew it, they were speeding down the road toward Lancaster. Dylan reached over and grabbed her hand. "Don't think the worst."

Maddie squeezed the fingers that held hers. "He's eighty-nine." Then she turned to Dylan. "I've had no experience with this. But you—"

"Yeah."

She leaned her head back and closed her eyes. Yes, he'd seemed a little down lately. Tired the last few days. And he hadn't been eating with his usual gusto. What was their last conversation about? She'd rushed through breakfast that morning, so looking forward to her outing with Dylan that she'd only half-listened to him. Oh. The leases. They'd met with Mr. Bingham yesterday. He was going to handle the sale of the land and her grandfather had been telling her how to distribute the money. He'd left instructions in his study, he said. She'd kissed his cheek and hurried out, saying she'd see him at dinner.

She felt a tear run down her cheek. No. She didn't think she would see him at dinner after all.

CHAPTER FIFTY

Dylan had been driving them to Lancaster General Hospital when Randy called. Called her. Not Maddie. Her hand had been shaking when she answered.

They were going back home now, driving slower than normal. Maddie hadn't said a word since the call. She'd broken down, of course, and Dylan had stopped the truck and had comforted her as best she could with a console between them.

Now, though, Maddie was sitting there silently, staring straight ahead, her tears having stopped. Dylan wondered what thoughts were racing through her mind. Regret? Yes. That had been her first thought when she'd gotten the news of her parents' accident. Regret that she hadn't spoken to them in a week. Regret that she hadn't gone to see them the weekend before. Then trying to remember their last words. Had she told them she loved them on their last phone call? Had they told her?

"My family was never very affectionate," Maddie said, her voice quiet. "My mother. Evan. There were never hugs, never endearments. My grandmother was a little more affectionate, but still stoic. Maraks, you know, are supposed to be impassive. Indifferent." Maddie turned to look at her. "Emotionless."

"Not you."

"No. I used to tease my grandfather that maybe I'd been switched at birth. Then he reminded me that I favored Isabel too much to not be a Marak." She wiped at a tear that ran down her cheek. "Isabel didn't fit that Marak mold either." Maddie took a deep breath. "The other day when I showed him your place, we stood by the firepit, admiring the valley and we talked about that very thing. I told him I didn't have to pretend with you. I could be myself with you. I could be Maddie with you. She is a completely different person than Madilyn Marak. That person is not real. She's a robot, going through the motions."

"I'm sorry."

Maddie turned to her. "I don't want to be that person anymore. Because that person wasn't very affectionate either, just like the other Maraks. That person didn't love." She wiped again at a tear. "That day when we were out there talking—talking from the heart—I told him I loved him. And he told me he loved me. Do you know that was the first and only time we'd said those words to each other?"

"Oh, Maddie."

"I know. So sad, isn't it?" She hung her head down and fresh tears fell. "I can't believe he's gone."

She reached over and took Maddie's hand again, feeling her squeeze it tightly. She kept the "I'm sorry" she was about to utter inside. She drove that way, with one hand, until they reached the gate to the Marak property. She punched in the code, waiting while the gate swung open. Maddie had recovered again, but she still kept a tight grip on her hand. When she was about to pass by the road that would take them to the orchard and her house, Maddie stopped her.

"I'd like to go to your place. I…I need some…" Maddie looked at her. "I haven't processed everything. I'm not ready to see them. I need some time." She was trying to hold back her tears. "And I could use a hug."

Dylan nodded. "Okay. I'm a pretty good hugger."

* * *

Dylan parked in her usual place, and they sat there quietly. "You want to go in, or…?"

"I'd like to go out back if that's okay."

"Sure. Come on."

They walked around the house to the back sitting area. She didn't know if Maddie really wanted a hug or if she wanted to talk. Maybe both. She got her answer when Maddie went to stand by the firepit.

"I've lost my friend." Maddie stared out at the valley. "I've realized that I don't have any." She shook her head. "Well, I didn't *just* realize it. But I've never had friends. You know, real friends. I never trusted anybody. That's an awful way to go through life, by the way. But my grandfather was my friend. I could talk to him. We were always close, but these last two months—"

"I'm your friend."

Maddie turned to her. "Yes. Yes, you are. Actually, I've talked more to you about my life, my feelings, than I have anyone else. Ever. Including him. You're so easy to talk to. But it's scary and I feel alone. He's gone. My mother and Evan are…somewhere." She waved a hand. "Greece, I guess, planning a wedding. And I'm—"

She moved closer. "I'm here, Maddie. You're not alone."

Maddie's lower lip was quivering. "I'm all mixed up now. We kissed. I haven't wrapped my head around that yet and now he's…he's gone, and I won't get to tell him about you."

Dylan pulled her closer, sighing quietly as Maddie buried her face against her neck. She felt her shaking, knew she was trying to hold back her tears. Dylan rubbed her hands across Maddie's back soothingly, pulling her a little tighter against her.

"It's okay to cry, honey."

Sobs came then and she cradled Maddie against her, feeling such a surge of protectiveness she wanted to wrap her in a cocoon and keep her safe. They stood there for long moments, she rubbing Maddie's back and Maddie clinging to her. Eventually the tears subsided, and Maddie finally lifted her head.

"Did you cry when your uncle died?"

"I did."

"You were alone?"

"Yes."

"I'm sorry, Dylan. I wish I could have been there for you."

She nodded slowly. "I wish you had been too."

Maddie touched her cheek and Dylan wondered if she would draw her closer for a kiss. Then Maddie's hand fell away, and she stepped out of her arms, wiping at the remaining tears on her cheeks.

"Thank you, Dylan. I don't know how I would have handled this if you weren't in my life."

"You're a strong woman, Maddie."

"Am I? Yes, I pretend to be. And if I was alone here, I would be. I wouldn't be afforded the opportunity to have a breakdown and a good cry. Marak women are stoic, you know."

"Except for you and Isabel?" she asked gently.

Maddie nodded. "Isabel cried so when Lorah left her. Cried for days." She wiped at another tear and tried to smile. "I cried when I read the diary. What does that say?"

"That says you've got a gentle, caring heart, Maddie."

"Oh, Dylan." More tears fell and Maddie impatiently wiped at them. "I do, yes. I just haven't been able to show it before."

"I'm glad you've shown it to me."

Maddie turned back to look at the valley, still wiping at her tears. Dylan went to the plastic box she kept by her grill and pulled out a napkin. She handed it to Maddie.

"Not exactly soft, but…"

Maddie gave a small laugh as she took it. "Thank you." She blew her nose and dabbed at her eyes. "I guess I should get back. I have calls I need to make."

"Will there be a big funeral?"

"Oh, no. Never."

"No? But he's a prominent figure, right?"

She nodded. "My grandfather was one of the wealthiest men in the Commonwealth, yes. However, the Maraks were never well-liked. That goes back to James Marak, Isabel's husband. To hear my grandfather tell it, he was ruthless. He made money, not friends. He, like my grandfather, never sought the limelight." Maddie moved around to the front of the firepit, her gaze back on the valley.

"The family plot is out here. When we buried my grandmother, there was no one there but our family and Loretta. I hadn't read the diary yet, so I wasn't curious about the other graves. Now I'd like to find Isabel's grave."

"Will there be like a service somewhere?"

Maddie turned around. "Like a religious ceremony? No. My grandfather said a few words when Grandma Belle was buried. Why? Does that seem strange?"

"I guess for most people, yeah. There's usually some kind of service. But my uncle? No. He didn't want anything. It was just me and Tanner there at the cemetery."

"My grandfather would be totally appalled if I organized something. He wasn't shy about giving away money. There are hospital wings with his name on them. College buildings have his name. But he mostly operated behind the scenes. He lived his life out here, with his Belle. I'm not implying that her passing urged him on. I don't think that's the case anyway. She'd been sick. He'd been prepared. They both were." She shrugged. "But he was eighty-nine. He liked to say he'd been living on borrowed time. All of the Marak men died young. In their sixties and younger."

With a sigh, Maddie turned around and came back over to her. "Thank you, Dylan. I'm so glad you're here."

She nodded but said nothing.

"Will you…will you come by the estate for dinner? Please? I don't think I could bear to see his empty chair."

"Of course."

"We didn't get lunch and you didn't get to do your shopping. I'm sorry for that."

"It's no problem. I can go another day. Maybe I'll sneak off early in the morning."

They stared at each other for a long moment, then Maddie leaned closer and brushed her lips across her cheek. Dylan closed her eyes, feeling Maddie's breath on her skin. When she opened them, Maddie was still there, watching her expectantly. It was one of those moments that she'd heard about—read about—but never experienced. The world stopped spinning and time stood still. The bird sounds faded, and the gentle breeze disappeared. All she heard was her heart beating in her ears. Maddie's eyes seemed to pull her closer and Dylan didn't resist. She cupped Maddie's face with both hands.

Their kiss this time was slow, gentle. Maddie's lips seemed incredibly soft, like satin against her own. A tiny moan escaped as Maddie's hands clutched at her waist, pulling their bodies closer. For a few glorious seconds, yes, time stood still. Then, as if getting back on track, everything seemed to speed up, including her racing heart. She felt dizzy as the world spun again, faster than before it seemed, and she found herself holding on to Maddie as they kissed.

How long they stood there—kissing—she didn't know. Maddie was the one to pull away. There was a look of wonder in her eyes—desire? Yet Maddie took a shaky step away from her.

"I like that…god, I like kissing you. You make me feel safe."

Dylan nodded. "Yes." Then, "I'll take you back."

Maddie took one last look at the valley, then took her hand and they walked back around the house. Instead of her truck, she got in the Gator. It would be quicker to get to the estate by taking the trails instead of the long road around.

They said nothing more about the kisses they'd shared that day. In fact, they said nothing else at all until she pulled up at the house. Maddie paused before getting out, as if gathering her thoughts.

"Dinner about six? Will you still come?"

"If you want me to."

Maddie turned to her. "Yes, I do. Please."

"Okay. I'll be here."

Maddie moved to get out, then stopped. She reached over and took her hand. "The kiss—well, I'm glad we kissed." She smiled. "Now I know how Isabel felt when Lorah first kissed her."

Before she could reply to that, Maddie was out and heading up to the house. She sat there for a while longer, conscious of the smile on her face. Then that faded. What was happening?

Were she and Madilyn Marak about to have an affair?

CHAPTER FIFTY-ONE

Madilyn stood in her grandfather's study, looking out to the gardens, feeling that she'd gathered herself enough to tend to business. The fact that she and Dylan had kissed wasn't quite the shock it had been earlier. She hadn't taken the time to dissect her feelings and she couldn't take the time now. That would have to wait. So, she pushed Dylan—and the kisses—from her mind.

The rose bushes that her grandfather had wanted had been planted and she spotted two that were blooming. She wondered if he'd gotten to see them. She moved around to his desk, absently glancing at the papers there. She sat down in his chair with a sigh, not knowing where to even begin.

She had consoled Loretta, who had been visibly shaken. Loretta had known—and worked for—her grandfather her whole life. Whether her grandfather would have ever admitted it—Loretta was like family. Actually, she was probably closer than family. Loretta had been there with him through it all.

She'd already called Bob Reeves at the Foundation. She'd called Mr. Randal, her grandfather's attorney, and Mr. Holdren, his accountant. She'd called Eric Bingham too. She picked up the papers on his desk, sorting through them, seeing his scribbled notes on how to disburse the funds from the sale of the leases.

Funnel some to the Foundation, Maddie, but I want you to keep the bulk of it. I know you'll say you don't need it, but that's not the point. It could go back to the trust funds, but I don't want Margaret or Evan to have it. Do with it as you want. More orchards? That seems to make you happy and that's all that I want for you. Be happy, Maddie.

She wiped at a tear and shook her head. Was it the orchard that made her happy? Or was it getting out and doing something productive? Or was it simply Dylan?

The mention of her mother, though, reminded her that she had yet to call her. She glanced at her watch. What was the time difference? Six or seven hours? Didn't matter. She took out her cell and placed the call. Four rings later, her mother's breathless voice answered.

"Madilyn? What a surprise."

Yes, she supposed it was. She rarely called her. "Hello, Mother." Should she just blurt it out? "I have some bad news, I'm afraid. Grandpops passed away this morning."

"Really? What happened?"

Madilyn wasn't very surprised at the indifference in her mother's voice. "He was eighty-nine, Mother. He collapsed here at the estate."

"Well, this is certainly not a good time for me, Madilyn. Not at all. I'm knee-deep in wedding plans at the moment."

"Good time? I'm sure he didn't choose this particular time on purpose, Mother."

"Yes, well, I imagine not. When do you plan to bury him?"

"I suppose as soon as you and Evan can get here."

"Oh, darling, that's not possible. Evan is on a yacht at this very moment on the Mediterranean Sea with some new friends. And I can't possibly fly back now. My wedding is in four days. Can't you handle it?"

"Handle it?" Unbelievable. She spun around in her chair, facing the flower gardens. "He was your father. Don't you want to be here?"

"Oh, Madilyn, I so wish I could, but it's just not possible. He would understand."

"Would he? Don't you care just a little?"

"Madilyn, you're almost twenty-eight years old. Don't suddenly think the family dynamics have changed. You always wanted things to be warm and fuzzy between us all and that was never the case with the Maraks. Father may have been gentle with you, but with me, he ruled with an iron fist. I was never close to him like I was with Mother."

Because Grandma Belle spoiled you rotten and Pops tried to rein you in, she thought.

"Now, what do we need to do?" her mother continued. "Do I need to sign something?"

"Do? Sign something?" she asked.

"About his money. His affairs."

She blew out her breath. Of course, that would be the only thing on her mother's mind. "There's nothing to do, Mother. I haven't seen his will, but he told me that most of his assets will go to the Foundation."

"*What?* The Foundation? But what about me? And Evan?"

"His death doesn't affect the trust funds, Mother. You know that."

"What about the estate then?"

She brought her gaze to the red roses. "I'm not going to sell the estate."

"You? Why do *you* get to make that decision? Evan and I should have a say. We—"

"Because I'm the executor and those were his wishes."

"He had planned to sell after Mother died. What changed?"

"He was bluffing. He was never going to sell. This is Marak land, and it shall remain as such."

"You're going to live there? By yourself?"

"I am," she said, surprising herself. "For the time being."

"What about Palmer?"

"What about him?"

"Doesn't he have a say in it?"

"Why would he have a say, Mother?"

"Well, I doubt he will want to move there after you marry."

"Marry? I'm not going to marry him. I've already told him that."

"And I told you he was a perfect fit for the family. Why, he would—"

"I'm not marrying him," she said forcefully. "I plan to stay here by myself for now. There are some decisions to be made for the Foundation and I imagine I'll need to go to Philly for that, but as of right now, I plan to make this my home."

"So, you're just taking over? Is that it? You're going to be making all the decisions for the family?"

"I'm carrying out his wishes, that's all. He left explicit instructions for everything. There are not really any decisions to make. Besides, you never took an interest in the Foundation."

"Well, I suppose it doesn't matter anyway. Whatever money the sale of the estate would bring is probably only a trivial amount to Richard, I'm sure. I won't need to worry about money." Madilyn could hear the smile in her mother's voice. "Did I mention that he has no children?"

"Yes, you did."

A laugh. "You should see the villa. It's spectacular, darling. And all I have to do is snap my fingers and someone is here at my beck and call."

"How nice for you."

"Well, I should get back. We're having champagne on the terrace. I simply love it here." Another laugh. "I hit the jackpot with this one, Madilyn."

"That's great. I hope the wedding goes smoothly. Goodbye, Mother."

"I'll send you pictures. You'll love it. Goodbye, Madilyn."

She leaned back and blew out her breath. *Unbelievable*, she thought again. But was it really? Her mother had probably already forgotten the reason she'd called in the first place. She doubted her mother would shed a single tear for him. She wondered if she would even bother to call Evan to let him know. God, how could they all be from the same family? No, there certainly were no warm and fuzzy feelings to be had.

There was a knock on the door, and she spun around. "Come in."

Loretta poked her head around the door. "Miss Maddie, I wanted to ask about dinner."

"Oh, yes. I'm sorry. I invited Dylan to join me. I didn't want to be in the dining room alone. I hope that's okay."

"Of course. Then I'll plan something—"

"No, no. Don't go to any trouble, Loretta. Nothing fancy."

"Wine?"

She shook her head. "Not tonight. And can we make it at six?"

"Six?" she asked disapprovingly. Six was an hour earlier than her grandfather's normal time.

"Yes. Please."

"You probably didn't have lunch. I could fix something up for you if you like."

Madilyn shook her head. "I did miss lunch, but I'm really not that hungry. So, don't make a big deal about dinner. Just a little something to eat."

Loretta nodded. "Very well. Six it is." She turned to leave, then paused. "I know this is all so sudden and you probably haven't had time to even think yet, but do you know what you'll do? I mean, should I look for a place to live?"

"Oh, Loretta, no. This is your home. I'm going to stay here like we'd planned, through the summer. After that, I really don't know how much I'll be here, but rest assured, I don't plan to sell. My grandfather wanted the estate to remain in the family. I'll honor his wish."

"That's such a relief, Maddie. You have no idea." Loretta gave her a smile before leaving. "Thank you."

She pushed away from his desk and went over to the credenza, picking up a framed photo of Pops and Grandma Belle. It had been taken years ago and they both looked so happy. Now, two months apart, they were gone. She brought the photo to her chest and closed her eyes, picturing her grandfather as he'd been that morning at breakfast.

Had he looked tired? In her mind's eye, he looked like he always did. She was the one who was preoccupied. She was the one who rushed through the meal. She shook her head. No. She wasn't going to feel guilty for that. Instead, she was thankful that she'd had this time with him. So thankful that he'd asked her to stay. She put the photo down again and went back to his desk.

She had no idea what he kept there, and she pulled out the center drawer, finding it neat and orderly. A few small pads of paper, four or five pens, and a pair of scissors. She pulled out the top side drawer on the right and the first thing she saw was a white envelope with her name printed boldly across it. It was his handwriting, and she took it out, staring at it for a long moment before opening it.

My sweet Maddie,

First of all, let me thank you for the joy you've given this old man by agreeing to stay here with me. After Belle left me, I really did intend on moving away. The reason being, I am sick, and I know my time is very short.

Her eyes widened. *What?* Sick?

I didn't tell Belle. She had enough to worry about. Randy is the only one who knows. He was my transportation to the doctor visits these last six months. I have a heart condition, Maddie. The doctor told me he was surprised I was still ticking! But after my Belle died, I no longer really cared. I stopped going to see the doctor. All these pills he's had me taking and then he wanted to do some kind of surgery on me. At my age? No. As I told you once before, I feel like I've been living on borrowed time as it was. Marak men don't get to experience all these extra years like I have. I'm thankful for that.

I'm sorry I didn't tell you. But like Belle, I didn't want you to worry. My wish is that you will take over the estate and make it yours. And what I mean by that, make it yours, not mine. Do with it what you want. I only ask that you take care of Loretta.

It makes me so happy that you've invested in the orchard again and that you seem to enjoy living out here with me. I hope I'll be around for a while, but something tells me that won't be the case. I wanted you to know how much I love you and how proud I am of you. You could have so easily followed in your mother's footsteps. That would have been the easy path to take.

When I'm gone, you know who all to contact. All of my affairs are in order. Your mother and Evan are to get nothing other than their yearly allotment from the trust funds. Everything else is yours. You now have the power to dissolve the Foundation if you choose, but I hope you will not. For all the wealth the Maraks have had over these many years, it is the first time it has gone to something good. With that said, make the Foundation yours too. I know you had some ideas to change the way we offer grants. Do what you want. You have my blessing.

Again, I'm sorry I didn't tell you. You are the most precious thing to me, Maddie. It pains me to know that I'll be leaving you all alone here. Promise me you won't end up like my mother, walking alone in her beloved orchard, still searching for what was missing in her life. If something is missing…go find it!

I know I didn't say it to you enough, Maddie, but I love you so very much. Be happy for me when I'm gone. I'll be with my Belle again.

Pops.

P.S. Remember that bottle of cognac I showed you? Open it for me. Have a toast in my memory. Then have a toast to the future. Your future, Maddie. Make it a good one!

Maddie dropped the letter as tears fell down her cheeks. She leaned back heavily in his chair, letting her tears come. It was almost too much to take it. No. It *was* too much. She got up and went over to the bar, taking a couple of napkins. She wiped her eyes and blew her nose, trying to regain her composure. She was in charge now. This was all hers.

Just what in the hell she was going to do with it, she had no idea.

CHAPTER FIFTY-TWO

Dylan stood by as Maddie struggled to open the bottle of cognac. She went over to her.

"Would you like me to give it a try?"

Maddie gave her a weak smile. "Please."

The bottle—Martell Chanteloup XXO—was sealed with a metal jacket. Once she got that off, she found a dab of wax over the cork. She removed that, then slowly twisted the cork until it popped out.

"This was a ritual after dinner," Maddie said. "At first, I wasn't really enthusiastic about it, but after a while, it became routine. We always had brandy, though."

Dylan could see the puffiness around Maddie's eyes and knew she must have had a good cry earlier. Dinner had been a mostly silent affair with her eating much more heartily than Maddie had—seared lamb chops with some buttery potatoes.

"Then why cognac? Because I'm certainly not an expert on it, but I thought XO was the best. This one has XXO so…"

"Yes. This bottle was special. He originally bought it for their sixtieth wedding anniversary, but Grandma Belle was in the hospital during that time, and he found another occasion special enough to open it. It wasn't the cost—I think he said he paid seven hundred dollars for it—but the fact that it had been aged eighteen years. He said the XO means it was aged ten years. The XXO means it was aged for at least fourteen years. He said there would have to be a very special occasion to get him to open it."

Dylan poured a small amount into the two glasses Maddie had put out.

"He told me to open it now." Maddie picked up one of the glasses. "He left me a letter and forgive me if I start crying again."

"Don't apologize for crying."

Maddie stared at her for the longest time before speaking. "Why haven't you mentioned the fact that we kissed?"

"I...I didn't think you wanted me to."

"You think I'm sorry that we did?"

"I'm thinking that you've got a lot going on and I don't need to add to it."

"Are *you* sorry we kissed?"

Dylan met her gaze. "No."

Maddie smiled at her. "Good. Because neither am I." She walked over to his desk and picked up a piece of paper. "He'd been sick. Or that's what he called it. A heart condition, whatever that means. Randy had been taking him to his doctor's appointments up until Grandma Belle died. After that, he stopped going."

"Do you think that's why he wanted you to stay here with him?"

"Yes. That's part of it, I'm sure. I think he was hoping I'd fall in love with the place, which I have." She put the letter back down. "He asked that I open this bottle and have a toast in his honor. And you were the one I wanted to share this with." She held her glass up. "To my grandfather. He was special and one of a kind. I will miss him."

Dylan nodded. "I'm sorry I didn't get to know him. May he rest in peace."

Maddie nodded too. "Yes. I hope he's reunited with his Belle."

They took a sip of the cognac at the same time. She was surprised by the sweetness of it. Of course, she supposed smooth would be the proper word to use.

"This is nice," Maddie said.

Dylan smiled. "Yes. It's a shame neither of us know a damn thing about cognac."

Maddie laughed lightly. "You're right. Do we even know how it's supposed to taste?"

She moved to the sofa and sat down, then patted the spot beside her. Dylan joined her there.

"With your grandfather gone, well, will that have a bearing on how long you stay? Or with him gone, will you have to sell all of this?"

"I'm the executor of his estate, yes, so I get to make that decision. I'm not going to sell, no. This land, the estate, has been in the family far too long to sell it. Besides, I have a sentimental attachment to it now."

"The orchard?"

"Yes. The orchard. Isabel and Lorah." She paused. "You."

"Having me here makes a difference?"

Maddie smiled. "I've grown quite fond of you, Dylan. You've brought out a side of me that I didn't even know existed. Or maybe I did, and I just suppressed it. I feel free to be me with you. I told you that before. I don't have to pretend. I don't want to go back to that life. If I left here and went back to Philly, that's what would happen."

"So, you're going to stay?" she asked hopefully.

"I'm going to stay through summer like I'd planned. With my grandfather gone, I'm fully responsible for the Foundation now. If I let things run like they have been, then I can work from here. If I make changes—like I want to—then I'll need to be at the office some. But I'll worry about that when the time comes."

"You think you'll be happy living here? I mean, once we get the orchard planted, there's not a lot to do. Keeping the trees watered through the summer months is the most labor. I won't do any pruning until February."

"Are you asking if I'm going to get bored here?"

"Do you think you will?"

"No. Because I *was* bored living in Philly. That's one reason I spent so much time at the office. If not that, then my days were filled with lunch dates and dinner parties and sometimes shopping sprees to kill time between those events. Out of my mind bored. But what about you? Will you get bored?"

"Me?" She shook her head. "No. But my life in Philly wasn't what I would call boring. I had my regular friends and I had work friends. We'd do happy hour and go out and bitch about bosses and all that. I was busy all the time. No downtime, really." She took a sip of the cognac. "I was happy. It seems I was out doing stuff all the time. Then when I moved here, I told you I tried to keep that going. Tried to go there on the weekends and hang on to that life. But it's different. Being out here, things are slower. And when I'd go there, I'd come back exhausted. It would be a whirlwind weekend, trying to cram all these activities in with different friends. Go out to eat, out to the bars, parties, drinking. I mean, it was fun, sure. But then you come back, and you're wiped out. And the older I got, the more I embraced the pace out here, the slowness of it." She laughed. "My old friends would think I'm terribly boring now. I'm at peace sitting on my little back patio, watching the valley, listening to the birds, staring at trees. You can't ever get that relaxed in the city."

"Yes. There's quite a bit of difference between being relaxed and at peace and being bored."

"Yes, there is. It took me a few years to figure that out."

"What about the friends you've made here?"

"Oh, yeah. I've made a few, but really, it's Tanner. We just clicked right away when we met. At first, he was someone to hang out with. Like he was a substitute for the friends I'd had. But when we were one-on-one, the friendship was so much deeper than what I'd had in Philly. Those were more superficial, I guess. Casual friendships where you don't really ever talk about anything deep, you know. I have that with Tanner. We can talk about anything, even though he's a guy." She looked at Maddie. "I feel like that with you, too. I can talk to you about anything."

Maddie smiled at her. "Anything? Anything except for that which makes us uncomfortable."

She smiled too. "You mean like kissing and stuff?"

"Yes." Maddie took a sip of her drink. "I want you to read the diary." She pointed to the desk. "I brought it down. I had it hidden in my bedroom. I was terrified of my grandfather finding it. I can't imagine what his reaction would have been."

"You mean finding out his mother had an affair with a woman?"

Maddie met her gaze. "He said she always seemed so sad. She always looked like she was searching for something. He told me I had that same look in my eyes. But I know Isabel wasn't searching for anything. She'd already found it. That look in her eyes was because she'd lost it. She wasn't strong enough to leave with Lorah when she asked her to."

"Did she ask?"

"Yes. Isabel said no." Maddie held her hand out. "Lorah gave her this ring."

Dylan touched the gold band on Maddie's finger. "The ring mentioned in the letter."

"Yes. I found it in my grandmother's old jewelry box upstairs. I didn't know what it was at the time. It caught my eye is all. Then I saw it in the picture." She got up then and went to the desk. She flipped through a book—the diary?—and came back with an old black-and-white photograph.

"This is them. Lorah and Isabel."

Dylan took the photo, a smile forming on her face. "My god, look at them. This is beautiful." Dylan glanced up at her. "You don't need to read it in a diary to know they were in love with each other."

Maddie smiled and nodded. "Yes."

Dylan touched the photo. "I see the ring. But who took the photograph?"

"I don't know. It's not mentioned at all in the diary. I guessed that maybe Hattie took it. Maybe she didn't give it to Isabel until after Lorah was gone. Maybe that's why it was just stuck in the diary like that."

She handed the photo back to Maddie. "I would like to read it."

"Yes. Of course." Maddie leaned against the desk. "And it won't be lost on you—the parallel."

Dylan arched an eyebrow. "You and me?"

"Yes. To be honest, it scares me to think about it in that way. Lorah mentioned it in her letter about them having loved each other in previous lives. And that they'd be together again in a future life."

Dylan got up and went to her. "Maddie, we're not Isabel and Lorah. As romantic as it is to think that they'll have another chance at love in another life, it isn't this one. They had their turn. Now it's ours."

"Never once in my life had I ever entertained the idea of being with another woman."

"And now?"

"And now I think about what it would be like to sleep with you."

Dylan nearly choked on her breath. "You're going to throw that out there, huh?"

"When we kissed out in the orchard, I was more aroused in that moment than I'd ever been before." Maddie moved away from her. "Now I have all these thoughts running through my mind. Some of my old fears pop up. Can I trust you? Do you have ulterior motives? Are you using me?" She shook her head. "And new fears. Like what the hell am I thinking? You're a woman! And yes, is this *us* or are we playing a part for Isabel and Lorah. Are we like puppets in an alternate universe or something?"

Dylan didn't know which of her fears to touch on first—the old or the new. For that matter, did Maddie expect her to?

"There are only a few things I can say to you, Maddie. Yes, I'm attracted to you. Yes, I've wanted to kiss you for weeks now. And yes,

I've thought about making love with you. But I can't address your fears. Those are *your* fears. You've got to work through them on your own. And now is probably not the right time. With your grandfather passing, you've got a lot to deal with. Let's don't complicate it any more than it has to be."

"I sometimes think you're more afraid than I am."

Dylan smiled. "Maybe. Is it that obvious?"

"Yes. I—"

Before Maddie could say more, her phone rang. She sighed and picked it up from the desk.

"Palmer. He has such impeccable timing, doesn't he?"

Dylan took a step away. "I should go anyway."

Maddie put the phone back down without answering. "I'm sure he's heard about my grandfather."

"Yeah. So, I should go."

Maddie came closer. "I afraid too, Dylan. Being attracted to another woman is something I have no experience with obviously. I think—"

Her phone rang again, and Maddie tilted her head back with a groan. "Oh, god, Palmer."

"Answer it. I'll see you tomorrow."

Maddie hesitated, then sighed. "Okay, Dylan. Tomorrow."

She nearly fled from the room, not knowing if Maddie answered the call from Palmer or not. Yes, she was afraid. Madilyn Marak, straight or not, was way out of her league. She had no business having an affair with her. But as she drove back to her little house, it occurred to her that it wasn't Madilyn Marak she was attracted to. No.

It was just Maddie.

CHAPTER FIFTY-THREE

"I didn't think you were going to answer."

"I'm sorry. I had...company," she said as she moved back to the sofa. "I assume you heard about my grandfather."

"Yes. I'm terribly sorry, Madilyn. I know how close you were to him. I suppose you'll be coming back home now."

"Home?"

"Yes. Back here. We can get together. Have dinner. We can talk—"

"Palmer, no. This changes nothing with us. I appreciate you calling, but you didn't have to." Apparently, her tone was a bit sharper than she intended.

"What is wrong with you? I call to offer my condolences and you treat me like this?"

"Like what? Palmer, you never even met my grandfather. You know nothing about him other than his last name. But I do appreciate you calling."

"Wow, Madilyn. I never really saw it before, but you actually *are* the Ice Queen, aren't you?"

"Call me what you want, Palmer. I don't care. Perhaps you and Brandon Raush should have dinner sometime. You can compare notes. And Palmer, this is the last time I will take your call."

She disconnected without a goodbye and immediately went to her contacts, blocking his number. That was something she should have done the last time they spoke. Even if she ended up going back to Philly and resuming her life there, she didn't want Palmer in it.

No. She also didn't envision going back there to live either. Like Dylan had found her peace out here, she felt the same. She felt connected to the land, the orchard, the estate. Really, for the very first time, she felt connected to her last name.

There were no constraints, no roadblocks. Her grandfather had given her his blessing. She could do things like she wanted to. She could make changes without having to answer to anyone. She could make the Marak name be anything she wanted now. *She* could be anything she wanted.

For the first time ever, she felt free. That thought brought a contented smile to her face.

CHAPTER FIFTY-FOUR

Madilyn rode with Randy in his Gator out to the family burial plot. They were to meet Mr. Wortham, the funeral director of the Wortham Family Funeral Home based in Lancaster, out here tomorrow afternoon and she wanted to make sure everything was in order. When she'd spoken to him yesterday, she'd been surprised to find out that her grandfather had everything already arranged. He had brought them the suit he wanted to be buried in weeks ago, he told her. And he'd picked out his own casket. While she found that to be a little bit morose, she knew that her grandfather had simply accepted the inevitable—and was probably anxious to join his Belle—and didn't want to burden her with any of that.

"I suppose he swore you to secrecy?"

Randy glanced at her and nodded. "I'm sorry, Maddie, but yes. He threatened me with my job if I told you."

"Do you know what kind of condition he had?"

He shook his head. "He just said his heart was wearing out. He said the doctor told him he should have been dead years ago."

"The romantic side of me wants to think that he held on for Belle. He couldn't bear to leave her here alone."

"I think you're right about that. As soon as Miss Belle passed, he told me he was done with the doctor."

Yes, she could almost hear her grandfather saying those very words. She also thought that perhaps he felt confident enough to leave this place, knowing that he'd transferred the family business on to her. And trusted her enough to handle it.

The family plot was on a small rise on the opposite side of the property from the orchard and estate. She'd been there only once before Grandma Belle had been buried and that was when her grandfather had taken her on a mini tour of the estate when she'd been but a teenager. The plot had held no interest to her at the time, though she remembered him walking among the graves and pointing out where his parents were buried.

What was different then was how well maintained the graves were. Bennie had kept up the family cemetery as well as he did the grounds around the estate, right down to planting flowers. Now? No. Her grandfather had someone come in and clean it up before Grandma Belle was buried but that was it. The road they were following now was overgrown as well. When Randy parked beside the wrought iron fence, she motioned to the overgrowth of weeds and grass among the graves.

"I know tomorrow is Sunday, but can you please contact the guys who have been maintaining the grounds and get them out here to do something with this? I'd like it to be cleaned up before they bring my grandfather on Monday."

"Of course. I'll call them as soon as we get back."

"In fact, Randy, have this be a part of the weekly routine. When Bennie was here, he had this looking so nice. Flowers and all."

"I'll see to it."

"Thank you. And I think it would be a nice touch to have some rosebushes planted near his and Grandma Belle's graves."

"Yes. Miss Belle used to love her roses."

He held the gate open for her and she walked in, going to her grandmother's grave. Grass was starting to grow over the fresh pile of dirt. She wasn't really surprised to find markers in the ground next to it. She pointed at them.

"He picked his spot out, I see."

Randy nodded. "He had me bring him up here one day last week." He moved in front of Belle's grave. "He stood right here for the longest time. Fifteen, twenty minutes, probably."

She could see that in her mind, him leaning on his cane, his eyes staring at the headstone. Was he only seeing Belle's name there or was he picturing his name chiseled in the marble as well?

She turned around, wondering where Isabel was buried. She didn't remember where he'd shown her. Besides, all the headstones were practically buried in the weeds themselves.

"They are coming up tomorrow afternoon to prepare the site. Please make sure the grounds crew has this cleaned up by then."

"I sure will. What time will they bring Mr. Albert out?"

"Monday morning at ten. I'd like you and Loretta to be here, of course. Julia too."

"I'd like that. Mr. Albert was always so good to me."

She smiled. "Even though he threatened to fire you if you told his secret?"

Randy laughed lightly. "Despite his age, he could still be intimidating."

"Yes, he could." She moved back to the Gator. "Thank you for bringing me out here."

"No problem. But if I may ask, are you going to stay here at the estate? Do I need to look for another job?"

"Nothing is going to change, Randy. I'm going to stay here for the time being, at least through summer. But I need you to oversee the grounds crew, for one. And I know Loretta relies on you to take her shopping. Nothing will change."

"Okay, good. That's a relief. Julia and I were talking about that last night, wondering what we'd do if you were going to sell or something."

"Not going to sell, no."

"And you're going to continue on with the orchard?"

"Absolutely."

He nodded. "I drove out there this morning, just to take a look at your progress. I saw Dylan leave."

"Yes. I believe she went over to Millersville this morning for grocery shopping."

Dylan had texted her a brief statement—*Going to my old favorite grocery store for shopping. Be back by noon.*

She had thought of mentioning to her that she could always have dinner with her every night. But she could tell last night that Dylan wasn't comfortable with the formality of the meal, even though she seemed to enjoy the food.

"I guess you're glad you hired her and not one of those men, right?"

She laughed. "So happy, yes. I know they were all more qualified than Dylan, but I needed someone who I could work with on a daily basis. Plus, I needed a friend. Dylan has become that."

"Yes, she seems to have fit in nicely out here."

Yes. Dylan fit in perfectly. And for only having known her such a short time—barely two months—she couldn't imagine Dylan *not* being out here. She was also sorry she'd listed off her litany of fears last night. She knew she could trust Dylan. That was silly of her to even think otherwise. As if Dylan was feigning this attraction between them for monetary purposes or something.

She should apologize to Dylan for that, she knew. Maybe later today, she would. Right now, she needed to get back. She had obligations to tend to. Her grandfather's attorney had called and left her a message earlier. It was about the obituary. Apparently, Pops had written it himself. Mr. Randal wanted to know if she wanted to look it over and perhaps add to it. Yes, she wanted to read it, but she knew she'd leave it just as her grandfather had wanted it.

Bob Reeves had been calling too, passing along many messages of condolences, and she knew there were some that she needed to call back personally—those donors that helped support the Foundation. He'd also said that they'd had several flower arrangements sent there, and he'd placed them in her grandfather's office, an office that he hadn't been to in years, she knew. She'd told him to place them in other offices so that someone would get to admire them. She doubted she would make an appearance there anytime soon.

She took another look at her grandmother's grave, then slid her gaze to where her grandfather would soon join her. She let out a heavy breath, then nodded.

"Thank you, Randy. I should get back."

CHAPTER FIFTY-FIVE

Madilyn leaned back in her grandfather's chair with a sigh. She felt like she'd been on the phone for hours. A quick glance at the clock told her that was indeed true. She spun around, her gaze going out to the garden flowers, which were bathed in sunshine. Amazing how quickly the new grounds crew had gotten everything looking as good as when Bennie had tended to it daily. This particular crew came out three, sometimes four times a week. She'd seen anywhere from three to five guys working at once. And poor Bennie had handled it all himself for all those years. She had wanted to contact him and let him know about her grandfather. She'd been saddened to learn that he'd passed away last year.

Her phone rang, interrupting her thoughts. She glanced at it. Bob Reeves again. With a shake of her head, she ignored it. She simply couldn't take any more right now. When the ringing stopped, she snatched up her phone, calling Dylan instead. The sound of Dylan's voice seemed to calm her instantly.

"Hey," she quietly returned Dylan's greeting.

"What's wrong?"

"I'm…exhausted. Mentally. Emotionally. I've been on the phone all day, it feels like. And I haven't had a second alone for me to process my feelings."

"It'll take some time, I'm sure."

Madilyn smiled. "My feelings for you, Dylan. Not my grandfather."

"Oh."

The smile left her face as she tried to put her thoughts into some sort of order. "I need to be honest with you. I'm terrified of making love with you."

"Because I'm a woman?"

She stared out the window, her gaze locked on the red roses. "No. Surprisingly, that's not it at all." She paused. "I don't think I know how to make love." She swallowed. "They call me the Ice Queen."

"Who calls you that?"

"The men I've slept with. There've only been three. And a fourth one who calls me that, I never even slept with. That should tell you something right there."

"And this is your warning to me?"

"Maybe. Yes." She sighed. "I'm not affectionate. I don't know *how* to be affectionate. And I guess I don't know how to make love."

"That's not true, Maddie. You are affectionate. You touch me all the time. When you're talking to me, you touch my arm. You are affectionate."

She leaned her head back and closed her eyes, feeling a tear escape at each corner. "I'm sorry."

"Maddie? Do you want to come over and talk?"

"No. I'm sorry. I'm just a mess right now, Dylan. I'm sorry I called you."

"Do you want me to come over there?"

"No." She got up quickly and went to her grandfather's bar, grabbing a couple of napkins. "But thank you. I should go before I make this any weirder than it already is." She cleared her throat. "I'm very tired. I'll talk to you tomorrow."

She put her phone down, letting her tears fall. God, why was she crying? What brought on the tears? She sat back down in his chair and blew her nose, trying to compose herself.

Why was she crying? What was she afraid of? Dylan? Why? Well, she's a woman, for one thing. She stared off into space. Had Isabel been afraid? Yes, she'd said she was. At first. But then later, no, she didn't think Isabel was afraid at all.

She shook her head. No, that wasn't why she was crying. Being afraid of making love with Dylan wouldn't cause tears.

Then what had? Emotional exhaustion? Yes, maybe she was overcompensating for her grandfather's lack of it. She glanced at the multiple notes scattered about. Notes from him, telling her where to find all his records, where she could find certain paperwork, what drawers to look for things in. Everything was all so matter-of-fact. Not emotional in the least. Judging by everything he'd left out for her to find, he must have known his time was short. Even then, he kept his emotions under control—the Marak way to the very end.

Yes, he'd left it for her to handle. Alone. Her mother couldn't be bothered. Evan probably didn't even know he'd died. And here she was, all alone, tending to his businesses, his Foundation, his fortune. Handling it.

The ringing of her phone reminded her of that. His accountant this time. With a sigh she picked it up.

"Yes, this is Madilyn Marak."

CHAPTER FIFTY-SIX

Dylan sat in one of the chairs, watching the night sky. Watching it but not really seeing it. She held a glass in her hand. She'd added more than the normal splash of the whiskey she liked—her Uncle Frank's Knob Creek. Her dinner had been a simple meal. She grilled two hamburger patties, then topped them with some steak sauce. A baked potato and green beans she'd opened from a can took up the remaining space on her plate. She supposed the dinner had been good because her plate was empty. She didn't really remember eating, though.

No. Her thoughts had been on Maddie. They still were. She'd sounded so tired. She'd sounded emotionally spent. And she'd sounded scared. She had almost driven over there even though Maddie had told her not to. In the end, she'd talked herself out of it.

She tried to push thoughts of Maddie away again. Instead, she thought back to those two old mother trees at the farm. She really couldn't believe that they were dying. After all these years, why now? She supposed she should go ahead and cut them down and save whoever bought the place that chore. Besides, she thought she might do something with the wood. Not that she was talented enough to build something, but she could take the wood somewhere. Have a cutting board made or maybe an outdoor cooking table that she could use here. Something like a butcher's block. She could even keep scraps for use in a campfire to add flavor to a steak.

She took a sip of her drink, then crossed her legs, one foot swinging idly back and forth. She should just go on to bed. She'd already showered and cleaned up the kitchen. Sitting out here trying to solve the world's problems was getting her nowhere.

She stood up and walked a little way past the firepit. It was a breezy night and she listened as the wind rustled the tree limbs around the house. Yes, she should go on to bed, but she felt restless, and she knew she couldn't possibly sleep.

She pulled her phone out of her pocket. It was almost ten o'clock. Was Maddie still awake? Or had her emotional day sent her to bed early? Didn't matter. She wouldn't call her.

Go to her.

She tilted her head. Go to her? Go see her? No. She couldn't just drive over there unannounced. Could she?

She shook her head, surprised at the urge she had to see Maddie. Like, see her right now.

Go to her.

She looked up, as if the words were spoken aloud. She turned back toward the house, half-expecting to see someone standing there. The shadows seemed to jump about as the wind blew and her eyes darted in all directions.

Go to her.

Without much thought, she went inside. Instead of going back to her bedroom, she found herself walking out the front door. Before long, the Gator was cruising along the trail, past the orchard and on to the shed. She stopped there and got out. There was a slight chill in the air tonight and she walked quickly around the shed and on to the house. She paused halfway there, frowning. Why had she parked by the shed? Why not drive right up to the house? For that matter, what in the hell was she even doing here?

She had half a mind to turn around and go back, but her feet seemed to move of their own volition. She was through the gate and up on the porch in a matter of seconds, it seemed. Would the door be locked? There was a gated entrance to the property nearly a mile away. Why would it be locked? She turned the knob and the door opened easily.

Wonder if there's an alarm?

She waited, but the house seemed eerily quiet. She moved up the stairs, taking each one slowly. Two soft lamps glowed along its length, lighting her path. She realized that her breathing was slow, shallow, measured. She also realized that the opposite was true of her heart. It seemed to be pounding nervously.

She paused at the first door for only a second, then opened it. It was a small room and even in the darkness, she could tell that it was empty. The bed was undisturbed. She closed the door again and moved on to the second. Before she even turned the knob, she knew that she'd find Maddie inside.

She opened it quietly and her breath seemed to be sucked right out of her. The curtains were flung open, the window raised. Starlight seemed to stream inside, illuminating the bed. Maddie lay there, on her side, facing the door. Dylan found herself staring at her, thinking she'd never before seen such a beautiful sight.

She swallowed nervously, wondering what she should do, wondering why she was even there in the first place. It was obviously a stupid idea. For one thing, she was probably going to scare Maddie half to death if she woke.

But no, that wasn't the case at all. Maddie's eyes fluttered open, looking right at her. Then she sat up on an elbow, her voice thick with sleep.

"Dylan?"

She swallowed again. "Yeah."

"What are you doing here?"

"I…I'm not sure, really. I had an urge to see you."

Maddie smiled. "An urge, huh?"

She sat up fully, the covers slipping down to her waist, revealing a baggy sleep shirt. It looked to be one of the new ones she'd bought on their shopping trip. Dylan moved closer and sat down on the edge of the bed beside her.

"I guess I thought maybe you might want to talk or something. You sounded, well, not yourself earlier."

Maddie shook her head. "I don't want to talk. I don't even want to think."

When Dylan would have moved, she felt Maddie's hand on her arm, felt fingers wrap around her. "Stay with me. Please."

"I…I should—"

"Isn't that why you came over, Dylan?"

Was it? No. Not consciously. Hell, she didn't know why she was there, sitting on Maddie's bed in the darkness, her heart hammering so in her chest.

"Take your clothes off, Dylan. Come to bed." A pause. "We'll talk or something."

She met Maddie's gaze, surprised at the gentle confidence she saw there. Not fear. Not panic. No. Maddie seemed quite composed. Unlike her, who was starting to tremble with fright. Were they going to make love? Right here? Right now?

"Don't be afraid, Dylan."

She managed to smile. "Shouldn't I be telling you that?"

Maddie's hand slid from her arm to her own fingers, wrapping hers between them. "Show me how to make love. Show me what it's like. Show me what Lorah and Isabel had."

Is that why she came over? So that this would happen? Hoping they might make love?

Yes.

CHAPTER FIFTY-SEVEN

Madilyn had a flashback to long ago dreams, back when she dared to dream about love. She always imagined someone coming to her, stripping her of her fears and making her delirious with desire. Making her wanton and bringing out her passion—she imagined them daring and dashing.

She never once imagined them as a woman.

But right now, as Dylan got into bed beside her, as Dylan reached for her and pulled her sleep shirt over her head, Madilyn couldn't imagine anyone else in her bed *but* Dylan. Dylan's fingers traveled along her face, her cheek, urging her back down. She was surprised at the calmness she felt, surprised that her mind wasn't darting in all directions. No. Dylan's touch was almost familiar, natural. Lips replaced the fingers along her cheek and then a mouth claimed hers, kissing her with both tenderness and urgency at the same time, making her moan as Dylan's body moved closer to hers.

She didn't know what to expect, didn't know how she should feel. Would it be like when Palmer touched her? When any man had touched her? No. She already knew it wouldn't. Dylan's touch was slow, gentle. Her mouth moved from her lips to her neck, nibbling there without hurry. Madilyn closed her eyes, feeling Dylan removing the one barrier still separating them. Dylan pushed them down her legs and she kicked them away impatiently as her hands pulled Dylan closer. Lips moved across her mouth again, drawing her into a deep kiss, one that made her shiver with want. Then Dylan moved lower, grazing a nipple, making her moan as a tongue bathed her. She moaned louder when Dylan's mouth settled over her. Her hands cupped her head, holding her tight against her breast. She closed her eyes, reveling in the feeling of her mouth and tongue bringing her to heights she'd longed for but never thought possible.

Dylan's knees urged her legs apart and she spread them, letting her settle there. Her hips arched up, meeting Dylan's first thrust. She let her hands travel across her naked back, settling at her hips. She pulled her close against her, arching up again to press them together. She knew she'd never been this aroused before, knew now that she'd only been going through the motions with others, with Palmer. Because this felt so completely different. Before it could even register how wonderful it felt to have Dylan pressed intimately against her, she moved lower, kissing across her skin, nibbling at her stomach, at the curve of her hips.

She knew then that she should be afraid. She should be scared to death by what was happening. But Dylan's mouth moved lower, and when her hands cupped her hips, any thoughts of fear vanished. Any thoughts at all vanished. She almost felt like she was floating on an ocean wave, rocking her up and down. She felt herself arching up, seeking Dylan's mouth. Her fingers were grabbing the sheets, clutching them into her fists as if trying not to fall. A loud gasp escaped followed by a deep, guttural moan when she felt Dylan's tongue move into her wetness.

She cried out when lips settled over her clit, making her nearly rip the sheets as she held on tightly. Her eyes were squeezed shut and she heard herself drawing ragged breaths. Then it was as if her mind faded to black and went completely blank. She let herself get swallowed up by that ocean wave, let it carry her off into a blissful, magical place where shooting stars and colorful rainbows collided.

She felt herself climax—she did. She felt her orgasm rip through her—she cried out from the pleasure of it. But still, she floated away, drifting out into her peaceful ocean and away. It was a beautiful place where she went. Magnificent. She heard her name being called from far below. Dylan's voice. She felt lips on her skin again, felt hands touching her.

Then all was quiet. A gentle peace settled over her. She felt an arm snake across her waist, felt the sheets being pulled around them. She tried to open her eyes. She really did, but they wouldn't cooperate.

"Let's sleep for a bit."

She felt her mouth open, but no words came out. She turned her head and snuggled into the warmth beside her. The arm at her waist tightened. She finally found her voice.

"That was fantastic."

CHAPTER FIFTY-EIGHT

Madilyn stood at the window, her gaze locked on the rose bushes. The coffee in the cup she held was probably long cold and she put it on the desk without tasting it. She moved a little closer to the window, as if wanting to feel the sun on her skin. Yes. She wanted to be outside.

She left the study and made her way through the back of the house, going to the large double doors that opened onto the sprawling back porch. She went out and down the steps, moving onto the walkway that would take her to the gardens. She walked up to the rose bushes she'd been admiring from afar. She bent closer, inhaling their fragrance.

She was beyond exhausted, yet the smile on her face belied that. She didn't imagine that they'd slept more than three or four hours total, but the night—and morning—had been far too exhilarating to make her feel tired.

Surprisingly, her thoughts went to Palmer, not Dylan. She'd never had an orgasm with Palmer. He knew it, too. She blamed herself, as did he, she was sure. She was the Ice Queen, after all. She'd always been embarrassed by it, but Palmer hadn't seemed to care anymore.

It had been effortless last night, though, and she'd learned a lot about herself. She'd been surprised at how natural it felt to touch Dylan, how easily she was aroused, how comfortable she'd been making love to another woman—and bringing another woman to orgasm.

She nearly blushed now as she recalled all that they'd done. She folded her arms across herself and moved down the walk. Yes, they'd done unbelievably intimate things with one another, and it so eclipsed all the times she'd been with Palmer, she had to question why she'd continued to sleep with him.

She knew why and it wasn't her normal fallback answer—safe and familiar. No. That wasn't it. It was because she truly thought that was all there was to it. At least for her. Ice Queen. She thought she was incapable of enjoying a fiery sex life. She had doubted she would ever know what it felt like to have a soul-shattering orgasm. One that rendered her speechless and unable to move. One that made her see stars as she climaxed and left her nearly paralyzed with pleasure.

Not only once, no. She looked up into the sky and smiled. Not only once. God, who would have thought her capable of reaching such heights multiple times? Not her, certainly. Of course, she now knew how Isabel had felt. She'd gotten the diary out earlier, rereading the entry that Isabel had posted after she and Lorah had made love for the first time.

What a magical night it was. I thought I would be scared (and maybe I was) but Lorah's touch felt so natural, so real, I didn't want her to stop. I have never been more thoroughly loved before. It was magical, yes, but so very sad at the same time. Sad, because I'm married to a man who never once touched me that way, who never once loved me that way.

Yes, she saw the parallel, obviously, between herself and Isabel—and Palmer and James. Isabel hadn't been strong enough or confident enough to leave James and go with Lorah. That was the really sad part of it all. Isabel sacrificed her own happiness—and her life, as it turned out—to stay with a man she didn't love.

Regardless of what happened between her and Dylan in the future, she was particularly thankful that she'd come to her senses about Palmer. She was better off alone than pretending to have a life with him.

What she really wished, though, was that she and Dylan could have some time. She wished they could have a lazy day today, maybe holed up at Dylan's house, hiding away for a few hours.

Dylan had escaped just as dawn was breaking. A few long, lingering kisses, then she'd dressed in the darkness and fled down the stairs before Loretta could catch her. Maddie had then fallen back into bed in an exhausted heap, but even so, she was too aroused to sleep. Scenes from the night replayed over and over in her mind, and she finally got up, chasing them away with a nearly cold shower.

She had business to tend to this morning. Calls were still coming in, and she wanted to be at the plot when Mr. Wortham's crew came out to prepare the burial site today. Dylan said she was going to be at the orchard, digging holes. She smiled, wishing that was on her agenda too. But not today. No. Today she had to be Madilyn Marak. She would bury her grandfather in the morning and then, finally, she could just be Maddie.

Maddie. A woman who was on the verge of falling in love. What a novel concept that was.

She was smiling as she headed back into the house, pleased that the prospect of falling in love with Dylan didn't send her running. No. She felt like singing. And dancing. With a grin, she did a little skip as she hurried up the steps.

CHAPTER FIFTY-NINE

Dylan walked slowly along the edge of the orchard, admiring the new trees they'd put in. While she'd told Maddie she would dig some holes today, she just didn't have the energy—or the want to—to work. Instead, she strolled among the apple trees, stopping at the cluster of old trees she'd left. She inspected the branches, smiling when she found young apples growing there.

Or maybe she was smiling for a completely different reason. She walked on, going to the maple trees at the overlook. She still had a hard time wrapping her head around the fact that she'd not only crept into Maddie's bedroom last night, but that she'd stayed until morning. And what a morning it was. Again, a smile as she stared out at the valley. While they hadn't talked about where they would take this, that steamy kiss Maddie gave her as she was leaving left little doubt. Well, she supposed there was *some* doubt. You don't just jump into an affair with a straight woman and think it'll all go smoothly.

She shook her head. No. Maddie wasn't straight. She'd only thought she was. Assumed that she was. Dylan could still hear the words Maddie had uttered last night.

God, so this is what making love is supposed to feel like. Who knew?

She smiled again as she remembered Maddie rolling them over, picturing Maddie resting her weight on her. She—

A sound came from behind her, and she turned, finding Maddie pulling up in the golf cart. Dylan leaned against the tree, their eyes locking as Maddie got out. Was that fear in them? Or uncertainty? As Maddie hesitated, Dylan decided that no, it wasn't fear there. Insecurity, maybe, as if Maddie didn't know how they should act around one another now. Dylan pushed off the tree and went to her.

She didn't say anything. She simply leaned closer and kissed her. She could feel the tension leave Maddie as soon as their lips met. Maddie's arms went around her shoulders and Dylan pulled her closer, mashing their bodies together as they kissed. She moaned when she felt Maddie's tongue touch hers.

Maddie was the one to ease out of the kiss, then, as if she'd not had enough, she came back again. Dylan molded every part of their bodies together as her hands moved freely down Maddie's back and to her hips. Maddie arched against her, then pulled away, her eyes nearly wild with desire.

"Good god, Dylan," she breathed. "I feel like I'm on fire."

Dylan ran a hand through her hair, trying to catch her breath. "So…hello."

Maddie smiled. "Hi."

Dylan grinned back at her. "Miss me?"

"I did. I've been on the phone all morning, it seems. And I've just come from the family burial plot. They are preparing it for tomorrow."

She nodded. "Are you holding up okay?"

"I am, yes. There will be a lot to sort through in the coming weeks and I don't even want to think about all that yet. I'm tired. After tomorrow, I just want to take some days to…well, just some days where I can be myself. Be Maddie."

"Do you want those days alone? By yourself? Or—"

"I think we have trees to plant, don't we?" Maddie took her hand. "Actually, I was hoping that I could stay with you."

She raised her eyebrows. "Stay with me?"

"Yes. For a few days. Would you mind? Or would that be awkward?"

"No, I'd love for you to stay." She squeezed her hand. "In fact, you can stay tonight if you want."

Maddie dropped her hand and went to the golf cart. "I brought you something. The diary. I'd like for you to read it." She held it cradled in her hands. "I know you said that I wasn't Isabel, and you weren't

Lorah." Maddie handed the diary to her. "I wasn't sure I believed you. Until last night, that is. Last night, I felt like I was reborn." She smiled. "I felt whole. Like all the missing pieces were falling into place. I felt like *me*. Like what I always thought I could be. I didn't feel like Isabel any longer."

Maddie came up close to her. "Read the diary. I think it'll explain how I'm feeling. And then I think we should talk. And yes, I'd like to stay with you tonight." She leaned closer and gave her a light kiss on the lips. "If you want to run after we talk, I'll understand."

"If you think I'm afraid of this, you're mistaken."

Maddie squeezed her hand tightly. "You might not be, but I certainly am." She moved away then, back to the golf cart. "I've got a call scheduled with his attorney at three. I should go."

"You want to have dinner?"

Maddie shook her head. "No. When I come over, I don't want to eat. I just want to be with you."

Dylan nodded. "Okay." Then she smiled. "Come early."

Maddie smiled too as she drove away. With a sigh, Dylan went back to the tree. She slid down its trunk to the ground, relaxing against it, much like she used to do at the old apple trees at the farm. She gazed out over the valley for a minute, then opened the diary.

I walked to the orchard today. The apple blooms are mostly gone, but they were oh so beautiful while they lasted. This is my second spring to see them. I can't decide which season I like the most in the orchard...

CHAPTER SIXTY

"You want to eat when? At five?"

"Yes."

"It's because you skipped lunch again," Loretta fussed. "If you would—"

"Loretta, that's not the reason." She took a deep breath. "I have something to do this evening and I won't be here. So, if you could have something ready at five for me. And something light, please. Don't go to any trouble."

Loretta stared at her for the longest time and Maddie wondered if she would dare ask her what she had planned for the evening. But no. Loretta had worked for the Maraks all her life. She knew not to ask questions.

It might be simpler to just tell her that she'd be with Dylan, but she reminded herself that she was the boss and Loretta worked for her. Loretta didn't need or require explanations as to her whereabouts. Yes. Her grandfather would be proud of her for that thought, at least.

"Very well. Five it is."

Maddie sighed. "Loretta, I'm going over to Dylan's house tonight. I'm going to stay with her for a few days—and nights."

"Oh. Well, I guess with Mr. Albert gone, you—"

"No. That's not it at all."

She met her gaze and Maddie saw recognition set in and the slight blush on Loretta's face confirmed it.

"*Oh*. I see."

It was Maddie's turn to blush. "We've become…close."

Loretta smiled at her. "My Aunt Hattie always said that the orchard was a magical place full of love. Said that's why Miss Isabel used to go there so often."

Maddie let out a relieved breath. "Yes, it is. Thank you, Loretta, for understanding."

Loretta nodded, then turned to leave. She stopped at the door. "Will you require meals while you're with her?"

Maddie shook her head. "I don't think so, no."

"Well, then I'm wondering if it might be possible for me to take a few days off then? I haven't visited my sister in more years than I can recall."

"Oh, Loretta, of course. It never occurred to me, I guess. You were always expected to be here, weren't you?"

"Yes. And that was my job. Mr. Albert and Miss Belle needed me here every day and I was."

"Everyone needs a break from their job, Loretta. Yes, please. Go visit your sister. Take a week if you like."

"Really? A whole week? You wouldn't mind?"

"Of course not."

"She lives in Cleveland. Do you think that's too far for Randy to drive me? I could maybe take a bus, I guess."

"You will not take a bus," she said firmly. "I'll speak to Randy. Go call your sister and make plans."

"Thank you, Maddie. She's going to be so excited."

Maddie smiled as Loretta nearly danced from the room. For as fond as her grandfather had been of Loretta, he still had treated her like a servant. She wondered if Loretta had ever had a true vacation from work. She supposed the weekly shopping trips with Randy were her sole escape from the estate. What a lonely life she must live. It had probably been ten years already since her grandparents had started shrinking the household staff. Julia and the cleaning ladies who came twice a week were her only means of conversation now. How sad for her.

She picked up her phone to make arrangements with Randy while wondering if she should speak to Julia about hiring a full-time staff to live here at the estate. She dismissed that thought almost as soon as it popped into her head. She was one person living here. What would she need a staff for?

CHAPTER SIXTY-ONE

Dylan was nearly embarrassed by the tears in her eyes as she folded up Lorah's letter to Isabel. She put it back into the diary and took out the old photograph instead. She stared at it for the longest time. You'd have to be blind not to see the love between them. Just this one snapshot in time had captured it completely. She, like Maddie, wondered who had taken the photo. And, like Maddie, she guessed it must have been Hattie.

She leaned her head back against the tree. Yes, the similarities between Isabel and Lorah and Maddie and her were glaringly obvious. And she could see how Maddie had thought they might be living in this alternate universe as she'd called it. She also knew why getting the orchard going again was important to her. The orchard had been a refuge of sorts for Isabel and Lorah. The apple trees had become a symbol of their love.

And a reminder of it. She couldn't imagine the strength Lorah had needed to walk away from the love of her life. She hadn't wanted an affair with Isabel. She wanted a life with her. Isabel, on the other hand, wasn't strong enough to walk away from her loveless marriage. In the end, their love affair had done nothing more than ruin two lives.

They had one summer of love and romance, then nothing. Isabel had wasted away but not Lorah. She wondered at Lorah's state of mind when she'd read Isabel's obituary. Had a part of her died right then too? She closed her eyes for a moment, trying to grasp the depth of Lorah's love—and loneliness.

Were she and Maddie traveling the same path? Were they falling in love? Were they going to have these same decisions to make a few months down the road?

Because like Lorah, she didn't want an affair. And yes, she *was* falling in love.

CHAPTER SIXTY-TWO

Maddie was feeling a little shy and perhaps embarrassed to be going to Dylan's house with the sun still shining over the valley. Not going visiting, no. She was going with the intention of having sex with her. She shook her head then. No. Not sex. What she and Dylan had done last night was far too intimate and personal to be labeled that simply.

When she went onto the porch, the door opened and the look in Dylan's eyes chased any apprehension away. She didn't hesitate as she moved into her arms. Their kiss turned heated immediately, and it occurred to her that she was finally having that euphoric, head-over-heels-in-love feeling that she'd always longed for. Like she couldn't kiss deep enough, couldn't get close enough, couldn't love hard enough.

Dylan ended the kiss and there was such a sweet smile on her face, Maddie was left in wonder of it. She gently touched Dylan's cheek, then ran a finger across her lips.

"This is going to sound strange, but I feel like I'm not really here."

Dylan raised her eyebrows. "What do you mean?"

"It's like…I'm watching a movie about someone else. Not me. Because there is no way I should be feeling like this." She slid her hands up Dylan's arms and around her neck. "I feel so alive. Like every cell in my body is smiling and singing and…and dancing."

Dylan pulled her close. "Do you need to talk?"

Maddie shook her head. "No. Not yet. Let's just go to bed."

Dylan's answer was a slow, sensual kiss that nearly buckled her knees. No, she didn't want to talk. She just wanted to make love.

CHAPTER SIXTY-THREE

Dylan leaned against the pillow, smiling as Maddie rested her head on her stomach. She ran a hand through Maddie's hair, feeling a contentment she never expected. The bed—the sheets—were a tangled mess and she closed her eyes, enjoying the feel of Maddie's fingers as they moved slowly up and down her leg.

"I think I'm insatiable," Maddie murmured.

"I'm not complaining."

Maddie rolled over, laying sideways on the bed now. Her head was still against Dylan's stomach, and she felt lips move against her skin.

"Do you think Isabel and Lorah felt this way? Do you think they tried to cram in a lifetime of loving in a few months?"

"Is that what you feel we're doing?"

"Not in the same sense that they must have. They knew James would return and their affair would end. No, for me, it's more like making up for lost time." Maddie looked up at her. "You know, the Ice Queen and all that."

Dylan smiled at her. "After everything you just did to me, you dare use Ice Queen to describe you?"

Maddie sighed. "God, that was nice, wasn't it?"

"I'll say."

Maddie laughed quietly. "Like I said, insatiable."

Dylan watched as Maddie's smile faded. "Are you ready to talk?"

Maddie sighed. "I guess we should, huh?"

Maddie lifted her head and righted herself on the bed, plumping up pillows next to her and leaning back.

"I read the diary this afternoon, up against that maple tree there at the overlook."

"Their picnic spot," Maddie stated.

"Yes. And I can see why you felt like Isabel and Lorah had come back to life."

"Did you fall in love with them?"

Dylan nodded. "I did. And it had a tragic ending."

"Why do you think Lorah never came back? I mean, James was gone all the time. They could have easily continued their affair. Hattie and the others were loyal to Isabel and Lorah. They would never have told James."

Dylan took her hand and entwined their fingers. "Lorah was madly in love with Isabel. If their affair was only sexual, then I think, yeah, she might have come back around."

"I keep thinking that it was 1933. Maybe divorce was unheard of. I don't know. But still, as much as Isabel loved her, why didn't she just leave with Lorah?"

"Maybe she liked the big house, the servants, having money. With Lorah, they would have nothing."

Maddie shook her head. "No. I never got the impression that Isabel was swayed by money. I think it was more of the obligations she had. She was the lady of the house. A Marak. There were expectations."

Dylan met her gaze. "And for you too now?" she asked hesitantly.

"Yes. My mother is planning her wedding and can't be bothered to come and bury her father. Evan is on a yacht somewhere," she said, waving her other hand in the air. "And I'm left here to handle it all." Maddie moved closer to her. "But I'm not Isabel. There is no one here to dictate what my obligations are or what expectations they have of me. I'm free to determine those things on my own."

Dylan asked the one question that had been weighing on her mind the most. "Will you stay here? Or go back to Philly?"

Maddie sighed and squeezed her fingers tightly. "If I tell you something, will you promise me you won't freak out? Or run?"

"Okay. I promise."

Maddie locked gazes with her. "I don't want to leave here. I don't want to deal with the family business right now. I just want to be with you. I want to spend some time with you. Like this."

Dylan held her gaze. "Why?"

"*Why?*"

"Tell me why." She could see Maddie swallow nervously.

"You're going to make me say it?"

"Yes."

Maddie finally looked away from her gaze. "I'm afraid to, Dylan."

"Tell me," she nearly whispered.

"What if...what if I'm wrong?"

"Oh, Maddie. Say the words."

Maddie looked back at her. "I'm in love with you. There. I said it."

Dylan nodded. "It was the picnics. It was you with dirt on your jeans. It was you with mortar on your cheeks. It was you crying over Isabel's letter. I fell a little bit in love with you every day, Maddie. And I was freakin' scared to death," she said with a smile.

"Is this real, Dylan?"

"Yes. It's you and me. It's not them. Like I said before, it's our turn."

CHAPTER SIXTY-FOUR

Maddie didn't know why she felt the need to dress up in one of her nice suits—there was no one there to judge her if she'd not. Regardless, she'd dressed in the same suit she'd worn when they'd buried her grandmother. Randy and Julia stood in front of Grandma Belle's grave. Loretta stood next to them. Maddie stood at the base of her grandfather's grave, her eyes on the beautiful casket that he'd picked out himself. A large display of red roses adorned the top and Mr. Wortham stood several feet away, giving them some privacy. He'd been there for her grandmother's burial, and he knew there would be no ceremony.

She had rehearsed what she was going to say, but those words failed her now. She turned and looked at Dylan. Dylan nodded at her.

"I didn't know Mr. Marak, of course. Not like you all did. From everything Maddie has told me, he was a kind and generous man."

Maddie took her hand and squeezed it, silently thanking her. "He told me once that his father would have been appalled to know that he'd taken the family fortune and created a charitable foundation. And yes, he was kind and generous. But most of all, he loved Belle more than anything in this world. I think Randy can attest to that. Once she was gone, I think he lost the zest to keep living."

Randy nodded. "Yes. He told me he was through with doctors after that."

Loretta held a tissue to her eyes. "I'd known Mr. Albert my whole life. I keep thinking I'm going to hear his cane come tapping along the floor."

Maddie laughed quietly. "I know. I miss the sound of it." She took a deep breath. "Albert Marak, my dear grandfather. May you rest in peace beside your Belle." She looked over at Mr. Wortham and nodded. "Thank you."

"Yes, ma'am."

She moved with the others away from the site. She motioned to the other graves. "Everything looks so nice, Randy. Thank you for getting it cleaned up."

"Sure thing, Maddie. And I told them to make this part of the routine. And they're going to get some rose bushes planted up here too."

"Very nice. Thank you."

He motioned to the truck he'd driven up there in. "I guess we're going to get back. I have a few things to do. Loretta wants to leave first thing in the morning."

"How long of a drive is it to Cleveland?"

"About six hours, I think. Julia is going with us. If it's okay, I thought maybe we'd stay overnight, take in a fancy dinner or something."

Maddie nodded. "Absolutely. In fact, if you want to take a few days off, that's fine with me. There won't be anything going on here."

"Really? Well, thank you, Maddie. We might take you up on that offer. It's been a while since we've both been away."

She smiled at them and nodded. "And, Loretta, enjoy your visit with your sister. We'll need to make this an annual thing from now on."

Loretta surprised her by coming closer to give her a brief hug. "Thank you, Maddie. That means so much to me."

Maddie waved them away. "Have a safe trip. See you next week."

As soon as they left, Dylan leaned closer. "Let's find Isabel's grave."

Yes, as she'd told Dylan that morning, she was anxious to see it. Now that everything had been cleaned up, it was easy to find. There wasn't a joint headstone with James, however. They each had their own.

Maddie stared at it, slowly shaking her head.

"Loving wife and mother," Dylan read out loud. "Taken too soon."

Maddie shook her head again. "That's awful. Isabel would have hated it."

"So let's change it."

Maddie turned to her. "Can we?" she nearly whispered.

"Why not?"

Maddie grinned. "Yeah. Why not?"

CHAPTER SIXTY-FIVE

"Can you believe we're the only ones here?" Maddie turned a circle with her arms held out. "I mean, no one's at the house, no one is anywhere on the estate. We have like a thousand acres all to ourselves. No. More than that. There's five hundred right here on this side of the creek."

Dylan smiled at her. "Want to run around naked?"

"We could." She went to Dylan and kissed her. "Yesterday was nice. Your steak dinner was excellent. The campfire was cozy." She kissed her again. "Sleeping with you last night, waking up with you…perfect."

"Raiding Loretta's kitchen for our picnic?"

Maddie laughed. "That was fun, yes."

She stopped at the edge of the bridge. It was a beautiful day for a picnic, and she'd decided on the bridge instead of the overlook. Dylan carried the basket, and she held the blanket. She walked across the bridge carefully, going to the opposite side of the creek where they'd picnicked before.

She spread the blanket out and sat down. Dylan joined her. From the basket, Dylan produced a bottle of wine. One of the sweet varieties that she liked, and Maddie was curious to taste it. She was also anxious to taste the pasta salad that Dylan had whipped up for their lunch.

"I was thinking that maybe next weekend I could invite Tanner and Jenna out and we could do a real cookout," Dylan said. "What do you think?"

"Yes. I like them. That would be fun. But a real cookout?"

"Yeah. Cook over the fire, eat outside."

She nodded. "You know, there are like eight bedrooms at the house. Why don't you invite them to stay overnight?"

"Really?"

"Yes. All those rooms just go to waste. I'm sure Loretta would love to do up a big breakfast." She watched as Dylan carefully unwrapped the wineglasses they'd packed. "I've been thinking about that anyway. The house is far too big and not something I would want to live in."

"Too impersonal?"

"Yes. Exactly. It's a showcase. There's no warmth there. It's...the Maraks. The opposite of that." She smiled. "And as I've told you, I don't want to be like the Maraks."

"So what are you thinking? You said you didn't want to sell it."

"No, I couldn't. But what about turning it into a bed and breakfast sort of thing?"

Dylan poured wine into a glass and handed it to her. "Tell me what you're thinking."

"It would give Loretta a purpose. And I could hire a couple more full-time ladies to live there. The servants' quarters where Loretta lives has three bedrooms. There's a large bedroom downstairs where my grandfather stayed plus one more. There are six bedrooms upstairs. It's enormous." She took a sip of the wine and smiled. "Yes. Sweet. I love it."

"You won't find this at any fine restaurants," Dylan warned with a smile. "Scandalous."

"And I don't care. I imagine the homemade wine that Lorah brought for Isabel was sweet, wouldn't you think?"

Dylan took a sip from her own glass. "Go on. Tell me your plans."

Maddie looked past Dylan to the woods behind the creek where the giant hemlock stood. "I think I want to build a house. Over here on this side of the creek."

"Really?"

"Yes. Nothing extravagant. Something functional." She smiled. "With an outdoor cooking area."

Dylan leaned back on an elbow. "Seems like you'll need a cook then, huh?"

"Yes. I'm hoping to hire one." She grinned. "Interested?"

"Well, I'll have to check with my boss. I'll have three hundred trees to tend to, you know."

Maddie leaned back too. "I feel so free, Dylan. Like all of a sudden, there are no rules. No limits on what I can do. No one judging me. I didn't realize how confined—how constrained—I'd been. And I'm totally free of that now."

"If your grandfather were still alive, would you have allowed yourself to be with me?"

Maddie considered the question. It was one she'd asked herself already. "I was attracted to you from the start. I knew I was. I just didn't want to put words to it, didn't want to name it. And the more time we spent together, the more I wanted. So yes. Whether my grandfather was here or not, I'd still have fallen in love with you."

Dylan met her gaze, holding it. "That doesn't answer my question. Isabel fell in love with Lorah too. But their affair ended."

"My grandfather would not have approved, no. Not necessarily because you are a woman." The word *commoner* came to mind, but she would never say that to Dylan. "That wouldn't have mattered. I'm twenty-seven years old. You're the only person who has ever made me feel this way. I would have run from him and my name before I'd run from you, Dylan."

Dylan smiled at her. "Well, you know what? If you'd run, I would have chased you. No way I'd be like Lorah and walk away."

Maddie leaned closer and kissed her. "If you had done like Lorah and left me, I would have come to find you." She kissed her again, a deep, nearly smoldering kiss that made her breath catch. "Have you ever made love on a bridge before?"

CHAPTER SIXTY-SIX

"Whose idea was it to get three hundred trees? I swear, you're trying to kill me."

Dylan laughed at her. "We have nineteen more to go, then we're done. Can you believe that?"

Maddie sat down fully on the ground. Her hands were filthy. Her knees were filthy. Her shorts had stains on them that she doubted would ever come out. "I say we stop now."

Dylan put her hands on her hips. "Nineteen, Maddie. That's a drop in the bucket. We can whip those out in couple of hours."

Maddie laid down and closed her eyes. "No."

"So you're done?"

"I want a beer."

"It's two o'clock. If we stop for a beer break, we'll never get started again."

Maddie turned her head to look at her and smiled. "I know. See how clever I am."

Dylan laughed. "Okay. You *are* the boss. Beer break." She held out a hand to help her up. "So, we'll finish tomorrow?"

"Let's hire somebody."

"No, no, no. You hired *me*, remember?"

"That was a year ago. I *knew* we should have finished planting the orchard then."

"Oh, come on! It was *your* idea to stop with two hundred trees, not mine."

She linked arms with Dylan. "Yes, it was. I had other things I would have rather been doing with you than planting apple trees." She bumped her shoulder playfully. "Still do."

Dylan turned them around to face the orchard. The trees they'd planted last year were already significantly bigger than the new ones they were putting in now. It looked like a real orchard again.

She leaned her head on Dylan's shoulder, smiling as she looked at the sign Dylan had made. *Isabel's Orchard.* Dylan had gone out to the farm before it sold, and with Tanner's help, they had cut down those two old mother trees. They had salvaged the wood and Tanner had taken it to a cabinetmaker in Lancaster. Besides the sign, Dylan now also had a nice butcher block table on her little patio. A patio they used frequently. But that would be coming to an end soon. The house they were having built on the other side of the creek would be finished in another three weeks or so. Dylan had designed the outdoor kitchen and patio, and she imagined they would use it most of the time in the summer months.

"I'm so happy, Dylan. I'm so content with my life." She turned to her. "I can't wait to move into our new house."

"I know. It's going to be great. It's getting to be too crowded over here."

Maddie laughed. "Yes, I know. Who knew the bed and breakfast idea would take off like it has. I've never seen Loretta so happy before. And now that Tanner and Jenna are going to get married out here, that's all she talks about. You'd think it was her own granddaughter getting married."

"That'll be a fun wedding."

"Yes. It's been nice getting to know them better. They've accepted me into your little group and treat me like we've been friends for years."

"What are we going to do with our little house when we move?"

"I don't know. It's become home, hasn't it?"

Dylan nodded. "It has. But our new one will be too."

"I wonder if Loretta would want to move into it. Now that there's people there all the time plus two other ladies who live there, she might want a place of her own."

"Maybe so."

They turned as a golf cart came along the trail. Some of the guests were out for an afternoon drive. Randy had been in charge of making new trails around the estate. The valley was off limits, though, as was the little road to their house. Surprisingly, the family burial plot had become quite the attraction. The grounds crew had it looking like a vibrant floral garden now, and Randy had put several benches under the trees to sit.

"You're right. It's getting too crowded around here," she said quietly as she raised a hand to wave at the couple in the golf cart. She smiled at Dylan. "Now. What about that beer you promised me?"

Before long, they were buzzing along the trail to the house, the wind blowing her hair around. Dylan slowed when they passed a clearing with a view of the valley.

"This has been the best year of my life," Dylan said quietly as she stopped the Gator. She glanced at her. "I never thought I'd find someone to love. I'm so happy, Maddie."

Maddie leaned across the seats of the Gator and kissed her. "I'm happy too, Dylan."

Dylan smiled at her, then continued on.

Yes, it was a good life she had. She too, was so happy. The last year had seemed to fly by yet so much had changed in her life. All for the better, she knew. She had changed course with the Foundation but not drastically. Besides offering more grant opportunities to universities, she'd also earmarked some to environmental groups, that at Dylan's urging. She made the trip to Philly three or four times a month, but most of her work she did here from her grandfather's study.

She'd spoken to her mother only once in the last year. Amazing, but she seemed genuinely happy being married and living in Greece. As far as she knew, Evan had not been put to work. He apparently spent most of his time sailing. She'd been shocked that neither of them mentioned her grandfather's money. Shocked, that is, until she found out that her mother had married a man whose net worth was over twenty billion dollars. Yes, she had indeed hit the jackpot.

She leaned her head back and closed her eyes, feeling the breeze blow against her face and hair. Again, that feeling of freedom settled over her. She smiled when she felt Dylan take her hand.

"I love you."

She opened her eyes at the sound of Dylan's words, turning to smile at her. Yes, the year had flown by, but it had damn sure been a good one. Actually, the best one she'd ever had.

"Instead of a beer break, why don't we grab a bottle of wine and head down to the creek."

Dylan arched an eyebrow. "With a blanket?"

"Yes. We'll hide from the workers at the house and do naughty things."

Dylan laughed. "The last time you suggested that we almost got caught!"

"But it was fun."

"Are you sure you don't want to finish planting the apple trees?"

"I'm positive."

"Okay. Let's go to the creek and do naughty things."

She leaned closer and kissed Dylan on the mouth. "Good. Because I think Lorah and Isabel would have done the exact same thing."

"Blow off work to make love?"

"Yes." Her expression turned serious. "I still feel so sorry for them. Every time I think about their affair, I wish they could have had the same opportunities that we have."

"Like getting married?"

Maddie smiled at her. "We should probably tell someone, don't you think?"

"Tell someone we ran off and got married?"

"Uh-huh. I can't believe you haven't told Tanner yet."

Dylan laughed. "I can't believe you haven't told Loretta."

Maddie looked down at their clasped hands, her gaze on their rings. On one of her visits to Philly, she had taken Lorah's ring to a jeweler and had a duplicate made for Dylan. She had given it to her one night while they'd been sitting by the firepit, watching the flames. She'd had no qualms at all about getting married. Dylan was the other half of her soul. And whether Lorah's prediction would ever come true—that she and Isabel would love again in another lifetime—she certainly believed that a part Isabel and Lorah lived on through her and Dylan.

"What is it?"

Maddie looked up and smiled. "Nothing." She squeezed her fingers tightly. "Let's go. I believe we have a date with a blanket and some wine."

Dylan stared into her eyes, then leaned closer and kissed her. "I'll love you forever."

"And ever."

Bella Books, Inc.
Women. Books. Even Better Together.
P.O. Box 10543
Tallahassee, FL 32302
Phone: (800) 729-4992
www.BellaBooks.com

More Titles from Bella Books

Hunter's Revenge – Gerri Hill
978-1-64247-447-3 | 276 pgs | paperback: $18.95 | eBook: $9.99
Tori Hunter is back! Don't miss this final chapter in the acclaimed Tori Hunter series.

Integrity – E. J. Noyes
978-1-64247-465-7 | 28 pgs | paperback: $19.95 | eBook: $9.99
It was supposed to be an ordinary workday...

The Order – TJ O'Shea
978-1-64247-378-0 | 396 pgs | paperback: $19.95 | eBook: $9.99
For two women the battle between new love and old loyalty may prove more dangerous than the war they're trying to survive.

Under the Stars with You – Jaime Clevenger
978-1-64247-439-8 | 302 pgs | paperback: $19.95 | eBook: $9.99
Sometimes believing in love is the first step. And sometimes it's all about trusting the stars.

The Missing Piece – Kat Jackson
978-1-64247-445-9 | 250 pgs | paperback: $18.95 | eBook: $9.99
Renee's world collides with possibility and the past, setting off a tidal wave of changes she could have never predicted.

An Acquired Taste – Cheri Ritz
978-1-64247-462-6 | 206 pgs | paperback: $17.95 | eBook: $9.99
Can Elle and Ashley stand the heat in the *Celebrity Cook Off* kitchen?